D0049590

INTERFERENCE

ALSO BY SUE BURKE

Semiosis

INTERFERENCE

SUE BURKE

A TOM DOHERTY ASSOCIATES BOOK NEW YORK

This is a work of fiction. All of the characters, organizations, and events portrayed in this novel are either products of the author's imagination or are used fictitiously.

INTERFERENCE

Copyright © 2019 by Sue Burke

Edited by Jen Gunnels

A Tor Book
Published by Tom Doherty Associates
120 Broadway
New York, NY 10271

www.tor-forge.com

Tor® is a registered trademark of Macmillan Publishing Group, LLC.

The Library of Congress Cataloging-in-Publication Data is available upon request.

ISBN 978-1-250-31784-1 (hardcover)
ISBN 978-1-250-31782-7 (ebook)

Our books may be purchased in bulk for promotional, educational, or business use. Please contact your local bookseller or the Macmillan Corporate and Premium Sales Department at 1-800-221-7945, extension 5442, or by email at MacmillanSpecialMarkets@macmillan.com.

First Edition: October 2019

Printed in Canada

0 9 8 7 6 5 4 3 2 1

To Jerry, for his love and patience.

INTERFERENCE

1

KAROLA—EARTH YEAR 2303

For all the danger in that forest with its tumbling-down ruins, the beauty pulled me back one last time. Old walls created cliffs and ravines, lushly overgrown by vegetation. Birds sang to each other. The wind smelled of wildflowers bursting through springtime earth. And there, on that late afternoon, I planned to injure Shani.

I waited for her, sitting on a mossy brick wall in front of what was once a grand building. The stones of a colonnaded entrance lay behind me amid daffodils and saplings, while in what had once been the street, flowers sprang up between black chunks of asphalt, with holes here and there caused by collapsed old tunnels. In my visual overlay, I saw them outlined in red for danger.

With a blink, I turned the overlay off. Shani was still out of sight, coming with other members of the task force, hiking down a path that twisted around dangers as it wended from the old main road. The unnatural landscape shimmered in the afternoon sunshine. The rustle of pliant young leaves blocked the sounds of the university and its interminable excavations and restorations. A kilometer away? An epoch.

She sang as she hiked with an easy vibrato on the high notes, a vocal smile, for she had every reason to be happy. I accessed the lyrics, signaled my location, and hid my plans, my public mind and private mind as separate as continents, as distinct as the present and memories.

All I could think was the truth: I will remember you always.

Her thoughts mirrored mine as she emerged on the path and smiled with a wide mouth made for joy. She sang, "Come to say goodbye, Karola and I. . . ."

She balanced on the edge between laughter and tears. I stood as they arrived, some to say goodbye, some to make plans. I would smile and weep with her, too, and we opened our arms and hugged, two young women. If I could have seen through her eyes, what would I have seen of me? But that was not the moment to look.

She would not see this place accurately. I would cause that. Amid the others, with their own mixed joys and sorrows, I hugged her and wept. Again.

Earlier that day, in the morning, more than one hundred souls had gathered in our finest formal clothing beneath a high-beamed ceiling painted with cherubs and allegories. We were surrounded by walls of fine carved wood and marble. The treasures of an Old Washington Dee Cee government complex had been restored and were reserved for scholarly assemblages of the highest merit, such as ours. Soon we would explore the living past. We would visit the Pax Colony, if it still existed half a light-century away. The planet Pax orbited a star barely visible to the naked eye just after sunset in the west of our springtime skies.

Or rather, only thirty of us would journey there, but which ones?

"It is an honor merely to be part of this task force," our chairman said in a voice like an axe, as if anything stated with sufficient force could wedge open the truth. He stood on a podium next to a formal witness-robot, a sleek black memory spire with a pleated white antenna echoing the collar of an ancient human judge.

Three of us were competing for the post of linguist. Shani and I knew that the third candidate would decline because his children had convinced him to remain on Earth to help raise his grandchildren. That left us, sitting side by side. I twisted the ring on my finger and waited. The sun slanted in through grand windows.

"Those who go must sacrifice much, perhaps everything, in the pursuit of knowledge," the chairman chopped on. "But the entire task force will be needed to prepare for their departure."

Shani and I had confirmed our opinions the night before. Each of us was as deserving and as determined to go.

"Now," he said, "after we have lost so much during the last centuries, we know the value of lives and hopes, and we will willingly risk ourselves to unite all branches of humanity again. Now I shall release the names of those selected."

He gestured at the robot. The names came to our minds. We read silently.

Shani would go on the expedition, and I was the backup.

We leapt up and hugged, weeping out of joy or disappointment. We had known we would react that way and had supposedly reached mutual comfort with our rivalry. But my life depended on going. She didn't know that because no one did.

The night before the announcement we had celebrated NVA Day, the commemoration of the Great Loss. Like all children, I had once delighted in it, playing with false terror, but now it meant unspeakable farce. But how could I fail to participate without hinting that I was the target?

In my dormitory room, I draped myself in a white body veil, the traditional ghost costume I brought out every April first. It obscured my face without even a slit for eyes to represent the idea that we were all the same in death, faceless. I set my visual overlay high to see better than I would with my real eyes.

The Pax Task Force had organized its own celebration, a small reiteration of Earth's first global holiday held everywhere on the first night of April as the sun set around the globe. We were holding it in a crossroads at the edge of a reclaimed section of the city, with our new dormitories on one side of a street and collapsed buildings on the other. The steel-framed rubble rose taller than the wild trees sprouting among it, and the glass that had once sheathed them, now shattered, sparkled amid green overgrowth.

On our side of the crossroads, squat cherry trees with pale pink blossoms decorated the spaces between the new buildings, which glowed with self-sufficient light. Our white costumes were tinted by sunset to echo the color of the trees.

If ghosts existed, they would be here in this city, in this once bustling street, one of countless emptied out one hundred fifty years ago by a great plague. But the dead stay dead, except for the architect of the Great Loss, NVA herself, punished eternally. People—some people—like to watch her suffer.

A stack of deadwood gathered from the forested ruins sat in the center of the intersection. I wanted to spend as little time as possible at that cruel ritual, although attendance was required by law, waiting until finally Shani called me to come. She said I was missing the fun. She was too kind, too thoughtful, to let me do that—my best friend, the first best friend I had ever had. I paused at the doorway to locate her. One more time, I would try to talk her out of going.

Almost two hundred people were celebrating, members of the task force, support staff, and their families. Children rushed around squealing with delight, a few disguised as ghosts but most as cute little animals. Almost all the adults were white ghosts like me, but a half dozen red ones circulated, even two men, and I flushed with anger at their disrespect. Anthropologists should know better. The red ghosts represented NVA, and there was only one of her. There should be only one at the celebration.

Task force members had settled into work groups around tables of drinks and snacks set up on the grassy, broken pavement. The pilots and engineers, who always had more energy than introspection, danced and sang to music I didn't care to log on to.

Shani stood among the biologists at the far side of the intersection. She heard me searching for her and called me again. I wove through the festivities to get there. On the way, I passed several children dressed as animals who surrounded a tall red ghost. A little-boy cat hissed at it, a couple of girl-puppies barked, and a bird cawed and squawked and giggled.

The ghost raised its arms. "I'll get you!" a man squeaked in a falsetto. "I'll kill you all! You can't run away! Hahaha!"

"You only kill people," a puppy retorted, and took a step forward.

"This time I'll kill animals, too! Animals! You!"

The children squealed and ran away. For them the ritual was merely about a scary person, and like all adults I had learned the true terror later, unfathomable to a child. NVA had poisoned the food her corporation distributed and had killed five billion people, everyone in the American continents and up to half the population elsewhere. She had done so deliberately, even eating the poisoned food herself, and she died before the disaster had been diagnosed. She had been pure, murderous evil, and too cowardly to face justice. Or so we were told. Debate was prohibited.

I passed the astronomy group. Many of them gazed with lost expressions at some broadcast information and discussed it animatedly. The few who noticed their surroundings called out greetings, and I returned them. "Good luck tomorrow!" All our voices were tense.

When I arrived, Shani draped an arm around my shoulder.

"We are practicing Globish. Can you help?"

We knew the Pax colonists had spoken Classic English. If they had survived and had descendants, and if we wanted to communicate with them, we needed to speak it fluently. That was the linguist's job. The rest of the task force had to learn simplified Globish English, which was hard enough, and it made its speakers sound like simpletons.

"I can do that," I said in Globish. "I like Classic English too. I learned it for work and now I love it, even though few people understand it."

The biologists were discussing a proposal to create new colonies in the Americas despite the effect they would have on the ecology, which had been left to grow as wild as possible.

"Everyone who goes to Pax," I said, "will never see the decision." I meant to guide the conversation in the right direction to dissuade Shani.

A young man named Mirlo laughed. "But we will see it when we come back. We will see the results."

"You are not going," a woman told him. "You do not have good skills for species identification. The task force needs me."

"I can count ant teeth as well as you can."

Everyone laughed. It was a running joke, even though Mirlo was a botanist, so he counted petals.

"But," I said, "what about your families?"

"My family has good teeth," Mirlo said.

"Are you having second thoughts?" Shani said. She tightened her arm to comfort me, pleasantly warm across my shoulders. "I know how you love your family, we all love our families, but your family will feel happy for you. Mine thinks this is the best thing I could do." Her family prided itself on exploring.

I took a deep breath. Globish couldn't express complex ideas well.

"Do not worry," she continued. "I know it will be a long and danger-ous trip. But think. We know the colony was established. And we know that the planet had very much life with many kinds of animals and plants."

"And then its satellite died and stopped sending reports," an anthro-pologist said.

She ignored him. "We know exactly where and when. We will go to a good planet."

"We will be famous," he added, "like other explorers."

"I want to go," she said. "We all want to go."

Various people chimed in, "Yes."

"But," I tried again, "only one of us can go."

"I know, I would love it if we could both go. We must under-stand that. If you can go and not me, I will be sad for me and happy for you."

This wasn't working, but I loved her for her kindness. She wanted to go no matter what, and I knew her nurturing personality would prob-ably rank her above me, despite my superior linguistic skills.

"I understand," I said. "I do not like to wait, that is all. I wish we knew now. If it is you, I will be happy for you." I hugged her, trying to imagine what else I could do to get off Earth, cherishing her soft body and its warmth.

As cheerfully as I could, I participated in the party. I lifted up my disguise to eat and drink, even laugh a little, until the axe-voiced chairman climbed up a chunk of masonry near the bonfire's woodpile and began the ceremony, reminding us all of NVA's crimes against humanity. The dummy that represented her was dragged out, a life-size doll made of old clothes stuffed with paper and brush. As people jeered, it was thrown on top of the firewood. But before the rain of stones fell on it and before the chairman set fire to it, he reached into her shirt and pulled out a doll.

I disconnected from the feed. I couldn't stand to listen. But I knew what he would say, something like the words I had heard since my earliest memories:

"She will pay forever! She is in prison, but her clone lives among us. When the time comes, it will take her place in prison. Look into your hearts. Could you do what she did? Could you be her clone? Show us by your behavior that this will never be you."

Any woman could be her, that is: another way to keep us submissive.

Without the feed, I heard his distant voice, the rustle of trees in the wind, the chatter of children. An anthropologist named Zivon, who stood next to me in a red veil and fancied himself a rebel, muttered in Globish, perhaps thinking no one important—I wasn't important—would understand Globish:

"I do not think that. If this is true, we would see her, we would see her face. We can see everything else from the past, and we can see her body now in her feed, but not her face. She does not have a mirror. Have you heard of Halloween? This is just a new kind of Halloween. It was an old holiday with evil spirits to frighten us."

"People did die," I said. I wondered how often he watched her feed.

"Right. We polluted everything, and people died. Everyone polluted the Earth, but it is better to blame one person."

"But you can log on to her in prison, you can see what she suffers."

"A lie. You can log on to fiction stories, and they seem just as real, right? It is a lie like them."

I was barely thirteen years old, and by coincidence it was the day of my menarche. For a history assignment I had accessed an old library and was rooting around, since I had little else to do but lie down and suffer cramps and ignore the younger children who played nearby. I knew barely enough ornate Classic English to know that I was bringing up records from the first half of the twenty-second century, primitive in their encoding.

I found a cluster of business news that no longer meant anything to anyone. I was supposed to be investigating early communications design, so I hoped I might find something. I slid through the pictures idly, and in one of them I spotted a woman who looked like an older version of me, with the same wide forehead and sharp chin. Her name was Nancsi Vasileios Altbusser, and she was attending a training class at a food corporation. . . . Was she NVA?

That couldn't be, I thought, though the time period would be correct. I looked for more photos of this Nancsi and found two. She had my cheekbones and the same curl in her smile that made her look uncertain of her happiness. I overlaid my face and hers: a perfect match. I knew I'd find no photos of NVA herself because all children goad each other into searching, so I'd already tried. I learned a little more about Nancsi, then her face disappeared from history after she had founded her own food company and named it with her initials.

She was real. I was a clone like most children, selected by the government for what it deemed positive traits and assigned to a family clan. But I was really her, the NVA clone who would be punished when the current incarnation died. No one knew who the clone was; only a witness-robot carried that information locked behind layers of encryption. But I had seen her face every day in the mirror.

By then I could hardly breathe from terror as I paced in the little play area, so upset that a medical program intervened and one of my mothers came with a cool drink. They decided it was a hormonal spike, normal for a day like that. I got some medication and lots of sympathy. Two days passed before I could eat again.

While family members fussed over my health, I spent those two days considering what I knew about NVA. In the celebrations, they said she was cold, logical, determined, and cruel. I would have to be like her to save myself, and by the third day I had a plan.

Within a week, I was before my fathers, properly obedient and respectful. Our house was as absolutely ordinary as almost every other one in our region, with six mothers, six fathers, servants, and thirty-seven children in a self-sufficient compound. The architecture, though, reflected our location in Greenland. The walls resembled wood panels, and glowing orange globes hung in front of the windows, mimicking the sun that in winter did not rise above the horizon. The fathers' formal reception room intimidated me with its tall peaked ceiling, elegant with flowing draperies and old-fashioned glittery furniture.

Although the men seemed old, I realized later they were barely middle-aged or younger. One or two of them came to the girls' quarters briefly every day to play or help us with lessons or occasionally join us at mealtime. They were like visiting celebrities.

I had carefully prepared a formal request outlining the success of my studies and proclaiming my fascination with the robust grammar and vocabulary of Classic English, and detailing the utility that the dead language would have in my employment and benefit to our house. I didn't mention that a profession might save me from becoming a mere minor wife, and especially, that I could learn more about myself, about NVA, the first step toward escape.

Now I would hear their response.

After formal greetings, I repeated my petition. "Our house dedicates itself to language. I want to specialize in Classic English. It's a difficult language, and I'm prepared to work as hard as I can to master it."

A secondary father rose to speak, so I was being granted scant importance. I felt enormous relief because this meant they didn't know who I really was.

"Of course you can, Karola!" He didn't seem as solemn as I had expected. "You're determined—and very logical. You've done very well at languages. But you'll have to study history, too, since Classic English is history and you can't understand it if you don't know history. It just won't make sense. How about that? Do you want to study both Classic English and history?"

I felt myself smile before I fully understood how helpful it would be to learn everything I could about the past and myself. "I'd love to study history!"

"Then it's decided. You'll do both. We'll handle all the permissions." He looked at the other fathers, and they nodded with faces hard as glass. "And we know you'll make us proud as well. And yourself proud. You've made the right decision."

Then they dismissed me. Dinner was waiting—for them, in that fine room. For me, dinner would be served at the table in the kitchen in the girls' wing. On my way out, I glimpsed the food that two of the mothers were bringing, meat, soup, two kinds of vegetables, and rice. The meal that awaited me would be only one simple dish, although plenty of it.

While I had been reminded of where I ranked, at least I had stopped being a child, and if I had been a normal young woman, I would have felt perfectly happy.

NVA's feed is always public, always connected, always one-way. She surely knows that everyone sees through her eyes and hears through her ears because she was like me until suddenly she discovered she was like no one else in humanity. One day in my teens I connected to her for the last time and shared her captivity:

She stares up at the glass roof of her prison, watching a sandstorm. Clouds of dust whip past at insane speeds, leaving a trail of twisting, twitching dunes. The wind howls. Her own breath comes fast and loud. An emotion-meter in the right corner of our view shows that she is close to panic.

She lives in a prison, a wide bomb crater blasted into living rock, and she may know that, as punishment, she has been infected with a pathogen engineered to cause fear. She may dread against all logic that the roof will fall, and she may even know that the emotion is artificial and uncontrollable. Would that hurt even more keenly than true fear?

Her vision jerks, eyes darting from one place to another. The crater is large, two kilometers wide, full of black rock shattered by the bomb. She never sees her jailers. She is naked and alone.

Almost alone. Something moves behind a boulder. She cringes, ready to bolt. It's a huge dog, and she is terrified. It bounds to the top of the rock and barks, ears back. She turns, and then the landscape bounces crazily as she runs and searches for a hiding place.

Her sight spins wildly as she falls and yelps in pain. She rises, looks at her leg, and dirty fingers brush away sand to reveal a jagged, bleeding cut. Behind her, the dog growls, and she runs again.

Finally, she drops behind a rock, eyes low to the ground, panting and cowering.

That was when I broke off the feed.

We're told she deserves it, and some people watch all the time, but there's a Classic English word for it: pornography.

Anyone subjected to that kind of stress could not live long. When the time for her replacement came, they would come for me.

I tried to learn more about NVA, about myself, and find the clue I needed to escape my fate.

The public record offered little. NVA had no recorded childhood; she had started a successful food business; and at some point she had begun adding a protein to her products that slowly destroyed the human brain stem and reduced people to vegetative states. Eventually too few people remained healthy to be able to help each other, and they all died as civilization fell into a nightmare. I could hardly bear to read the details.

I had caused that, or rather, I had the latent personality so twisted and evil that I could do that. My DNA, supposedly, carried that flaw. But I myself had done nothing, and I had been raised to be virtuous. I would be punished as NVA for what I would have done simply because someone had to be punished.

"Stupid girl," one of my fathers said, the youngest one and the least patient. Other fathers treated us the way most men treated women, merely with condescension. The sister he spoke to dropped her head in shame. He rarely came to visit, and the sight of his short, square-shouldered silhouette in the doorway to our wing never brought us joy.

"Mars? You don't know about Mars? After all we did for that planet, they revolted. We helped them and they gave back nothing. You don't know that? I'll send you a history lesson. You—all you stupid girls have to read it. You'll be tested."

I was sitting next to her. After he left, I murmured, "If no one ever bothered to tell us, it's not your fault."

"That's right," another sister said. Most of the rest looked away, too cowed to offer sympathy and annoyed at getting extra studies.

But once I read the history, I rejoiced. During the Reorganization after the Great Loss, Mars had objected to the terms, and though the colony could barely subsist alone, it cut off relations with Earth. And there the matter stood. Technically, the planets were at war, but in practice, nothing could be done.

The Reorganization had included NVA's punishment. Mars did not punish NVA. If I could get to Mars, I would be free.

Women and girls as well as a few men crowded the little merchants' gallery, the only market of its kind in our mountain-enclosed town. The glowing beams in the peaked roof lit the twelve shops offering trinkets and luxuries that mothers, daughters, and servants could buy with their allowances. I had come with a sister.

"Should we sample some perfume?" she said. "Maybe we could buy some rose cologne. It's always cheap."

"Maybe we could," I said, then in a shop window I saw a tiny flash of color, orange-red like rust. "But let's look there first."

We slid between the people to stare at a jewelry store display.

"That ring is interesting," I said, "the one with the round orange stone." Round and orange like Mars.

"It's used."

"Then maybe I can afford it. I want to try it on."

The shopkeeper greeted us with the graciousness of a natural saleswoman and fetched the ring from the display, talking all the while.

"This is coral. It's such a beautiful color, isn't it? They told me the ring was scavenged from the Americas. Licensed scavengers, of course, don't you worry. Try it on. Coral's very old in its use for jewelry. And this design around it to look like a rope is very traditional. Genuine silver, of course. The black tarnish is natural and helps show off the silversmithing. It's worn, but you can still see the design. It's so pretty. Do you like it?"

As she continued her patter, I slid the ring onto my middle finger, a stone as wide as my fingernail that looked like the most beautiful thing I had ever seen, for it meant hope.

Used jewelry was inexpensive, but I would have paid anything, and I wore it out of the shop.

For four centuries, the Institute of English Studies in London had occupied a nineteen-story white building with narrow windows that overlooked the grand diked city. It abutted a squat library whose climate-controlled rooms contained a wealth of old paper books and antique-coded memories incompatible with current general public record technologies.

I entered at a respectful distance behind two professors I knew. One had taught me "Information Nodes, Redistributions, and Their Uses," and considered himself liberal for accepting female students as equals. "And your skills will be helpful as an assistant to researchers, Karola," he had said.

I had my own research and a three-part thesis based on my theories of meta-history. I wanted information at least one hundred years old. It needed to originate from informed sources, and they would be defined as sources that appeared in nodes, especially nodes that connected to other nodes. And they would be in Classic English, not Sino-Arabic Creole, so the debate would have been sheltered from popular opinion and politics. The Great Loss had ended a half century earlier, and NVA would have been recently exhumed and her DNA extracted. By then the shock would have dissipated and the consequences would have emerged.

As I searched, I became familiar with the little computer booths and their exotic equipment and databases, and with the long aisles of steel vaults that held shelves of delicate paper. The librarians proudly helped me explore the library's ignored treasures.

The thesis took some fine-tuning because the debate I wanted had taken place before her grave had finally been located and desecrated, because the information in her grave changed everything.

I spent a full month refining my Classic English skills, and during that time I found frequent references to an analysis by a historian named Li Ming. It had been erased from Chinese-language records but had been cited in Classic English works that escaped the less educated hands of censors. From those citations, I reassembled his argument:

"We must praise the Heavens for the Great Loss. The progress of mankind had brought us to the stage of barbarism as the result of excessive population. People lost the correct relationships among individuals and societies, and among institutions and nations as they fought to survive. Soon warfare threatened to engulf the world and destroy it.

"Among these miseries was pollution, which caused disease. The Heavens saved us from war by means of disease, which blessed not one generation but hundreds. Where there was overcrowding, now there is space. Where there was competition, now there is cooperation. Where there was pollution, now there is a clean world. Where there was poverty, now there is wealth.

"Thus the Heavens benefited the world with illness. A great flood was drained before it could wash away the very rivers that had created it."

Nancsi's grave had been discovered and opened not long after Li had made his analysis, and a testament had been buried with her: "Only disease can prevent war, a fate worse than pestilence, for the coming war will kill us all. I chose to save humanity through kinder means. I weep for the loss and rejoice that some will survive."

Could that be me? Had I saved the world?

"Try to locate to this."

A blond middle-aged man pushed a button on a small box, and I closed my eyes. I saw and heard the ordinary background noise of my own feed, tailored over the years. Messages, reminders, items of possible interest, half-completed projects, storage, news, the locations of family and friends, weather, several conversations . . .

"Be patient," he said. "First you have your own frequency. Everyone has their own. Now try to lose your own signal. Everyone can do that, and it's bloody annoying. But don't do it by accident, do it intentionally."

This was my third try. On the first two, I had gotten nowhere, but this bitter man in an old-fashioned plaid coat had been patient.

"Every time I've lost it," I said, "it's been when I was switching off and on."

"Then do that. Everyone is different. If that works for you, do it."

What I sought to learn would have been illegal if any lawmaker had believed it possible, if they knew enough about the centuries-old science of one of the universe's most basic forms of energy, the electromagnetic spectrum. You could adjust radio-wave frequencies with a radio transmitter-receiver, obviously, so those were banned for private ownership, but you could never do it with your mind and your own chip.

No one was supposed to be able to do that, at least. No one in Greenland could, but London had always festered with rebellious subcultures. The blond man, an original Brit who made sure you knew he was, considered himself subversive: he strove to undermine the world union and assert ancient independence by eliminating controls over the population and reestablishing freedom. That's what he said, anyway. I had met him through a friend of a friend who belonged to a group dedicated to maintaining "pure" English.

I switched off and focused on my surroundings. I was sitting on a hard, orange chair in a sub-subbasement next to the water-recycling unit. A series of translucent white tanks lined one wall with only enough space around each tank for repair access. Light fibers above them created complex shadows. The dusty tank next to me gurgled softly, and the damp air smelled of the must of bacteria eating the building's waste.

Within that distraction, I switched off and then tried to reconnect to my feed, failed, and tried again. Instead, as if from far away, I heard a whistle being broadcast almost exactly on my own frequency. I tried to draw it closer but it was like trying to remember something I never really knew, something I had to learn anew rather than remember, until finally I heard it in full.

"I've got the tone."

He switched another button on his transmitter box.

"Now I hear music."

"Now follow it." He slowly turned a dial.

I tried to follow, dragging my memory and attention like an anchor toward the music. I reached it and realized I was sweating and panting and swaying to its rhythm.

"Ah, you're good. No one ever gets it that fast. Really. Rest a minute, then we'll try again."

After some deep breaths, I nodded. He turned the dial again.

Again I tried to move toward the sound. It was a little easier. But my head was pounding.

———

Each time I practiced, my head ached, but less than the last time. And each time, week after week, I tried to master another technical detail.

Music let me tune in to other people's feeds as well as my own because I used their reaction to music as a means to locate the feed. Feeds were broadcast from relatively few antennae, something everyone had been taught but few understood consciously. The recipients' actions, such as moving to music, offered clues to determine exactly which feed from which antenna they were receiving, but there might be other clues to identify their feed. I wanted to see how far I could go.

With a hood pulled forward to hide my face, I followed a language professor with a lazy teaching style and a weak vocabulary. I didn't know where he was headed, but like most people he doubtless relied on his feed rather than really knowing where he was. He paused to check the way at every cross street—yes, he was using his feed. I began searching for it.

Before he reached the next corner, patiently waiting since even petty offenses like jaywalking were monitored and prohibited, I had found the antenna and feed for his visual overlay. The right direction to reach his destination would be marked green, and the wrong way would be red. I concentrated and reversed the colors the same way that if you stare at something, then close your eyes, you see it in reverse. I sent that as a preferred feed—or at least I tried to do that. Everyone could send and receive on their own frequency, and with the training I'd received, I could send on other frequencies as well. For geolocation he might receive messages from several sources, but one would have consolidated the others and become the preferred message. The process wasn't secret, but only technicians needed to know how the wavelengths reinforced each other. I had learned it, or so I hoped.

He reached the corner and turned left instead of continuing forward as he should have. He had seen what I wanted him to see, not what he should have seen.

I sat down on a bench to rest as sweat dripped between my breasts. I no longer got blinding headaches, instead merely bad ones, and I felt as if I had sprinted three hundred meters. More than that, I felt triumphant. Hopeful.

This subversive skill might somehow help me escape, if I ever got the chance.

In the aisles of the Institute of English Studies library, a librarian stopped me. She was old, businesslike, and seemed to notice everything. Her gray hair was pulled back and tied, and she wore plain, simple clothing, as if she could afford nothing more, and perhaps she couldn't if she had been abandoned by her family to the wages of a mere academic assistant.

"Do you know about Pax?" she said. "That colony, the one that sent a few messages back to Earth in the 2280s? They're going to send a task force to see if they can find it."

"Now, after so long?"

"Bureaucracies move slowly. Anyway, they'll need a linguist, and with your history background, you'd be good. If you want to go, that is. It's a long trip and you'd lose everyone you know. But things might be different when you get back." She didn't need to say what those things were, especially for women, or that few interstellar explorations needed linguists.

That might have been enough, but if I left, I could also escape NVA. I answered with less emotion than I felt. "I might want to go."

She used a feed to show me the task force proposal, and it hung in front of my eyes and glowed with my own excitement. The colony lay fifty-eight light-years from Earth, and that far away, someone could live free and independent.

"Let me think about it." I could go to Mars or to this place called Pax. Either would do.

"Of course. If you decide yes, I'll get a professor to give you a good recommendation. A lot of professors owe me."

I did some research. I discovered that before the colonists had left, they had written a Constitution in ornate Classic English that devoted its bulk to matters of governance, but its "Article II: Principles and Purposes" declared plainly: "The Commonwealth declares and affirms its special responsibility to promote the full and equal participation of all its citizens in its activities and endeavors without regard to race, species, color, sex, disability, wealth or poverty, affectional or sexual orientation, age, national origin, or creed."

My family granted permission for my application without comment and agreed to pay for lodging and food in the least expensive women's dormitory in Old Washington Dee Cee. A fine recommendation got me accepted, although in truth few people sought to leave the planet on a mission so dangerous it approached suicide. But suicide had its attractions.

I was down in the musty basement again. For helping me develop illegal mental skills, my "teacher" was going to want his payment, but he didn't know how much I had practiced on my own. And there was only one thing a man without a wife would want from a woman, something he probably would have considered as subversive to the system as his lessons, and therefore as liberating, but it would have left me less free.

His eyes flicked on something in his enhanced vision as he fiddled with his transmitter box again. I located it, a feed from a different, more distant transmitter. He was watching the entrances to the building. I had worried about discovery, too, worried enough to have fully imagined it. I interrupted his feed with my own version of reality.

"Halt, police!" a voice commanded in his head. The feeds showed a blur of motion at one of the entrances.

He jumped to his feet, eyes wild. He looked at the box, then at me. I was evidence.

"Get out! Get out now!" he shouted at me. "The back way, take the back way!" He shoved me at a staircase. I heard him smashing the box as I ran. I never heard from him, or about him, again.

People trust what they see. They trust the system that sends them these visions even though it is as fragile as the paper in ancient books—

because they have never read those books. They know nothing about their own environment. They trust it the way people once trusted the food they ate.

In Old Washington Dee Cee, a few days before the announcement of who would go to Pax, Shani was swinging her arms and moving her feet to a feed of dance exercise music in a corner of the patio of our dormitory. At a nearby table, I pretended to be studying something in my own feed, but instead I watched her shadow. I was sitting between her and the antenna. I scanned for her music, tuned in, listened, thought of another song I had stored in my own feed, substituted it as if it were part of the exercise plan, and sent it.

She interpreted the change as a programmed alteration of her routine. Now her feet moved to my rhythm. She raised her arms over her head and swung them from side to side as her hips swayed the opposite way. The music shifted to a refrain, and she bent and turned, her legs spread wide to maintain her balance as she draped her arms ever wider, front and back, left and right, with the grace of a bird navigating air currents. I glanced and saw her smiling wide: she loved to dance. She bent her knees and turned, swayed forward, stepped, and turned again, her hips making wide arcs.

I turned away and slowed the music slightly, and her shadow moved from side to side at my command, one two three four left right . . .

I continued until the headache made my eyes water. Or maybe I was weeping—for her or for me? For inflicting harm on my best friend or for proving that I was NVA, determined and cruel? I had to be prepared in case she won the chance to go to Pax. I only needed to injure her enough so that she couldn't go. And if I failed, Mars still beckoned.

Several hours after the team to go to Pax had been named, on a warm spring afternoon, women working on the project had come to our favorite place in the green ruins of Washington for a happy-sad good-bye. Some would fly to another planet and some would stay behind. We all shared the bond of inequality and, beyond that, like the men, the burden of a system that decided our families, our work, and as much as it could our thoughts. I would have never doubted that the world was as it should have been had I not been able to see the world as it once was, and everything I had learned had left me with one horrible choice.

The men who ran the Earth wanted a monster, and they created one. To survive, I had to do something abhorrent.

"Karola," one of my co-workers said, "since you're staying, maybe you can join this other project."

"What is it?" I tried to look attentive.

"It's about artificial photosynthesis. We'll need help understanding old research, and for communications."

Shani was elsewhere talking with a trio of women, all of whom would be leaving. As usual, they chatted by feed while they wandered separately through the ruins and its overgrown cliffs and ravines.

"Photosynthesis for food or for energy?" I asked.

"Both. It's a big project. Complicated. And long-term. . . ."

Shani was out of sight, but I found her feed easily. She and the others were discussing ways to coordinate their work. She was too involved with that to notice her visual overlay beyond avoiding dangers marked in red, and when she looked up at a singing bird, I switched the colors.

"The project is going to go to Mars," my co-worker told me.

Shani was in immediate danger, and I wished I could know exactly how much so I could control it, make it no worse than it needed to be. I wished I could do something besides hurt her. Then I understood what I had just heard.

"Mars?"

"Right, I knew you'd be interested."

The wind made the yellow daffodils sway. Maybe I wouldn't have to hurt Shani.

My co-worker continued: "Earth and Mars are at war."

I twisted my ring. "They have been for a long time."

"Yeah, but now the idea is to create a new colony on Mars because the rebels are only in one place and they haven't gotten much beyond subsistence, so if Earth can establish its own base, a superefficient base, then Earth could fight and win."

Of course Earth would win. I looked down at my feet because everything inside me was collapsing. I struggled to maintain the color change for Shani and twisted my ring until the band bit into my flesh. No matter what happened, no matter what Pax was like, I could never come back to Earth or Mars. There was nowhere else to go.

Shani was surrounded by wild beauty, walking toward a wide and very bright green line on the ground, and then, a sudden shift in her visual feed spun into darkness.

What had I done?

My co-worker said: ". . . and it will need to capture every kind of radiant energy—Oh!"

An alarm sounded across all feeds and showed us where the trouble was. Everyone rushed toward her.

"Shani!"

I was already weeping. I located her medical readout and it showed extremes, all of them wrong.

2

ARTHUR—PAX YEAR 210
SINCE FOUNDING

Something poked up at my shoe, and I froze. Through the thick sole, I couldn't tell what it was. Coral, burrowing owl, or maybe, finally, a red velvet worm? Or maybe I'd just snapped a twig, but I hadn't heard anything.

We didn't want surprises.

I whistled Glassmaker sounds for *trouble* and *perhaps* and pointed at my foot. A lot of things recognize the vibrations of a voice as a sign of prey, but some ignore a whistle. Would velvet worms?

"Heard you," Cawzee squawked behind me. Right behind me. I told the Glassmaker to stay back. Stupid. No surprise there.

I didn't move, except for my eyes. If it was a velvet worm, its swarm might be nearby, and with the bare branches of winter, I might spot them . . . if I knew what to look for. Dark red, about the width of my thumb, so they said. The locustwood trees kept reporting them here in the south forest, but those trees spooked easy.

I saw only dry underbrush, patches of snow, and tree trunks. I heard nothing, smelled nothing. I had a long knife in one hand, a spear in the other, both ready, and wore heavy leather boots up to my knees. That was as good as it was going to get.

The thing under my foot poked again, then scraped along the sole. It was alive, and I wanted to find out what it was.

"Back off," I whistled.

"Where?"

I gestured with the spear at my foot.

The thing underneath it began to push up hard.

Cawzee leaped ahead of me in a flash of gray-brown skin and fur, and stood just out of reach. He squatted on his back legs, held his body and long head straight up, raised his front legs and arms, and froze. But a perfect imitation of a stump with bare branches, wearing a winter coat, wouldn't help. I gestured to move away fast. Fast!

The worm exploded from the ground and rose up as high as my knee, and I reacted a half second too slow. My knife cut only air. Cawzee jumped up and screeched loud enough to stun. I swung again and this time I whacked the worm.

But it had already squirted glue strings that hit him on the belly. The strings tightened and yanked the lopped-off head against him. Freshly dead, it could probably still bite, and its poison could kill a lion.

Cawzee panicked. He dropped to all four legs and started running, still shrieking.

"Get back here!"

Something else burst through the dead leaves. I looked, but it was gone. Cawzee had stopped, his big long head bobbing. I ran toward him, shrugging off my backpack to get the antidote.

"Stay there. I'm coming to help you, Cawzee. Stay there."

He reached for his belly, tugged at the worm head, and made a rattling sound. Glassmaker faces don't show emotion, but he scented *fear* strong enough to make my eyes water.

"I'll help you." I was standing next to him now with a fruit out and shoved it into his hand. "Eat this." I grabbed the worm head and yanked it off. Blood ran fast. Good, it would clean the wound from inside. I groped in the bag for another fruit, crushed it in my hand, and ground it into the bleeding hole.

Cawzee started trembling and whining. He held the fruit in long, thin fingers, but he hadn't eaten anything. Well, I wasn't going to lose him. The hassle of him dead would be even worse than having him alive. I put an arm down around his shoulders and pushed the fruit at his mouth. Something rustled off to the left. I jerked my head to look. A boxer bird, harmless.

"Come on, eat that, it's good for you. . . . Yeah, there you go. There's no seeds, just bite and swallow fast. Here's another one. You know you have to eat this. Here, chow it down."

He shook worse and dropped his head. Don't throw up, I wanted to say, but that might give him an idea. His stink was making me queasy. I let go of his shoulders, fell to my knees, grabbed another fruit, and rubbed its pulp into the belly wound again. It was bleeding less, and the flesh seemed firm. He rested his head on my hat. I heard him chewing. Good. I'd get that brainless insect home alive.

"You say move back, but you not tell me where," he squawked. "I not know where I go-me."

Right. With Glassmakers, it's always our fault, us Humans. Whatever we do isn't good enough.

"Can you walk?"

He took a couple of shaky steps. "You will help me."

"Let's go to the camp." I stood up, my elbow at the same height as his shoulder. "Here, I'll help you hold up your head." His big, faceted eyes glittered. A thread of saliva dripped from the bottom of the vertical slit of his mouth. I wasn't sure where to hold his head, so I wrapped my hand around where his chin would have been if he had one, and we began to walk. Supposedly there were things like this on Earth called insects but tiny and truly brainless, and some old records said a species that looked a lot like Glassmakers was called praying mantis, or preying, or whatever. No matter what, "insect" was *not* a polite word on Pax, but somehow it had never been forgotten.

I stayed alert for anything underfoot or in the brush, but it was winter and quiet, except for the crusty snow and dead leaves crunching as we walked. Cawzee was young and new at hunting, I reminded myself, and the Hunter's Committee had assigned me the job to take him on his first winter hunting camp, since I was young but experienced. If it worked out, we might make a permanent pair, but of all the Glassmaker majors in the city, I'd never want him. Their queens assigned them, and we Humans could only agree. Next time, I was going to argue. Stupid queens.

Instead of teaching hunting, I could have been doing real hunting. Or exploring. Both would have been more fun. Maybe after I got him home, I'd just take off on my own.

Within an hour, I had him resting in our tent, had a fire going, got him some tea and then some food for both of us.

He said, "I perhaps live-me, yes?"

"I gotta say yes." Glassmakers whistle and chatter and squawk and emit scents, and we understand them mostly, and they understand Human speech mostly, so I could entertain myself with sarcasm he wouldn't catch. "There's no chance you'll leave me alone."

"I be-me cold."

"Take my blanket, too. Here, take all the blankets. Take everything."

"We will go now home?"

"The sooner the better. I wish I could throw you all the way there."

It was about noon, so after we'd eaten, I struck the camp. He didn't lift a skinny finger to help me or carry a thing besides his side baskets, empty because he felt too weak, so I had everything on my back, and had to help him tremble through every rough spot. That night, he stank and snored worse than ever. I moved my sack outside and lay there, staring up. It was cloudy, no auroras to light the sky, no moons or planets or stars to help me track the time.

I thought about red velvet worms. Most people thought they were just worried prattle from the locustwoods. Those trees were always reporting eagles where there were merely owls. They weren't the brightest species of tree, except for the huge ones, but we had planted them in the south forest on the deal that they would keep watch, and they took their job seriously.

There had been a lot of little changes in the south lately. We needed to do something about it, and I decided to volunteer. I had the proof, a red velvet worm dead in a sack. We needed to go hunt red velvet worms. With the right team, it would be the best sport yet.

It began to rain the next morning, and we were cold and wet hours later when the trail took us out on a little ridge at the river. Far off, we saw the domed glass roofs of the city. It looked better than ever. We just had to hike along the river past the fields and orchards, cross the bridge, march up the bluff, enter the gates in the city wall, and we'd be home.

The bamboo in the city stood green even in winter. We were too far to see the rainbow stripes on its stems, but the colored glass in the roofs was arranged in circular rainbows, and we could glimpse that. It was called Rainbow City for a reason.

"It's great to see home," I said. Best of all, I thought, when we got there, I could dump Cawzee on someone else.

"We build good city. Home for us, not for you."

"Home? You abandoned it because you wanted to be nomads again. You thought you were going to lead better lives. While you were gone, we rebuilt it for you."

"And you keep it for you, not us."

If he wanted to fight over ancient history like his queen, so could I. "We invited you to live with us when you came back after you failed as nomads, but no, you had to have a war."

"We have now little room."

"There's still plenty of room to grow. And there's more of you now than there used to be. Life is good with us."

He puffed the scent of rotting fish. "You cheat and use plant to fight or we win-us our old home."

"That was a hundred years ago, and Stevland is for all of us."

"He be-he plant."

"And you're a stupid tulip."

"Fast tulip. With you, I have bad trip, and you almost kill me."

"You seem to be doing fine. Wanna carry something? Maybe your own food?"

His four legs began to wobble again. "I go to clinic in city, get good care."

"I'll take you myself and leave you there. Don't ever partner with me again."

"Bad hunter, I learn nothing."

"Shut up."

We hadn't talked much before and we didn't talk at all after that. The path took us past fields covered with stubble. Not even caterpillars were out crawling over the dirt, and of course we saw no farmers. They didn't work in the cold rain like us hunters, water seeping into my boots and squishing in my socks. But on the far side of a field a team was digging, and when a Glassmaker worker saw us, he came running over in boots covered with mud up to his first knees.

He greeted Cawzee with whistles and a cloud of alcohol for *welcome,* and they sniffed each other, as if they had to. Even I knew the worker was one of his brothers, Chesty or something like that. He chattered and looked at Cawzee's bandaged belly, took him by the hand and screeched back to his team, "I now go-me with family to city."

Good, he could carry something.

His team members waved him off, then waved at us, and one wore a black hat like mine. I waved my hat at her. She didn't wave hers back. I couldn't charm women at all.

Chesty took Cawzee's side baskets and didn't offer to help me carry anything, but I dropped his bedding and weapons into them anyway. The worker puffed laughter and something fishy.

I entertained myself by ignoring them and inspecting the scenery. A hunter had to be prepared everywhere, since we defended the city, too. A checkerboard of trees and shrubs grew on the side of a little rise and nothing was lurking between them, but closer to the river, a dragon gecko hunkered under a little palm tree for shelter, looking miserable. It probably just got kicked out of its own burrow by a boxer bird. I knew how it felt.

Close to the river, a team in a flax workshop paused to wave.

If I wanted to hunt velvet worms, I needed to start a campaign, just like a politician. "He got hurt by a red velvet worm," I called out.

"Will he recover?" a man said.

"I think so, but where there's one worm, there's more."

"Be careful." He returned to his work.

Where was the panic? I was going to have to explain exactly how dangerous red velvet worms were to get the panic I needed.

Right at the river's edge, I took a look at the old statue of Uncle Higgins, dead for a hundred fifty years, the first one to talk to Stevland. The children's flower garden around it was green and colorful even in this weather. I couldn't remember how we did that as kids, exactly what we planted so the garden was always in bloom. I'd been fascinated by the jewel lizards who lived there. None were out sunning themselves now on the statue, though, since it was raining. I wanted to get out of the rain, too.

We crossed the rope bridge over the river one by one, Cawzee and Chesty chortling nonstop. The fishing boats were tied up. In the workshops, Humans and Glassmakers were bent over wood or leather or reeds, and no one looked up until Chesty made a nutty sort of smell and all the Glassmakers turned to look, and then the Humans turned to look at what they saw.

"He got attacked by a red velvet worm," I called out. "They're in the forest now, not just in the Coral Plains."

"How's he doing?" a woman asked.

"He'll recover, but where there's one worm, there's more. They're in the forest now."

"Good he be-he back at city," her partner said. And they went back to work. So did everyone. I was going to have to campaign hard to get my chance for some fun hunting.

The pavement of the road up the bluff gritted under our feet from the sand sprinkled to provide traction in sleet. We walked through the big wooden gate in the walls and we were home. Stalks of extra-tall rainbow bamboo arched overhead at the entrance. I waved up at them. I knew Stevland would be watching and he'd be concerned. The rest of the city was quiet in the rain, except for drops spattering on the glass-and-stone houses and on the dirt in the gardens between them.

We made it to the clinic without much notice. The medics hurried to help poor, cold, wet, poisoned, injured Cawzee. I delivered a quick report on what had happened.

Ivan, the lead medic, put him on a bed, removed the bandages, and inspected the wound and then the bandage. "It looks good." He checked Cawzee's breathing, listened to his heart, prodded his thorax, and looked into his mouth.

"Good first aid. He'll be fine."

"I'm worried," I said. "There are more red velvet worms out there."

"Spread the word among the hunters who go down south, then."

Up until that moment, I had always admired Ivan's calm in the face of everything. But I wanted some drama. I wanted to hunt.

I'd get my chance with my report that evening in the Meeting House. Usually I'd rather hunt flesh-eating slugs than talk to thirteen politicians sitting at a table pretending to listen, so I hardly ever went.

The minute I walked into the Committee meeting that night, I didn't like what I saw. It's a big building, actually three round buildings connected by wide halls to make sort of a triangle, and it was almost empty. Just a couple dozen people in the main room. The far ones weren't even lit. Where was the panic? Worms were about to attack! Not even all the Committee members were there, just seven not counting Stevland, a bare quorum.

Worst of all, Cawzee's queen, Rust, was one of the two Glassmaker representatives on the Committee and the only one who had shown up. Proportional representation, but disproportional noise. Not just because Glassmakers were high-decibel. They were always looking for a fight, especially her. And there was a lot on the agenda I had to sit through before the item on velvet worms.

But Fern was in the audience, the woman I'd marry if she'd ever talk to me so I could ask her. I found a place near her so she'd have to notice me. She was carving some bit of wood in calloused fingers, a sculptor, the best in the history of the planet Pax, some said. I wanted those calluses to touch me.

She had a very young pet fippokat at her feet playing with the shavings. I tapped the floor so it would come to me. It turned its little ears, then hopped over. Its pink nose was sniffing my hand when another hunter sat next to me with his baby boy in his arms. Show-off. I picked up the little kat in one hand and held it for the baby to look at. The kat still had a few patches of brown baby fur, but mostly it was bright green. The baby squealed and reached out, and I guided his hand to gently pet the kat.

I cooed at the baby, and I glanced at Fern. She looked at us, laughed, then returned to her carving with a smile. *Look at me again, I'm trying to show you I can give you the best babies on the planet!*

She had looked at me, at least. I made her smile. Victory was mine! Someday.

Eventually the agenda got to me. "Cawzee and I spent four days hunting in the southern forest. We were training."

Queen Rust stood up and interrupted. "You were to teach him to hunt, not let him be attacked." She was as tall as me, with brown-on-brown patterned fur, but her body was long and wide compared to workers and majors. Her skinny legs didn't look like they could hold her up. All queens were clumsy compared to majors and workers, but she was the worst. And somehow, maybe the way she bent every joint in her legs and arms at a different angle, she looked fierce. I wanted to be that scary. It was all attitude. I wanted that attitude.

"Sorry," I said. "First thing to learn about hunting is that you can be hunted, too."

"Thank you, Arthur," said Ladybird, the co-moderator, showing the warm smile she gave everyone, warm but don't cross her or it turned cold. "Cawzee should make a full recovery thanks to your quick attention." She wore a big skirt, just in case anyone forgot she was a woman. Stevland was the other co-moderator. The Human moderators were always women. Women were always in charge.

I knew I was supposed to sit down then, but I had more to say. "A red velvet worm attacked him. There are red velvet worms in the south forest, and they've come in from the Coral Plains."

"Just one," said the cooks' representative on the Committee.

"They never travel alone," I said. "The locustwood are still saying there are more, right?"

"That is correct," Stevland said. "I get frequent reports from them and from other plants to the south about many kinds of intruders from the plains."

He was using a strange, echoing voice that night. Some old Earth or Glassmaker sound technology had been re-created to give him a loud-speaker unit so he could talk, and he liked to play with sounds. A box with a speaker was clamped to one of the thick stalks of bamboo grow-ing out of a space in the flooring. Technicians worried that Stevland would feel pain when the wires went in, but he said he felt light, and light fed plants, so it was good.

"Sometimes there's more slugs than other times, too," said the farm-ers' rep, Geraldine. "Nothing new."

Ladybird saw that I had more to say, and she gestured for me to speak.

"We need to look for them and hunt them down," I said. "They bur-row. They could come up anywhere where there's dirt."

"Two days' hike away," Geraldine said. "We don't farm down there."

"I know it's frightening, son," said Ivan, the medical rep, "but one isolated incident is just that, an isolated incident."

"We could really use more meat," the cook said. "More and better hunting."

And that was why I never came to Committee meetings. No matter what anyone talked about, it turned into a bicker, and good ideas got tortured and left to die as slowly as possible.

"But they're new." I pointed up to the dome where glass bricks made a circular rainbow. The big crack had been repaired, but they all knew what I meant. "Something happened out on the plains with the earth-quake, and animals are moving, and we don't want them coming here."

"That was two years ago," the farmer said.

A woman in the audience who did a lot of fishing stood up. "Some-thing did happen. Right after the earthquake, the river went low for a while. We were all worried about that, remember? Now we have fewer crayfish and hardly any natans. There's that new crab, the pink one with three big claws, and spiky corals keep trying to anchor on boats and bridges and even nets."

"Corals are always doing that," Geraldine said.

"Not so many!"

"We should investigate every new danger," Stevland said.

"Have you seen anything?" Geraldine said.

"My roots are thin that far south, and I have few stalks," Stevland said. "But I get other reports. I believe this is serious and action is needed."

"Then let's have a planting expedition for you!" Geraldine laughed. "Forget the worms. Strange weather makes things move around. Come spring, they move back."

Farmers. Most people were farmers, so my idea died there. It came to a vote and was eviscerated five to one. Ladybird and Stevland abstained, as usual, but it wouldn't have made a difference.

I stayed and watched more debates for a while. I felt glad I wasn't Ladybird, who had to try to keep the debate moving. I liked the way Stevland announced data and information at just the right time to nudge the debate, or at least he tried to. We'd have starved without him. Death by incompetence.

I thought about the way we were all divided by our main jobs, and we didn't understand what other jobs did. Then we were divided into Humans and Glassmakers, men and women, animals and plants, and old and young. None of them understood the other.

We were divided by generations, too, counting back to the First Generation, the Parents, who came from Earth. Each set its own rules and had its own marker. I was Eleven, and we wore black hats, Ten shaved their heads, Nine wore raindrop shapes, Eight wore stripes, and Twelve wore red belts. Thirteeners were too young to have decided yet. Each generation thought it was the best.

And teams. Each project had a team, selected by the team leader. With everything else in play, teams usually included the people the leader liked best, not the people who were best at their jobs. That's why so many teams failed.

We were incompetent because we couldn't get along. We were stupid.

———

Late the next morning, I escaped. I perched in a hunting blind less than a half-hour hike from the city, waiting for something to go past that I could kill. I was tired of tramping all over in the slush for people who didn't care what I thought. Then I heard a shriek for help. I recognized the voice, a working-caste Glassmaker, probably farming. I didn't want to help, but I had to come running. It was the law.

I found a crowd that included some of my least favorite people, so I would have gone back to the blind except I thought I heard Geraldine yell, "Velvet worms!" She was having a fit. I took a closer look.

"It's full of them!" She pointed at something in the brush alongside a field. Then she looked around with huge panicked eyes at the bare, plowed ground, as if worms were about to pop up out of anywhere. She grabbed her Glassmaker worker and ran away. Coward.

That left four other farmers plus me standing there, and I was the guy with weapons.

"Lemme take a look for you," I said, nocked an arrow on my bow as cocky as I could, and sauntered over.

A little trap for crabs or geckos sat in the brush, and inside something slithered, scarlet-brown. A head snapped up and pressed against the mesh to shoot glue toward me. Then a second worm in the same trap attacked.

"I told you," I said. "There's red velvet worms around."

"Okay, you were right," said a woman, annoyed to admit it. She carried a basket filled with twigs and bark. "What do we do?"

"The woods aren't as safe as they used to be." I took a big step back and knelt down to look at the trap from another angle, then realized a worm could jump out of the ground and bite my butt. I stood up, made it look casual. "Those traps are just baskets, and I don't think they'll hold forever. Let's see, I have these arrows, a long knife, a sling, a spear. The kind of things you'll all need to carry now. And I'm telling you, these worms move fast."

"Are there more around?"

"No way to know. We don't know much about them." I took my quiver of arrows from my shoulder. "I've got some barbed tips here. I wonder if that'll do it. One way to find out." I selected an arrow with a narrow shaft and tiny point, and I guessed it could pass through the mesh without breaking open the trap. I hoped, at least. "Hey, everyone, get back. These worms don't die easy."

They all stepped back twice as far as they needed to.

I couldn't miss at that range. I hit a worm, and it roiled around so much it knocked over the trap. By then I'd released two more arrows into the other worm. I had a fourth ready and waited for a while. I didn't want to make it look too easy. The worms fought, then twitched, then seemed to be still. I let the fourth and fifth arrow go just to be sure. The worms didn't move.

I got a sixth arrow ready to make things look more dangerous. "By the way, are there any more traps?"

"Geraldine and Tweeter would know."

"Yeah, but they ran away. Here, I think these are dead." I poked at the trap with my spear. Nothing moved. I looked at my audience, and behind them, across the fields, more people were coming running. One of them was Jose, the chief hunter, gray-haired and wrinkled but still strong and fast. And smart. He'd be happy with my work.

He was. We tracked down the cowardly farmer, learned where the other traps were, and found one more worm. It had crawled into the trap to attack a little owl in it, and once we'd killed the worm, we took a good look. Its poison or saliva had dissolved the bird from the inside. The worm had sucked it dry, leaving an empty sack of skin and spiny feathers.

That night, terrified people filled the Meeting House to overflowing, but they cleared a path to let me and Jose make our report.

"It's time for an organized hunt," Jose insisted.

"I'm ready to serve the city," I said. This was going to be fun.

Then a woman stood up. "It's more serious than that. I said last night, the red velvet worms are just one change out of many. To me, as a geologist, this pace suggests a permanent change since the earthquake, and it's taken two years for us to see the results. That is, there may be a change in the Coral Plains. We need to authorize a team to investigate."

Stevland spoke up, this time in the most beautiful woman's voice I'd ever heard. "I have never had a seed germinate in the plains. Or perhaps they germinated but were killed as seedlings. It is an environment hostile to me and to you, too. That may be why no Human has gone there for seven years, and no Glassmaker ever. The corals constantly try to encroach northward, and we plants constantly repel them, but we are fighting harder than ever. Something has changed."

There was silence. Stevland had spoken. Then he added, "I can understand the reticence to go. Winter carries certain inconveniences, but it is the safest time to go, since corals and other predators are relatively dormant."

More silence. No one wanted to go, since not everyone came back.

Finally the woman who managed the lentil orchards stood. "Remember all those little brown lizards last summer? They ate a lot of lentil buds, and we had a small crop. We don't want that again."

Geraldine nodded. "It's not just bad weather."

"Then," Ladybird said, "we agree to send a team to investigate?"

"Arthur," Queen Rust said. "We perhaps will spare him."

Vindictive old lady. I began to object, but Jose started talking.

"Yes, Arthur is a good choice. He likes to explore, and it's time he led a team. I nominate Arthur to lead a team to explore." He looked at me firmly. "I'll help him out, of course."

I couldn't say no to him, not without making him look bad, which would come back to me soon enough, and, well, yes, I did want to be an explorer. Just *not* of the Coral Plains. But he said I could lead a team! And he would be on it.

"I'll do it," I said. I'd come back alive and face down Rust. I'd show them how it was done.

"If he perhaps find change," she added, "we send genuine expedition."

I opened my mouth, but Jose kicked my foot, and I could take a hint sometimes.

Motion made, seconded, and passed on a voice vote.

Then they talked about a "moving star" that a guard had spotted the night before, which could be a little moon no one had ever noticed before or a giant floating cactus or a superfast comet. Investigating a harmless light in the sky seemed like a good idea to everyone, while the near death of a major like Cawzee hadn't made velvet worms seem like a problem. They had to scare Geraldine silly for that.

The first thing I learned after the meeting was that Jose meant he'd give me advice, not come with me. I asked a couple of other hunters to be on my team, but they all had excuses.

The next morning I posted a general call for volunteers on the boards at the Meeting House and dining hall and asked Jose to help.

By noon, nothing. I began to think I wasn't popular, somehow. At lunch, I was sitting in the dining hall with two Black Hat friends when Honey walked toward me carrying a big roll of paper.

There were more than five hundred Humans in Rainbow City, and I knew everyone more or less, and I'd never had a reason to get to know her better. She was the youngest of the Raindrop generation, so she was their coddled baby, and younger than me, and she had big blue drops tattooed on her cheeks. Like big teardrops, like she was crying all the time.

She was spoiled and bossy. She'd never gotten a haircut in her life, to prove she wasn't a Baldie, and her hair hung down to her knees, not as long as you'd think because she was short, too.

She sat down with a big grin and spread her skirt on the bench. She wanted to volunteer, I knew it. This team stank already.

"I want to volunteer," she said. "I'm a geologist, so I'm a natural for your team. Well, a geologist in training, but I need to learn, and that's the way, isn't it? Jump in and see if you swim!"

"Well, it'll be dangerous. Very."

"And I'm a woman, right? Women are for safe, important things, right? This isn't safe enough, is it? It's not important, is it? I knew you'd pull that on me!"

"I just wanna be honest up front."

"I know the risks. I've studied coral, too. See?" She held up her left index finger. There was a scar on the pad where a hunk of flesh was chopped out.

"Stung?"

"I know the risks."

My Black Hat friends were already laughing at me.

I wanted to say she was a risk, too. She'd try to take over the team. Women were like that. If we hadn't been in the dining hall surrounded by everyone, I'd have said that. Instead I said, "Geology, huh? How can that help us on this team?"

"A lot!" she said. "We have maps and reports going back more than a century for the plains. I know it all! I think the key's going to be hydro. Water. Corals thrive on moisture. The plains are part of an enormous watershed. Did you know the ground level has been sinking in part of the south forest? Six full centimeters in some places! The locustwood trees give us constant reports."

"They do like to talk."

"Next to Stevland, they're the smartest plants. In my opinion, anyway. I know some people are impressed by the pineapples, but they don't have the memory and scope that the others do. They're just a group intelligence. And we don't know about the corals at all. Maybe they're intelligent, too. We have so much to learn!"

"We'll be traveling by river. What do you know about the rivers in the plains?"

"Everything! Several rivers converge at different points in the plains to create ours, and they all meander." She unrolled her paper. It was a map. "I created this from all available sources. I've been working on this for months!"

It was big and detailed. Maybe too detailed, but everything was there, swamps and landmarks, hills, major life concentrations and zones. I studied it a while, then looked up. She was watching me, waiting for me to be dazzled.

"This'll be useful."

My friends laughed. She glared at them. I didn't want her on my team, but I wanted that map. I needed that map. It was the best map I'd ever seen. And she probably came with it.

I stayed serious, like a leader should be, to remind her I was the leader. "What else can you do?"

She'd been waiting for that question. She launched into the story of her life. Before she was halfway through, my Black Hat friends wandered off with excuses because they were dying of boredom. So was I, but I had to listen. Being a leader had downsides.

". . . so I've done fieldwork before. You know everything about every animal visible to the naked eye, or that's what they say, and I can do that with anything mineral. And with corals, at least the ones we have in the forest. Well, like you too, probably."

"They say that about me?"

"Is it true?"

"I haven't seen everything."

She clapped her hands and laughed. "And you're an explorer! You've climbed mountains!"

"Lots of people climb mountains. Just not as high as me."

"I've never climbed one. I want to see everything, too! Starting with the plains."

"It'll be dangerous and cold and wet and uncomfortable. It won't be fun."

"I have warm clothes! I want to come."

Jose had told me that the first thing you want from a team member is enthusiasm, and next knowledge and skills. This conversation had only one outcome, and I didn't like it.

"Okay. But I don't know when we're leaving yet. We still have a lot to plan."

"Then I'm on the team?" She gave a little shriek and got up and danced around. Danced! People looked at her and laughed. I wished I could make this trip alone. But that wouldn't be safe. And a team leader mustn't say things like that out loud, and people were watching, so I couldn't get away with it.

Honey calmed down, but only a little. "I'm going to the Coral Plains!"

"Remember, this isn't a real expedition. If we find something, then they'll send a real one."

"Right, we do the hard part, which is to go into the unknown, and once it's known, then the real work begins? No. This is the real expedition. You know that. And I'm on the team!"

I had to say something nice, so I said, "You're a great addition." That was the formal welcome, though mostly only old people used it, and I suddenly understood why. It gave you something nice to say when you needed to say something other than what you were thinking. I wasn't sure I'd wanted to learn that.

I had Honey on the team. I'd need at least one more person. I also needed to start planning the trip. Jose was out hunting, but I'd arranged to meet him in the late afternoon. I told Honey to be there with her map. I hoped he'd approve of her. I knew he'd like the map. Meanwhile, I'd talk to Stevland. He knew a lot.

The Meeting House was empty, and inside, Stevland was making noises. I ducked under the doorway and listened. They were animal noises, each one exactly right. He was going through bird species one by one, by clades, all their barks and woofs. Even eagle jabber. I'd never seen eagles, but maybe someday I'd be lucky. They liked big prey, including Humans, and I liked challenges.

"Stevland," I said, "do a bluebird reef." Anyone could do one bluebird, but only Stevland could do a couple of dozen birds at once.

After a pause, a lot of noise came from the speaker, first just ordinary barks, then an alert of approaching danger, then the whole reef reacted to try to scare it away.

"Wow, that was good. They saw a spider coming."

"Correct."

"You got it exactly."

"I appreciate your praise. You are an expert." Then he switched voices and sounded exactly like Jose. "You have come here to discuss your expedition."

I laughed again. "You can do anything."

"Sound analysis is as easy as chemistry. Your trip will bring back important information."

"That's what I think."

"Not everyone shares Queen Rust's opinion."

"Farmers do."

"Farmers think circularly and repetitively. They are inclined to assume that what has happened before will happen again. They are tied to seasons."

I thought a minute. "Hunting is tied to seasons, too."

"Correct. But you expect things to change, so you will see changes more readily. This is why you are a proper choice to lead this team. Honey is on your team now. She will provide good balance. But you need a Glassmaker, too. Every team should have one. I recommend a worker known as Scratcher whose queen is Thunderclap. She is not like Rust. She listens. Scratcher is an older worker, but he is strong and active and very experienced. He can run your camp so efficiently that you and Honey will be free to explore without other concerns."

"If you think so, I'll ask for him." I knew that Thunderclap ran the carpentry workshop, and no one hated her even though she was a queen.

"I appreciate your trust. She has the raft you can use. And I must trust you with one key piece of information, since you are leading an important team. I do not believe that velvet worm venom is fatal to Glassmakers, although it is to Humans. It may not even make them ill. In any case, the antidote will do them no harm and will reverse the mechanical action of the venom."

So Cawzee was just faking it! Figures.

"But you tell everyone it will kill them."

"There are already enough divisions on Pax. The saliva will dissolve any flesh, so the antidote must be applied to the wound. Also, any bite is trauma and requires prompt attention. As a team leader in a remote situation, you must have all the facts to make immediate, correct decisions. I wish I could go with you. The electronics workshop is creating a radio transmitter, and we are almost ready to implement that, but not in time. We need a little more metal."

"We'll take bats."

Stevland switched to bat language. "Warmth. Food." His traditional goodbye.

I tried to answer "water and sunshine" in Glassmade. Maybe I said "water and lizards."

After I'd left, I thought a lot. We always believed that Stevland was honest by nature. And I could understand his worry. This used to be the Glassmakers' city. They left, abandoning Stevland, we Humans found the ruins two hundred years later and took over, the Glassmakers came back a century ago, we fought, Humans won, and the surviving Glassmakers wanted to live in peace with us. But rumors said they'd like to wipe us out and take over. I didn't believe the rumors, but I couldn't forget them. Rumors also said Stevland never forgave them for abandoning him, either.

I went to see Thunderclap. There were eight queens, and for all that they were supposed to be integrated, I didn't know them well because I'd never tried. I found her directing the carpentry workshop, a tall, wide wooden building close to the river but above the normal flood stage. She and two Glassmaker workers and five Humans were all busy measuring, cutting, and pounding. It smelled like fresh-cut wood, sweet as a forest. Tools and boards and logs were everywhere. She wore a smock over a simple dress, and seemed a little swollen. Pregnant. Another worker or major on the way.

She saw me, put down a box she was working on, and dashed over to greet me, taking my hands the way queens like to. The air smelled like roses, she was that happy to see me. Was she expecting me?

"I'd like to ask Scratcher to be on my team."

She wiggled happily and held my hands tighter. "Scratcher be-him very happy to come with you. He travels much, enjoys travel, but not yet goes to the Coral Plains. He has many skills. I will send for him." She squawked something to one of the workers, who dashed off. "I desire he make a great addition to your team."

"Stevland says so."

"I desire say-you Rust say wrong things. We always must investigate. I perhaps come with you if queens perhaps take such grave risks. You be-you very brave. In that-far plains live terrible species and killers, you never know with every step what be-it beneath your foot or aim at your back."

"It won't be that bad."

"I will instruct Scratcher to obey you like you be-you me."

Finally, someone who understood chain of command. I wanted to thank her, but she kept talking.

"We need travel, we Glassmakers. To stay in one place is like be-us plant, and we be-us animals. Travel forces test of ideas to see if be-they true everywhere, testing roles and duties and learning which be-them correct. Places must change, we must find ideas which remain the same."

I was about to say I was an explorer because I changed when I went places, because I wanted to grow like a plant, at least mentally. Maybe some other day. "Scratcher will be a great addition to the team."

She took me by the hand and led me out of the workshop to the docks. A wide raft was tied there, with a little cabin that straddled two of the four fat white logs. She gestured at it like it was a prize.

"Your raft. It be-it perfect for travel. Sail for fast travel, pole to push if no wind, rudder to guide."

I pulled it close and stepped onto the back deck. The raft barely dipped under my weight. In any river race on a windy day, this kind of boat won. Sturdy and fast. With a quick leap, she was standing beside me. My smile was rewarded with a cloud of perfume. Then she rubbed her hands on her neck and reached out to anoint me with her scent. That would help Scratcher feel loyal to me, so I let her. She stroked my cheeks, my hair, and my clothing in a way that seemed a little personal. It smelled like pine and leather. I liked it.

A worker appeared at the riverbank, tan fur with reddish-brown patches like her. He bent his front legs to bow to her. She said something to him in Glassmade too fast and quiet for me to understand well. Something about "important" and a lot of "you." She gestured to me, and we both climbed off the raft onto the riverbank. He bowed again to her, and then to me, and walked over to my side.

"Where you go, I go."

I wasn't sure I wanted that kind of loyalty, but I knew what I had to say one more time. "You're a great addition to the team. Our team. Now I need to talk to people about the plains, and I'd like you to come with me. You should know everything I know."

"Where you go, I go."

I turned to the queen. "I'll need to know all about the raft. I've used them, but not enough."

"Very wise," she said, rosy again. "You will return-you both tomorrow when Lux is high. We will teach you to use it and cross war zone in river."

"Great. I'll bring Honey. She's on the team, too."

Halfway to Jose, Scratcher took my hand like a child, but his grip was strong and his hand was dry and rough like someone who had spent a lifetime working hard.

The hunters' headquarters was in a room attached to the north gate to the city, mostly a place to store and repair weapons. Honey had her map spread on the workbench and was showing it to Jose when we arrived. Would he approve of her?

He looked up at me, then at Scratcher, and nodded. "You've got yourself a great team. Let's start."

He went over everything he knew about velvet worms and the plains, and soon a biologist and another hunter joined us. Honey constantly asked questions and took notes. Scratcher asked what was edible, afraid of fire, or attacked at night.

But it turned out that Honey could hardly shoot an arrow and Scratcher had never wielded anything bigger than a kitchen knife. So I was in charge of security. Good. No competition. By then it was almost sundown.

"Let's meet again tomorrow right after dawn for breakfast," I said. "We've got training and preparation all day, and we leave the day after tomorrow at dawn."

"All right!" Honey said. "We're leaving! This will be exciting!"

Scratcher smelled sweetly content.

I went home. I share a house with five other guys, kind of crowded, but we're all lazy, and that way we split housekeeping down to nothing. Pretty soon Scratcher was knocking at the door, carrying a thick blanket and wearing a pair of side baskets with a few things in it.

"Where you go, I go."

I was even less sure I wanted that, but he was happy to curl up on the floor and hardly snored at all.

He wasn't easy to wake up at dawn. An hour later, I had laid out plans for the day, surprising Honey with all the details that went into a trip like this. I hoped she might resign from the team, but instead she got more enthusiastic. I started with a review of security, things like always staying in the line of sight of someone. I could guard them, but they had to avoid being stupid. If they could.

At midmorning, when the bright star Lux was high in the sky, Thunderclap showed us every detail about the raft, with tedious details like tacking with the sail, bright orange so we could be seen and rescued if needed. We practiced crossing the war zone. At the end of the forest, the trees made sort of a net across the river with their roots. We'd have to cross that carrying the raft, but we could detach the mast from the cabin, the cabin from the platform, and the platform from the logs. The logs were foam-wood, so even little Scratcher could carry one alone if he had to, and they would float high. Everything was made light so the raft would move fast with the slightest breeze or push by a pole.

We had a great raft, a great map, and an enthusiastic team. I was hyped, hyped, hyped for the trip. We'd be smart and fast.

We spent the afternoon gathering supplies and picking out three homing bats to return to the city with a message in case of trouble, training with them, then reviewing the maps to plan each day's trip. Seven days at most, two to get to the edge of the forest, three or four to roam around the Coral Plains, and then back home in less than two, since we could float downstream on the current. I sent Scratcher with Honey to pick out the right clothes for her. He came back after twice as long as I thought it would take.

"How did it go?"

"Many questions." His herbal scent said he was tired. He wanted to pack the cabin, so I helped carry down supplies and left him there and went to fetch my stuff.

On the way back, I walked past the Meeting House, and I heard Stevland talking with Fern like they were best friends, advising her on some new project.

After she left, I slipped in. "You should tell me more about her."

"Certain aspects of Human interaction lie beyond my expertise."

"Come on. A lot—"

He interrupted. "I have a root just for you."

"I bet it's packed with memories."

"It is only partially full, and it can continue to grow. I expect there will be much to know about you in the future."

"You keep track of everyone that way? Fern, too?"

"Some people I wish to forget, though it is unwise to act on that type of emotion. Most people I wish to remember long after they are gone."

"You're already waiting for us to die."

"I live for centuries. You will be very much worth remembering. Your trip will add significantly to our understanding of the plains."

I knew he tried to stay out of romances even if he had to change the subject, but it was worth a try.

"Did Fern mention me?"

"Like everyone, she is curious about the velvet worms."

He'd changed the subject. Oh, well. "What do you think we'll find out?"

"If I knew, you could stay home. I detect significant changes to the south, and, like you, I am curious. I cannot travel to the plains. But . . . will you take some seeds and plant them? Perhaps one will live."

"Sure."

"In case of danger, abandon them. I abandon groves as necessary. I wish I could be on your team."

"You'd be a great addition."

"You will be a great team leader."

I got some seeds and took them and my weapons and gear to the raft. Scratcher and Honey were arguing about how to store the food. I had the final word, and I used it. "We'll sort this out tomorrow."

Then my worker and I ate an early dinner. We had finished up and were outside in the cold headed home when Cawzee approached. Scratcher gripped my hand tight. He smelled something I couldn't.

"I be-me going with you," Cawzee announced.

"I've got my team already."

"I will prove my skill to my queen."

"We're leaving tomorrow and things are set."

"You need a warrior. Honey and Scratcher be-they useless. I will guard-you the team."

We did need a guard, but he was no expert, and not even Honey was useless. I heard someone approaching. Four feet, by the pattern of the footsteps, a Glassmaker, and a heavy one. A hint of clumsiness, also the way Cawzee tensed up, told me who it was.

"Good evening, Queen Rust," I said in poorly imitated Glassmade just to annoy her.

"You know me?" She sounded more annoyed than usual. "You not smell me."

"I know you by the sound, Queen. I'm a hunter. I listen."

"You will take-you my major."

"I have a team."

"He will be-he on your team."

I tried to bluff. "He will need weapons, lots of weapons. We don't know what we're facing. You might really lose him this time. And he needs clothing, enough to spend all day and all night in the worst weather, because he will be on guard all the time. And he needs all this by one hour after dawn."

I glared at her but didn't hint that we were leaving exactly at dawn, so he'd arrive late. She scented something rude.

"He will have-him all this." And they walked off, no anointing, no goodbyes, and I didn't say that he'd be a great addition to the team.

"We need-us more food," Scratcher said. "I get-us it." There was that tired smell again.

I went to bed early, but I didn't fall asleep fast. Scratcher came in a little later, curled up, made a happy smell, then a tired smell, then fidgeted for a while.

———

I woke up to the birds and crab calls before dawn, and coaxed him awake. We got the bats, fed them, grabbed breakfast, got a big basket of travel bread at the bakery, and headed for the raft.

Little plaques of ice had formed on the logs. No one had come to see us off and wish us luck, not my family or any Black Hats or hunters or Scratcher's family or city leaders. No one except for the guard lounging up on the wall at the gate, who waved and shouted good luck. That's how important we were. We began loading up the raft.

Honey arrived. She looked to be dressed properly, with a rain poncho over a winter coat, a brimmed rainproof hat, heavy slacks and boots under her knee-length skirt, and her hair braided and out of the way. Scratcher had done his job. But she was carrying a fippokat.

"This is Emerald." She hugged the animal. "She has lots of experience digging for geological work."

"You're not taking her."

"I'll take good care of her. We'll need her."

"She'll get killed the first time she tries to dig. You can't walk in the plains without boots and protection. Does that kat have boots?"

"There are kats in the plains."

"Not that kind."

"She has tough paw pads. Look."

I took the paw, then pinched Emerald hard on the ankle. The kat whined and squirmed. I don't like hurting animals, but I had a point to make. "It'll be that easy for her to get stung and killed."

She pouted. "I don't want to go without my Emerald."

"Okay. Stay here."

"If I can't go, you can't have my maps."

"I've already got your maps."

The sun was about to rise, and I didn't see Cawzee. Maybe we'd get away without him if Honey didn't make us waste too much time. I looked up, and the guard on the wall was waving and pointing so I'd know a team member was on his way.

There came Cawzee, staggering fast down the river bluff road with side baskets loaded with weapons and clothes. Scratcher made a tired scent.

"Cawzee's coming," I told Honey in a taunting tone. That made him good for something.

"Why? We don't need him."

"Tell his queen. Go ahead. Try."

"If he's coming, I'm coming."

"Good. You're a great addition. Without the kat."

She looked at me, at the kat, at Cawzee, at me again, then at the kat again. "I'll be right back."

"Run," I said. Scratcher was already rearranging the tiny cabin. I helped him, and I was surprised he made it all fit, and we were done before Honey got back so she couldn't object, and all the while Cawzee stood by on guard, as if we could get attacked at the dock.

We cast off and I raised the sail. I noticed the stand of rainbow bamboo growing near the docks and knew Stevland was watching. Someone was seeing us off. In fact, there were scattered groves of him here and there all the way up the river. He'd be with us until we got to the Coral Plains.

The first day nothing happened. The current was slow, the wind got funneled onto the river, the sail worked great, we punted as needed, and the raft floated as gracefully on the river as a cactus through the air. We set the bats' roost on a corner of the roof, and they flew around occasionally but didn't say much and weren't ambitious. It was cold, but I was used to it. Honey shivered but didn't complain. Cawzee did. Scratcher either made himself useful or sat with his legs underneath him on the roof of the cabin and looked around in sweet silence.

We tied up for the night. Scratcher cooked and fed us a good meal. I thought about the hunting sites I'd seen along the river. Cawzee paced nervously on the deck and the roof. Honey scribbled in a notebook. Eventually we all crowded inside the cabin and slept.

The second day, the same. We got near the war zone a little early and tied up, then stacked ourselves into the shelves that passed for beds and slept.

Bird calls woke me a little before dawn. I also heard bat calls, but it wasn't the language of bats from Rainbow City, and ours were eager to fly. I let them go and set out food so they wouldn't forget to return. By then the rest of the team was waking up. Scratcher prepared food while Cawzee took a little patrol. Honey was jumping for joy because we'd be at the Coral Plains in no time.

We poled the remaining little way up the river as fast as we could to the war zone. None of us had seen it, but we couldn't mistake it. Suddenly up ahead, a wide mass of tree roots crossed the river, topped by leafy shoots and branches. It looked like the river was dammed, but it continued to flow through a net of roots below the water.

"Agate trees!" Honey said. "They thrive on the war! That's how they get silicon, they kill the corals and absorb the shells." She continued to explain the ecology and how little symbiotic animals amid the roots helped one side or the other. Meanwhile I sent Cawzee to find a path across the roots. Scratcher began to dismantle the raft. The bats flew around and had nothing more to say than "No trees! Come! See!" so at least there was no danger they could identify on the other side. But these bats had never been to the Coral Plains.

Cawzee called, "I be-me on other side, easy way! Come! I have done-you your task!" It wasn't that easy, and the dam was almost a hundred meters across, but we could do it. Soon we had moved the four logs, then some pieces of the cabin frame, and were setting them up on the logs. As I was tying them down, something struck my heel.

I turned, grabbing my spear. The biggest venomous crayfish I had ever seen was climbing onto the raft, and other crayfish were reaching up behind it. I swung the spearhead like a scythe and knocked it off.

Before I could warn Cawzee, he screamed, "Crayfish! I fight them!"

I ran toward the side near the cabin, where more were climbing up, and slipped as the logs shifted. I dropped the spear to grab a cable. The last thing I wanted to do was fall into the water. It would be the last thing I would ever do.

Cawzee came running around from the other side. "More! I kill them!" He stabbed at them a little clumsily because Glassmakers have strange elbows. But he moved quick, hitting one, then two. On the third, he bent down to strike low. "I make raft safe. I be-me good guard!"

"You're a fine guard," I said. I picked up my spear and watched him toss away the dying crayfish. Somewhere, sometime, he had learned something.

We heard Scratcher and Honey arguing even before they came through the little forest that topped the dam, carrying the final load. They looked at us and our unfinished task as if we had been goofing off. We got to work again, Cawzee and I with an eye on the water at all times, and soon we put up the mast. We were done. Ahead of us stood no more trees, just wide plains pocked by low growth.

"Let's tie up and explore!" Honey said.

"Let's just go slow and look," I said. "Listen. We're not alone."

Near and far, things were clicking and buzzing, totally different from the forest. No leaves rustled because there were no leaves. It sounded wrong.

The soil on the banks and plains shimmered light red and looked rocky, but many of the rocks and pebbles were alive, different kinds of coral. We could see a long way, across flat, wet land that gradually gave way to low rises separated by rills carved by rainwater. Clumps of brush grew on the tops of the rills. Some were mere sticks hung with brown ruffles, some were shaped like upside-down bottles with green bladelike leaves on top, or squarish boxes covered with blue thorns thick as fur. Sprays of red quitch grass grew wherever there was enough empty dirt.

The river bottom sometimes felt sandy, sometimes mucky. Occasionally something struck the pole. The air smelled like wet decay with a hint of sulfur.

I pulled out a small telescope and didn't see anything different far away. I don't know what I'd expected, signs of civilization?

Behind us, the forest rose like a wall, a dark layer of short agate trees in front of taller locustwood and pine, and among them, maybe, a rainbow bamboo, or maybe I was just hoping too hard. It was winter, so most trees stood bare, but even still, the ones closest to the plains seemed sickly. A swamp lay between the forest and plains. Fuzzy red filaments rose up from the water to wrap around trunks of trees that had fallen into it fighting for us. What a way to die.

Honey saw me looking through the telescope. "There's a whole ecosystem at work here," she said. "It's so different!"

"It be-it ugly," Cawzee said.

"For once," I said, "I'll go with him."

Something splashed and thudded on the far side of the raft. Scratcher was there! We all jumped and ran to help him. He held up a big two-tail fish in one hand and a little hooked spear in the other.

"Food."

I raised the sail and we took off, tacking through the meanders of the river. Honey sat on the roof of the cabin, narrating nonstop about whether the land and the map agreed, and scribbled down everything we saw. We had to report back, but not all of us might make it.

Cawzee spotted a pair of crabs scrambling among the plants and corals on the far side of the river, patterned red, yellow, and green, big enough to have killed Honey's kat easily. She made a note and was silent for a little while, but not as long as I would have liked.

We beached for lunch, by then maybe ten kilometers upstream. The landscape had become thicker with corals and plants. I stepped gently out onto the ground. It felt spongy under a surface layer of scattered corals like pebbles, some round but others shaped like branches or horns or fans, red, pink, purple, blue, or dead and white. The dead ones crunched under my soles, empty. I stood still and felt tiny knocks from the live ones, corals sending out darts to attack.

"Watch out," I said. "Big corals will have big darts. Keep your distance."

But Honey had to try to prod a boulder with a pole. The dart sprang out longer than her arm. "Whoa, that's good to know!" she said, and made a note.

I stabbed some holes in a clear area with a pole and planted a few of Stevland's seeds. Good luck, friend. Maybe the stink meant the soil was fertile.

I felt glad to be back on the boat. We ate. The fish was delicious. Two hours upstream, Honey motioned to stop.

"Look, fippokats, sort of!" she whispered. "There by the trees!"

For a second, I saw nothing, but the shape of a shadow gave away a fippokat colored in red, black, and white that blended perfectly into the landscape. It even had red-tufted ears that looked like grass. There was a group of them, maybe twenty, now obvious since I knew what to look for, including a couple of little baby kits that were the cutest things I'd ever seen. The adults were three times the size of Emerald. Their paws and legs were thick with fur.

"We don't want to draw their attention," Honey whispered. "Carnivorous kats. They hunt in packs."

"My kind of pet."

"A long time ago, they killed two members of an expedition."

"What you-see?" Cawzee squawked.

His shout got their attention. The two biggest ones took a few hops toward us. They could have easily hopped from the shore to our raft.

"I not see something."

"They're part red," Honey said. "Glassmakers can't see red well."

I grabbed a pole and shoved us away upstream. The carni-kats hopped along the bank to keep up. One snarled. It had big fangs.

Honey began scribbling. "There's another kind of kat that lives in the hollow trunks of the box trees with blue thorns. Those have blue fur. We don't know much about them. Maybe we can look for them!"

"We're here to see if anything changed."

"Oh, right!"

We were there to look for danger. Carni-kats in our forest would be a big one.

As we moved on, we noticed more and bigger corals, some round and more than a meter tall, arranged in lines. The weather stayed clear and cold. Scratcher brewed tea over embers in a pottery brazier, and served it with dried fruit.

"Thanks," Honey said. "You know, with all the predators, there should be more animals in general."

"Why?" Scratcher said.

"To feed them."

He watched the landscape slide past. "Yes. Water and food."

"If I were food," I said, "I'd be hiding. The reports said that there are a lot of caterpillars and herds of giant land trilobites, at least in summer. Maybe a lot goes on underground, or maybe the animals are hiding. Even in the forest, it's hard to find the animals, but they're there."

Honey draped the map over the back of the cabin and pointed. "We're here right now, I think, and you can see that just up there, the river splits. We have to choose."

"We'll decide when we get there."

When we got there, it was obvious. The branch to our right, to the southwest, flowed full and apparently normal. But the southeast branch was dry. There was a backwash for a ways, and farther up a dry, rocky riverbed. Dried weeds stood stiff, and some of the corals along the edges looked dead and dry.

"It hasn't been dry for long," I said. "A year or two, probably."

Far up the riverbed, seen through the telescope, stood a now dry waterfall over a ridge of light-colored rocks.

"Well, now we know!" Honey said.

"How water stop-it in river?" Cawzee asked.

"That's the question!" she answered. "I think it was the earthquake! The books say earthquakes can alter riverbeds."

I pulled us out of the main current. "Now we know. We can turn back." But I really wanted to climb that ridge and see what was on the other side.

"No," Honey said. "We should see what's on the other side of that hill."

"Cawzee?" I said.

"How water stop-it in river? We find answer there."

"Scratcher?"

"We go-us to hill, see."

"We all agree, then."

I punted us up as far as I could and we dragged the raft onto sort of a sandbar. The water wasn't safe, the land wasn't safe, and the sandbar seemed to be neither water nor land and all the safety we were going to get. I decided we'd hike to the hill first thing the next morning, since the sun would set soon and storm clouds were blowing in, nothing too bad, I hoped.

We tried to examine a big pink coral near the riverbed without getting too close. Its surface was rough and pitted, openings for eyes, ears, stingers, or whatever, Honey said. An animal lived inside and sucked nutrients from below and from anything that came near. Scratcher caught a little fish and threw it at the coral. A stinger flew out and hit it. The dead fish landed on a carpet of little corals around it.

"It could all be one big animal," Honey said.

"Sort of like Stevland," I said, "with groves all connected by roots." Without trees and big hills, the land stretched all around us, and I felt exposed, the way I did standing in the middle of big fields. Nowhere to hide. But I could also spot anything coming.

"Could we live here?" she asked. "Humans and Glassmakers?"

"I don't know. The forest hates the plains. This whole place is poison. And the ground vibrates like things are moving under there."

"Yes! Look how wet the soil is! This is rich soil, but maybe not for us."

Then it started to sleet, and we headed for cover. The rain hadn't let up by the time we were ready to sleep, and when Cawzee and I made a final patrol, we saw that some of the corals were glowing. The air had filled with the sound of clicking, mostly in unison. But nothing was attacking, so we went back in and slept.

We woke up to a clear dawn and began hiking as soon as we could, Scratcher laden with first-aid supplies, Cawzee and I with weapons, and Honey with the telescope and a notebook. We wore our toughest clothes. We'd need to avoid the round corals, and I spotted a good path higher up.

When we got there, I knelt to study it. "There's three kinds of tracks. Kat, bird, and something big and heavy with a tail. This is a popular trail, and everyone in the neighborhood knows about it."

Cawzee and I took the lead, armed and ready. Soon we saw a big dead coral sphere about twenty meters from the path. Just to see what would happen, I put a clay bullet in a sling and threw. The coral shattered. Caterpillars and land trilobites tumbled out like a squirming wave, and a foul breeze wafted toward us.

"They were eating it!" Honey said. "That explains a lot. It must be densely nutritious. See how many animals there were in there!"

An hour of slow, careful hiking later, we were almost up the rocky hill. I was looking at the way the land could be great for an ambush. But the dirt was thinning out, and so were the corals. The Glassmakers got there first, Cawzee waving weapons. At least he was doing his job.

"Big," Scratcher called back to us.

I scrambled to his side and looked. A wide, long, shallow, empty lake bed filled the valley behind the hill, and it had been empty for a year or two.

Honey ran up. "Wow! This is new! Look! There's still a big pond down there near the middle." It lay over two kilometers away, ringed in red, probably the same filaments that grew in the war zone. "Let's go there!"

"Let's take a long look before we do anything. A lot of things live there."

Dead, dried-out water plants and animals and corals and stiff clumps of red quitch grass covered the ground, except on the bare sandbars. I gave Honey the telescope so she could scan the far side.

"There's another escarpment! The river came over it before, I can see the entry. I bet the river is flowing around it now!"

"Here be-it now no river," Cawzee said. He smelled like a mix of very overripe fruit, nervous.

"Right!" she said. "The earthquake moved the ground, and the river shifted."

Scratcher tapped me and pointed to some tracks with a whiff of stinking *fear*.

"Carni-kat," I said. "It's good hunting here. Let's not get hunted."

"Can we go down now?" Honey said.

"Why?" I said. But a nearby sandbar glittered like a yellow jewel lizard. Maybe gold. Maybe I could bring Stevland a present he'd love.

"Well," she said, "we can see what lived here. Maybe take some samples."

"Okay," I said, "let's head for that sandbar."

Far away, I saw a shadow move and checked it out with the telescope. Carni-kat. Another one next to it. I warned everyone, as if we weren't on edge enough already. But we made it to the sandbar safely.

Honey saw the gold. "That's useful for making wires for radios and things. We knew it came from somewhere in the plains. Let's take what we can!" She handed me a sack for samples.

I made sure my gloves were on tight, then scooped sand, pebbles, and gold into the sack.

"Aren't you going to sort it?"

"We don't have time."

"Are we going to keep exploring?"

Scratcher answered with the scents of *fear* and *flee*. Cawzee, at the far end of the sandbar, didn't seem to be paying attention.

"I don't think so," I said. "We can figure out what happened already. The lake dried up. I'm guessing that as the corals died, the populations went up of the animals that ate dead corals, like caterpillars and trilobites. That had a ripple effect. Velvet worms are higher up in the food chain, and their numbers went up. Now they're hungry and looking for food."

"Wow!" Honey said. "That's smart!"

"Thanks." I saw a red velvet worm sliding toward her. "Honey, run! Towards me! Run!"

She looked up wide-eyed, and after a second of hesitation began running. I started slinging bullets. The worm turned away.

But it turned because a carni-kat was leaping at it. One, two—no, five, maybe more kats were skulking in our direction.

I heard hooves and glanced back. Cawzee was running toward us, weapons raised. Scratcher was staying where he was in the middle of the sandbar, the safest place around. Good. Honey was at my side by then, tense, ready to sprint again.

The kats crouched, eyes on us. They began to squeak, one answering the other with complex sounds. I could guess what they were discussing. I slung a bullet and they scattered, then regrouped with the grace of practiced hunters.

"Cawzee, shoot some arrows!"

"Where? I see-me nothing!"

"There, next to that big clump of grass. On the left."

That's where three were crouched together, making plans.

Cawzee shot a pair of arrows faster than I knew he could. The first arrow hit a kat square in the ribs. The rest scattered, squealing, and disappeared into the landscape. The injured kat took a few short hops and fell.

"Let's get out of here," I said. But Cawzee had dashed off in the other direction, and by the time I'd turned around to tell him no, he was holding up the arrow with a twitching kat hanging from it.

"First big kill. Me! Mine! For queen!"

"Fine. Make sure it's dead. Whack it on the back of the head. Now let's get out of here!"

We ran to the top of the ridge, took a long look back to see if we were being followed, and began climbing downhill.

A half hour later we were close enough to see our raft. Three big, shiny, purple things were hulking around it. Through the telescope, they looked like giant trilobites with blunt heads. Each was half the size of the raft.

I handed the telescope to Honey. "Those are new. Take some notes."

"Let's go look!"

"Let's not. Anything that big in this environment is tough as stone and mean."

One of them nudged the raft.

"I think it's biting it!" Honey said.

Scratcher was ready to bolt and smelled, surprisingly, like *attack*. I put a hand on his back.

"Hold on. They can crush us like lizards. And they're a bright color. That's a warning. They're dangerous and they want everyone to see them and stay away."

"Queen make raft."

"Yes, it's a fine raft and we need it." I tried to think about what to do. I didn't have any good ideas. We were in big trouble.

"Cawzee, let's go, you and I. Slow, very slow. Let's see what we can do."

He handed the dead kat to Scratcher, and we began walking.

The giant trilobites kept nudging the raft until it moved. One lowered its head and started to push. The raft rose up, up, and tipped over with a crash.

"No no no no no," Scratcher squalled behind us.

The trilobites kept nudging the raft's logs, ripping and crunching like a carpenter's workshop. I decided we were close enough.

"They're feeding!" Honey called. "They're eating the logs."

"We will attack-them," Cawzee said, reeking of aggression.

I put an arm around his shoulders to hold him back. "We've never seen these before. We don't know what they can do. But they're dangerous, we can see that. I know we need the raft. But if we shoot some arrows, they could charge at us. We'd lose the fight. We need our lives more than the raft. Just stay calm."

We should have left someone behind to guard it. . . . No, that wouldn't have helped. No one would have been safe alone, and even all four of us couldn't have stopped three giant purple land trilobites. But without the raft, we couldn't get home.

If we had to stay in the plains it would be tough survival. I was trembling. I forced myself to stop. We'd left the bats inside the cabin, safe. If the bats were alive, we could send them home for help. I listened for them. They should have been screeching. But I heard nothing.

I stood there, useless.

The trilobites ate most of the logs, then they reared up and smashed what remained of the raft. The bats darted out of the wreckage and flew around, screaming the word for danger. They must have been huddled inside in terror. The trilobites rooted around in the wreckage, munched a little more, then began climbing the riverbank away from us.

Cawzee tensed, ready to run.

"Wait until they're far away. The raft will be the same if we wait or if we don't, but the first thing is to stay safe." There was something we should be doing. "Cawzee, you speak bat. Call out 'home, rescue.' You're louder than me, they'll hear you."

He took a deep breath. I covered my ears. He began to call loud and clear. The bats answered with "Danger! Flee!" They exchanged calls a few times with him, then turned and flew like arrows northward.

"Good job, Cawzee."

"They will fly-them one day and one morning, I think. The city will send-us help."

"Maybe even less time than that. They're in a hurry to get home."

I knew that half of all homing bats failed to arrive if the distance was more than a day and the terrain was new to them. And if we didn't know about the big purple trilobites, what else was out there? And what was keeping the trilobites in the plains, out of the forest? But I didn't say that. Everyone was scared enough.

I decided the trilobites had gotten far enough away. I motioned to Honey and Scratcher. We started walking. Carefully. Everything else that was wrong with the Coral Plains was still there and trying to kill us.

The raft looked like what I'd expected instead of what I'd hoped for. The logs were chewed up, with not enough solid pieces left to make a little raft for even just one person. The cabin's contents were spread out, some of it nibbled, and the food had been trampled. The same for the clothes and bedding.

"They liked the wood," Honey said. She sounded like she was going to cry.

"Why wood?" Scratcher had picked up a gnawed fragment and was stroking it as if he could make it feel better.

"The wood probably tasted good," she said, her voice catching. "I think this kind has lots of potassium, even for wood. Kats, our kind of kat, like to nibble these trees. And some crabs and birds."

Scratcher began searching methodically through the debris, stinking of suffering. Honey helped him, stone-faced. Cawzee danced around, checking the horizon. I didn't like the storm clouds I saw coming our way. It was early afternoon and getting windy.

"All right, we have some food and clothes and most of our gear. Let's make a shelter out of what we have for tonight. Cawzee, stand guard while we work. Carni-kats might have followed us."

Scratcher mumbled about his queen as he took stock of what we had, then pantomimed a way to reassemble the cabin, more or less, with the roof set down as a floor to protect us from the ground and the orange sail serving as the new roof.

We got to work. Soon Honey was tying the sail mast in place as the roof beam as I held it steady. She had inspected the ropes for dangerous hangers-on and then taken off her gloves to pull them tight. But as she was looping the ropes for a knot, a coral lashed out from a fold in the sail and stung one of her fingers. She screamed.

As fast as I could, I grabbed her hand, pulled the finger clear, pinned it against the wall of the cabin, and chopped half of it off with my hunting knife.

She kept screaming but didn't resist. I gripped the finger tight, the third one on her left hand, to stop the bleeding.

"I'm sorry," I said. "I'm sorry."

She sobbed but was trying to control herself. She raised her injured hand high and took over from me, holding the stump of the finger shut. Good first-aid procedure. I hoped I had cut away enough. Scratcher was pulling out the first-aid kit. I took her upper left arm and squeezed to hold a pulse point shut to keep it from bleeding more.

Cawzee stared at us, frozen in place.

"Cawzee, keep your guard up! The smell of blood will attract things."

He took a few steps back, then began a careful circle of the raft.

Honey panted, staring up at her hand, then down at the tip of the finger lying on the ground.

Scratcher motioned for her to sit down on the remains of a log so he could examine the wound. I couldn't look at it. It wasn't the blood, it was something else. I had failed. I'd lost the raft, and a team member had gotten permanently injured.

Scratcher fussed with her hand, then guided my hand to hold hers again. It felt slick with salve or blood or sweat. He picked up a needle and thread and began sewing. Honey tried to hold her hand still, but she needed my help. I tried to distract myself by looking around for approaching predators.

When Scratcher was done, he gave her some antibiotics, painkillers, and tranquilizers and sent her inside to her bunk, which was now on the floor instead of a shelf on the wall, since we had no shelves. I found the coral that had stung her, flat and orange. It tried to sting my gloves. I dropped it and crushed it under my boot into sticky powder. We finished assembling the cabin.

Then I got buckets of water and washed the blood off the cabin and the area around it until I was sure I had done enough, then I rinsed it some more. I buried the fingertip a good distance away. I wished we could have moved the cabin, but it was too fragile. I helped Cawzee skin his trophy kat far away from us, downstream. We tossed the corpse into the river.

"What be-it your first big kill?" His voice warbled. He was still scared.

"A fitch. Remember how excited Stevland was? He thought they were extinct. Okay, now we need to stretch this out to dry. I think on these bushes over here. The fur looks good. When you lay it flat, you can see the pattern."

"Queen will like-it." He did not seem convinced.

"She'll be proud of you. That was some good shooting." He was slowly getting more competent. I hoped he would feel more competent. That was what we needed in order to get through, competence. Even if I had to fake it myself.

The wind had picked up and it was going to snow. The sun was setting. I ordered him inside.

By then Scratcher had food and salty tea ready. We insisted on making Honey eat, although she was sleepy, then we went to bed. I lay down next to her so she'd be warmer and not alone if she needed something or had convulsions. No one was going to die on this trip. I hoped.

I kept waking up all night, and every time I did, I looked around at the wrecked cabin, lit and heated by a little oil lamp. I heard snow rustling on the roof, saw a few flakes blowing in through cracks, and tried not to think about anything besides what to do next. I got some ideas.

At dawn I got up, grabbed my weapons, and went outside. Snow lay a palm deep, and the air was very cold but windless.

Something moved downstream when I stepped out, but I couldn't see what. A set of carni-kat tracks came up to the cabin, paced back and forth as it had inspected the wall where Honey had bled, and then left, unhurried. The tracks were fresh. Snow had melted over some of the corals. They were warm. I'd try to remember that to tell Honey. Something made a hooting sound far away. Tiny things under rocks clicked and clattered as usual. Cawzee's kat pelt was still there on the bush.

I went inside. Everyone was awake. Honey looked up and smiled, a forced smile that meant forgiveness. She had her notebook open and was writing.

"What's the plan, team leader?" Her cheer was as fake as her smile.

"I'm working on that. Cawzee, I need you to come out and help me clean snow off the roof."

Once we were out, he said, "I go for help. Glassmakers be-us fast."

"I thought about that. It's too far and too dangerous, and we need two guards to be safe around here, you and me. Honey and Scratcher can't be guards."

"I be-me—"

"And I have a job for us that will be crucial. Okay, they'll send help, but how do they find us? They'll see smoke. That's what stranded hunters do, smoke signals. So we need to find stuff to burn, and it needs to be smoky. Just gathering fuel is going to be a two-person project, one to gather it and the other one to protect that person."

During breakfast, Honey had ideas about what could burn. Scratcher assembled tools for us. We took them and went out, keeping the cabin in sight by one of us at all times. Cawzee helped me prod and poke and drag burnable material out of the landscape.

Two hours before sunset, we were on the best nearby hill we could find with a safe, bare, stony top. The woodpile, so to speak, looked more like a garbage pile, but a small test fire had burned well, especially the bits that had been coral guts, and plenty smoky. And stinky, which we agreed might help Glassmaker searchers find us.

As far as we could see, the plains looked more or less the same everywhere. Ridges and ravines created by runoff marked the land. Coral clustered in the damper parts of ravines, and vegetation topped the ridges.

"There's a lot we don't know about this place," I said.

"I not return-me here. Dangerous. Ugly. Sad." He smelled *angry*.

"I'm with you there." But I didn't agree about ugly. Hostile, incompatible even, weird for sure, but beautiful.

We could see a section of the river below the fork, its banks outlined by corals. And, far away, a moving dot. A bright orange dot, the search-and-rescue color. Moving fast. A canoe! Cawzee started scampering around in place and bellowing so loud they could have almost heard him. I started up the fire and black smoke billowed.

The canoe would be at the fork in the river soon.

"Run and meet it," I said. He took off like an arrow, dodging pink corals and patches of vegetation. I ran down to the cabin.

Scratcher and Honey had heard the noise and were outside.

"A canoe is coming!" I said.

They cheered and looked downriver. I climbed up on a rock. At the fork in the river, Cawzee screeched and danced on a safe, bare patch of the sandbar at the bend. Several screeches answered. The canoe came into view, a small one, with two—no, three Glassmakers. But one was too large. A queen. That was stupid! Queens should stay safe in the city. The plains were for expendable, unimportant people. We probably shouldn't even have sent a Human woman.

The canoe stopped at the bank where it was pocked with big pink corals. The queen rose to get out.

"Stay in the canoe!" I shouted.

Cawzee was making explosive sounds, bounding toward her.

The queen squawked something in response, but did not pause and walked right at a coral. She had no training in the plains and couldn't have known how deadly they were. But she should have guessed.

She staggered. Cawzee leaped and dragged her into the canoe. The Glassmakers pushed off and paddled toward us as fast as they could. I ran down to the water to meet them.

"Scratcher, first aid!" I called. An amputation, a mere amputation, I hoped. We could do that.

As the canoe approached, I recognized the queen drooping in Cawzee's arms. Rust. That explained a lot. She would listen to no one, not even her own major trying to save her life. But a dead queen would be a bigger disaster than if all of us died. A family couldn't live without its queen.

"You will help-her!" Cawzee bawled. I met the canoe and held it stable as the three Glassmakers carried out their limp queen. Scratcher began to work. Honey held the first-aid kit. She looked as scared as I wished I felt, but I felt worse. Hopeless.

Scratcher had them turn her to look at a dripping wound on her chest, poured something on it, then on another wound like it farther down on her belly. He looked into her drooling mouth, put his head on her neck to listen, and felt along her belly. He didn't seem to be finding what he was looking for, and he was looking for signs of life. He searched again and again, and finally grabbed her limp hands and keened, the Glassmaker sound of grief. The other three clutched her and wailed.

My eardrums rattled in pain with the noise. I sneaked behind the cabin to hold my hands over my ears and think.

At least it wasn't my fault. Rust should have known better. No one should have let her come, no one, not her family, not any other Glassmakers, not any Humans. But there she was, dead, and I was the team leader, so this was my problem now. First, all that noise might attract something. I couldn't stay hiding behind the cabin.

The three screeching Glassmakers had sunk to the ground and held her limp body. Cawzee, another major, and a worker. Scratcher and Honey had backed away and looked at me to see what to do. I checked for predators, then motioned them to join me.

"Do we have to kill them?" Honey said.

"No," Scratcher said, his voice still rough. "They kill-them each."

"Not here, not while I'm in charge," I said. "We have things to do and we need all hands. Scratcher, will they understand that?"

"Not kill-them here. At city, at ceremony."

"Good. The sun'll set soon, and we need to have this sorted out before then. First, Scratcher, we need them to stop making that noise. It will attract something."

"Yes," he said, and walked toward them, emitting a complex smell.

"I'm sorry for them," I told Honey. "But she was stupid, and look what she did." Honey nodded. A queen's family depended on her too much. Right now, those three were blind with grief, blind with fear, blind with abandonment, all alone in a world that needed a queen to provide guidance and control.

I looked at the canoe again and bailed out some water. It could hold three at the most. I tried to figure out a way to get us home safe. We wouldn't all fit, so I'd have to send some ahead. I'd go last. I made a plan and had time to think it through three times.

When Cawzee seemed coherent, I took him aside.

"Cawzee, tomorrow you must take your queen and Honey to the city."

"I will kill-me."

"Not yet. You must honor your queen by taking her home and by escorting Honey to get medical care."

"My queen be-her dead!"

"And now more than ever you must show how great a queen she was because she has such great majors."

He stood still, barely breathing. I looked at all three members of her family and hoped I had their attention.

"It will be night soon, and we must prepare. Your queen will be prey to scavengers here. We must take her inside. We will hold a vigil. Understood?"

"Yes."

"We obey."

The smell of *subservience*. And *misery*.

By the time we were done, it was night. A writhing green aurora lit the sky. It was too cramped inside, so I decided to spend the night outside, guarding, in order to escape the dead body and reek of grief. Honey said she would guard with me, and maybe she belonged safe inside, but I understood why she wanted out.

We took some blankets, the cooking brazier for a fireplace, and some boxes both to sit on and to make more room inside. We left the Glassmakers whining on the floor, grouped around the corpse that was wrapped in her own blankets.

Honey got flames going in the brazier while I inspected the canoe and all sides of the cabin. We decided to burn the remaining bits of log from the raft, since they might attract more big trilobites, and besides, the night was cold, and flames would frighten away most animals, we hoped.

I sat down, slung a blanket around my shoulders, and thought about how to get home. Rust's other major had told me his queen had become frightened because the moving star in the sky was a spaceship. She didn't know what would happen, so she wanted her family together. Her trip hadn't been well planned or even announced. People were too upset about the spaceship to notice her leaving.

We needed to get back to the city. Fast.

A spaceship. Honey had interrogated the major, but she hadn't learned much. Viewed through a telescope, it was definitely a fair-sized spaceship or something else artificial, and its orbit made it fly over Rainbow City regularly, which couldn't be an accident. We were being watched from above. By who? Or what? Why?

More trouble was about to happen.

We stared glumly at the landscape and the aurora curling overhead. "Maybe we can see the spaceship!" Honey said.

A pale pink curtain radiated from the horizon and lit the landscape. None of the stars seemed to be moving.

"The sky looks so big here," she said.

"Yeah. I saw a sky like this, even bigger, when I climbed the mountain. I could see the land below me and the sky down to the horizon. I saw how little the city was compared to the forest, and how the forest was surrounded by mountains and the Coral Plains, and downriver we know there are more plains and the ocean, and beyond them more continents, but we don't know much. That's what I thought."

"We're small."

"Yeah. I'll never be bigger than the things around me, bigger than the city, my team, what we do. But those things can be big."

Around us, the coral boulders contrasted with the rough rocks and vegetation like the smooth rounded roofs of our city. The corals closest to us began to glow, then others farther away, and soon they were blinking in unison. I pulled my blanket tighter.

"Honey, did you ever think the corals might be aliens, like us and the Glassmakers, but really aliens, at least compared to the forest? We fit in there, in the forest, and we try to, and we've made friends and allies, but these corals are trying to take over and get rid of the forest because they need room to live."

"Every biologist wonders that. Their chemistry is odd compared to the forest, but not too odd. It might be native, it might not be. We don't know."

Another thing to add to the tally of potential danger. "What about the ship up there? It really is a ship, right?"

"The telescopes spotted antennas and things," she said. "It's a ship. Stevland and the radio technicians heard pings like radar and sensors. It couldn't be here by accident. Someone came looking for us. Earth."

"Maybe. Or it could be Glassmakers."

"Glassmakers always say, 'Home Mothers not search for us.' They don't say why, and they might not even know why, but they're sure. So I think it's Earth, and Earth is horrible. The First Generation that settled here almost killed everybody." She went on for a while, and I wondered what was going on back in the city. That farmer Geraldine, for example, would be in a panic. The moderator Ladybird would need help.

"It could be something else, too!" Honey said. "If Humans came and Glassmakers came, some other life-form could come."

"It could be just someone else looking for a green planet. Or a pink one. The Coral Planet, if there is one. Oh! Look at that!"

The corals had started to blink in patterns. We stared silently. The patterns became complex. Soon her lips were moving as she counted. I realized I was holding my breath, my hand clenched on my knife.

"I'll make a note of this," she whispered.

I desperately wanted to flee and knew I needed to stay there and say something brave. "We've never seen them move. They can't really do anything if we stay far enough away."

"It's probably just communication."

"Fireflies blink," I said. But not like that.

Eventually they stopped blinking and the lights faded.

"A Coral Planet," she said. "Maybe."

We were quiet again for a while, a long while.

"You've been a good leader," Honey said.

"No, I think the trip's been a failure. You got hurt, a queen died, the raft was destroyed."

"We discovered a lot."

"Still, no one's going to pay attention with the spaceship stuff. I won't be a leader again soon."

"Yes, you will. But you intimidate people, so they're scared to be on your team."

"I intimidate people?"

"You're smart and experienced and sure of yourself and, well, that. They don't feel equal."

"I'm not that sure of myself."

After a while, I got up to patrol. The corals stayed dark. Soon after that, Scratcher came out with the scent of mourning clinging to him.

"Sad. Not my queen, not my sad."

I put a box next to mine, and he settled down on it, wrapped in his blanket. Soon, his head dropped into my lap. Honey curled up and slept. I kept watch over the dark plains, wondering about aliens and Earth and being sure of myself. I kept the fire bright. Once I saw some glowing eyes looking at us, I threw a rock, and it went away. A few hours later, Scratcher woke up and told me to go to sleep while he kept watch, so I did.

He was awake when the hint of dawn woke me. The fire was bright and warm.

I sent the canoe off as soon as possible. Rust's major and worker remained, moping around like it was the end of the world, which for them it was, but the major stood guard reasonably well and the worker helped Scratcher. I got bored, lit the signal fire in case someone else was coming, then went to plant the rest of Stevland's seeds in the dry riverbed. I found some gold nuggets and flakes there. At the sound of shouting, I looked up to see four canoes coming up the backwash toward our raft.

I wasn't surprised. A queen couldn't go missing for long. Each of the rescue canoes held a Glassmaker major and a Human, all experienced hunters and friendly faces. I felt a hundred kilos lighter to see them. We organized our trip back in record time. I'd never wanted to get away from somewhere that bad. With the help of a stiff wind at our back and constant rowing, we were in the city by the next afternoon. They told me a lot while we paddled, and I still had plenty to do to wrap up the trip.

But the city was in an uproar. Who was coming from the sky?

Messenger bats and Stevland had announced our arrival, and Ladybird, Jose, and Thunderclap were waiting to greet us. They were already wearing old clothes for mourning for Rust's funeral. I thanked them for coming, caught up on some of the news, none of it good, and said goodbye to Scratcher. I knelt down to be eye level with him, and he smelled like a bouquet of flowers.

"The next team I head, you'll be on it. You'll be a great addition."

I escorted Rust's Glassmakers to the Meeting House. Everyone in the city seemed to be rushing around, and a scent of worry hung in the air, but it was quiet and sad-smelling in the Meeting House. Her body lay in a basket in the chilly north bay of the building, and nine members of her family were settled on the ground facing her. The two Glassmakers with me took their places. I sat next to Cawzee for a while in shared silence. His carni-kat pelt lay in front of him.

Not every member of a queen's family had to die when she did. A Human could adopt one and act like his queen if the Glassmaker agreed. I'd gotten so used to Cawzee that I didn't want to see him go. There was a process to follow and the Committee would have appointed someone to handle it. I'd find out who.

Then I stowed my gear and visited Honey at her parents' home, another island of calm. She was healing fine and had lots to say while her kat Emerald sniffed my boots and coat and finally jumped onto my lap. Honey had already given an hour-long report to the Committee and promised there was a lot more to say, so I should be prepared.

"But," she said, "don't expect a real expedition to the plains now! Not with the Earthlings coming."

"So I've heard. They're sending us radio messages. They're landing tomorrow."

"Yes, everyone's talking about them. Sometimes we can understand them, so we think that's what they're saying. I'm surprised Ladybird could get away from the meetings to greet you at the river. We don't know what the Earthlings want, but I have an idea. They're coming to settle Pax. They ruined Earth, we know that, so they need a new place to live. But they'll ruin Pax, too! Maybe we can make them live on the other side of the planet."

"Ladybird said we don't know how many they'll be."

"On a ship that big? I think a lot of them." And she explained in detail why.

Finally, I went to see Stevland at a little greenhouse with its clear glass roof, since the Meeting House was occupied. It was a short walk through a busy city, and a lot of people stopped to say welcome back and share their theories about Earth's return.

Halfway there, I stopped to think about it myself, staring at a little garden between some houses. It was ordinary and mostly bare, since it was winter. Some thorny stalks would sprout flowers in spring and cherries in summer. A ponytail sapling decorated the center, and its long thin leaves hung brown and dry, rustling in the wind. Above them arched the rainbow-striped stalks of Stevland, his leaves still green.

Honey and I had talked as if the corals were the aliens, but maybe green plants were. Maybe the forest was the intruder and had taken over plains that used to be coral. But some small and mostly harmless corals grew in the forest, and some plants were growing in the plains. Things weren't as separate as they seemed.

The forest wanted to destroy the plains. And yet a lot of things lived in the plains, and they were beautiful. Beautiful and dangerous. Learning that had been a success in a way. Three intelligent species lived in the city, Humans and Glassmakers, both aliens, and Stevland, the last of his kind. Rainbow bamboo used to be the dominant species. He blamed wars between bamboo for its near extinction.

And now Earth Humans were coming, and they weren't Pacifist Humans. We didn't know them, and they didn't know us. We'd all find out about each other soon. I was small, but the things around me could be big.

I felt I was being watched, and not just by those cell-sized eyes on Stevland's stalks. I turned and saw Fern pretending to be merely walking past. I watched her until she turned a corner. Someday she'd talk to me. I hoped.

I went to the greenhouse and felt more relieved at every step. I'd be glad to talk to Stevland, and he'd be glad to talk to me, and no matter what the spaceship brought, nothing could change that. And Stevland was big.

"Water and sunshine, my friend. I brought you a present." I opened a little cloth bag and held it in front of the stalk so he could see it. "Gold. We got what we could before carnivorous fippokats came at us. This will help you build radio parts."

"Warmth and food. You are more important to me than gold."

"I'm really sorry about the queen."

"She acted imprudently. She is responsible for her own death and the deaths of her family. We will miss them."

I nodded and thought about the loss of an entire family. "I hear Humans from Earth are coming."

"Tomorrow. Everyone's getting ready, and there is no calm in the city."

"Yes, there is, right here in this room. Me." I still remembered how to talk tough, even if I didn't mean it anymore.

"You would make Ladybird happy to know someone is calm. You have shown good leadership skills. Be aware that the plans include keeping my sentience secret. We do not know if these Earthlings are peaceful. But we will go ahead with the Glassmaker funeral no matter what."

"Yeah. About that. I want to adopt Cawzee."

"Did you become close on the trip?"

"Sort of. I'd really rather adopt Scratcher."

"Scratcher is close to the end of his life span, sadly. Cawzee should live for at least forty more years. It would be a fine opportunity for him."

"Yeah, an opportunity."

"I see these Earthlings as an opportunity, although we are right to be anxious. I doubt this is a one-way trip. I could send my seeds to Earth."

I laughed.

He said, "I believe I could adapt to its ecology well."

"You'd end up running the place."

"Every change or endeavor always brings the opportunity for success, no matter how difficult."

"Yeah, Earthlings'll be difficult, so we need to be calm. We can handle them."

But I was talking out of habit. We might be able to handle them, or we could fail and face disaster, and it might not be our fault, but in any case it would be our problem to solve. We'd find out soon, and I hoped I'd be ready.

3

OMRAKASH BACHCHAN—EARTH YEAR 2443, PAX YEAR 210

During hibernation, we wouldn't dream. That's what the medical staff on Earth had told us. They also said we would awake confused. But the moment I regained consciousness I was lucid, aware that I had dreamed for more than a century, the same sweet dream in endless iteration. I had envisaged that after the privations and sacrifices of this journey, I would return home to the comforts of Earth and write an anthropological masterpiece, a study of a secluded society on a distant planet and our success in reuniting them to our species. Oh, the insights into humanity!

I started immediately, making mental notes and recording them with my feed:

Arrival means awakening to illness and worry. It begins with the indignities of a life support machine and anxieties over whether we have arrived as planned at the planet Pax.

I lay in a close-fitting capsule, and a recording of a soothing male voice instructed me to push the green button to open the door. The voice explained how to deal with straps and needles and tubes. I re-

membered reviewing the recording before we left, secretly harboring a
hundred fears. But as the chairman of the task force, I dared show no
anxiety on Earth and especially now, at that moment, wherever we were.

I opened the capsule and saw that I was alone—no, another capsule down the row opened and the soldier in it rose into the weightlessness of the chamber. I barely saw his bulk in the dim light as he
methodically removed his connections. I began to remove mine, not
willing to be outdone by that bioengineered simpleton. He noticed me.

"Chairman, sir! Chairman . . . Bachchan. Captain Aldo Haus reporting for duty, sir!" Then he laughed heartily and looked in a bag next to
his capsule for supplies. He was an archetype.

I had objected to the presence on our team of someone sworn to
belligerence—and in addition, even more strenuously, to the last-minute
inclusion of the government observer. Our mission was science, not con-
quest or punitive politics, I had said. My objections were imperiously
ignored.

I felt both ravenous and nauseated, noting that beard, hair, and nails
had grown, evidence of about two months' biological time. I remembered a small bottle of water with electrolytes next to the bag of clothing. It tasted vile, and my stomach tensed. I was going to throw up, and
in weightlessness, floating vomit would mortify me and make others
sick. And that would only make me feel sicker and . . . At this spiral of
thought, my feed interrupted with an anxiety cycle inhibitor from the
central network. The wild speculations stopped and I relaxed. I took
another sip. The water still tasted vile and chemical, but I managed.

I looked up to see Haus.

"Do you need help, sir?" His square, lined face seemed sincere. "I
think we can leave the skin suits on until we are sure we have arrived.
But they stink, don't they?" He laughed again. "Here, your oxygen mask,
before we leave. And your flashlight." As if I were an idiot.

The chamber rested inside heavy plating and a water tank to protect us from radiation. He hefted open the portal and we floated out
and down—up?—a dark passageway. He inspected as we went and
seemed to find nothing wrong, shoved open the hatch to the forward
control room, and hit a switch.

"You first, sir! Let's see where we are."

I could not fathom his mix of deference and exuberance. Had we arrived? If the computer had erred, even if we could determine where we really were, we might not have enough fuel to reach the correct planet and eventually return to Earth. An error could be the end of all our hopes and plans. . . . But duty called. I entered the tiny room lined with equipment. In the little window, a sphere floated: blue, swirling with clouds, a twin of Earth, and it could be only one planet.

"We're here," I murmured. "We're at Pax."

He entered behind me and whooped in primitive joy. I stared at the planet's beauty, hot tears trembling on my cheeks. But I made no notes about my loss of emotional control. The "me" of the book was not the "me" of reality.

I punched a button to send a message to Earth and quickly returned to the capsules to awaken our physician. I was revived first not merely because I led the mission but because I was deemed expendable compared to specialists—as expendable as a mere soldier, in fact—an estimation I was determined to change. Together we woke the rest, a biologically messy process that proceeded only slightly better than our worst-case scenario. At least no one had died. The very next day, biological issues under control, we started to work—and the problem with Pollux, the government observer assigned to us last-minute, began to emerge.

The botanist Mirlo and a data specialist were calibrating a sensor to detect vegetation. Mirlo planned to check for both visual-spectrum and near-infrared light. Pollux floated up behind them. Mirlo's grimace was reflected on the face of a panel. Pollux had already irritated most people with niggling interference.

"You don't need to do either," Pollux said. "Just look out the window. The planet is plenty green."

Mirlo was young, blond, and ruddy: a Gallic phenotype. He took a deep breath. "We're measuring intensity. If we assume those are plants and they use something that functions like chlorophyll, they'll absorb certain wavelengths."

"Right. They're green."

Mirlo's piercingly blue eyes became stern. "Yes," he said slowly, "we can see that, but infrared will show their temperature. If they're like Earth, they need water to function, and infrared shows their heat, and if they're moist, they'll be cooler. That way we can compare both measurements and see how much is likely to really be vegetation."

Pollux exhibited the sallowness of a naturally tawny person who had spent a long sedentary life indoors, making his dark eyes and eyebrows all the more prominent. "You're here to look for people, not plants," he said. Then he looked Mirlo in the face with a sneer. "I don't mean to offend you, but we have a mission. Botany isn't central to it."

Mirlo remained still as stone. As chairman, I needed to defend him. With a gentle push, I drifted over to an instrument panel now crowded with floating bodies.

"We have a protocol, and we're going to follow it," I said.

Pollux turned and the sneer grew. "You don't have time to waste. How much oxygen do you think you have? If you don't look for the colony right away, you'll fail. We must return to Earth soon."

Everyone was watching. I opened my mouth to respond, to explain that step one was a bottom-up examination of the planet, and step two, a search for anomalies that suggested organized life, all with timelines, but he spoke first.

"I've headed missions before." His tone of voice lacked all respect. "Have you?"

I simply turned away. Senseless arguments couldn't be won, and I would diminish my leadership to engage in them. In addition, I was trembling, anxious, close to panic. I hadn't had a panic attack since I was a young man.

But he was lying. He hadn't led a mission. Even in the rush before we left, I had found time to glance at his professional history and was appalled. He had been one of NVA's jailers. Although I dared not say so—no one ever did—I abhorred the NVA institution for its systematic cruelty, its obvious lies, and its naked social control. A liar and a torturer: the worst possible person for this mission.

The day passed, and Mirlo discovered that indeed the planet hosted massive vegetation, surpassing Earth.

The next day, another problem with Pollux. We all had to exercise to recover lost muscle and bone mass from hibernation and weightlessness. I invested the required two hours per day on treadmills, bicycles, and resistance equipment as a duty, not a pleasure, and those first few days were particularly exhausting, even with the machines set at their lowest level.

Everyone was scheduled for their time, monitored by the computing system and overseen by the physician. That did not satisfy Pollux.

"Have you exercised?" he asked one of the technicians. Her feed was open, so I could follow the encounter although I was elsewhere. She merely nodded and continued checking equipment in the storage area, preparing it to be taken planetside.

He edged between her and the readouts. "Only one hour so far."

"I know." She possessed an inquisitive, calm personality and an angular, athletic build. "I'll do the other as soon as I'm done here."

"But you'll land and collapse, and you don't know what's down there."

"We won't land soon, and by then we'll know more. We thought all this through and created protocols."

"For an Earthlike planet."

"Which this is," she said. During training, her assertive character, so unfeminine, had surprised me.

"No, it's not. Gravity is twenty percent more."

"Yes. The air pressure is higher. Our blood volume is lower in space, which will cause immediate problems when we land unless we remediate it, so we will. Our suits will help us, too."

I forced myself to intervene again, pushing off to go float inside the doorway of the storage area. "Pollux, we've thought about all that."

He turned and looked at me. "You're not taking this seriously. We won't get back to Earth. You aren't fit to lead."

He shoved me aside and left. People stared at him and me. I wanted to fly after him and punch him, or to lock myself in the closest thing we had to a closet so I could tremble in secret. Both would be bad leadership. I should have intervened earlier, but I hadn't thought he would go so far so very fast. I had a personnel problem that threatened to undermine my stature.

I asked my feed to give me another anxiety inhibitor, then, while I marched on a treadmill, I looked closer at his history. It did not report misconduct. In fact, it reported no conduct—good, bad, or indifferent—which meant redaction. Which meant he must have conducted himself badly. Perhaps someone had done him the "favor" of assigning him to this mission to escape disciplinary action.

Or perhaps it meant something worse, I realized to my utter consternation. Long ago as a graduate student, I had researched a voyage embarked upon by Spanish conquistadors down the Amazon River in search of El Dorado. The travelers did not know that the purpose of the trip had been to gather together the most undesirable conquistadors—a ghastly lot, most notably Lope de Aguirre—beneath an incompetent captain and ship them off to the unexplored jungle, never to be heard from again. Most succumbed to malnutrition, mutiny, murder, and madness.

I knew from the beginning that, like myself, some members had left Earth with desperate hopes that home would be different when we returned after more than two centuries away—in a word, Earth would be free. We were undesirables, united by an unspoken secret. Now we had the enemy at our elbow, incompetence inserted at the last moment trying to impose himself—so we would fail and never be heard from again.

That possibility could have been paranoia on my part, but I had a duty to stop him by whatever means I could command. I would save this mission.

Meanwhile, our work progressed.

Earthlike first appearances create misguided expectations, and our examinations over the coming days reveal subtleties: an older planet than Earth with greater mass and gravity, shorter days and longer years, more distant from a brighter sun. Intense life fills every corner.

We debate a babble of possibilities as we anxiously search for our colony. Small continents, some linked by land bridges, lie in sapphire oceans. For a week our scans are strewn with false alarms of humanity until a heat signature in the southern hemisphere identifies a small town, astoundingly bright and busy even in winter. We rejoice. Soon

*we have identified a settlement with colorful round roofs surrounded
by well-tended fields. We estimate hundreds of residents in addition
to domesticated animals.*

*We have found humanity's frontier, and three weeks after arrival
we prepare to resume contact. More study would be welcome. In fact,
we are overwhelmed by data, but we are cramped and have a limited
supply of food and air, which we must replenish on the planet. We do
not know how we will be received, but we must go meet the natives.*

I wondered about including more details, the way *Death Downstream* by J. P. Rashid recorded minute preparations for his trip down
the Mississippi River during the Great Loss. The tale of our suffering
in that overpacked vessel and its toll would have been equally moving.
And damning for Pollux and his attempts to destroy morale and perhaps the mission itself, worthy of a full chapter detailing incidents,
insults, and impositions.

"We have to go back to Earth." He said this too often: it marked a
clue to his thoughts. His only goal was to return as fast as possible, overriding any interest in science or exploration. He had come under du-
ress. Worse yet, he threatened to dismiss me, quoting rules by section
and paragraph. I checked the mission charter, and unknown to me, it
had been changed when he was added to give the government observer
rights to assert control. I was chairman, but he was prosecutor, judge,
and successor.

Our mission had been sabotaged, deliberately and thoroughly.

I couldn't let that happen. In addition to my administrative skills as
a chairman—planning, fostering teamwork, coordinating activities
toward a shared goal, aiding members to contribute their best—in ac-
ademia I had navigated both scholarly and bureaucratic waters whirl-
pooled with infighting, character assassination, and rival personalities
and camps. I had observed masters at the art of office-milieu politics,
participating as needed. And still, a misstep had once brought me close
to incarceration, so harshly were iconoclastic opinions judged. Dissi-
dents at any level of society might even quietly, permanently, disappear.

I knew what to do and how to step lightly, and in the process, I could
enhance my respect among mission members.

The anthropologist from the Kingdom of Kongo, a voluble woman, was reviewing the original Pax settler list in the kitchen module as she sipped dulse-seaweed "soup," our staple food. I entered ostensibly to fetch fortified water and asked her if she had ever encountered Pollux before. "He's an anthropologist by training."

She frowned at the mention of his name and shook her head, her tight black braids waving gracefully in the weightlessness. "I've never understood why people study one thing and do another."

"He used it in penal work. Pollux was an NVA jailer."

Her eyes snapped open wide. And I heard a gasp behind me. Karola floated in the doorway. The two stared at me for a long moment.

I said, "Women tend not to like NVA."

Karola held herself so still she had to be concealing something deeply felt.

"She could be any of us," the anthropologist said, her voice tight.

"That's the point," I said, as close as I could get to condemning the institution without losing apparent neutrality. I had seen which side they would cheer for.

I added as lightly as I could, "He's functionally blind, too. I don't know what that will mean on the planet's surface. There won't be any fixed-camera feeds there to compensate, and a local network won't be in place." Thus I undercut his competence.

That done, I changed the subject and asked the anthropologist about the original settlers, all three of us exchanged a few Globish sentences for practice, and finally I left them to ponder the news. I had handled that well, I thought. I knew they would spread what they had learned to trusted friends, so soon everyone would know. When I defeated him on Pax, I would be a giant-slayer.

We hoped Earth had changed, and information was occasionally broadcast toward us, though it had to traverse a fifty-eight-light-year journey. The last message had been automatically intercepted two decades earlier, and there had been no change.

"What's happening on Earth?" Mirlo asked at a biology planning meeting.

"There's no reason to know," Pollux said. He was not welcome at that meeting, but the ship's size precluded privacy. "You should worry about what's happening here, or we won't get back to Earth."

"We're all fulfilling our duties," I said.

"Duties?" He was suddenly shouting and pointing at me. "If you call loafing a duty. You let people eat what they want when they want and work as little as possible. If people put in just one more hour per day—"

"We'd be where we are now. Please, let us continue with our work."

"We need to decide who should run this mission." With that, he floated away.

"The rules give him the right to remove me and take control," I said to the members around me. "They were changed to accommodate his presence."

The members exchanged looks. They now understood the urgency of the battle I was about to undertake for them.

All our radio hails to the planet went unanswered, although surely they would have maintained such basic, essential, universal technology. We continued to broadcast until the moment came to leave. Twenty of the thirty members of the team would travel to the surface, while ten would remain in orbit to maintain the ship and record the information we transmitted. Two heli-planes would carry us down while a third stayed behind for rescue purposes if necessary.

We disguised our fear as excitement. I had already guessed that Pollux's anger hid fear. On the surface, who knew what terrors we might find? But if he stayed behind, he could order the ship to abandon us and return to Earth—unlikely, but possible, and I had to prevent it. I asked the physician if Pollux was well. By the rules, I had access to medical records only in emergencies.

"Excessive anxiety. He's not stable."

I hid my joy. "Is he being treated?"

"No. You self-regulate, and you're doing fine. I suggested it to him and he refused."

We were silent a moment. Fear was weakness. I could exploit it only if I was less afraid than him.

"You could order treatment," the physician said.

"And he would depose me, take over, and refuse again."

"He's going to be trouble."

"I'll ask him to stay behind."

I knew Pollux would oppose any idea from me. I found him sweating on the treadmill. "Perhaps," I said, "you'd be more comfortable staying behind."

He reacted more strongly than I had expected: jumping off the treadmill without disconnecting the elastic cords. He was sprung into the air.

"No! I have a job to do." He waved his arms to find a handhold and control his writhing trajectory. "Down there—who knows what you'd do down there? You have no idea of what to expect and you're unprepared."

"You're welcome to come, of course. I just wanted to give you a choice."

"That's what I mean. You don't lead. We'll never get home and it'll be your fault."

I walked away, but now worried. What might he do on Pax? I had no way to predict.

And so, finally, we were ready to go.

"Goodbye, flowerpot," Mirlo said. "Hello, jungle." He floated steadily for his final check. The computer read out his data. His health was good. His gear had been properly stored on the plane, he was wearing a shirt and slacks over a bodysuit that would protect him from cold, precipitation, and small weapons and animals, and he had brought sufficient water to boost blood volume as we returned to gravity, so he was clear to go. He ducked into one of the planes.

Eighteen more team members were checked, and then, finally me. I entered one of the planes to deliver the discourse I had written the day before. Nine faces gazed at me while the pilot stared instead at equipment readouts. I said:

"We must imitate all friendly greetings and accept any offers of interest and help, but we must be prepared for hostilities from the natives or from the environment. We've seen large animals, and we will be unexpected. Maintain constant connection with the rest of the team.

The pilots will remain on board to manage the communications systems, prepared for emergency escape if necessary. At the end of the day, we will have a formal meeting, and you will be notified of the exact place and time."

That was the necessary speech, but this was worthy of writing:

We have already learned much about the place where we will land, about its climate, its general vegetation, even its population. But this has only made us want to learn more. Now, at great personal danger, we shall do what no one else has done before to further the reach of humanity.

Or, I could have said, "*We are going to our death. We will die of malnutrition, mutiny, murder, and madness—that is, we will succumb to Earth and the malice sent with us in human form to destroy us. Or we will prevail: I shall make that happen.*"

The technicians began the final preparations. I entered the second plane and repeated the prosaic speech before taking my seat. Pollux glared at me.

The flight encompassed two hours of tedium. I sat strapped in place as gravity slowly and unevenly increased, as did my thirst. I sipped my water and reviewed our official plan yet again. We would land both heliplanes a kilometer away from the city in what we hoped to be a fallow field. We expected the inhabitants, alerted by the sight of the crafts, to come greet us. Perhaps the entire city would come running. But so much could go wrong. We could crash, we could land in the wrong place, we could be treated as invaders, we could be attacked by local fauna, we could fall into division and mutiny or distraction spurred by Pollux . . . Finally my anxiety inhibitor kicked in.

Doubtless Pollux struggled, too. Our fears would soon battle each other. His personal feed was closed, at least to me, while mine was open. I received a few excited questions as around me, scientists and technicians anticipated what was to come.

When J. P. Rashid headed downstream, he knew exactly what he would find and what he would need. We did not. Rashid was welcomed by civilized settlements, but between them he was frequently beset by bandits. The human colony might have breakaway lawless factions. . . .

My inhibitor directed me to watch a projection from the flight deck's windows and enjoy the sight of that beautiful planet. Eventually, as we descended, we entered a wide, lush forest surrounded by mountains on three sides and by unique red plains to the south . . . closer and closer, and then the rotor whirled more noisily.

"Touchdown," a pilot announced, though I felt nothing. He checked some readouts while I listened to the second plane's roaring landing nearby. I got up, stumbling a bit in my first reencounter with gravity, then looked over the pilot's shoulders directly at the planet for the first time.

The vegetation was as we expected: farm fields with hedges of trees, mostly leafless in winter. The sun shone bright and the scene looked beguiling, almost Earthlike. Most importantly, several humans and pack animals with large side baskets came running toward us.

Haus and Karola had already released their harnesses and were preparing to exit with me—just the three of us, in case we met hostility. My environmental suit suddenly couldn't keep me warm or wick sweat away fast enough.

I glanced at Pollux. He looked petrified. I had duties to fulfill before our confrontation could begin.

"Let me take a look," Haus said, and wended around stacks of freight to peer through the pilot's windows. "They've got farm tools. Those can hurt you. A couple of spears. And look at those animals! Giant insects! Ugly, too. They're fast, too fast." Yet he smiled unceasingly.

The natives drew closer, and I observed the animals: four thin legs, two spindly arms, a ragged blanket worn over a long thorax, and a long blunt head like a zucchini with insect eyes. But "ugly" was a subjective judgment. I tried to think of them as *alien*.

Karola hurried to join us looking out the windows, smiling like Haus. "Four people, four animals. Three men, one woman."

"What are they saying?" I asked.

"I don't know, but it looks like hello. They're smiling and waving. Can we get exterior sound?"

"Sorry," the pilot said. "Not on this model."

"They're keeping their distance," Haus said. "They're short and beefy." He pulled on his coat, which concealed a variety of weapons. Would our environmental suits resist spears? Those animals? My anxiety inhibitor was still on. Haus gazed out the window, fingers tapping at his side. Karola took a few steps to shift her perspective, motionless in a way I had learned meant worry. I glanced behind me. Everyone was staring at their feeds of the view. This was the moment for success or failure.

"Let's go," I said, and heads snapped toward me. The pilot rose, hustled to the door, threw some latches, and slid it open. Cold, sweet air entered the plane, reminding me of the accumulated stench of voyage.

"Hillo!" called human voices. Their braying animals mimicked the greeting. "Wilcum to Pax!"

Did I really hear that: "welcome"? I looked at Karola.

She nodded. "Someone said, 'Welcome to Pax.'" She tugged her hooded coat tight.

We are greeted with joy.

I tensed my legs, jumped, and landed on moist soil covered by dead grass, the grass coated with frost from the engines. With the stronger gravity I felt like I was made of weighty iron, not flesh—just as I had expected yet not how I had imagined it, weight on each and every part of my body, including the most sensitive. The natives continued to wave and cheer. I raised my arms according to plan and waved back at them with bare hands so they could see that I carried no weapons. My hands were trembling, and I couldn't stop them.

"Hello!" I shouted, smiling, but I heard tension raise the pitch of my voice. A young man in a black hat and a necklace of what seemed to be large claws or fangs began to walk toward me. He carried a spear casually in his left hand. He—like the other humans—was short and sturdy, a head and shoulders shorter than us.

Haus thumped as he landed behind me.

"Hello, Pax!" he shouted.

Another, smaller thump. Karola.

"Hello! Hello!" she yelled.

Their shouts were answered by the natives. The young man's face, tanned like the others, had sharp features and lively eyes. His felt hat was old and worn, as were his rough tunic and slacks, which were topped by a knee-length open cloak. Everyone's clothes were faded and threadbare. Their tools and weapons were primitive. Disappointing.

We are greeted with preindustrial joy.

"Wilcum tar hom!" he said. "Wae taut hyew whur comin whin wae swa laiets in ta skai."

Karola didn't answer, and for a long moment I doubted her. Perhaps Shani, may she rest in peace, would have been better. Then she said, "Hyew saw tat? Did hyew heer us?"

"Hyes, laiets, an tru ar tiliscyops wee swa et wus a spais sheep en worbit, but hyeer hyew? Ai dund—"

"What's he saying?" I sent. "Doesn't he speak Globish? We thought they would speak Globish."

"It's the accent. We knew sounds would shift, but not how. Mostly the vowels. They've become diphthongs."

"Everyone spoke Globish when they left. Globish was the world language."

"Yes, but this project was based in the United States. It used Classic English. They'll understand Globish, of course. But talk slowly."

"Es dier sum sorda cunsirn?" he said, looking concerned at our apparent silence.

"Hyur language es a surprise," she answered slowly.

He laughed. "Hyou ah a surprise!" He spoke very slowly, and despite his wide-voweled accent I finally understood him a little.

She turned to me. "He said they saw our spaceship in the sky. They have telescopes, apparently."

"Ah hyew frum Eart?" he said, one word at a time, his face hopeful, and his accent falling further into a pattern. But why would he think we were from elsewhere?

I stepped forward. "Yes, we are from Earth. I am Om. I lead this group."

"Ai am Arter. Tees es Hosay . . ." He gestured to a taller—though still short—gray-haired man. "Scratsher," one of the pack animals. "Honee," a very young woman with large tear-shaped tattoos on both cheeks. "Blas," the fourth man, and the other three animals, "Cewkee,

Shain, Treell." Curious that he introduced the animals as if they were people.

Beloved companion animals, an instinctual relationship for humans on Earth, have been re-created from local species. . . .

Arter said something quite long, then gestured at people lurking across the fields.

Karola clarified some terms and translated: "Arthur says, 'I'm the head of this team, but we're just a farm team working in the fields today. There are more people in the city, of course. Are there more of you? The planes look big. We're very curious about you. And we're happy to welcome you.'"

Arter was *Arthur, hyew* was *you,* and so on. With time, I hoped, this would all be intelligible.

But, if they were very curious about us, why was our greeting handled by a handful of mere farmers? We were hardly a surprise. No, we were something to be feared, met by a small group to test our intentions.

Another thump behind us, then a few stumbling steps. I turned. Pollux had joined us. Terror could make a man do strange things—disastrous things.

I had to take the initiative. "This is Pollux," I said. "He is here to observe."

"I'm here to lead," he said. "Which you aren't doing."

I took a calming breath. I was about to dispute that, then I considered how terrifying leadership was, and how I wished to sow terror in his path. Before I could answer, he spoke again in Sino-Arabic Creole, Earth's common tongue:

"So you want me to jump back up . . . ? No? Once again, you're being passive." He turned to Arthur. "You were obviously expecting us. Exactly what did you prepare?"

Arthur looked at Karola. She turned to me. I turned back to Pollux, keeping my breathing even. "All right. You command the mission."

"What? You're just going to let me?"

"We don't need an argument right now at this delicate moment. Go ahead."

As we spoke, Arthur patted the animal Scratsher rhythmically. It made an odd whistle-crack sound. The girl named Honee stepped forward and took Karola by the hand and murmured something.

Karola sent privately to me with an utter lack of emotion, which meant she was seething with it: "They want to know if Pollux is on our team. I'm going to say he is starting right now, he is the new head, but imply that it's an imposition. He speaks no Globish, so he won't understand."

I assented. I should never have doubted her for a moment. She had divined my plan without the need to explain it to her.

She shook her head and took a step closer to Honee and said quietly, letting me hear distinctly over her feed, "Hee es new on ar teyam, hee es ta hid, ta new leedeh. Hee es . . . hee can dew tat, hee can saey tat."

The native girl nodded, and Arthur and the other two native men tightened their lips, suppressing smiles. The scent of strawberries suddenly and incongruously wafted past. Honee patted Karola's hands and stepped back with a knowing smile. They had seen that sort of thing before. At some point we'd have to learn about their leadership systems, apparently as rife with conflict as ours.

As she spoke, Pollux centered his attention on me. "You haven't evaluated all the danger here. To begin with, they have weapons. What kind of welcome comes with weapons?"

"They might be ceremonial. Or perhaps they're meant to protect us from some sort of danger. We mustn't rush to judgment." I was sure we were safe—from the natives, at least.

Something buzzed loudly to our left. Pollux jumped. I held my breath to listen. The natives glanced at it, unsurprised, then Arthur laughed and addressed himself to Pollux, "Pallogs," as he pronounced it, talking as he gestured with his spear and kicked at the ground with muddy wooden clogs worn over tall boots.

Karola translated: "'That's just a . . . crab,' he calls it. 'They're harmless. Not all the animals are. That's why we need weapons even when we're farming. Velvet worms are now this far north. But it's safe for you. Your shoes look sturdy.'"

"Tell them they're responsible for our safety," Pollux said. "If any-thing happens to us, they'll pay the price."

She smiled at the natives. "We tang hyew fuh ar sayftee. We ar eegur ta see mor uf tis place."

"Can I look at his spear?" Haus asked in Creole, glancing at me before directing himself to the new boss. Pollux looked down, frown-ing, and finally nodded. Haus said to Arthur in Globish: "Can I look at your, um . . ."

"Spear," Karola said, her head held straight, her face returned to its usual inscrutability.

"Sure," Arthur said, and held it out, handle end first, apparently un-afraid, still with an easy smile. Haus inspected it, especially the tip. One of the pack animals stirred nervously—disquieted by us or by something else? Hosay gave it a pat and murmured soothing words, and in response it brayed at the group lingering across the fields. One of those animals answered, and they traded squawks and hoots while Haus talked to Arthur.

"Stone?" Haus pointed to the blade.

"Yes," he answered, then offered an explanation.

Karola translated: "'Yes, glass, actually. A long, sharp spear is all we need to kill a worm. It's not meant for you, so don't worry. The worms are poisonous and fast.'"

"Those worms are a convenient excuse," Pollux said. "They're plan-ning something, and you're not prepared. You were never prepared. We should never have come."

"Is there something we can do about the worms?" Haus had Karola ask Arthur.

He laughed before he responded, a man in his element. "Be cahrful hwat hyew tudge." He looked at the other members of his team, then spoke at more length.

Karola repeated, looking at Pollux: "'Would you like to come to the city? I think there are people there who would be easier to talk to, and there are no worms or dangerous animals there. I can take you to our moderator. You can bring everyone on your team.'"

"Moderator?" I asked. Pollux glared at me, unaware of the meaning behind the word.

Karola nodded. "That's what he said. Perhaps they still use their Constitution, or some vestiges of it."

If they followed it, they might have freedom. But our government on Earth told us we were free, too. And here I was on another planet, still squirming beneath its thumb. But not for long.

Protocol said to seek Haus's opinion, since he was in charge of safety, but our new leader had not bothered to study our plans. He stared at the ground again, then the sky.

"No, not with those insects near," Pollux said. "Look at them. They have claws. I can't stand insects. Translate that."

She turned so he could not see her face and frowned. "He sajz he duz nat laik insects. He es afraeed uv dem."

"Insects?" Honee muttered, frowning. The others blinked or shifted slightly. They understood that word, and it seemed to be taboo.

Should I act? Or at least offer advice? In any case, I now knew the natives would also rejoice when I defeated Pollux. I had an idea, but to act . . . I took a deep breath. He was still more anxious than me, I was sure of it.

I tried to smile with a hint of patronization, and said, imitating Pax speech as best I could, "Ai will keep him wit me. Ert es a very diffren plais."

"It's hahd ta lead a team," Arthur said.

Despite a language barrier, we exchange messages of subtlety and complexity, sharing similar perspectives on issues of social order.

Karola sent, "You learn fast."

"What did you say?" Pollux snapped.

"I said I could stay between you and the . . . native animals."

"You and Haus."

"Haus's job is to keep everyone safe. You should ask him what he thinks of the natives' offer."

"Well?" Pollux said.

"Stone tools," Haus said. "We shouldn't underestimate their

effectiveness, though. They expected us and they had a plan, and part of it is to be friendly. They're afraid of us and trying not to show it. My advice, sir, is to reciprocate. Be friendly. I see no signs of aggression."

"Ask him what he plans," he said to Karola. "And look at how poor they are. And what's in those baskets? I want a full list of dangers, and what kind of hospitality they can afford to offer."

She asked him where they would go, if they had room for all our people, and what kinds of precautions they should take. He answered too fast for me to follow, gesturing toward where the city was, toward our surroundings, and added, "Hyew ar wilcum, al uv hyew." All of you. Oh, the subtle jokes!

"He said we're all welcome, they can accommodate us all in the city. They have houses and food. And there are no big dangers, but don't touch anything without asking, especially animals. The baskets are to help us carry things we might have."

We were about to take a physical step toward the unknown. I realized I had stopped breathing. Pollux was breathing fast. I was winning.

"Come out now," he sent. "Leave the planes and come with me."

On board, they cheered, even though they must have noticed that I was not in charge. They should have been glum.

One by one, mission members jumped out of both planes with delighted shrieks. Some spun in glee, hugged each other, or waved wildly at the Pax natives, who smiled and laughed and waved in return. Arthur and the other natives peppered Karola with questions. Mirlo landed, looked down, and stepped aside to make space for the next person before kneeling to study the grass, stroking it as if it were a beloved animal's fur. All of them were recording and sending in enraptured frenzy.

Pollux glowered, eyes fixed on feeds but appearing to stare at the ground. How much more disruptive would he become? Someone sent him questions about technical issues. Other questions followed fast. They knew the answers, so this was malice at work.

Of course, he knew even less than they did. "Oh, just do what you're supposed to do!"

Hosay—or Jose, according to what Karola sent—advised us to secure the planes against curious animals. He, Haus, and the pilots inspected the undersides of the planes, communicating by gestures and
simple words. Jose seemed relaxed. Haus sent that his advice seemed
earnest, honest, and helpful.

The pack animals, beckoned forward by the natives, approached the
new humans slowly, uttering reassuring cries to each other, ready to
help us carry our gear. They seemed intensely curious.

*We are greeted with preindustrial joy and welcomed with appar-
ent trust hiding understandable suspicion. Yet they know their environment and immediately start to share its secrets.*

I was not about to record anything about Pollux's coup. It would be
brief.

With that unceremonious start, we trekked up a dirt road toward
what they called the city, and I still felt disappointed that the entire
population hadn't come running. I scanned the feeds of the rest of my
team, and their eyes and equipment were taking in everything—the
state of the soil, the clouds scattered in the blue sky, and all the wonders large and small that lay in between. They chatted among themselves, eagerly sharing observations.

Pollux marched a step ahead of me, stiff and grim. The animal
Scratsher followed us at a discreet distance. It would be hard for Pollux to reconstruct his surroundings from that flurry of visions. Yet he
sent, "What dangers do you see? Report." He received a kaleidoscope
of sights and thoughts that even I found impossible to interpret.

"Everyone stay together!" he sent. But our people were still in close
formation.

Haus continued to speak with Jose, or rather, they gestured at each
other cheerfully. The tattooed girl, Honey, talked nonstop with Karola,
who walked a step behind me, two steps behind Pollux. Honey's hand
was bandaged. She seemed to have lost part of a finger—to what? I
pointed it out to Pollux, scanning for whatever else fearful I could find.
But I worried, too. So many things could take a finger: accident, illness, interpersonal malice . . .

The farmer Blas paused to snatch a small green animal like a cat or rabbit from the side of the road, and the zoologists rushed to examine it. Arthur remained talkative and tried to speak slowly, but it did little good for me, nothing for Pollux.

"Here we grow something, and there something, and those trees something something, but it's winter, so we something something something. And today, we will something something, something. I hope you something. Here are more people something something welcome."

A limited vocabulary reduces our discussion to childishness, which will no doubt make the growth toward mature, mutual understanding all the more satisfying.

"He's describing their farming practices," I said to Pollux. "But I don't know why he wears that claw necklace."

He did not respond, and as Arthur glanced from me to him, his eyes narrowed a bit. Pollux looked flushed and breathed fast and shallow, yet he barely responded to anything.

I nudged him. "Look, more natives!" Surely that would push him over the edge.

Two dozen people with quite a few insect-animals had been waiting for us alongside a dirt road between more fields. The animals brayed, and the people waved and cheered. I looked for weapons and saw only farming tools, but those could do harm, so I sent that thought to Pollux. I noticed more men than women, but no children. I sent that to Pollux: the situation might be too dangerous for children. And there were lots of those insects. I glanced back. Our group had begun to split up, perhaps out of spite for him. As we approached the second welcoming group, I smelled flowers, though I didn't see any.

But I did see what looked like small pterodactyls in the sky that swooped low and hooted at us, and some of the natives hooted back. A giant many-legged spider ran from one bush to another. Far across the field, several crabs the size of a man paused, apparently looking at us, but no one seemed concerned. Green tatters hung from trees, and a couple of bluish balloons with spines—creatures?—floated on the wind. I pointed to them and Arthur told me their names, carefully pronounced for my benefit: bat, spider, deer crab, ribbon plant, cactus.

Unsettlingly familiar, even the names, but beguilingly strange and not always beautiful to us . . .

One of the zoologists knelt to investigate the spider, but a native quickly tugged him back—obviously dangerous.

. . . but to the natives, each creature carries the weight of lifetimes of direct experience.

I added the names to the feed, more noise to deafen as well as blind Pollux. He could not walk easily unless someone looked at what lay before us at our feet. So I looked up, out . . .

We arrived at a crest of the hill, and below us lay a riverbed with a walled city on the bluff on the other side, surrounded by tidy fields and orchards. Despite the season, green fronds rose gracefully above the city, and its roofs sparkled in the sunlight with the hues of a rainbow. The wall around the city was crowned by colorful glazed bricks and with a well-decorated gate. Civilization in full bloom! Unlike the case with J. P. Rashid, who saw it in decline and fall. Our videographer rushed to capture the scene.

This would be the place to begin my direct attack on Pollux.

"Karola," Haus called, "come here. I need to ask about the wall. What's so dangerous?"

The second group of natives introduced themselves to our members one by one, and it seemed each of us had at least one native as a guide. Karola had already taught the central control for our feeds some basic pronunciation and names to aid in communication.

"It's a plan!" Pollux said. "Those guides, they're part of their plan. Don't do it!"

He was panicking. Finally.

"They want to welcome us," I said innocently. "They saw us in the sky. They knew we were coming, so they prepared to greet us."

He sent: "Everyone, stick together! That's an order. How many times do I have to tell you?"

I glanced around and I felt sure I saw a few of our people deliberately take a few steps away from each other.

I took several steps away from Pollux to study those fine walls and buildings. I kept my feed of what I saw and heard open, recorded, as an alibi. I was merely doing my job. And the sight reminded me of the great Ishtar Gate of ancient Babylon and the domed roof of Rome's Pantheon. Humanity had carried its magnificence to the stars! I recorded that: *I am reminded . . .*

"Wild animals," Haus said. He, Jose, Karola, and Honey had returned. He switched to Globish. "Big ones, small ones, all dangerous. Many kinds. Always wear shoes." The two men laughed. They had bonded quickly. Haus's archetype had met its kind: both he and Jose were men of action.

"The natives carry weapons, though," I sent to Pollux.

"Something else," Karola said, taking a step back. "There is some sort of funeral for what they're calling a queen. A glass maker, they say, and I'm not sure what that is, I suppose an artisan. They seem extremely distraught. The entire city is taking part in the ceremony."

I turned to Pollux. "Excellent. We'll get to see an important aspect of their culture immediately. You should have Karola inform the others, especially the anthropologists, about the funeral. She should also inform everyone about the wild animals."

"Uh . . . do that." Had he become incapable?

Karola squinted and was lost in thought, sending.

Pollux shook his head desperately as if to clear it. "Are the feeds failing?"

"Mine works fine." Perhaps his were being interrupted by strong emotion. Occasionally an overwhelmed brain could reject feeds. I might have been in luck.

He shook his head again and stumbled, trembling head to toe. "It's back." He still trembled. I was succeeding.

"Then let's keep going." I led him down the bluff to the river, which was flanked with long docks for a dozen different boats and rafts. Above the banks and the flood line were dense hedges. Our members became even more spread out, and the level of chatter seemed to increase, impossible to follow. We passed empty, closed workshops as we descended, and Arthur described the tasks undertaken in each. At the riverbank, he paused in front of a gloriously colorful flower garden surrounding a strange half-man half-animal stone statue, a work clearly worthy of a scholarly book by itself.

"Oh! It bit me!"

I turned back. A biologist next to a small palmlike shrub held his finger, too far away for me to see why, though I could guess. The physician and Scratsher rushed over, and the braying animal seemed as interested in examining the wound as our task force member was. A native approached and talked to them, and soon the physician announced, "It's fine. Nothing serious."

But Pollux stared at them, or at something. If he tried hard, could he recover? Leadership consisted largely of playacting, a false front. He didn't need courage, just a posture, a simulation, and his natural aggression could supply that if he was smart enough. I kept my anxiety inhibitor set high.

Karola followed a couple of meters behind, deeply lost in thought. She even stumbled once from the mix of unfamiliar gravity and diligence in her duties.

Drums sounded faintly from the city. Arthur turned, suddenly more somber, and called over Karola to explain something.

"It's the funeral," she said, then asked him a question before continuing. "We should join it when it leaves the city. They'll be taking the queen with her family to be buried. The queen is a kind of . . . the companion aliens they have with them."

Pollux did not respond, his face stiff. When was he going to do something that I could capitalize on?

"Should we go?" I asked him.

He raised his arms as if to protect himself from something. "How far are we from the planes?"

"About a kilometer. Should I take you back?" He was slow to answer. "Or we can cross the river and join the procession," I said. "It's for a funeral for one of those insects. A queen insect." He still didn't answer. "Or I can take you back." No response.

Finally, he said, "No, let's go. But stay with me."

I took several steps ahead. Arthur led us to the bridge. Even from the sky we had noticed the bridge seemed narrow. Up close, it amounted to some ropes and a few planks of wood. We would have to walk across it in single file.

"Why is the bridge so small?" I said.

"It's for safety." I listened to my feed, which was translating Arthur well now, thanks to Karola. "If a big, dangerous animal comes, we can destroy it fast."

"Is it dangerous here?"

He thought a moment and shrugged. "Well, yes and no. There are dangers, but we have a lot of experience."

I sent that to Pollux: dangers.

"We could die here," Pollux answered, his voice catching as if from a sob. "We won't get back to Earth."

"We knew the risks," I told him, imitating Arthur's shrug.

I followed Arthur across the bridge, repeating Arthur's instructions to leave space between each of us. As I stepped onto solid ground again, the first members of a procession left the city, marked now by flutes as well as drums. I moved to the side for a better look, rather than turn back and watch Pollux and share my feed with him to help him cross. There would be other feeds of people watching him, or he could loop my recording. I would not seem negligent.

Behind me, Pollux shouted, "It's gone! It's completely gone!"

I turned to look. He was halfway across the river, stumbling and grabbing a rope. He was about to fall into whatever danger lurked in the river. I hoped he would, and instantly forgave myself for the thought.

"Oh!" he said. "There it is!" He stood a little straighter, steadier, and raised his foot to step onto thin air, as if the bridge had made a sort of turn over the water. I held my breath, held my expectations, held a vision of our own funeral for him—all within a single second of time that passed with intense dilation.

But Scratsher dashed up behind him, crouched, leaned out, and guided his dangling foot to a plank and safe footing. It had moved with extraordinary speed and grace. And intelligence. Did it understand speech?

Pollux recovered his balance but not his composure. "I can't see again! Help me!"

A native woman came forward, her hand outstretched.

"There's an insect right in back of me," he said, and shuffled forward as fast as he could. As he finally reached the end, he lurched and fell. Scratsher remained in the middle of the bridge. Karola stood on the far bank, sweat glistening on her forehead. Had she been helping him with her feed? I had thought she was loyal to me. But then I saw that her eyes were closed.

The physician ran toward the bridge and crossed it, slow and clumsy. Pollux thrashed and stood up.

"Pollux, come here," I said. I could hold him until the physician arrived. A medical intervention would prove him unfit.

He ran toward me a few steps, then shouted, "It's back."

"Your feed?" I said. I put out a hand to steady him, but he stood outside of reach.

Meanwhile our mission members chattered in their feeds: "Glass makers are those animals, the insects, but don't use that word."

"There's probably a story behind that name, glass maker."

"A queen is a breeding female."

"Like an ant colony?"

"That would be interesting."

"If a queen dies, the colony dies, too, right?"

"It weakens until it's killed by enemy ants, at least on Earth."

"How smart are they?"

The physician arrived and put an arm around Pollux's shoulder and talked to him quietly, privately, and urgently. Pollux shook him off. The physician kept talking.

The procession descended on the road from the city down the river bluff toward us. I tried to study it despite the distractions; this would make a moving passage for my book. The procession was led by five humans and five large glass makers, all carrying spears—an honor guard? They were followed by eight or ten humans and a half dozen very large glass makers, longer than the humans were tall—queens? I sent the question to the biologists, interrupting their babble.

"It's a big funeral," an anthropologist sent, "so it might have consequences."

"Why have such a big deal for an animal?"

"Is that why they didn't all come to see us?"

"There's something we're not getting, something we don't understand."

"Are they animals? They seem pretty smart."

"Record everything. We can figure this out later."

They kept chattering. Karola and Honey crossed the bridge and came
toward us, squinting, listening.

Pollux grabbed my arm. "The feed! Where is the feed?"

"I have mine. It's just fine. Karola, do you have your feed?"

"Mine's normal." Hair clung to her wet forehead, testament to her
labors.

Honey asked her a question, and she began to explain, pointing at
her head and our heads and gesturing.

Pollux stood with his head in his hands. The physician and I exchanged looks. I should order an intervention, but not too soon. I
needed a full-blown crisis to justify myself.

I turned back to the procession, which had neared. Behind the
queens, if that's what they were, more humans carried a large basket
on their shoulders—a casket? About a dozen glass makers of all sizes
followed that, then drummers and flutists, and finally what had to be
the entire population of the city, including children. Everyone walked
in solemn silence. Many carried flowers, and a strong, sweet, aniselike
scent preceded them.

*Humanity's love for ceremony has also come to the stars, strangely
expressed and yet again familiar. . . .*

Everyone wore tattered clothing, some veritable rags, and threadbare blankets were draped over the animals. But clothing styles varied, from simple skirts and loose trousers to Greek-style chitons. The
near savages Rashid encountered on his trip had remained well dressed
by looting stores and homes, but these people were hardly savage. *Poverty does not preclude humanity. . . .*

They were all looking at us. Arthur stood at attention, so I followed his lead, suddenly aware that a pivotal moment approached. Pollux backed away, moving his feet carefully, apparently still feedless. Perhaps there was something wrong with his chip. What would he do?

As the procession passed, two women following the honor guard stepped out to speak to me—not to Pollux. Karola joined us.

"Welcome," one said. She wore perhaps the worst clothing of all, a tattered skirt, a leather vest that seemed half-decomposed, and battered wooden jewelry. A blanket full of holes was wrapped around her shoulders. "I am Ladybird, and I am the moderator." Then she said more too fast for me or the feed to catch.

"I'm connected again," Pollux sent. "Everyone stay together. And let me talk to her." He began to approach, but slowly. . . .

"'I'm sorry that we cannot greet you formally now,'" Karola interpreted her words. "'But I invite you to join with us. We can speak later. We're very pleased to have you here.'"

"Yes, thank you," I said. "Your welcome has already been more than we had hoped." If I spoke briefly, Pollux would arrive too late. Yet I felt aghast at the poverty, and felt my prejudices rise against a female leader—I knew better, but I was a child of my time and place, alas. No one needed to know that but me, however. I would respect her fully.

She and the other woman hastened to their places. Karola hurried back to Honey, who waited closer to the river.

Pollux shrieked, "Everyone back to the planes. Now! We're not safe. This is our funeral. That's the plan. They can interfere with our feeds! Back to the planes, to the ship!" He knelt to grab a rock as a weapon. "Everyone come with me!"

My moment had come.

"It's under control," I sent to the mission members. "Stay with your guides and join the funeral." Haus and Jose were running toward us. Karola edged closer. Scratsher ran up to Arthur, who told it something, and it whistled and buzzed, and others of its kind answered.

Pollux held the rock above his head. "Who's here!" He turned around and around.

Behind him, two large glass makers, apparently called by Scratsher, crept closer. Jose and Haus murmured to each other, then Jose moved his hands in a complicated series of gestures.

"They say they'll take care of this," Haus sent. "Disarm him, I mean."

All at once, the glass makers and natives jumped in synchronization. The men grabbed Pollux's arms as the glass makers leapt high and snatched away the rock. Haus stepped forward, talking to him, and gently pushed him to sit down, although Pollux struggled against his grip. The physician arrived, fumbled in a bag, then held out a pill and a bottle of water. "Take this. It will relax you."

"Are we going back to the planes?"

"We'll take care of things." The physician knelt down and kept talking and put an arm around his shoulders, although Pollux struggled against him. With sleight of hand, the physician put a patch on the back of his neck, unnoticed.

The mission members chattered.

"Pollux snapped."

"Did he hurt anyone?"

"He joined the mission too late. He didn't even want to. That's what he told me."

"Can we block his feed? I don't want to hear from him."

"I guess Om is back in charge."

"He always was, this was just theater to get rid of Pollux. Om knew what he was doing."

I had triumphed and won respect!

Honey had run off and came back with a gray-haired native man, a medic, she announced, with a glass maker. "'We have a clinic, and we can help,'" Karola began to translate between the medic and the physician. They could give him a bed and care. Sweat beaded on her face and she looked exhausted, but she kept working hard. Our day's success would be owed to her, although I was the one who had brought about the coup.

Pollux began to slump into unconsciousness, and the physician gestured at Haus.

"Let's carry him to the clinic," I said. "It sounds like a good place."

The medic's glass maker had brought a stretcher. I sent Karola to the funeral, and Haus and I carried Pollux. His weight felt massive, but my suit became a sort of exoskeleton to help somewhat. I tried to look concerned, even sad, not jubilant. I had retaken leadership! Scratsher followed for some reason.

Haus, at the front of the stretcher, looked back toward me. "'They moved too well together. And those glass makers, too fast. These people know how to fight. If they want, they could wipe us out."

"Even with your weapons?"

"There's one of me. A few of us—five, I think—have some military or security training, and they could help. But five against hundreds? No. We're at their mercy. We'd better be able to trust them."

But J. P. Rashid had been welcomed in most places. Humanity longed for company.

We entered the magnificent glazed-brick gate, and I saw the city for the first time. Tall plants somewhat like bamboo had rainbow stripes on their stems, and a large stand lined both sides of the entry and arched over it, still green in winter, like a ceremonial passageway. A road led on between domed houses with circles of colored glass bricks arranged in rainbows on their roofs. The gardens alongside them, despite the season's bleakness, showed indisputable signs of beauty.

It is like Eden in winter. . . .

These people did far more than merely subsist. They had prospered. And yet they wore rags.

Someday I would say so much more about that in my book, but about Pollux? Not a word. I also felt enormously calm and considered turning off the anxiety feed. I had been brave. I might be more of a man of action than I had ever thought.

Yet I would have preferred a less destructive course. I had been taught malice on Earth shamefully well.

The feeds showed what was going on in the funeral. The flowers exuded an overwhelming smell, oddly of anise. Several people complained of feeling tired, achy, and dizzy from the gravity and the fragrance.

The cost of discovery. . . .

The procession moved on alongside the river, then up into a forest. Soon, the road opened into a wide sloping field, and at the low end, a circular pit yawned far too big for one body. As the music continued and people and glass makers filled the field, the pallbearers descended into the pit and deposited the basket-coffin in the center.

Arthur, Karola, and Honey found a space toward the front on the far side from the path where we had entered. The crowd was subdued, almost silent. Our videographer stood in the front off to the side, respectfully.

Back in the city, we arrived at the clinic, a large rectangular building with an entrance that seemed very much like an emergency room in our own Earth hospitals, and on both sides were wards with wide windows, the most Earthlike architecture I had seen so far. We transferred Pollux to a narrow bed in front of a window, and the medic and his glass maker and our physician began to remove his shoes and overclothes with practiced efficiency. The bed boasted finely manufactured linens and blankets. The medical team could handle Pollux. We had to get to the funeral.

"Scratsher will take you," the medic said.

Scratsher moved toward the entrance to the building and waved for Haus and me to follow. We exited through a rear gate in the walls and walked down a path almost Earthlike except for such surprises as blue bushes with leaves that looked like butterfly wings and animals that looked like a bundle of sticks and chattered like birds as they ran past. Haus watched everything, silent and alert.

We were being led by an alien—a small, sentient, intelligent, arthropod-like alien. I had thoroughly misjudged the glass makers. How many more surprises did they hold? Were they equal to humans?

Our feeds showed Ladybird climbing onto a mound of fresh earth excavated from the pit, decorated with flowers and foliage. The music stopped and she began to speak.

"Numbers are something, and we are something now, something something." I understood "queen" now and then, and a few other random words. The feed provided a bit more translation. She was speaking about population.

Then one of the glass maker queens came to the stage, and she spoke.

The anthropologists had by then agreed that they had their own language, impossible for humans to speak, although apparently glass makers understood Classic English and humans understood glass maker language. The smell of anise, anthropologists said, was the glass maker scent-word for sorrow.

Our mission's members were elated by the quantity of surprises they had already learned. They would have work for months. *Discoveries await. . . .*

A very old woman with face paint spoke with great emotion. A shaman, perhaps? We had seen no one else with face paint. And a few people in the crowd began to weep. Another queen spoke, then a man with a shaved head. Some men and women had shaved heads, and yet some other natives looked as if they had never cut their hair or beards in their lifetimes. One man, but only one, wore clothing with long fringe. Several more people came onstage, and a child with a wide red belt declared something.

Karola sent to everyone: "She said she will remember the queen, who is named Rust."

About a dozen—no, eleven (an anthropologist counted) glass makers came forward, some large and some small. Every speaker greeted each one with tender hugs and words. Perhaps they were the deceased queen's immediate family.

By then I had reached the edge of the gathering, but the feed showed better what was happening.

Arthur took a step forward and announced something. One of the grieving glass makers responded. Arthur walked toward it. The insect—arthropod—held a red fur in its hand and seemed about to throw it into the pit. Arthur approached and took the fur. The two seemed to argue over it. Karola asked Honey what was happening. She responded with a look of surprise and uncertainty.

Two more natives came to speak to specific glass makers, though with affection rather than debate, and led them away. Arthur and his glass maker seemed to have reached an agreement, and they walked back to the crowd with his arm over its shoulders, and it clutched the fur.

A native came forward carrying a large basket and paused in front of each of the remaining eight family members. Each took what seemed to be a piece of fruit and ate it. I heard the wind beginning to blow, though I felt nothing and the trees around us did not stir.

The wind became louder, then resolved itself into a whispered chant. Everyone was whispering it, natives and glass makers, in the language of the aliens, with buzzes and whistles.

The song grew louder, and different parts of the crowd sang different harmonies with marvelous beauty. The odd voices of the glass makers only made it richer. The eight members of the dead queen's family filed into the pit. With a bit of a jostle, everyone else moved back, and in the pit, the members arranged themselves around the casket. The native with the basket of fruit followed and gave them more to eat. A final shared meal?

Children and dozens of those little green cat-rabbits moved into the area now open in front of the crowd. The song dropped to a whisper and the children lay down with the cat-rabbits in the same pose as the glass makers in the pit, though only briefly, yet the gesture could not be misinterpreted, and they rose up. *Beauty and symbolism. . . .*

Then a new song started with drums and flutes, slow and solemn, and the children and the cat-rabbits began to dance together in astounding synchronization. The children paired up, holding hands and stepping from side to side, back and forth. The animals hopped the same way in facing pairs like the children.

The little green animals could dance. The large insects—glass makers—could sing.

At the end of a verse in the song, the children switched partners. A few began to dance with some glass makers plucked from the observers alongside the field. Honey turned to Karola and showed her the dance steps. Soon Karola was singing along, at least to the chorus. Arthur and his animal were dancing together as they sang. The air was choking with that sad sweet anise smell.

I felt a hand on my arm and it was Ladybird. She had found me. She took my hands and began to dance, wordlessly inviting me to do the same.

Acceptance comes quickly, for after all these years alone, they are lonely for their species. We are not visitors here, but brothers. . . .

The steps were simple, and she led me into the crowd of dancers. When the verse changed, she turned me over to an old man in striped clothing. After him, I danced with a young woman with a shaved head who was weeping. After her, a boy. I gazed into his serious eyes. He knew what was happening and I didn't, but the singing, the movement, the smell, and the music were hypnotic with solemn grief. I glanced around, and most mission members seemed to have joined in. A few others were recording the event.

On Earth, our rituals leave us as passive spectators, and here in their odd poverty, sorrow becomes movement. . . .

The boy was singing, though I understood few words. My next partner was one of those glass makers, a small one that wore a necklace of beads. Its fingers had a ridge of tough keratin all along the back, ending in a claw, and it danced gracefully. By then I had learned how to change partners, and I did so many times. For a while four cat-rabbits danced with me, leaping high. I was tiring but did not dare stop.

Then a message came on the feed from the videographer: "They're dying. The ones in the pit, they're dying. Look!" The glass makers in the pit seemed to be sleeping, and a team of humans and other glass makers were draping worn old blankets over them, covering them completely, even their heads. The humans seemed to be sobbing. I had thought the glass makers there would rise again, like the child dancers.

"This is ritual murder."

"We don't know that," an anthropologist answered.

"When a queen dies," a zoologist sent, "the family dies, too. But not right away, not like this. On Earth, anyway."

"Is it murder if there's no malice?"

"Maybe they were sick."

"What about the ones that the natives took?"

"Can you get a better angle to see what's happening?"

"Look at how everyone is crying. And all the flowers."

"The glass makers are aliens. They could be very different from us."

"Even if it is, it's too late to do anything about it."

"They went in there willingly."

"We can't know that."

"Are we safe here?"

"Yes, are we safe?"

I had stopped dancing, as had some other members of our mission. We were disrupting the ceremony.

"Yes," I sent. "We've been welcomed. We haven't been threatened, in fact we're invited to participate. Everyone, continue with what you are doing."

"Participating in murder. We can't do that. I—"

"We're here to observe," I sent. I resumed dancing, hoping I was right. The natives had a beautiful city with a fine clinic. They were civilized. Yet on the Mississippi, J. P. Rashid's crew was trapped fully three times, with personnel losses each time. The river always lay close by for escape, more accessible than our heli-planes.

The music changed back to the first song, and everyone stopped where they were. A line spontaneously formed to go past the pit. The little green cat-rabbits were kicking dirt into the pit from the piles around it. One by one, people came to the edge to add their own handful. I came forward to look inside, adding my handful of soil so as not to cause a scene. The insects lay half-buried and motionless. Yes, they had died, or been killed, in an elaborate, sad ritual. I didn't understand, and everyone on the mission kept discussing it. Was this something done just to show us?

Arthur and the glass maker he took came up to me. Both carried spears. "This is my son now," he said, patting the alien.

"I am happy for you," I said, but I didn't really know what to say. He had rescued it from death, but at the cost of an argument. About what?

Karola sent, "Ladybird is coming to talk to you. We're with her."

We are welcomed immediately, and if our first few hours led to more questions than answers, they also led to a deep feeling of security, as if we were coming home, too.

If that wasn't true, it was what ought to be true and ought to be told—not that the natives had just killed eight sentient beings, and Haus said they could easily kill us all. Or that their environment was so treacherous that they had walled their city and persisted in maintaining a fragile bridge as a defensive measure. The natives had a plan for us, a welcome that had yet to be fully defined.

I still was breathing hard, although I had stopped dancing for long enough to have recovered.

If we made another mistake . . . if we broke another taboo . . . if I was wrong . . . if the environmental dangers overcame native preparation . . . I sought an anxiety inhibitor. If the feed broke for me, how could I remain calm?

The story I had been recording told lies—beautiful, wishful lies. Pollux, in his madness, had stumbled upon a truth. We were in danger.

We might not return to Earth.

Up until that moment, I had not believed it.

4

QUEEN THUNDERCLAP— 20 DAYS LATER

Ladybird knocked on my door early, trouble on her fleshy face—trouble, that was all we had these days. Could I meet with her and Stevland in his little greenhouse? She held her face tense, her mouth tight. Of course, the meeting would be secret. Everything involving Stevland was secret, but I would learn about another undeclared battle between Humans and Earthlings, and they would want me to get involved again.

"I must feed my baby, then I will come," and I caught myself scenting *this is wrongness* and stopped. Then I almost said no. No. No more lies and secrets. I could have said that. Like Mother Rust, I could have done anything I wanted, anything madness provoked, but that had brought her death. I had always been a good mother: I was responsible, I listened, I weighed alternatives. I was sane. And that must not change no matter what else did.

She nodded. "We need to act. Come soon. Thank you." She hurried off in the drizzle, so much to do, none of it agreeable.

And I was tired, worn by pointless conflict. They could ask, and I would listen, and maybe I would say no. Finally. Unless it was about health.

I turned back to my baby, Rattle. An irresponsible thought: I would not feed her! I would throw her out of my house already! But everyone, most of all my other children, would know I had done so. And that would be madness. I had to stay rational. Reasonable. Even happy. I used to be happy.

Within a half hour I had Rattle bundled into a basket on the back of my worker Chirp, and we left. Humans feared the Earthlings. Did they know one of the Earthlings wanted me to hate the Humans?

The rain had stopped, leaving the city's gardens filled with cold spring mud and the welcome scent of germinating seeds. Rattle reached out and grabbed a low, wet branch of Stevland and shook it, deliberately splashing Chirp. How had I borne such a vile baby? What kind of a mother would she grow up to be? She *laughed,* and he whined with a bit of playacting.

I took the branch from her hand and scented *protect.* "Mothers must show kindness and love. Now look how cold Chirp is." He whined a bit more. I took an extra scarf from the basket and handed it to her, then showed her how to dry him. She giggled heartlessly.

He puffed *question.* "Too many people, too quiet."

True. At midmorning, adults—Humans and Glassmakers alike—should have been working in the fields or the workshops, and children should have been in school. And if they had free moments, they should have all been preparing for the Spring Festival. Instead, too many people hustled between houses or paused at doorways, speaking in hushed voices. No laughter. Cloths covered their mouths and noses.

A man who worked for me in the carpentry workshop passed us.

"Blas," I called, and held out my hands. *Welcome.*

He approached and took them, and his hands felt hot.

"Your daughter?" I asked.

"She's at home. Her fever's broken, so she'll be fine." But he coughed. He looked tired, different from the tiredness at the end of a good hard day of work. And he wobbled on his two legs. He was very sick.

A cart clattered behind us. "Here's what we need," he said. A worker pulled a cart filled with jars and covered dishes: food, tea, and medicinal fruit, delivered to the door of households with sick members. Another of Ladybird's urgent projects—seven deaths already, and the epidemic had not peaked, not at all, so said the doctors, theirs and ours.

"Rest well," I said. *I wish you happiness.* He loved his daughter, and rightly so. The scents from the cart reached me: savory, sweet, and medicinally bitter.

He managed to smile. "I have to plan my change for the festival!" But tomorrow he might be in bed with aches and chills, and dead before the festival eight days away. Influenza, they called it, a latent virus hiding undetected deep inside someone's cells, a contagious respiratory infection common on Earth they thought they had deliberately left behind, yet our visitors had brought this like a gift and delivered it after being here for a score of days. It had only made the Humans hate and suspect them even more—behind that charade of welcome.

But influenza did not sicken Glassmakers. I did not want to be in the middle, yet the middle kept finding me.

I turned toward the greenhouse, a short walk away. Rattle was waving the wet scarf with the jerky movements of a baby, but with intent. "Be careful!" I said, and took it before she could slap Chirp on the head. I imagined slapping her, tensing claws and . . . no. No!

Ladybird sat on a bench outside the greenhouse, studying a wax tablet with the major who managed the city's defense and emergency plans. She murmured something to him and stood as we approached. I entered, took Rattle's basket and set it on a table, and sent Chirp outside. "This will be fast," I said. I hoped the warmth of the greenhouse would make the baby nap. I got ready to say no.

Ladybird entered and threw the bolt on the door. "Earthlings barge in almost anywhere," she complained. Then she took a deep breath and reached for my hands. "We need something, and we think you could have Scratcher get it for us. From the Earthlings."

Scratcher was working in the clinic—keeping watch on the Earthling doctors, whom Ladybird did not trust and who could not quite believe workers might be clever, so Scratcher saw and heard everything.

"You desire something from a doctor," I said. "To cure the influenza?" I felt hope and unease at the thought. If they had a cure, why not share it?

Rattle curled up. *Relax and rest,* I told her. Obey for once! I thought.

"We have a cure," Stevland said in a soft, Human male voice, almost monotone, like all Human voices, emanating from a beautifully carved wooden box, a speaker. "It exists, for what good it does. Some proteins can weaken the virus, but then the body's immune system must complete the task. Earthlings can make this protein with their equipment, and I can make it and put it in fruit faster, and we are giving it to the ill. The Earthlings' bodies have more experience with varieties of this virus, and they can fight effectively. Our Humans' bodies react with confusion. So the medicine they created helps too little. What we want instead is a small object that they call a neurotransmitter that is implanted in Earthling brains to permit communication."

"They communicate mentally by radio," Ladybird said. "We knew from the first that they do that, and now we know how." I tried to judge what she was thinking. Wide tense eyes, eyebrows close together and wrinkling her forehead, her chin slightly forward: fear, perhaps. What she knew frightened her.

Rattle dozed in her padded basket on the table, curled up, her baby fur like a bundle of tan wool waiting to be spun. She had been born the day after the Earthlings came, so for me, all the tragedy of raising a future mother was mixed with all the troubles brought by these newcomers. Troubles and lies that kept getting more complex and vexing.

I breathed deeply before I spoke, feeling my hands tremble. "You propose theft. I desire to avoid that."

"If we could make one of them by ourselves, we would," Stevland said. "Radio reception technology, which I have, is much simpler than radio transmission. I need to transmit, and I need their technology."

"But they will notice it is missing. They may blame my Scratcher."

"Their doctor has several with him," Ladybird said, "and he's careless and distracted. The clinic is in a tangle anyway with so many patients."

"Why steal? If they have so many, we could ask for one."

This question made Ladybird tense her lips.

"They have told us about it," Stevland said in that false voice, "but they do not want us to have this technology. They say they do not have the facilities to give it to Humans. This may or may not be true, but what is true is that it gives them an unquestionable advantage. But for what? I am listening to them, and I am worried. They have many factions, and they are willing to work secretly against each other, or against us. All they need is the courage to act."

Rattle fidgeted. She never slept properly.

"Perhaps you will tell me more." I had lost much trust in Stevland since the Earthlings came. He seemed to care more about them than Glassmakers.

"I can show you what I am receiving now. Their broadcasting antenna has been placed on one of my stems at Queen Chut's suggestion, and she has placed a receiver antenna for me in the same stem, so I can hear very clearly."

The speakers began to hiss and Earthling voices sounded, two men. I understood only their intonation and the word "Om" in a dismissive tone, then laughter. I seemed to smell *malice*—it was my imagination, but their tone reeked of it. One said, "Omparkash Bachchan z fukal!"

"I will explain," Stevland said. "These are Pollux and Mu Ree Cheol speaking via radio, linked by their transmitting equipment. They spend much of their time discussing the faults of Om. The word 'fukal' means 'tulip' or 'idiot,' roughly."

"Team leaders always are criticized," I said. "And perhaps rightly. Om is hesitant, afraid, perhaps. But afraid of us or his own team?" My words felt weak compared to those voices. And one Earthling never ceased to tell me how bad Humans were. That would include Ladybird as bad. What would they say about Stevland if they knew about him?

"Jose's told us about their weapons," Ladybird said. "Do you trust them?"

I feel uncertain, I answered. Uncertain about everything. Fear of Earthlings was a Human grudge that affected their judgment.

Ladybird curved her lips unhappily. "We can't trust them about what they can do to us or to each other," she said. "All you need to do is ask Scratcher to take a neurotransmitter. Once we have it, we can implant it in Stevland, then he can be part of their communications network."

"And there is more," Stevland said. "I can only show you the sound of their transmissions, but they share what they see, and certain of them look at Pacifists in a very worrisome way."

True. Those wet little holes for eyes could not disguise what they looked at, and Earthlings did not understand that I could see behind myself as well as forward. I had seen their looks of disrespect, and I had smelled the human's sexual arousal sometimes, too. I could refuse to cooperate, but that would change nothing except to leave the Earthlings with an advantage.

"If one of them learns something," Stevland said, "they can all learn it if they wish to tell each other. Also, with these neurotransmitters, they can retrieve information stored on their transmission equipment, and I wish to have access to that, too. And beyond that, their bodies send information about where they are and about their health. Thus they are diagnosed faster and cured more effectively."

I saw a flaw in his plan. "What exactly will you do when you have it? If they know so much about each other, they will know you are not one of them when you transmit."

Stevland repeated my words exactly in Glassmade, as if I were talking. "I can imitate anyone. I will only monitor them, but if necessary, I will enforce equality among us, the Pacifists and Earthlings. Communications can serve as a weapon, and I have many skills."

Ladybird looked at his speakers with tight eyes. Stevland could fight, but as fiercely as the stories said?

"I am so tired of lies," I said with *anger*.

"The lies trouble me, too," Stevland said. "I cannot sing at the funerals as I should. I will not sing at the Spring Festival. I cannot speak at meetings or anywhere but in private. And every Pacifist must lie about me. To keep secrets requires constant effort. You are right to feel tired and angry." His voice carried the emphatic tone Humans used for anger.

Ladybird nodded in agreement.

I was right. Angry and not alone in anger.

My baby dozed on. She was a little mother, and I and my family would care for her until she came of age and developed her own scent, which would be detestable to me and my majors and workers, as our scent would be to her. Then she would flee, or I would drive her out. Until then, I had to protect her. And my family. And all of Pax. But from what? A hunting team had seen the Earthling soldier destroy a band of eagles from a long distance. One Earthling was more dangerous than twenty eagles, and we had twenty Earthlings living among us.

There was one sane path ahead, though it made me a different kind of angry to follow it.

"Scratcher is very capable in all things," I said. "He can do this task for you." These words were scented with *resentment*. This conflict was about to get even worse.

"Thank you," Stevland and Ladybird said at once.

"I have no desire to fight the Earthlings," I said.

"None of us do," Stevland said.

"Perhaps."

I opened the door, called in Chirp, and placed the baby's basket on his back. After the courtesies of departure, we left, back into the cold wet day with low clouds, and headed toward the clinic.

We had not gone far when a voice called: "Queen Thunderclap!"

I recognized it. Zivon. The Earthling who wanted me to hate Humans, who said they used us as slaves. But he said that only in private, with no translator. And most of his fellow Earthlings did not treat us Glassmakers as equals. Did he think I was equal?

Arrogance in motion, Chirp puffed.

Zivon and the other Earthlings looked different from our Humans: tall, slow, fragile, and thin, just as Earthlings were remembered to be. Like the others, he wore strange clothing, a sort of tight suit that kept him warm and dry and even strong somehow. He also wore a Pax shirt over the suit, billowing over his upper half while the suit clung tight as stockings to his legs. He looked only half-dressed.

But I paused to let him approach. The day could not become worse than it already was. I did not bother to scent anything, since he would not understand, but Chirp told me, *Be careful.* I held out my hands, but he did not take them. Yet I knew he had been briefed about our culture when he arrived and several times since then. How should I interpret that? Arrogance, ignorance, or bad manners? He had a reputation for all three.

"Queen Thunderclap," he repeated in that simple English that Earthlings knew, heavily accented, then gestured at my worker. "And what is this little one's name?" He reached into a bag on his shoulder and pulled out a flat, square, transparent tablet. "We can communicate direct, you and me. You can write to me. Queens are the smartest of people on this planet."

He held it out, waiting.

I could write. In fact, I could write fluid English, and I had already learned how those tablets worked. They had radio transmitters, too, so my words would go to everyone, to the information storage, to all parts—so be careful. I took it and began to trace letters on it, which assembled themselves into neatly arranged words. For a moment, I imagined having one in my mind, like a window to elsewhere, to anywhere. Earthlings had great power.

"My worker is called Chirp in your language."

"Chirp. And Thunderclap." His face tightened up, wrinkled naked flesh. "Do you not think these are bad names? Humans laugh at you, at the sounds you make."

I laugh too, happily, Chirp told me. He made the sound of his name, a chirp in any language.

I took the tablet and in a moment of rancor decided to use my best English to see how good his vocabulary was. "My name evokes the power of nature, a noble name."

He read slowly. "What do you call yourself? What does your name mean?"

I wrote, "It is a sound and no more." I said my name, the low, brusque sound of a close flash of lightning. "What does Zivon mean?"

He read it, then lowered the tablet fast, his mouth curving down. He shook his head. "What do you call this baby? It is a queen, right?"

"Yes, a little queen. Rattle. A distinctive sound. Percussive. We can use it in songs to good effect."

He muttered something in Earthling language, but he shook his head inadvertently, a sign of no, of disagreement. He did not like our language. He knelt to pet Rattle, but she continued to sleep, even though he smelled like *alert*. All the Earthlings did. "It is a miracle you have survived on this planet."

"No," I wrote, "mere hard work."

"Your work. You do the hard work, the Humans use you."

I began to write and realized I would have to write too much.

He saw my hesitation and said, "You can trust me. Earth has changed since the original colonists left, and I am not like them. You live under Human rule, and it limits you. You are not equals."

"One person, one vote," I answered.

"They are more than you. They can do what they want."

"If they all voted together, yes, but they never do. How do you decide things? Back on Earth. And here. How?"

"That is not the issue," Zivon said. "I mean, we know things are unfair on Earth." He looked down and for the first time seemed to notice the carved stones in the pavement. The Human named Fern had made them, and they were part of a sundial, a beautiful way to measure the hours. Beauty was important to us, but to him? "We can talk about something else, then. Can you tell me about the onions for the festival?"

"It is what we ate when we traveled," I wrote. "Wild ones, not crops."

"We? Glassmakers or Humans?"

"Both. We celebrate traveling to this city."

"Can you show me how you gather them?"

"The same way as crops."

"How? Can you show me?"

"Onions right there," Chirp said, waving at a muddy garden.

"Those?" Zivon asked, pointing to the narrow children's flower garden surrounding the history museum.

Chirp *laughed*.

"No. Those are rare flowers," I wrote, "special tulips and deep-woods lilies and others. Chirp will show you onions."

He took a few steps and pointed to some thick green leaves bursting through the wet soil.

"Can you dig them up?" Zivon said.

Chirp stepped into the garden.

"But you, Queen. Why not you?"

"In the harvest, I gather fruit and grain, but I do not dig."

"Why?"

"I am a mother."

"So?"

"Digging is for workers."

He read that message for a long time. Rattle stirred on Chirp's back. He murmured a song to her. Finally Zivon said, "Queens do not dig, you say. Do you understand the word 'equality'? Do you?"

"Yes. Glassmakers and Humans are equal." And Stevland, I could have added, all three of us equal.

"But you are not equal to a worker."

"A family is one thing with many parts," I wrote. "An eye is not a hand or foot."

He made an unhappy face again, muttering in Earthling. Then he turned and walked away. Not even a goodbye. I had done nothing rude or unmotherly.

"He is scientist," Chirp said, still *laughing*. "But he does not know his onions."

"We must find Scratcher," I said. I had learned nothing—or something too hard to describe and not what I had wanted to learn. We were surrounded by Stevland. He must have heard. What did he think?

At the fountain nearest the clinic, we saw Scratcher filling buckets. I called his name. He set them down and came to take my hands.

Sad greetings. "We lose this morning an old man to the illness." He nodded at Chirp, who nodded back, a greeting workers had learned from Humans. Visual communication, much like all those facial expressions.

His hands in mine felt moist and calloused. *Be strong,* I scented.

"I am troubled, too. And I will ask you to get something for me. There is a small device the Earthlings have in their brains, and they have extra devices in their medical supplies. You will take one of them for me, but they cannot know."

He gripped my hands tighter, so tight it almost hurt. That was a surprise. He was usually the calmest person anywhere. "I know what you desire. The Earthling doctors try to explain them to the Pacifist doctors. Like all things, they do not agree with each other." *These many disagreements are tiring.*

"I was told the Earthlings will not give us that technology."

"They say we cannot understand, too complex, and they do not have medicine to give it to Humans, mistake will ruin a mind, even on Earth this happens, they say. To give to Glassmakers, not even something to discuss. *They are selfish and arrogant.* They have little medicine to share, they bring little from home."

"Do they suspect anything about Stevland?"

"They believe with difficulty that I can think. Plants? *Laughable.*"

"Do you trust the Earthlings?"

"No, but each for a different reason. Each is foolish in a different way."

Malice?

"For each other. For us, do you have malice for a child? They think we are children. But they always have interest for us. For me, since I am there. They take samples as if they are biting moths, blood and flesh and even urine and feces, they ask what I eat, how I breathe, how I see. *Tiring, I repeat. Now I must depart.* Many at the clinic are very sick and need care at all moments. You will come soon and I will have the neurotransmitter. Perhaps it is for Stevland?"

"Yes."

Good. He is safety.

He patted the baby and nodded again at Chirp. I bade him a loving farewell and watched him return with a bucket of water in each hand. He felt no trust for the Earthlings and wanted to be safe from them, and he was wise. Malice for a child? He could not imagine it, but I had burned with it every day for twenty days.

Rattle stirred again. If she woke, we could play—no, she and Chirp could play. He would enjoy it, and perhaps he would never notice how little I wanted to do with her. I lifted up the basket and set it on the ground. "Rattle, you can play with Chirp. Would you like that, Chirp?" I did not know how much the baby understood. A worker or major at that age would understand little, perhaps just names, but mothers learned faster. Much faster.

Chirp was ready to run. *Come!* he said.

Come! she repeated, and chased him between the buildings.

As I watched, I smelled Mother Cheery approaching before I saw her, a sulfur smell like poisonous fruit. She waved at Rattle. We greeted each other, but not hand to hand. Never hand to hand, not since she had developed her own scent. I had thrown her, my daughter, out of my home at the first whiff, and less than a year ago. It was instinct, and when I slammed the door, I fell to the floor, immersed in sorrow. Knowing that she felt sorrow and confusion and worse. Alone.

Thus it is with all mothers. Once I, too, had been sent out, rejected. I had a house waiting, but empty. Instead I went to the dining hall and told some Human friends, and they congratulated me. They did not understand. Humans cannot.

I went home that night and slept alone. Alone as seasons changed, night after night. My own mother and her workers and majors greeted me only from a distance. No touch, except from Humans. Sometimes I even slept in their homes for company. I had understood everything that was happening to me, how it was normal, how I could go on, but suddenly my own mother hated me, would hate me forever.

And worst, I hated her, her scent, remembering all the while how I once loved her utterly. All mothers hate each other, disgust each other. Someday I would hate Rattle, and she would hate me. I could not bear to feel that again. Until she developed her scent, Mother Rust had been high-spirited but affable, agreeable. When her mother threw her out, she changed, and those first few days of madness stretched out into years. Sometimes that happens.

I hated Cheery.

"I have news," she said *happily*. "The Earthlings desire to take us back with them."

"To Earth?"

"As an honored new species. You know how curious they are. The whole planet will be curious, they say. But it is a long journey, and it takes special medical preparation."

"They study Scratcher at the clinic. Perhaps that is why." I would not let them take him. But Cheery? Good riddance.

"I desire to go, no perhaps about it. I am curious about them, too."

"I learn things I do not desire to know. They desire us to hate our Humans."

"Oh, you must be wrong."

"Have you talked to Zivon? He speaks only of that. About how we are oppressed. How Humans make us work and they control the city." *Anger.*

"He is right in one way. We must all work very hard. They do not fear hunger on Earth. Can you imagine? We could study, could do nothing but music, but here, you must build with wood, I manage weaving, our workers harvest and cook and build and serve and all the other things every day."

Rattle came running back fragrant with laughter as Chirp chased her. She hid beneath me, as if my legs and the hem of my dress were part of the game. I tried not to flinch. Chirp lowered his head and came after her, and, with lots of whistles and clouds of laughter, they continued the chase. I suddenly wished I could play with her like that. But the thought made me ill.

"Someday she will be another mother," Cheery said with a whiff of *regret*. "A good family. But we all send our majors and workers out to hunt and toil and return to us exhausted. All of us must work, Humans too, and all of us must take part in the government and try to decide what to do, and none of us know, and all of us make mistakes and foolish decisions. Our errors could leave us hungry or dead. But we would be free on Earth."

She was swollen with her first child, so she was not speaking from experience. And yet she was right about work.

"We? They will take us all?"

"They have a big ship. You see it in the telescopes. Perhaps an entire family can go. We can be free. And we are meant to travel, us Glassmakers. This has been a good planet but we do not belong here. Humans can only live here with difficulty. We needed their help. They have been very good for us, so imagine a whole planet of them!" She smelled of *hope,* pure hope.

"Free? Imagine the voting."

"Free to be us. Free of Stevland. He is good to us, yes, but he is a plant, and we are animals. He has us stay in one place, rooted, like him, because that is how he lives. But that is not how we live. When we travel, we learn what is true. We can go somewhere new, and we will learn much."

"I trust no Earthlings, none of them."

"You must talk to them, and not just Zivon. Others are good, and they desire what is good for us. You will see."

I thought a moment. She knew nothing about the implant we were going to steal, and I decided not to tell her. Instead I said, "That can explain Zivon's attitude. Some of the Earthlings work together, and they desire us to go with them. So they desire us to hate our Humans."

"But they do not all feel like that."

I wanted to say something gentle and loving, to be what I used to be even if only for a few words. To be that way again all the time. "You are right. We are always working."

"Yes. Now I must prepare something to burn for the celebration. It will be what it looks like. That is all I can say. And you?"

"I do not know."

"You have little time." She puffed *goodbye,* turned, and left.

I called Rattle. She came hopping with Chirp, first on right legs, then on left, clapping to keep time. He had already taught her that! Then a memory made me troubled. We had always had music, but it was the Humans who had taught us to dance again. I put the basket back on Chirp, and we turned toward the clinic. The sky showed that it would rain soon.

But as we approached, I smelled *fear* and vomit and feces. The clinic

lay on the western side of the city, not in a round stone-and-glass building that we Glassmakers first built so long ago, but a square Human-
style one with many windows on all sides. Medics liked light. Stevland
liked to look in. Air leaked in and out, and on that air always rode many
scents—and sounds.

"I hurt! Hurt!" That was Cawzee. And groans and retching sounds.
Fear. Help!

And there were Human voices, not less fearful:

"Help him!"

"Here, I've got it."

"He feels hot."

"Cawzee, it will be okay." That was Arthur, his new mother.

"I'm coming."

"Can you get him to be still?"

Could I still get the neurotransmitter from Scratcher? And if Cawzee was ill, we too could be ill. Even if I hated Rattle, I had a responsibility. To see her suffer, sick? I dared not think of that, of how it would
feel. I would wish her dead.

"Rattle, stay with Chirp. In your basket. Maybe you two can sing.
The song about the moons?" That might keep her occupied for the
moment it would take to run inside. I entered carefully.

There in the reception room, crowded with chairs and tables and
shelves, Cawzee writhed on the floor, spewing vomit from one end and
diarrhea from the other. Arthur knelt next to him, holding him and mum-
bling. Our medic, Ivan, knelt on the other side, examining him. The
Earth medic looked into a small instrument he held in his hands.

"Fever, definitely a fever," Ivan said. "Influenza?"

"I need a better sample," said the Earthling.

I stood there stupidly, trying to believe it. Could we get sick from
the Earthlings? Perhaps. Perhaps.

Scratcher scurried into the reception room carrying a bucket and a
mop, then set them down. "Mother!" He touched a pocket of his smock,
ran to me, took my hands as if in greeting, and pressed a small box into
them. "You must go. Illness. *Danger.*"

Rattle came dashing under my legs, babbling the song and *laughing.*

Scratcher shrank back. *Flee. Urgent.* Rattle stopped and looked around.

The Earthling medic looked at us. I tried to hold my hand with the box out of his line of sight, but I also had to get my baby and go. Or should I leave her? No. I jumped and grabbed her, but there was no space in that room crowded with bodies and furniture to turn around, so I leaped out backward as fast as I could, the hand with the box snug beneath my baby's fur. She squirmed, but I held tight, wishing to drop her, to hurt her, to let her be hurt.

Outside, in the fresh air—the theft was accomplished! And Cawzee? Maybe the doctors were wrong. Chirp stood nearby, *apologizing.*

I set Rattle down into Chirp's basket. It began to drizzle. *We will go now.*

Go, go, she answered. *Hungry.*

Sorry, he said. "She jumped down and ran fast."

"It is not your fault." We were all sick already if we could get influenza, because we had all been exposed for days and days. And if Earth medicine did not work for Humans on Pax, much less then for Glassmakers. And what other illnesses would be on Earth?

I opened my hand to see the prize we had schemed to get. The box was the opaque yellow of the Earth substance called plastic, small, yet it seemed too large to hold a bit of electronics to put into a Human brain—much empty space lay inside, I supposed. The box weighed almost nothing and looked plain. All Earthling creations looked drab. They had no sense of beauty. I slipped it into a pocket. Stevland would have seen that I had it and would be waiting. I had questions for him.

But I saw behind me an Earthling approaching, Om, with Dakota, a Human who helped translate Glassmade for him. Mother Cheery had said I should talk to the Earthlings.

"Chirp, take her home." It had started to rain. "I will come home later." I petted him—not her! but I should have—and he dashed off.

"Queen Thunderclap," Om said, "can I have a brief word with you?

About the Spring Festival. What you think of it, and what it means to you. If you do not mind."

Om, the nervous one that some of his own team disparaged, was tall, slow, but not so pale or fragile, and spoke passably good English with less accent than Zivon. He wore Earthling clothing over his suit and looked out of place rather than odd. A cold, heavy raindrop fell on my left eye, beaded, and as it dripped off, it created distorted images of buildings, muddy gardens, and green Stevland. More rain began to fall, each drop like a noisy pebble.

He stood there, half turned away as if to protect himself from me, waiting.

"Let's talk in the museum," Dakota said, pointing to the building close by. She ran ahead and opened the door, and since I moved faster, I arrived first, followed by Om.

Inside, rain rattled on the glass dome, and the stormy light was barely enough to illuminate the display tables topped with clear glass, and the other exhibitions. I knew he had been there before, since all the Earthlings had received tours of almost everything in the city and its surroundings, but had he paid attention?

Dakota closed the door and smiled at me when he could not see. She wanted to have sex with Om, not because she liked him but because Pax Humans needed new genetic material, and Stevland had determined that he would be a good match for her. Stevland had shown us mothers a scent that would inspire sexual response, complex but not difficult, and not something they would consciously notice. Should I emit it?

"What does he desire to know?" I asked. She repeated the question to him with no hint that I should do anything for her. Yet.

He looked into the air at something his radio transmitter sent him, and he asked with his entertaining singsong accent, "What is your opinion of the Spring Festival? It existed before Glassmakers came to the city, so it is a Human holiday. Do you feel a part of it? If I may ask."

Dakota looked at me with apology drooping on her face, knowing how annoying the question was, waiting for my reply.

"It is a Pax holiday," I said, "not a Human one. We were all looking for this city."

She translated. He seemed to stare into space, probably doing things with the neurotransmitter. If Stevland was right, was he also sharing our discussion with other Earthlings?

"That is what you have been told, I think," he said. But his meaning hung like a scent: what I believed was not true. Just like Zivon, insisting we were used by our Humans.

"Come look at this," I said, and walked to the exhibit in the middle of the room that re-created in miniature the city as the Humans had discovered it, in ruins.

"We built the city, then we left, and while we were gone, the Humans came. Do you know why we left? Our health was failing because we could not survive on this strange planet. We had originally been a nomadic people, so we left to become nomadic again to see if we would survive better that way."

Dakota had not finished her translation when he responded. He did not care what I said.

"And you came back and the city had been taken over by Humans."

"Yes. By then we were in an even worse state, with very few survivors, very few mothers. But the Humans gave us homes."

I wanted to add that Stevland had helped the Humans, too, that we would all probably be dead without him and the other plants who helped us. And that Om and the other Earthlings should have stayed at their own planet.

"They gave you homes only after a war with a high price."

He knew the story. Dakota sighed and smelled my *anger*. I decided to answer as if he were Zivon, using precision as a way to express my feelings.

"Some Glassmakers tried to kill all the Humans. And they lost. But others of us had already been welcomed into the city, and the Humans protected us from the Glassmakers who fought. The Glassmakers who fought all died. We who hoped to live in peace then became citizens equal to the Humans, and now we work together, and the city is beautiful!"

"That is the story," he said. "Where are you from? Your home planet, where was it?"

"We forgot. Forgot almost everything. When we came back to the city, Humans could write our language better than we could."

"And you practice Human culture more than your own." He was sounding even more like Zivon. Why did they hate Humans? Perhaps it was like mothers hating each other.

"It is not the Humans' fault. Come and look." I led him to a side dome that re-created a Glassmaker nomadic tent. It held a small loom, wooden bowls, a few stone and wood tools, and some coarse blankets. "These are the riches that a mother like me would have had. We could not even make glass anymore. Look at that blanket. That is what I would have worn. Now look at this tunic."

I spread my arms to show him the brocade. It fell in wide sleeves from my arms and draped around my legs in a design that re-created the colors and even the textures of a bed of spring flowers. "It is warm and beautiful. Humans and Glassmakers made this together. And together we all eat and are well and safe."

"But do they need you? They were living well without you."

Dakota did not wait for me. "We're a lot better with them, a lot more productive. They do great work."

"But you do not need them."

She shook her head. "We would have failed if we hadn't found this city. We were lucky the Glassmakers made this city. Lucky lucky."

"You feel defensive about them."

"We . . ." She looked around the room, then up at the roof, where rain still drummed on the rainbow glass. "We're all the same."

"I have a question," I said. He looked down at me intensely. "Do you plan to take Glassmakers to Earth?"

His face did not change. "Well, yes, perhaps. We have the facilities to take back specimens."

I looked at Dakota. "That means Pacifists, right? Both Humans and Glassmakers?"

"I think so."

"Ask him to clarify."

She did.

He tensed his lips. "Well, the ship is not large, you know. And there are medical problems with hibernation travel. So . . . we were thinking perhaps a queen. She could come with us to Earth and establish Glassmakers there. I know we are asking a lot, so I will understand completely if you say no." He cowered just a bit as he spoke.

"Just one Glassmaker," I said. Maybe Rattle. He would take my baby and raise her far away. Where she would not be equal, for she would be alone. If she did not sicken and die. But I would send her away before I truly detested her, before I became truly mad.

Dakota translated, looking at me with narrowed eyes. Did she understand what this might mean to me?

"Ah, you think I mean your baby," he said. "Well . . . well, we can talk more later. Or perhaps just some DNA so we could reconstruct the species."

Dakota looked at him and at me. She waited. He turned to look at the replica of the ruined city.

"We must talk a lot more," I said.

"You are not the first alien species we have encountered," he said with a small smile like an apology. "We have been talking to one by radio, but it takes generations, and we will never see them. But we have you, face-to-face. You cannot imagine what it—you—tells us about the universe and about how life works." He had reached out and was idly touching the fronds of a miniature model of Stevland.

What if he knew about Stevland? Why not just tell him?

"On Earth," he said, but not looking at us, "when we have met other cultures, we have often killed them, and they were our own species, not to mention what we did to animals. But Humans have adopted you into our species. What is it about you that makes it possible? . . . I have trouble saying what I want in English. We must talk someday, you and me, with Zivon or another anthropologist, and I can say better what a surprise you are."

Adopted? Dakota, perhaps unconsciously, had taken a half step back from him. I scented *bitter laughter,* and she looked at me with a twisted smile, then shook her head to say no.

Humans had not adopted us. Stevland had adopted us all.

I had never thought about it quite so clearly.

The rain was still falling, but not as hard, and I had a delivery to make. I thrust out my hands to him. "I must go now and attend to duties."

"Think about it," he said as he clasped them with a little bow that was unexpectedly charming.

"I can do nothing else."

Dakota took my hands and squeezed them, her little wet eyes sharing a secret as expressively as anything that could be said or scented. I released the sexual scent Stevland had taught, and I wished her *happiness*.

I galloped to the greenhouse to shorten my time in the rain, entered, locked the door, and looked at the fronds falling all around me. I waited for him to speak. His attention was not always everywhere, but he would notice me soon.

Welcome, he scented.

"He desires to take Rattle to Earth."

"Not necessarily her, but a Glassmaker mother for certain," he said in Glassmade. "And seeds. I will make sure Earthlings take some of my seeds, but seeds for me are not like a child for you, especially a future queen. Or he could take yourself. I cannot tell you what to choose, but I know it will be a difficult choice."

Perhaps a joyful choice. "Cawzee is sick."

"Yes, and I wish I knew what his illness is. At the clinic, they are still trying to stabilize him. They are also working on another medicine for Humans based on its earlier failures. We may have good news soon."

"Did you hear what Zivon said to me?"

"He is always saying things like that. Do you think it is true?"

"Things are never perfect between Humans and Glassmakers. And us and you," I dared to say. "Or members of a family. That is truth. Our family is a normal family, the family of Pax." The wind gusted outside. I reached into a pocket. "I have the neurotransmitter." The plastic box was sealed. "Shall I open it?"

"Please."

I struggled with the snap lid a bit, then struggled to understand what I saw inside. Protected by a cover of clear plastic, nestled into a protective berth, lay a tiny flat piece of gold, its surface elaborately worked, and with a long tail-like wire on one end, looping around the berth. I held it up to show him. "It looks small."

"It fits outside the skull, and only the wire goes into the brain."

I thought about what it would mean to have a tiny radio in my head. Could I turn it off? A constant noise, a constant connection. "Does this connect everyone with everyone?"

"They seem to be able to choose whom to speak with. Often some individuals have periods of silence, so I believe they can control it. I will have a lot to learn. My roots are the equivalent to a brain, and one of them can accept the wires."

I had a frightening thought. "You will become more like the Earthlings."

"I will become more attuned to them. That does not mean I will like them more."

"Do you really desire to go to Earth? Send your seeds? Earth could be horrible." Or as Cheery said, it could be wonderful. What did he think?

"I desire to send my seeds everywhere, to places good and bad. It is my nature. Many plants send their seeds to float on the wind, to travel without any plan at all. Your nature is to travel. You are nomadic."

"Perhaps migratory. We leave home, but we come back. And we do not leave our babies to luck." But perhaps I would!

"You do not bear a hundred thousand babies in a season. I will not live forever, but I can try to live everywhere."

That made me *laugh*. And laughing surprised me. "I must attend to my work and my family."

"Please leave the neurotransmitter in the box on the table. Queen Chut will come to install it soon."

"I hope it works well. Water and sunshine."

"Warmth and food."

I left into rain and wind, and galloped home. Inside, Rattle and

Chirp were playing with dolls, both Glassmaker and Human dolls. I imagined a home without her, after she was grown—or sent to Earth!—and how relaxed I would feel. I walked over and petted her. It felt reasonable, like what a loving mother would do.

"We must think about the Spring Festival," I said. "What shall we make to burn?" It would symbolize what each one of us wished to change.

"I do not desire change in anything," Chirp said, "but changes happen."

"Earthlings?"

"I think a ball for me. It can be a planet, not this one. Earthlings will not understand."

"You dislike them so much?"

"They eat a lot of food but do not help us get it. They make more *tiring* work. They are going to eat a lot at the festival. Our Humans are too sick to prepare it, so we will work work work."

"Is it only the work that bothers you?" If we became ill, who would do that work?

"And what Scratcher said, what they think of us. And their illnesses. But I say this only to you, Mother. I do not speak to Earthlings at all."

"You are the most headstrong of my children."

"No, that would be the little mother. As it should be."

And what would I make to burn, a symbol of my willingness to change? Chirp was right. I had desired no changes, but changes had happened. More would come, great and small, and perhaps good. Perhaps.

5

JACQUES MIRLO—6 DAYS LATER

No one was following me. Good. I walked out of the west gate late in the day, when most colonists were finishing dinner, to a path through a newly planted field. Around me, animals chirped and chimed and barked, and every noise spooked me, but I was more terrified that someone might see me.

I knew where I was headed. I'd investigated earlier. The path continued uphill to a grove of rainbow bamboo shielded from sight from passersby. When I got there, I stood still and looked around. Bamboo branches arched over me like a vaulted roof. I listened. Creepy little animals, no colonists. Good.

I pulled a knife from my pocket. I needed a stalk of bamboo. A small one would do, small enough to hide, but mature. That one? No, too young. There? Yes, but I'd have to trim off the leaves. . . . I knelt and cut. Sawed, really. A tough stem. This was going to take too long. But I reminded myself that I was in a field in a forest, not in a building with alarms, and not on a planet with the technology to alarm its plant life. As far as I knew.

Done. I had my stalk. I needed only a half meter of it. I began trimming the top and leaves, and they were tough, too. Why didn't I bring a saw? I was stupid, unprepared.

I could hide the stalk under my coat, but I'd need to cut it into pieces. I knelt to brace it on the ground to begin cutting. Something rustled. I jumped. Probably just an animal. Why did I even think it was a good idea? But I needed to know more about the rainbow bamboo, the plant the colonists seemed to worship. No, not worshiped, respected. Maybe feared. The anthropologists had figured out that they'd even given it a name: Stevland. They'd seen it written at the museum. Why that name? Why any name?

The anthropologists wanted to know, but no one wanted to talk or even admit to it, and we were all worried about being too pushy after we'd seen them kill all those Glassmakers at the funeral. The colonists didn't appreciate our killer flu, either, even after the cure four days ago. No one can kill their way to friendship. Om had said to tread softly, and for once I agreed.

I was the task force botanist. The natives were farmers, most of them, so even when I wasn't trying to figure out the bamboo, everything I did was treading in their territory. I was an outsider.

But I had too many questions to ignore, and until that moment I'd had enough courage to want to find out any way I could. Well, no turning back now. I'd cut a third of the stem off. Another cut and the three pieces would be small enough to hide and I could leave. . . . There. Done. The knife in a pocket, the stalks under my shirt up against my suit, held in place by the waistband of my slacks.

And back to the city. No running downhill, just walk, out for an evening stroll, enjoying the beauty of the sparkly caterpillars and the music of the barks and chimes and squawks and a far-off terrifying roar, a bat swooping down at me and hooting—I didn't want to be there at all. I had to continue down the path, through the gate, down the streets. Walk normal. Maybe smile a bit as if I were listening to some entertaining feed. I passed some colonists. Some ignored me, a few nodded more politely than pleasantly.

And finally, the lab. I ducked in under the door and barred it shut.

Safe. I'd analyze that bamboo with every piece of equipment I had. I wouldn't dare to gather more samples anytime soon.

There, in the MR scanner, those cells again, easy to spot because there were lots of them. Long, thin—ten times too fine to be tracheid tubes to carry water. They carried electric charges. Nerve cells: I'd figured that out a week ago with samples from other species. Nerve cells in plants. I'd seen them in every sample—all the plants on this planet had a nervous system!—and this time I was looking at *Bambusa iridis*.

As slowly as I could, I rotated the stalk in the scanner, searching for a clue about what the nerves were for, what a plant needed them for. I decided to check the nodes, the joints between stalk sections, as logical a place as any to look for some purpose. . . . Yes, there. Neurons were entering . . . something, a little organ of some sort. I took a cross section of it. Another in a different direction, horizontal now because the organ was thin and long, about four micrometers long.

I took a series of images and put them on-screen to study. . . . Fairly complex for being only a dozen or so cells, with a clear top, long sides, and nerves at the end. Not like anything I'd ever seen in a plant on Earth. So far life here hadn't seemed as weird as we'd hoped. Earthlike, far too Earthlike for major surprises, both the animals and plants. But now, this. . . . Animals. . . . I tried to remember some zoology. . . . This could be an eye. A cornea, lens, and nerves to sense light—that's what it might be. I called up some reference materials and searched through them.

An ommatidium—it looked almost exactly like an ommatidium, a unit of a compound eye of an insect. A little eye complete with attached optic nerves. I had to be sure. If it could see, it would react to light. My samples were still alive, since I'd picked them just an hour ago. I could slide in a microhair-sized wire from a sensor to measure electrical charges. The equipment lay on another table in the lab.

Something rattled outside and I jumped. Then I recognized the sound, the string of rattles that the city guards carried, a pair making rounds. Would they stop in front of my lab? I was working in the middle of the night, and the central skylight would be glowing, so they'd know I was there. I had the door blocked so colleagues and Pacifists couldn't come in and see what I was doing. No colleagues because I wasn't ready to share what I knew, if I ever would be. No Pacifists because they would have stopped me.

Or maybe they'd do something worse. They had a lot of opinions about all the plants. You could pick some plants or fruit and not others, or just certain parts or at certain times. Above all, you could hardly even touch the rainbow bamboo, never ever burn it, even though it was huge and grew everywhere. And I was dissecting samples of it.

The rattle faded as the guards walked on, leaving me alone in the chilly, dark, glass-domed stone-walled lab with this plant that might have eyes.

I finished placing the sensors into the sample, set it gently . . . gently in front of the MR, and draped my coat over the machine so the stalk would be in the dark. I brought a lamp over and carefully pulled off the coat. The sensor jumped. The eye had noted the light.

I tried again. Again. Then I brought over a lamp that shone with ultraviolet light. Another reaction. One more time just to be sure. Then with another ommatidium.

Eyes. Tiny eyes. It had a lot of them. I put a stalk under a microscope and started counting the eye cells in a node chosen at random, the first one I grabbed. Thirty-four on that node, and three nodes in that half-meter-long culm, and it was a small culm compared to the monster trunks I'd seen elsewhere, and the plant grew everywhere. A total number of eyes in this valley would require scientific notation to write because we hadn't brought that many zeros from Earth.

Seriously, it would take a lot of brain-processing power to handle all that data from all those eyes. I'd already seen brains—that is, bundles of neurons—in some of the roots I'd collected from other plants and examined with microscopes, scans, comparisons to known animals on Earth and Pax—thanks, colleagues, for your notes. I found what I was looking for, long cords of ganglia in the roots along with vascular bundles of xylem and phloem and all the other things a root might have. It had secondary growth, too, with new cords and ganglia. Interesting.

The bamboo must have roots like that—a brain. And it could grow more brains. Every plant on this planet had nerve tissue and many had brains. None as big as the rainbow bamboo, though. None of the plants were anywhere near as big as the bamboo. It could do a lot with a brain that big and information from, effectively, every part of its habitat.

Could it hear? That is, detect vibration? And smell, too? Probably. On Earth, plants sensed chemicals in the air, and noted movements and gravity. There were enough nerve cells in the stem for lots of kinds of sensory reception. I needed to investigate more.

And oh, how I wanted to! I wanted a plant, any plant, to sense me, to interact, to communicate, to think in a way I would understand.

There had to be a way to communicate with an intelligent plant alert to its surroundings. On Earth, I could interact with, say, a goldfish, teach it to solve a very simple maze, but not an oak tree, and an oak could live for centuries, maybe growing wiser than me. I'd never believed plants were mere automatons, living self-operating machines going through the motions. Plants made fruit to be eaten. That demonstrated their awareness of us as frugivores, dim awareness, perhaps, but real. How much more did they know?

If only we could . . . measure a response, watch it make a decision, something. For all that plants could do, for all that I stared at them frustrated, imagining their secret lives, nothing. Now I had a way to find that something.

The Pacifists knew, and they wouldn't tell us.

But it was late, and I was tired and needed to get to bed, and I still had to clean up very carefully. Where to hide the bamboo samples? As I turned off equipment and put it away, I worried about that. Then I had a flash of genius: I'd drop it in the latrine—gift center, they called it. Gifts? For whom? The bamboo, which occupied the city. A plant that big needed lots of nitrogen.

And so I left with a bag of samples, dumped them while I used the latrine—something for you, Stevland!—and went to bed in the little house I shared with other scientists, the Mu Rees. I thought I'd be too tense to sleep, but I dropped off fast to exciting thoughts. From the moment I'd seen the bamboo, I knew it could make me some good money if I could get it home. What garden plant could be prettier? Big, beautiful bamboo.

But now I wouldn't just be rich, I'd be famous, at least in the scientific world. And even if Earth was still a fascist lunacy when we got back home, money and fame would protect me—but only if I could find out more about the bamboo, about the enormous plant that could see and think. *Bambusa sapiens.* The Pacifists knew a lot. How could I get them to tell me?

Oh, and its fruit, such possibilities. . . .

The next morning the Mu Ree triplets dragged me out of bed, three identical clones, and if they turned off their ID display, which they did a lot, you couldn't tell them apart, not in looks, not in personality, not in knowledge. Mediocre zoologists who liked being three parts of one thing.

I didn't want them to be suspicious, so I got up, tugged on a suit and clothes, and left for breakfast with them. The sky looked clear, the air felt a little chilly. The zoologists were chortling about some giant spider they'd finally documented.

"They're everywhere," the Mu Ree next to me told me. "But camouflaged."

"Here?" I played along, gesturing at the big rainbow bamboo we were passing.

"No, not in the city. They don't come here. The colony has trained them not to. But the minute we leave the city, they're everywhere."

That big rainbow bamboo we passed, was it watching us? It had to be. Those eyes had no lids. What was it thinking? About me? It had to be thinking about something with all those brains. Animals had brains to control their bodies' processes, to move, to find food, to do things. Plants on Earth, even sequoias, got along just fine without them, as far as I knew. Why here?

"How much do you think the colonists have changed the environment?" I asked.

"Globally, insignificantly. It's all still wide-open. You've seen the global surveys we're getting from the ship. Amazing stuff. In the immediate area, besides a couple of domestications and some conditioned responses, not too much. It's a small colony."

"But here's something interesting," another Mu Ree said. "The colonists tell us they didn't domesticate the fippokats and fippolions. They were domesticated before they got here, and not by the Glassmakers, either, who got here a little before them. The colonists believe that intelligent species preceded them. But they have no proof. They just believe that."

In unison, they shook their heads in amazement.

"Right," I said. "They know things and they're not telling us."

"How did they domesticate so many crops so fast?" one of them asked.

"Good question," I said. "If I could get anyone to talk to me honestly, I might learn the answer."

In fact, that was an obvious question. I'd been asking it and not getting many satisfactory responses. And if all the plants could think, the questions got more complicated. Why would, say, the pineapples cooperate and be domesticated? Was there some sort of deal? How? Did it involve the bamboo? And if the colonists found out I'd filched samples of the bamboo and examined them, would they ever talk to me at all? Or would they just kill me?

We walked into the big, square building next to the kitchen where everyone ate, a lot like a school cafeteria. Food service and buffet at one end, the rest filled with tables and benches, lots of light and lots of windows, and big doors to open in nice weather. I looked around and tried to remember what I'd learned about sociology, because if I could figure out where the weak links were, I could pry some information out of someone.

Colonists tended to sit by generations, each with its marker—like black hats or bald heads—but not all the time. Sometimes they sat by work group or families. Could I spot a work group of farmers? They could tell me something.

If they would talk to me. During the flu outbreak, they'd stayed far away, as if I were poison ivy come to infest their crops, as if I were the source. (I checked, I wasn't.) After the antiviral was developed that got all but the sickest cases back on their feet in forty-eight hours and everyone else immune, they were still looking at me as I scanned the room as if maybe I were about to mutate into poison nettles.

Om said to be humble. I could fake that. I could go with them, pull weeds with them, and talk with them. And listen. Learn. Sooner or later they'd let something slip. I'd sit at that table over there, with Geraldine, too much of a coward to be rude, but yet a knowledgeable farmer. She'd let me invite myself along to the fields.

First, some food. A table at one end was loaded with bread and nut spread and fruit—rainbow bamboo fruit. I had checked that fruit carefully. It had caffeine in it. Great breakfast fruit. Delicious. Fruit like that would sell big on Earth. I grabbed one and put it and a bread turnover on a clay plate, grabbed a cup of what they called reddog tea, and—

Behind me a man began talking loud enough to distract me.

"Velvet leaves? You could boil them a week and dip them in butterfly oil and they'd still be inedible. What were you thinking?" The translation sent through my connection didn't match the indignation of the original voice. That was the trouble with translation. That's why I had learned as much as I could of English and forced myself to get used to the Pax accent.

I turned. Behind me was the little table where cooks put experiments. If you tried something there, you had to give an opinion.

The cook, a plump woman, just shrugged. "I was thinking that Glassmakers might like them. It was brave of you to try."

"Put a warning sign on it next time."

"I thought 'velvet leaves' would be enough."

They glared at each other a moment and went back to whatever they were doing. The anthropologists had explained that the culture here was very direct.

Velvet leaves. Something else, yet another thing, that might warrant investigation.

Someone touched my arm. Om.

"Would you mind sitting with me?"

"Of course not." Well, yes, I would, but I had no choice. So I followed him to his table in the middle of the room. He liked to be the center of attention, the senior person by location. Karola and Honey were there, too, and one of the Mu Rees. Om let me sit down and begin to eat while he asked me polite questions about how I slept and whether I had finally fully adjusted to the food, which had given us diarrhea and worse at first. I assured him I was fine.

"I think you know that we've discovered that the corals here have DNA, while most other life-forms use RNA."

I nodded. "No plants with DNA either, only RNA."

"And that's what we want to explore. We want to go to the Coral Plains and take some samples."

"Good idea."

"Fine. Mu Ree Fa is organizing the trip tomorrow." He gestured at the Mu Ree at the table. "He'll fill you in on the details."

I swallowed hard to avoid choking. "I'm going?"

"Yes."

Karola murmured something to Honey. Those two were a pair. Like Jose and Haus.

"You'll love it there!" Honey said. "I just got back. It's beautiful and very interesting. I can tell you all about it. Some of the plants are the same, but some are completely different. And of course the corals are fascinating!" I understood some of what she said, and the feed took care of the rest.

"They can hurt you," I said.

She raised her hand with a stump of a finger. "Wear gloves and don't take them off. And don't be stupid like Queen Rust. The corals hunt, and they have a pretty good range. I wrote a full report about our visit. You can read it!"

A long report, probably, in Classical English. I didn't reply.

After a moment, Karola said, "I'll read it and send you a summary."

"Oh," Honey added, sitting straight up with enthusiasm, "and you want Arthur to be on your team. He's great there, and he'll keep you safe. And Cawzee, if he's well. I hope so!"

"Has Arthur been there?" Mu Ree Fa said.

Honey began a description of their recent visit. A detailed description, and Fa seemed interested. I tried to pay attention, and the rest of the time I tried to convince myself I really wanted to go. A one-day trip, in and out fast, wouldn't take too much time, but if we found interesting samples, and from what she said we would, they would need analysis. I already had more interesting samples than I could deal with. We should have brought two botanists, but everyone cared about animals more than plants, probably because we humans were animals ourselves. But there would be no animals without plants.

Like Stevland. The most interesting plant of all.

"Is there any rainbow bamboo in the Coral Plains?" I asked.

"We planted some seeds, but s— But we don't know of any bamboo."

Stevland . . . Did she almost say Stevland?

Later that day I was talking to Zivon, one of the anthropologists, up on the city walls. I had gone there to spy on colonists to see what they did around Stevland and to marvel at the landscape. Every growing thing there had nerves and brains. He saw me up there and joined me. I felt a little disappointed by the interruption. If I could stare hard and long, I hoped I might see something, some pattern, to show me how they thought, how they interacted, what I might do. . . .

"I have a question for you," he said. "It's weird, but I have to ask it. It's about those trees named Stevland."

"Ask away."

He leaned on the wall and looked out, squinting. "Yesterday a four-year-old told me she talked to him—him, she called the tree him, not it. I thought that might be a childhood fantasy, but maybe not, so I kept her talking, and she had details. He talks with a machine, she said, and he talks a lot at the meetings they have almost every night. I said we've never heard him speak there, and she said he was turned off. He won't talk to people from Earth."

"What's wrong with us?"

"Yeah. I asked her why and she got incoherent, which probably means she doesn't know. But my question for you is, could this be possible?"

"Talking plants?" I weighed my words. "I don't know. I can't say yes,

I can't say no. The plants here seem to have a nervous system. I'm still researching. But it bothers me that the colonists are lying to us about it."

"This tree is central to their culture. So is a belief that we destroyed the Earth, which is why their ancestors had to leave, so we might destroy this planet. If the bamboo is so central to them, they might want to protect it. These are practical people. I disagree with Om about that a lot. He sees superstition or romanticism, and I see a good reason that we haven't figured out yet."

"Om. He's going to write the final report."

"His final report," Zivon said. "I'll have my own."

"When we get back to Earth. What's happening there, anyway? We should be getting reports. That was in the project plan, regular radio contact."

He stared at some people working in a field. "If we weren't getting messages from Earth, Om would be fretting. He's silent, so I suppose we're getting them. Maybe Pollux won't release them, if he's back at his job. He's still, um, unstable. I don't have the exact diagnosis. And I wish he'd stop complaining and trying to make us agree with him. Anyway, Om is a government tool, too. They don't want us to know what's going on."

"I take that as a good sign. No news is good news."

Zivon continued to stare. "Yeah, but at some point, we might have to do something to find out what our real situation is."

"We might."

Dawn. Me, Haus, Mu Ree Fa, a visual recorder, a data recorder, and Arthur with Cawzee, both of them loaded with primitive weapons, waiting to climb into the plane as the pilot on board made some checks. Around us fields and forests, aware, watching.

"How's Cawzee?" I asked Arthur. Cawzee was standing next to him, like a loyal dog. I could guess, but I wanted to be on Arthur's good side. He knew a lot, according to Honey's report. He was a hunter, not a farmer, and an explorer, and a leader, and something else. Something the natives wouldn't say.

Cawzee squawked, and my link provided a translation: "Fine. Not an Earth virus, it was a Pax bacteria, easy medicine. I am strong. I recover quickly." He took Arthur by the hand, a gesture that bothered me for some reason. He pointed at the environmental suit Haus had insisted every mission member wear. "Good clothing for the Coral Plains. But perhaps not enough. We should call it Hunger Plains, perhaps. You will be careful of everything you see and even more of what you do not see."

"What are we going to see?"

"Big corals," Arthur said. "Stay far away from them. They have a long range with their darts, up to three arm's widths. And animals, all of them dangerous. A lot of the life is underground, so watch where you step. And plants. You'll see some strange plants. We didn't look at them closely, but they're probably dangerous somehow, too."

Haus had wandered over. He grinned. "We can handle this. We've got suits and weapons"—he gestured at their spears—"a hundred times better than yours."

A technological mismatch. Our suits could change color for camouflage and resist bullets, gases, fire, rays, and radiation. The colonists wore high leather boots, heavy coats, and leather gloves. Haus had a combined projectile-ray gun slung over his shoulder, and pockets and pouches filled with smaller weapons and equipment. Arthur and Cawzee carried glass-tipped spears, a bow and glass-tipped arrows, stonewood knives, and pouches filled with items made from wood, clay, fiber, glass, leather, and stone. Pax had almost no metal, so its inhabitants were stone age.

Haus carried his helmet under his arm. It bore 360-degree sensors for the visual spectrum and beyond, audio amplifiers, communication links, and a link to his weapon for pinpoint far-distance aiming. Arthur had a black hat and alert eyes. Cawzee's wide compound eyes offered close to 360-degree vision, but the physician said they had a limited visual spectrum.

I smelled strawberry, which meant Cawzee was laughing.

Arthur glanced at his Glassmaker. "The best weapon is caution. It's hungry there, that's the truth."

I said, "Don't you like the plains? Honey said you think they're beautiful."

He nodded, frowning. "Yes, beautiful but deadly. I don't really want to go back, but I can't let you go alone, so I had to accept joining this team."

Haus shook his head, still grinning, and sent: "A man with stone tools thinks we need his help." At least Arthur and Cawzee didn't hear the insult.

We got on board. Haus opened a panel and handed Arthur and Cawzee earphones. "We have links in our brains, you know. These are like links but external. You can wear them, and we can communicate." He looked at Cawzee. "Somehow."

Arthur took the earphone with big eyes and held it in his palm, gazing at it with surprising reverence and a big grin. It was the first time I'd seen a Pacifist get excited about something technological. He slid the loop over his ear, pushed in the earbud, and listened. Haus reached out and adjusted a slider on the loop. After a moment, Arthur's eyes got even bigger and he bit his lip to suppress his excitement.

Cawzee watched, checked his slider, muttered something about "two ears," and tucked his into a scarf tied around the base of his neck. "We can speak with this?" he said.

"Oh, sure. Mics." Haus returned to the panel as Arthur watched him intently. Haus handed them some microphones on clips for their collars.

Stevland talked by a machine, the girl had said. A radio was a machine. Arthur could see the usefulness of a radio.

We took off. The two colonists were fascinated by the view out of the windows and stood together, pointing things out to each other. I sat at the next window, almost as fascinated. We passed over the end of the forest and the start of the plains, a line so stark it seemed artificial.

"Why does the forest just end that way?" I asked.

"The forest fights against the plains," Arthur said.

An interesting metaphor. If it was a metaphor. "What do you mean?"

He pursed his lips, then shrugged. "Each one has its own ecology. So they fight to keep separate."

"How do you know that?"

He thought a moment. "I have eyes." He wasn't a good liar.

"Did you know that we think one might be native to Pax and one might be from another planet?"

"Yes, that's what it looked like when I was there."

"You see a lot for someone with no technology to speak of." That was out of my mouth before I realized I had insulted him.

"I keep my eyes open," he said, aware of my real question and avoiding it. Cawzee made a noise too fast to be translated. Arthur reached out and patted him on what passed for his shoulder. "You learn fast," he told him.

The plane began to descend.

"No, don't land there!" Arthur rushed to the pilot and began talking and gesturing, but the noise of the engines kept me from hearing them. The plane moved about a kilometer forward and descended again. I looked at the landscape below, wondering what was wrong, and saw it. The site we had been headed for had a lot of lines of big white and pink ball corals converging on it. We'd have damaged some of them landing. I knew from Honey's report what that would have meant. I must have been the only one to have read it, at least the summary—and it had been worth my time. She could have earned a Ph.D. with it.

We touched down in a barren area, the top of a rise. Honey had described the terrain well. Uneven ground with lots of rills. Brush on the hilltops in odd shapes and colors: plants, she supposed, but she hadn't examined them closely. The ground seemed covered with tiny balls and fans and horns in a variety of colors. Corals, she said. I looked for something moving. Nothing. Good.

Arthur came back and talked to Haus about something that seemed very serious. Haus looked into the cockpit, then talked to Arthur again. They both seemed concerned. When the noise of the engines subsided, I heard Haus ask, ". . . if we crushed them?"

"You could. I think they're easy to break, and they're deadly. If we crushed the center ones, the rest would attack. I think. I don't know. But I know to take them seriously. Those are the kind of corals that killed Queen Rust. You"—he gestured to Mu Ree Fa—"if you want to take a sample, take small ones." He made a circle with his fingers of a couple of centimeters. "Avoid the big ones. But the little ones will attack, too. And I think they're connected underground, so stay far away from anything big."

"Noted," Haus said. He put on his helmet and headed toward the door, the first one off according to plan. The door opened, he jumped out, and we heard a far-off buzz, then something closer, clicking loudly. A breeze blew, damp with more than a hint of methanethiol, the aroma of flatulence and marsh gas. That confirmed something about the ecology. After a minute we got an all clear. But that click had spooked me, so I let Arthur and Cawzee go first, then Fa, and then it was my turn, because to let the recorder techs go first would have been a breach of rank and proof of cowardice.

I checked that my gloves were on tight and wished that everyone had been wearing helmets. That way I could check their feeds and know where I was jumping and not look overly cautious. I could see Haus asking Arthur which way we should go. I prepared myself to leap, still not used to falling faster than on Earth.

I landed hard and the ground gave way under my feet, and for a moment I panicked, but the ground sank maybe only a centimeter. Calm down. Just soft ground. Haus, Fa, and Arthur were talking and pointing, Cawzee faced the other way, his bow in his hands. A light breeze blew. I looked around again.

All those colors on the ground were like a field of low wildflowers in bloom. Lots of red and pink, not much green. And those big white spheres here and there were the oddest thing I'd seen yet. I could spend a lifetime here researching. I could spend a lifetime researching what I already had. I could spend a lifetime researching just one thing, Stevland.

Let's get this over with, I thought. Get some samples and go.

"Let's go there," I sent to Arthur to test the radio system, pointing at a clump of what seemed to be stems hung with brownish undulate leaves. Odd to see brown plants growing above water. The solar spectrum here was ideal for green plants, better than Earth. So a brown plant would be a good place to start if I was looking for aliens to Pax's native ecology.

Arthur touched his earpiece but didn't stop looking around. He pointed to giant, shiny, purple beetles far away, maybe a kilometer. "Those ate our raft when we were here the last time."

"Big, dangerous, and no other thing known," Cawzee said. "It is noisy here on the radio."

"They're far away," Haus said. "And about the radio, sometimes it's noisy, background noise. It's called static. This isn't bad, though."

"I don't know how fast those things can move. Anyway"—Arthur looked at the ground closest to us—"we need to worry about small, fast, close, dangerous things. Cawzee, see any?"

"Hey!" a technician said, jumping. "Something hit my foot!"

In a single leap, Cawzee was at his side, spear ready, and inspected the ground. He relaxed. "Corals." He pointed at something on the ground with his spear tip. "They send darts. You will be alert for big bump of worm."

Arthur glanced at me, then at the plants. "You want the ones over there? Well, here's sort of a path leading that way, and that's how I'd go." He pointed to slightly more bare soil that formed a line on the ground.

"Will you go with me?"

He looked at Haus, who nodded. "Cawzee, can you help them gather corals without getting killed?"

"A difficult work, but I will make success."

I let Arthur lead. He walked slowly, alert. The ground under my feet seemed soft and crunchy.

"Your partner's pretty funny," I said.

"He really does learn fast. They all do." He paused, poked at something on the ground with his spear, and began to walk again.

"He's a partner, right?" Or a slave. That's what Zivon said.

"Officially, he's my son, but partner is a good word, too."

I looked around, marveling at the alienness of the plains. Then I remembered my goal. "You don't seem very interested in our technology."

"You mean the guns and stuff? That's interesting, but when you leave, it'll be gone, so there's not much point to learning about it."

"But you like the radio."

"Better than messenger bats." He stopped a few meters from the plants. "What's your plan?"

"Take a sample or two. A whole plant, that is. Roots, if we can get them. I brought a little shovel."

"Digging's interesting here. A lot happens underground. I'd prefer a shovel with a longer handle."

"I'm wearing a protective suit."

"Fine, but let me check for surprises." He approached the clump, spear ready, and then whacked the trunks and the ground. Insectlike things skittered away. "Which plant?"

"How about that second one. . . . Yes, the one with lots of leaves. It looks healthy."

He whacked it again, then poked the ground. "All clear."

I approached and inspected. A woody stem, stiff linear leaves with parallel veins, a thick bristly cutis. "Now let's dig."

"You dig, I'll guard."

The ground was damp and full of things that seemed to be colorful stones and pebbles, but some of them jumped and wiggled. I avoided them. Animals were the Mu Rees' problem. Fa sent that they were going down into a damp rill to pick up some samples, and he was exulting as if he'd found a gold mine. Fine, if he had time for it.

I kept digging and asked Arthur, "So why don't you have plant scientists?"

"Hmm . . . Hold it, what's that?"

Something reddish darted through the hole, out of the soil on one side and back into it on the other. There seemed to be a tunnel.

"Gone. I hope for good, but watch out." He moved a stone to block the tunnel. "Farmers know all about plants. And when we first landed, there was a scientist named Octavo. He wrote the rules about plants."

"Rules?" Maybe rules for rainbow bamboo?

The brown plant seemed to have extensive roots with nodules. Would they contain symbionts as on Earth? I wished I could get the entire root ball but it was just too big. Brains? There only seemed to be fine roots, fibrous, probably not for information storage, so I began to cut roots with the shovel ten centimeters around the plant. Tough roots, hard to chop. I jumped when something buzzed close to me.

"Yes," Arthur said, looking in the direction of the noise. "The rules say that plants can count, they can see, they can move. Stuff like that. That's what he said."

"Stuff like that. . . . It's true, they can."

"Here," he said, "I'll grab the plant for you."

I had finished digging around the roots. He picked it up, root ball and all, and set it in a specimen bag that I held open. "Do you trust plants?" I asked.

"Keep a watch on that dirt. Who knows what's in it? Be careful when you open the bag. Trust? They move slower than me, so I'm not worried."

He'd said nothing about plants outthinking us.

Static roared in the link to the other part of our team. Maybe they weren't in the ideal range for the plane. We had only one retransmitter. But I had my job to do as fast as I could so we could go home. "Can you spot any other plants here that don't grow in the forest?"

He could, lots, and five of them were right around us, smaller and superficially quite unlike forest plants. As fast as I could, I had them packed up and was ready to go. "Let's get back to the plane. Fa has what he wants and then some."

"I've heard them. It's funny how the radio translates Cawzee. It gives him a Human voice. He says the corals they took were much too big. Too many of them. Much too dangerous and foolish. This was quick, at least. I'll be glad to go."

We arrived first at the plane. The rest were still climbing up the hill, excited by how reactive the corals were when they collected them, and Cawzee complaining that they were more dangerous than they realized. "More than perhaps foolish." The static had gotten even worse. He held out his hands to show how big, at least a half meter.

"Can you hear me well?" I sent.

"Horrible, horrible," Cawzee answered.

"It's not that bad," Haus said. "But not good, either."

"Something's wrong," the data tech said. "I'm getting interference. . . ." Then her voice dropped out. They approached, she and another tech, speaking directly about how the planet had high magnetic fields and was hit by a lot of highly charged solar winds. Arthur said something, but my chip didn't translate it. This was no time or place for network problems. Something on the ground near us started clicking.

"Let's go home!" I shouted to Fa.

He and Haus carried a huge bag between them, bulging with samples. They stopped outside the door of the plane. "Open up," Fa sent to the pilot, who had remained inside. I hardly heard it over squeals and static. I turned off my connection. Fa seemed to send it again. He pounded on the door. He tried the handle.

"It could be automatically locked, but it shouldn't be," Haus said aloud. "I can override it." He took off his glove and put his hand on the door latch. It might have clicked, or that might have been the noise from something in the area, but he opened the door and hopped in.

"Mosegi!" he shouted, the name of the pilot. "Mosegi!"

Arthur said something about the pilot. Cawzee answered with hoots. I tried my link again, but the noise would have given me a headache in seconds.

"The links are more than failing," I told the data tech.

She tried it and winced, then shook her head to clear it. "This is new to me." She pulled out a piece of equipment and turned it on. Her mouth dropped when she read the screen, and she showed it to the other technician.

"Dear Lord," he said. He looked up. "There has to be a transmitter here. Transmitters, more than one. We're being jammed."

"Fa!" Haus shouted. "Come in here."

Fa climbed in as fast as he could, clumsily, and Arthur followed in one jump.

The rest of us stood there. Cawzee motioned for us to stand close together near the plane, and he stood ahead, facing out, guarding us. A few hours ago I'd have laughed at him. Now I felt grateful. The air smelled like rotten bananas, probably some Glassmaker scent.

Voices shouted inside, and finally Arthur: "Sick. Lungs. Full of fluid."

"Will he die?" Haus said.

"Maybe. In the city, no. Who else can fly?"

"I can, basic flight," he answered. "But without the radio, I'm sunk."

"Do the instruments work?" Fa said. "Velma!" he called to the data technician. "Come here and check the instruments."

She shoved a scanner into her vest pocket, turned, and began to scramble in. I laced my fingers and gave her a leg up. Out of the corner of my eye, I saw Cawzee rise up on his back legs and grip his spear in two hands. Then he turned to us, squalling something and gesturing at the two of us to climb in, the visual recorder and me. When we were in, he leaped in himself and called to Arthur. This time he smelled like oranges.

"Trilobites," Arthur translated. He was holding the pale, sweating pilot erect in a seat in the passenger compartment while Haus strapped him in. "Purple. You saw them. Now there's one on this side." He pointed and added something I didn't understand. Haus found an oxygen mask and strapped it on Mosegi's face, then tipped the seat back as far as it would go.

Fa rushed to the window and called the visual recorder to look. I found a window to look out of. A giant purple trilobite, five or six meters long, was climbing the hill toward us. Another, twice as big, followed.

"How dangerous?" Fa said in English.

"Very," Arthur answered.

"Giant horseshoe crab," Fa said.

"I've got to shoot it," said the visual recorder. He held his camera tight and began to open the door.

"No!" Haus and Arthur and Cawzee shouted together, but he was out. No one seemed to know what to do, so I shut the door, careful to leave it unlocked. Whatever the purple things could do—and I'd seen lots of Pax animals already—they couldn't open a heli-plane hatch.

The visual recorder hit a button on the chest of his suit and seemed to disappear as the camouflage kicked in.

Haus and Velma continued to examine instruments. Haus slipped a radio receiver on one ear and plugged wires into it and the panel. He listened, then shook his head. The two continued to talk quietly, cheerless about what they were learning.

Something big hit the back end of the plane. None of the windows gave us a good look in that direction, so Cawzee quickly opened the door, stuck out his long head, then pulled it back in and shut the door. He babbled at Arthur, still reeking of oranges.

"Maybe it can damage the plane," he translated, with gestures to make his meaning clear. "Haus, weapons?"

Haus smiled, picked up his gun, and locked his helmet in place. Then he dashed to the door, opened it, and jumped out, leaving Cawzee to slide it shut again. I crowded next to Arthur at a window.

Haus aimed and fired. Then something—the crab?—screeched. It was answered with other screeches. That was bad. It had friends. The crab hit the ship again, harder. Haus fired again. Again. A crab was coming toward him.

Arthur ran to the door, opened it, and shouted and pointed. Haus turned and fired. A huge crab dashed at him and knocked him over. I knew there were more weapons stashed in the plane, but where?

Arthur closed the door, his face grim but thoughtful. Cawzee said something. Arthur came next to me and crouched at the little window. He stared a moment, then rushed to Velma.

He talked and gestured. She didn't seem to understand. He picked up a tablet and stylus and drew a picture. Fa came to look. He and Velma disappeared into the cockpit. Arthur returned to the window. The crab seemed to be trampling or chewing on Haus.

"What did you say?"

"Use the plane as a weapon."

"How?"

"The engine. Noise and fire."

Fa shouted from the cockpit, "Where's the recorder?"

Cawzee answered, pointing.

"Shadow," Arthur translated. "There, near the blue plants."

I looked out of the window, and after a moment I made out a shadow in the shape of a man, that idiot who ran out to make a visual recording of all this. He was standing far away and safe, camouflaged.

The engine began to whir, powering up. Then it roared and the plane lurched. I thought I heard Haus's gun, then dismissed that as wishful thinking.

The plane lurched again, engines thundering. The crabs stood still. The plane thundered again. Set to lowest efficiency, the engines spewed fire instead of frost. Hot exhaust flashed. A crab ran off, gone in a second. The other one, apparently injured by Haus, moved away more slowly, but obviously hurrying. Farther away, a coral exploded from the heat and burned brightly.

Arthur opened the door and jumped out. He ran to Haus and helped him up. He shouted at the recorder, the meaning clear even if the words were not. The recorder's shadow began to run toward the plane. Cawzee, at the door, grabbed their arms and yanked them all in one by one, then shut it and motioned for me to lock it.

Dirt clung to Haus's suit. Something fell off. Arthur moved like a flash to stamp on it, then grabbed him with gloved hands to inspect the suit and quickly knocked off something else and crushed it. Haus took off his helmet. He seemed unscathed but deadly serious. He shot the recorder a look like a projectile and entered the cockpit. Fa and Velma came out and strapped themselves into chairs. Arthur checked on the pilot. The roar of the engines got louder, and we took off.

We sat, silent, relieved. I checked my link. Still static. A few minutes later, with the forest in view, I tried again. It worked fine. But what did I have to say? I remembered my goal, to learn about Stevland. So I sent to Arthur, "Good work."

"All hunters are fighters. I'm not used to losing." He looked out a window as we crossed the boundary with the plains. "I never want to go back there. It's too hungry. Can we call ahead for help for the pilot?"

"Done," Haus said. "And yes, good fighting."

We rode on, Fa and Velma fascinated by the recorder's video. Haus landed the plane in the field near the city perfectly. He must have used automatic pilot. A team with a stretcher was waiting and whisked the pilot away as fast as they could. I was left with several bulky bags to carry back, but Arthur and Cawzee lingered to help me.

"It was beautiful there," I sent to start a conversation, then realized they'd have returned the radios, so they couldn't hear me.

"Beautiful," Cawzee said. He reached into a deep pocket of his coat, took out something red and furry, and held it gently. It stirred, and a wide-eyed head popped up and looked around. A baby fippokat? But those were green. And how had he heard me?

Arthur's mouth dropped open, then he laughed and slapped Cawzee on the shoulder. "You think we can domesticate that?"

"Yes. I have us a pet. Perfect for hunters. Perfect for you to give to Fern."

"What are you going to name it?" I sent to be sure of what I suspected.

"Fippokats have green names," Cawzee said. "This must be a red name."

He still had his radio set. Arthur wasn't wearing his, but I hadn't seen him put it back, either. He'd spent all his time getting the pilot off the plane. He'd probably kept it.

By afternoon, the plains plants, tucked into flowerpots outside our lab, were attracting more interest from the colonists than from my fellow explorers. We were all overwhelmed by new things, and this was just more newness. But the colonists knew that plants mattered, too.

I spent the rest of the day examining my samples. As expected, they were morphologically distinct from the "forest" plant life and from Earth. No nerves or sense organs that I could find. They had common biochemicals with the corals, even a little methane, and like them, they had DNA. Fa's corals, placed in a brick-walled pen for safety, sat as if they were inert.

Four kinds of life on Pax: Human, Glassmaker, forest, and plains.

The most beautiful native species, perhaps the smartest, grew above my head on rainbow stalks, apparently mute, but I wouldn't believe it.

That long day got me nowhere closer to what I wanted to know. At the end of it, Om came to congratulate me for a "worthy mission on this strange, wonderful planet." All he did was delay my going to bed.

"Wake up," Arthur's voice whispered inside my head. "I have something to show you."

After a minute of drowsy confusion, I remembered. He had kept a radio. He knew how to use it. The Mu Rees were snoring. It was dark.

"Get up, get dressed. I'll tell you where to find me."

Stevland. He was going to show me Stevland. All my fishing for information must have gotten through to him.

"I'm coming."

I pulled on my clothes as fast and as quietly as I could and added a Pax scarf with a rainbow design a woman had traded for some socks. I ducked under the door into the cold. The east held a hint of twilight. The sun would rise soon.

"You're hungry. Get some food. We can have breakfast together."

I tried to trace and identify the transmission. It came from nearby. We had an antenna in the city. But the transmission had no identity confirmation from the central transmitter. It seemed to be merely a smart instrument transmitting data in the system, like a refrigerator or portable weather station. Clever disguise.

I found my way in the dark more by memory than sight. But Arthur wasn't at the dining hall. All I saw was a table holding trays of fresh bread and fruit, dimly lit by a cage of glowing insects. The bread smelled beautiful, of wheat, of plant life. I took a small loaf and grabbed a couple of pieces of bamboo fruit. I ate one as I left, sweet and energizing. Stevland's fruit.

"Where are you?" I sent.

"Go out the west gate."

I passed a few colonists on my way. They greeted me more or less politely and didn't seem surprised to see an Earthling wandering around so early. I wasn't sure of the way to the gate and got lost once. But Arthur wasn't there, either. The sky had grown bright enough that I could see more easily.

"Keep going. Take the path straight ahead, then the branch on the right that leads up a little hill. There's a grove of rainbow bamboo at the top."

"I know where that is." That was where I had taken my samples.

The path led through a field of what colonists called yams, where the plants were now young shoots. Spiny glowing caterpillars crawled among them, and a bat swooped low and called out to me. The bats spoke a language that the colonists understood.

I sent the sound to Arthur. "What did it say?"

"A greeting. It contains the offer to be of service. The bat must be hungry. They carry messages in exchange for food."

It circled around me again, calling, then flew off. In the fields, lizards were chirping, noises that sounded like little chimes. A bird was barking near the path. I tried to spot it, knowing it would look so much like a clump of dried weeds that I probably wouldn't identify it. But even the weeds had nerves. Even these yams. And that felt . . . right, like something I had always been searching for and was finally going to find. The landscape abounded with sentient entities.

"You know," I sent, "I have a lot to learn about this place, but it feels familiar. On Earth, we were in a place called Dee Cee that was surrounded by a forest, and it feels like that. I loved to walk in the forest there."

"From the beginning, the colonists felt like they were at home here."

He said "the colonists." Not "we." That was odd.

The field ended with a line of palms and what looked like shrubs but were really a benign coral—in the forest and not the plains? The path headed uphill, through some thistles. Familiar, too, thistles, like a fence around the bamboo. Finally I reached the grove, which had a little grassy space at one side. Boughs reached out like arms ready to hug me. But no one was there. I pulled out my breakfast and prepared to wait.

"Thank you for coming." The voice was different this time, as if Pax lizards could speak in their chimes. "Sit down and we can watch the sunrise together."

Many people mastered the trick of sending in a different voice. So this could still be Arthur. Or—I gasped with hope.

"Who are you? You're not Arthur. Who?"

"Stevland. It is a pleasure to be able to introduce myself to you. You are aware that I use radio, and I have learned to use your transmissions. It is like having roots that touch people, much as my roots touch other plants. I can speak to you as I might to a locustwood tree, although we have much more to discuss."

I held my breath. Stevland! I could talk to Stevland, to a plant. Or it might be a trick. "Why do you want to talk to me?"

"With you. I wish to speak with you, that is, to listen as well as to talk. But first I wish to say that you chose well two nights ago here when you took a sample of me, a young but mature stalk, large enough to be revealing but small enough to hide. And then you tossed it down the gift center."

"I'm sorry."

"I am not angry."

"Did it hurt when I cut you?"

"A little. But deer are now nibbling some new leaves nearby. If it hurts too much, I can cut the connection. I am a plant, not an animal, so all my parts are disposable. Indeed, most are temporary, especially those aboveground. What did you learn from me?"

"You have eyes. You can see."

"Correct. I see that you are wearing a scarf patterned after me, and you have bread and a piece of fruit, but you seem too awed to eat."

True. And I was hungry. Or I had been. Now I had questions.

"I know that you have nerves in your stalks and ganglia in your roots. Is that where you think, in your roots?"

"Correct. I photosynthesize in my leaves, and it is morning. Sunshine and water give me strength."

"How does that feel?" I'd always wanted to know.

"It is like power flowing from my leaves to my roots, and from what I have learned, it is much like the satisfaction that food gives to you."

At that moment, it seemed like the time to eat some bread. I sat there, looking up as I chewed, as sunlight began to sparkle on his upper leaves. His leaves—he, not an it anymore. This plant was a person. A personality.

"I think we can work together," he said. "More than anything, I enjoy the company and stimulation of other intelligent beings, and I think we can become good friends. I do have one important request for you."

I knew before he asked that I would do anything for him.

6

STEVLAND—THE NEXT DAY

A spark of ethylene freezes a few of my rootlets as the auxins are inhibited. The main locustwood speaker wants my attention and strikes where a patch of our roots overlap. It is odd that he should greet me in an almost nondestructive fashion. He is the new speaker for his grove of trees but already behaves typically for his species, with aggression. The biggest and most belligerent tree in the local grove becomes not merely the spokesman but the only breeding male, so the entire species aims for size and hostility.

No doubt he wishes to ask about my service animals. The recent arrivals from Earth have created a noticeable change, to understate the situation absurdly.

"We have a question," he says.

No demands? No bluster? He must be distressed. "Yes," I answer. "A migratory group has arrived for a visit."

"We do not understand."

"The service animals. No doubt you have observed a change, but it is temporary."

"We are concerned about the fires."

"The fire tonight is for a celebration and will be strictly controlled." I add, "As it is every year." He ought to remember that.

"These fires have already occurred. They were along the border with the Coral Plains."

Fires at the plains? I know nothing about that. But I keep my response calm, if only because an excited locustwood is a dangerous locustwood, and they get excited easily. "Tell me more."

"Our southern groves saw small fires over the past two nights. They started in the Coral Plains and did not spread into our forest, but five fires are too many. Our other groves can show you where. Your service animals must investigate."

"They will do so. Thank you for the notice." Five. Fire is our greatest danger, although locustwoods tend to overreact. Swamp fires are not forest fires. Methane is the likely cause, since it can ignite spontaneously and at a low temperature, thus harmlessly, if that is what happened, yet such fires are uncommon. Five may be far too many.

"But," the locustwood continues, "about your animals, we have heard of odd movements and some new strange members. They can fly, for example, and they are not bats or cactuses."

"The visitors will eventually fly away, and the city will remain the same."

"And we wish to have the trunk of the previous speaker harvested."

I did not expect that. When the old speaker died, his death hastened by this rival's quest to achieve speakerhood, we had agreed to leave the dead tree standing in honor of his service. "Why do you wish it removed?"

"It lies in the way of new growth. Have your animals cut it down promptly. They will appreciate the wood."

Perhaps, for the speaker, it is a reminder of his dishonorable deeds to displace the incumbent. Or the dead tree may genuinely be in the way of new growth, new female trees for the speaker to add to his grove. But in any case, the wood has a remarkable pattern, called "checkerboard" by Humans and "plaid" by Glassmakers, and it can be used for items of beautiful utility and decoration, so this is good news for the city.

I must not sound too agreeable, however, or the locustwood might interpret that as weakness. "I shall order it done. And we must set the quota for this year's harvest. Perhaps, given your success, it can be expanded. Your wood is very useful."

"Provided it is only used for durable purposes. We do not wish to be burned any more than you."

"We will discuss this further."

"In the summer. Meanwhile, keep the fire tonight under control."

"We have sufficient experience."

"And keep your animals under control."

"Of course I will. I also have long experience with these species."

My deepest roots remind me that I have not always had successful experiences with these species, both with individuals and with groups. While I have extended my understanding in many ways over the years, this wisdom does not always serve in new situations, and every day is a new day with new problems.

For example, I have begun to learn how to use this new radio feed, and I can easily understand why the Earthlings depend on it. It is like having a root that reaches inside people, though the operation of this radio is complex and requires energy.

At the clinic, doctors and the medic are arguing over the care of an Earthling pilot, Mosegi, who has coccidioidomycosis, an illness we know well, so we have a stockpile of the cure, jars of white powder purified from some pineapples who produce a specific fungicide in exchange for the usual planting and care concessions. Actually, they are arguing not over the care but over the source of the treatment.

"These pineapples," an Earthling doctor says, using radio-based translation, "how did you discover their medicine?"

"I don't know," says Ivan, our medic, although of course he does. I helped discover it and negotiated with the pineapples for its production, as I have also helped to find, develop, and procure many other medicines. "This came into use several generations ago. It's been passed down with more concern about its use than its discoverers."

"You get a lot of different compounds from the pineapples."

"There are many kinds of pineapples."

"No, our botanist says there is only one variety. The RNA is identical, but they produce very different fruit, and you know a lot about it."

"They grow in different places. The sponges in the soil come in different types and form local colonies. That affects the plants that grow there. The farmers know all about this. They do the harvest."

An Earthling doctor sends via radio to Om: "I'm getting another stonewall here. Probably Stevland again."

I check the meaning of "stonewall" in the network, yet another of the radio's amazing conveniences: "Delay or block a request, process, or person by refusing to answer questions or by giving evasive replies." Ivan does not want to mention me.

Om replies, "Well, we've learned one more thing, that this secret also involves medicine and its creation. By plants. Once again, there are plants involved. And probably Stevland. Good work."

They are looking for me, but would they believe me if they found me?

At this moment, Ladybird is consulting an Earthling recording crew in the field where the bonfire will be held. Technicians record the exchange, and I watch it proceed.

"Nakedness represents a willingness to change," she says.

"Do you know how that began?" the anthropologist says.

"I think the custom began when the city was first settled, in the time of a moderator named Sylvia. Apparently the settlers in the original village went naked to show they were willing to move."

"Sylvia. Her knife is on display in the museum, with a list of moderators who possessed it, Tatiana and Lucille and Stevland. Were they all moderators?"

"Yes."

"Why does it stop at Stevland?"

"That was when the Glassmakers first came back. You know about the battle, and after that, many customs changed." She smiles sweetly.

One of the recorders sends a note, "Stevland was a moderator," to a collection of notes about me in the computer. I look at these notes:

"Sort of like Higgins, a semi-legendary figure."

"A taboo prevents his being spoken of."

"Perhaps some sort of superfarmer. Connected to crops or native vegetation. Perhaps a personification of ecology."

"The name for the rainbow bamboo."

"Confirmed."

"Possibly a powerful deity."

They think I might be a god, a powerful god. That idea entertains me.

Karola and Honey are sitting outside in a plaza next to one of my stalks, creating their representations to burn. Honey's task was to domesticate Karola, and she has done a fine job. She has also given her love, which she seems to have lacked on Earth. Karola is creating sort of a stick figure, obviously a person. Custom forbids asking what someone's contribution to the fire represents, but Karola might not know that, which may be why Honey asks.

"A person on Earth," Karola answers. "She's legendary, a criminal, or they say she's a criminal."

"What did she do?"

"She killed a lot of people, and they keep her clone alive and punish her. Her name was Nancsi, and . . . well, I just never liked the legend, and they burn her image every year in a bonfire, maybe an effigy like these sticks but big, and I guess it doesn't make sense to burn it in fire to change things, to end it by burning it in a fire, but that's what I want to do, what I want to change. What's yours?"

I look up Nancsi in the network library and find much information and a recording. I still have difficulties interpreting images. Mirlo told me that the Human brain simply works differently, but I can learn to process the data since my roots can grow and adapt so easily. I must practice, however. As if reflected on a rippling river, I see Nancsi's clone, her descendant, in punishment: naked, dirty, injured, and frightened. This is unspeakably horrible and Earthlike. I am glad Karola wishes it could end.

Honey has made an elongated oval shape from soft wood. "It's my finger, the piece I lost. Time to say goodbye and get used to living without it. There's no going back!"

In his lab, Mirlo has made a bundle of twigs tied by bark twine. I can observe him through a camera turned on to record an experiment that no one has turned off, even though neither he nor his companion is sending his thoughts. This way of viewing is intensely strange, peering through only one "eye" and listening through only one "ear."

"You have to get naked for it to work, you know," a Mu Ree says.

Mirlo blushes.

"What does it mean, anyway, that thing?"

Mirlo hesitates, then says, "Things I used to believe before I came here."

"Well, we don't want to change. Except clothes. We need new clothes."

Om is with Queen Cheery as she oversees food preparation for the festival, Haus is with Jose as they hunt, and all others are working except Pollux. He sits and stares, listening to a feed. I have trouble hearing it because it is private, so I switch from the chip Queen Thunderclap stole to a radio receiver our technicians built two years ago from a quartz crystal. It can capture a wider range of frequencies; the chips have built-in limitations.

I hear a voice that Karola has spoken of to Honey, the voice of the network, which occasionally speaks. She said it would sound like any normal Human voice, but it carries an identification as "Abacus" and possesses a kind of machine intelligence. It would seem alive, she said, but it is not and does only as ordered, orders that can be complex and even hidden.

"[Something] received a report from Earth," it says in a strong male voice. "It informs you of the conclusion of the war between Mars and Earth. It requires [something]."

Pollux does not react as he listens to the report. I understand little because I do not know the history of the war and I have not fully mastered their language.

"Earth government capitulation due to fifth column action. Reorganization was reversed." I have to look up "fifth column": a clandestine subversive organization working to further an invader's political and military aims. That is, traitors. And "reorganization" yields a long explanation about political and social changes that took place after something called the Great Loss, which would also take too much time to pursue in depth right now. What kind of action is required from Pollux?

Pollux dismisses the report before he has heard it all, without reaction. He returns to sitting and staring, now in silence. If he were a Pacifist, I would recommend the medics pursue his mental health. My initial diagnosis is depression, although they understand emotional illnesses better. But do I want him well? And surely the Earthling doctor is aware of his condition, but he has not acted. Pollux is unpopular with many of the members of the mission. Observing him has led to more questions than answers.

In a workshop, two technicians are reviewing data by scans of the surface of Pax from the orbiting spacecraft, and they are sharing it with anyone who will tune in. The images are intensely beautiful. I had known that Pax was a planet and knew what that meant, but to see it exceeds expectations. Blue seas, green islands, white snowcaps at the poles, and swirling clouds. I copy this vision into a root to enjoy at will in the future.

"Nothing but forests," says Velma, a technician specialized in recording. "Virgin, this whole planet is virgin."

Ernst, the technician team leader, orders a few changes in the image. "With false colors, you can see how the ecologies are different in different places. The science guys are going to love this." He makes a few more adjustments. "Here, these are the parameters for this valley. Let's look for a match."

After a moment, the scan rotates to a continent far to the east they have named Laurentia, then to a specific area.

"Closer," Ernst says.

I see it before they do.

"Look," Velma says, "rainbow bamboo."

I am the only survivor. This cannot be.

Ernst adjusts the resolution. Yes, arching branches like mine, colorful stems.

"Wow. A lot of it," he says.

I do not know what to think, only what I feel. More bamboo. More of me. I am not alone. If this is correct.

He calls for more views from previous scans of that specific area from different angles. This one is fairly directly above the area. Another is at an angle in early morning daylight. He asks for high resolution at the edges of what seem to be stands of bamboo. Yes, rainbow-striped stems, large ones, and many too small to identify the separate colors, but clearly bamboo. Forests of bamboo.

A civilization. My civilization. My people. There, on that continent.

These humans can fly. They must go to Laurentia. I must meet these—these people, these bamboo. I am not alone.

There are more of me. I was never alone.

Here in this valley, waves of wind toss my branches. Below them, my service animals work. They are my friends, my equals, my partners, my beloved, but never like me. All my seeds are self-fertilized. All my thoughts, except for some centuries-old roots, are my own. All my accomplishments are solitary. Until now.

I have been lonely for my entire life. I knew that, I ached over it, and now, my life is different.

And it is the same. I have a city to help lead and conflicts to manage. And a party to enjoy tonight. I have something to celebrate, and I must make arrangements for that.

With scent, I invite Queen Thunderclap into the greenhouse, and as she enters, I catch a whiff of *sadness* and *uncertainty*. Glassmakers sometimes scent inadvertently, like the facial expressions of Humans, and it rarely serves to ask someone why they are sad. Instead I say, "Mother, will you make something for me and burn it at the festival?"

"Anything."

"I am thinking of perhaps a small wooden box with nothing in it."

I have selected that because I now have something instead of nothing, and I commit myself to the change of exploring this new way of being. As a woodworker, she can create this without difficulty.

"Easy to do. Perhaps I do not say it is for you when I throw it in the fire? Earthlings think you do not exist, but they are not sure."

"Earthlings do not know what to believe about me. They think perhaps I am a god that you secretly worship."

She laughs sweetly.

"You are right," I say. "Perhaps this should not be announced. But you can tell others discreetly if you wish." She enjoys gossip. This will be a fine secret to share.

"You never participate in the fire before."

"Rarely. I have learned something that makes me very happy."

"If you are happy, I am happy."

"Warmth and food."

"Water and sunshine. I go make you it now."

She smells happier as she leaves. I hope I have done her some good in exchange for her service to me.

I continue to observe with new and old senses. Meals are prepared for the festival, including the traditional traveler's meal: roasted trilobites and wild onions, and my dried fruit, but only the fruit is eaten with gusto. Cooks bustle to create additional, more delectable dishes in quantity. Lettuce is especially plentiful this spring.

Lumberjacks arrange the fire out in a field that could use ashes as fertilizer. They want it to burn fast and spectacularly, and they place hydrogen seeds inside some images to explode. The location caused a small controversy this year since it is some distance from the city, but in its favor, it offers more room for performances.

Dancers are making their final rehearsals. In a fallow field next to the city wall, children and fippokats practice a complex exchange of partners that involves synchronized jumping. It should thrill onlookers. My nearest stems enjoy the sight and vibrations.

Inside the city, stilt walkers prepare their participation in the festivities. Originally, stilts let Pacifists imitate the taller, slimmer, First Generation Human colonists. Now Earthlings are back, a head and shoulders taller than most Pacifists, and Zivon, one of the Earthling anthropologists, has joined the stilt walkers, asking about their inherited information concerning the Parents. Velma, who has finished examining planetary scans, is recording their replies.

"Well," says Geraldine, "they were tall and frail. Sickly. They all died back in the old village and couldn't manage the trip here, even though they wanted to come."

History tells a slightly different story. The remaining elderly First

Generation Humans refused to come because they were afraid of me. But Geraldine is no scholar, and I have no self-interest in correcting many common beliefs.

"What do you know of Earth?" Zivon asks. He stands face-to-face with her as she wobbles on the stilts.

Geraldine scowls. She takes a few steps to maintain her balance. "They say it was hard to live there." She turns around, almost falling in the process. "Oh, and there were millions and millions of people there."

Zivon's face remains encouragingly interested, but he sends to Velma, "More like billions."

Mirlo walks past, heading toward the kitchen.

Velma connects. "Hey, analyze this." She shows him the forest of rainbow bamboo in Laurentia, then returns to recording the stilt walker practice.

Mirlo receives the image, then freezes. He seems to stare blankly at the air for a long time. Then, slowly, he begins to grin. He looks around and spots one of my stems. He is about to speak to me, then stops. He does not want to initiate conversation in public, but I realize he does not know how to initiate contact with me via radio.

I know what he wants to tell me, but how should I react? What would be best for me?

"Mirlo," I send, "do you want to speak to me?"

He jumps a little, startled. He sends, "How do you know?"

"I have eyes on every trunk, and minds in every root. I am talking to one other person and three plants right now. I think. Distributed consciousness is not always distributed equally. But I am also here, now, with you."

"Can you see these pictures?" He sends them to me, excuses himself from Velma, and takes a few steps away. Earthlings are used to someone in their midst pausing to have a radio conversation.

"Yes," I say, "I can see them, but I do not recognize that grove. Where is it?"

"On another continent."

I pause, as if reflecting. "I do not understand."

"Here." He shows me a view of Pax as a globe with an area marked by a red circle. "We are here, in this valley in the mountains by the sea. This picture is from here, a place we call Laurentia." Another red circle forms on a wide, flat peninsula on another body of land far away.

"I am not there," I answer. "I am only here. There is only one of me."

"No, look," he says, his face full of happiness and excitement. He moves the picture to show how much of the distinctive foliage can be seen. "There's a lot of rainbow bamboo. A major community."

Velma interrupts. The stilt walkers have finished their practice. "What do you think? That's a find, right? More of that pretty bamboo."

Mirlo blinks. "Yes. This is amazing. It will mean a lot to the people here."

"I hope they like it," she says. "I gotta go. Big party tonight. We have to plan our documentation."

"Thanks," Mirlo says.

"I want to meet those trees," I send. "I want to know all about them. You can understand."

"Of course. They're your species." He looks at my stem, then up at my leaves. "Wait, you said 'meet.' How would you do that?"

"I would send my animal partners. I would send you."

"I want to go!" He turns toward the laboratory. "But first I have to learn all we can about the trip. Plan an investigation. This will take a while."

"I live for centuries. I can wait, although I am very eager. And you should not forget to eat lunch. Thinking is more efficient with food."

"Oh." He smiles and turns back toward the kitchen. "Yeah. Lunch. Thanks."

I think I handled that well, but I have one more thing to say. The woman who leads the Philosopher's Club asked me to help spread certain information. "I have something to ask of you for tonight, Mirlo. This is difficult to explain. Traditionally, for Humans, the festival can be prelude to amorous incidents." I word it that way because Earthlings are not as blunt as Pacifists, especially about reproductive acts. "The Humans here need renewed genetic material. If the opportunity arises, please help Pax."

Mirlo's face and body tense. He is reflecting cultural differences, as the anthropologists are fond of saying.

"That makes scientific sense," he says, looking down. "I'll . . . yes." He leaves, his face full of uncertainty. I have given him many things to think about.

In another part of the city, Om has come to talk to Pollux. They rarely interact rationally, and Om receives mental health support from the network itself. Pollux, who does not, looks at him with an expression of fear, but not as much fear as he usually displays in the company of Pacifists. Om stands in front of him in a stance of intimidation: with his hands on his hips to appear larger, and standing a little too close, both to invade Pollux's space and to impede his ability to stand and achieve equal footing—this in addition to the aggression of his facial expression and the angle at which he holds his head. Pollux shrinks back.

"You've heard from Earth," Om says.

"Nothing interesting."

"Share it."

"Music. And climate, a shift in the climate again."

Om leans slightly forward. "Government."

"Government." He looks away and does nothing, neither moves nor sends anything.

"Bad news, then."

"Mars. The . . . the Mars War is over."

Om smiles. "Who won?"

"I don't know. I need to look at the report again." He stares at the end of the bench.

"We can do that together. Can't we?"

"Government news is classified."

"But if the government has changed, you've lost your classification, and it would fall on me as the chairman. Let's see it." Om sits down on the same bench, a little too close.

Pollux looks away again.

Om stares as if he is reading something.

"We have to go back," Pollux says.

Om continues to read a while before answering, "No."

"But the government has changed. Our mission's canceled."

"What happens a hundred light-years away doesn't matter now, except that now you're nobody. You've lost your rank, and I'm in charge."

"I still represent the government. Whichever one there is."

"Government is an association of men who do violence to the rest of us. Tolstoy said that, Leo Tolstoy. Heard of him? Nineteenth century. The government made me do and say repugnant things in exchange for a simulacrum of freedom. No more. No more violence. That's also from Tolstoy."

"We have to go back. Our mission is over. We have orders. You saw them."

"We'll go back when I say." He stands up. "And you. You're not terribly useful. But maybe you can do some good."

Pollux squints up at him. "I'm the ranking government observer."

"Your rank is assistant anthropologist. That puts you above data techs, below pilots." He begins to walk away. He stares for a moment.

Over the radio connection, I hear Pollux giving orders to the central system as fast as he can. Om issues counterorders, and the report is made public.

"You can't stop me anymore," Om says, "so don't bother trying."

I witness another moment in which the action takes place within the space of information. I am not certain how decisions are made there, how actions are carried out, but Om prevails. In any case, I do not know how other members of the mission will react to the report.

Om leaves. Pollux goes to his house. I will need to watch them both, and now Velma notices the report, reads it, and notifies all the members at once. "Mars won! Look."

That is all they talk about for the rest of the afternoon, in addition, of course, to the festival. Some express their joy, but they do not express it to everyone. A few express regret. Mirlo is delighted but hides that from the Mu Rees. Yet soon the Spring Festival commands their attention.

And mine. We plants have yet to celebrate our Spring Festival. We are waiting for warmer weather, for although some plants obey the angle of light as the sunlight shifts, most of the rest, including the belowground ecology, respond to warm moisture, which has yet to come. The forest and fields are mostly quiet, and in about two hours, the sun will set.

I will pay close attention to the border with the Coral Plains tonight, as well as attend the festival as an involved observer. I see Queen Thunderclap showing my box to other queens and, downwind, I detect spicy puffs of *curiosity*. Little Rattle picks up the box and shakes it and seems perplexed when it makes no noise. The babble of voices of the festival is already too loud to hear even queen voices from where I am, off to the sides in patches of garden.

The plaza is crowded. The wide stone-and-brick walls at its side will be used to serve the feast, and the traditional meal awaits at the head of the plaza.

A few Earthlings stand together close to one of the entrances, and they are broadcasting their discussion, so I listen in:

"That was a century ago. In fact one hundred sixteen years and almost three months."

"And if we left now, we'd get there a century later than that. Anything could happen."

"But something did. We may as well enjoy it."

"Why go back at all?" Velma says.

"What? Explain yourself," Mu Ree Fa says. "What did you mean by questioning whether we should return to Earth?" This remark comes with a notice to others to pay attention. He wants everyone in the mission involved.

"We're here, it's safe, it's nice, we survived," she says. "And they treat women like equals here. Going back, I mean, what would we discover? It could be even worse than when we left."

"You know what you agreed to," Fa says.

"You know what we secretly agreed to, which was to escape. We did. Why go back?"

Some distance away, Karola is talking with an anthropologist. They have both stopped and are listening to Velma and Mu.

"Did you hear that?" the anthropologist says. "Velma doesn't want to go back."

After a long moment, Karola answers, "Do you?"

"Well. I need to know more. First we weren't getting messages, now we get this."

"I was sure Mars would lose. You don't need Velma to get back, anyway."

"Without her, we'd have room to take more samples. Maybe someone native."

I look for Mirlo. Being an Earthling, he's tall enough to find relatively easily, but his radio is turned off. He is in the crowd talking to a young Pax woman named Paloma. He seems very serious, and she is smiling. She steps closer and touches his forearm. He still looks serious. She says something with a lot of wide gestures. He smiles a little. I hope they are talking about procreation.

I see Om, outside the plaza with the stilt walkers, recording his thoughts for future publication on Earth:

Earth and its inhabitants receded from Pax memories to become nothing more than vague ideas of height and frailty and failure, since the colony's very founders considered Earth a planet ruined and its people doomed: they had escaped an oversize, decaying society. The founders, in turn, became the embodiment to their children of what they had tried to escape. For the Spring Festival, this concept of Earth returns as the so-called Parents will be the first to eat the meal that symbolizes exploration, maintaining the irony that while they were ultimately rejected by their children, their inaugural explorations led to this now prosperous city. Yet the term "parent" is an insult, and the reenactors wear rags, their faces painted to look pale and haggard with hunger.

I am surprised. He has understood the history more or less correctly. It seems, though, that he is not attentive to the conflict that has just arisen among his mission. He may have that part of his radio reception turned off, which is irresponsible since he will have to become involved eventually.

Pollux rushes over to Velma. "This is treason," he says, and sends for all to hear.

"You're not dangerous anymore," she answers.

"I still have the power to make judicial decisions."

"That's right," Mu Ree Fa says.

"And I have the power to quit. Or is Haus going to shoot me?"

Om says, "What makes you sure the natives will want you?"

I was wrong. He is listening in.

He adds, "Look at the stilt walkers. They represent the original colonists, Earthlings. Like us."

Velma peers over at the beginning of the show. The Parent imitators enter the plaza, greeted by derisive shouts.

Om returns his attention to his publication and records:

Like buffoons, they respond to derision by inviting more of it, by wobbling and shouting insults back in ritualized anger. One chases a group of taunting boys, and when they easily outrun him, he hurls threats at them. Another Parent is surrounded by a ring of mocking dancers. Even Ladybird, who ordinarily maintains a front of good-will and concern, joins in, organizing a satiric chant, "Children never speak. Children never vote." Finally some youngsters begin to pester the Parents: "Look, food. Lots of food. You can eat. You're hungry. We have food." They indicate the "traveler's meal" at the head of the plaza. Soon the Parents wobble over, manifesting exaggerated enthusiasm over what they might have considered delicacies but current Pacifist eyes appraise as less than second-best.

"So you see," Om says, "the natives might not want you to stay."

"They've always treated me well," Velma said. "Nobody likes Pollux. I've seen that. But the rest of us, it's different. We're individuals, they know that."

"That was history, that little show," an anthropologist says. "The present really is different."

Zivon shakes his head. "Everyone here belongs to a group, a generation, a family, a work team, something. And we have our group. Big, clumsy, stupid. Pacifists are always trying to help me do things, as if I'm handicapped."

"The women love us," Ernst says. Velma shoots him a look.

"Fraternizing is forbidden," Om says. Ernst laughs.

"And then there's that whole Stevland thing."

"Well, yes, they lie all the time."

"I wanted to go on a farming trip," someone else says, "and they said it would be too difficult. Yeah, they think we're weaker."

"Arthur, the hunter, seems pretty fed up with us," Velma says. "But that's just one person."

"I think all the Glassmakers hate us."

"Well," Mu Ree Cheol says, "they won't talk to me at all, so I can't tell."

Om listens as they continue. Eventually he records: *A few members of our team, tall and lanky like Parents, watch this and ask each other if they are seen the same way. One anthropologist says no, the ritual relates to historic incidents, but then some mission members begin to relate small, accumulated slights to show that Pax hostility to Earth has not waned. Earth had cooled as a memory, but we reignited it.*

As the discussion among the Earthlings over the question of staying continues, the rancor becomes personal. While many regard Pollux as the representative of something they hate, a few consider Velma stupid. They even call her a tulip: they have learned something during their stay, one new word. She responds in kind.

I do not like how this situation is developing. Ladybird has already noticed that the Earthlings are quarreling, and she issues an order that whispers from mouth to mouth: separate the Earthlings. The Pacifist mentors assigned to each one approach to guide their charges to participate in the festival, just as they isolated individuals at their arrival on the planet. But this problem will grow more acute, and guides would surely prefer to celebrate rather than work, so discontent may spread among Pacifists. I must share my observations with Ladybird.

Food—quality food, a delicious feast—is eaten, and then a song-and-dance spectacle distracts everyone as the sky begins to show its first hints of pink sunset.

I also patrol the border with the Coral Plains. I get two notices of fire that seem to be merely sunset reflected on still pools of water. Other than that, we trees and plants chat as best we can, for they do not have my size or intellect. But our rootlets touch, calcium ions move, and each wave of ions with its enzymes and chemical pathways creates meaning.

"Springtime," says a ponytail tree.

"No rain," a village of ferns complains.

"Water flowing deep," a free aspen answers.

"Owls digging," says a grove of palms.

"I am happy," a young locustwood says. "I am chosen to be male here."

"Congratulations," I say. "You will progress far."

"I am dominant. You will see how much."

"I have observed that much domination is possible." The tree is still too young to be as helpful and annoying as the valley's main locustwood speaker, and yet I am pleased that a large, intelligent tree will grow so near to the edge of the plains. He will no doubt prove himself useful.

In the city, Human and Glassmaker children and fippokats engage in a complex dance. The older children arrange themselves, dancing in a precise grid alternating with kats. Toddlers come forward with younger kats and try to imitate them in a way meant to be humorous, and they succeed. Rattle tries to dance on two legs, and Human children on either side take her front hoofs in their hands. It is charming. Finally the older children simplify their movements, the younger ones invite adults to dance with them, and the older children pick up torches, light them one by one as they dance in swirling patterns, and lead the way, singing, out toward the bonfire in the field, a dance of flames.

Mere words cannot convey the beauty and spectacle of the show, and in fact, any single viewpoint misses some details. I can see it from various stems, and the Earthlings also share their viewpoints and marvel. For a long while they even cease to bicker.

Once everyone arrives at the bonfire, the Earthlings face the question of removing their clothes as Pacifists are, both Humans and Glassmakers.

"It's too chilly."

"They're going to look at us as outsiders again."

"I don't have anything to burn anyway. I came to observe, not to go native."

"This is such a beautiful ceremony. I want to be part of it."

Mirlo silently strips off his clothing, quickly, perhaps nervously. He takes his bundle of twigs from a pocket to burn. Of the twenty Earthlings, only six have removed their clothing: Mirlo, Karola, Velma, Haus, the physician, and Om.

Pacifists continue to sing, and some compare the items they created to burn. One after another, they dance forward to place or toss their pledges of change onto the pile of fuel, including Queen Thunderclap, who throws two small items and then helps Rattle toss something. Child dancers come forward and set their torches at the base. Loggers begin to move the crowd back as tinder catches fire.

I fear fire, but I watch, fascinated and safely distant. As the flames grow, they light hydrogen seeds, which flash and bang. My box is burning in there, somewhere, my pledge to meet this other bamboo. Despite what I said to Mirlo, I wish to go as soon as possible, and I envision complications. First, some Earthlings like Pollux wish to leave Pax immediately. I must delay that. Second, although Mirlo truly wishes to go, perhaps not all Earthlings do, since it is a long, uncertain trip. They would go if they understood, as Mirlo does, that they would visit yet another sentient alien species who might fascinate them as much as the Glassmakers do. Yet I do not wish to make myself known. I see no advantage to me or my people.

At the city, I am watching fire and pondering change. At the edge of the forest, I am searching for fire and pondering ecological stability. The young male locustwood, admirably, wants me to share what history I know, so I describe the nature of the Coral Plains and the consequences of its recent earthquake.

"No trees in the plains?" he asks.

"Only bushes, and very different."

"We must colonize it." He is already aggressive.

"It will be difficult to colonize. I have not succeeded."

Another of my groves gets a message from several plants of various species at once: "Fire!" I pass the news on and concentrate my attention. Another false alarm? From the top of a stalk, I spot a bright light at the edge of the forest. It is not, as I expected, centered over the water, but at the far edge, on the Coral Plains.

The fire is small, the size of a Human, growing slowly over logs floating in the water, but wet wood will not burn. Perhaps this fire will endanger only the plains, or it may be simply swamp gas.

The forest plants who see it are screaming with fear, the terror expanding to those too low or far away to see the flames. I report that the fire is on the far side of the swamp to try to calm them, but for some, the idea is too abstract. They understand "fire," a chemical word almost identical to danger. They would understand "safe," but that might be a lie.

Should I call for help? It would be hard to mobilize a team. At the Spring Festival, the fire has reached its peak, roaring like a pack of fippolions. Its uppermost flames swirl and sparkle. I notice that the loggers have buckets of water nearby and watch to see where sparks fall. Even from far away, I can feel the heat.

Dancing and singing have resumed. Mirlo is still with the Pacifist woman toward the front, while most of the Earthlings are standing far back, watching and sending among themselves. Then whooping cheers catch everyone's attention. Arthur is talking with Fern. I cannot hear the words, but I see him point to his penis, which, I imagine, is erect. She answers with an embrace and kisses.

I believe this will be the start of a family. The Earthlings share scandalized comments, but I could tell them this is hardly the first love consummated on the night of the Spring Festival. Pacifists are used to it. Spring is the time for flowers and fertilization, although flowers lack the emotional complexes that Humans must suffer for love. Arthur and Fern have been encircled by dancers to reinforce their joy.

And then at the city a sudden sharp wind blows across the fields, a foehn wind from the mountains. The fire is pushed higher and brighter, crackling with new life, while loggers scramble to maintain safety and vigilance. But no one is surprised. These winds happen from time to time, depending on the exact weather situation.

This wind, however, will travel across the valley all the way to the edge of the forest. I have never observed its exact effect at the border with the plains. A flame will tell me a lot, but I do not know what I am about to learn. I wait.

One by one, my groves between here and the city report the arrival of the wind, but the speed of transmission is barely faster than the speed of the wind itself.

At the edge of the forest, the tops of trees rustle as they are tossed in the wind. The sound moves closer. My own branches wave, first the top ones, then all the way to the ground in the fierce wind. The fire suddenly grows brighter. Birds bark and dash away while plants scream again.

I watch as calmly as I can. The fire roars and sparks like a smaller version of the festival bonfire, and it leans—away from the forest, toward the plains. It creeps along the ground, burning whatever litter it can find. It flares with a bang, perhaps fueled by gas or a dry bush. It flares and bangs again, then seems to cease growing. I feel hopeful. Yes, after a minute, it has definitely begun to die. Within another minute, it is gone.

"Safe!" I announce.

"Good. Good. Good."

"What happened?" the young locustwood asks. Locustwoods cannot see.

"The fire died. It was blown into the plains, but it could not find enough fuel, and it died."

"The plains do not burn?"

"I do not know. I am not exactly sure what happened. I can see little in the dark. I will look in the sunlight, and perhaps I will send a service animal to make closer observations. The fire is out. I can assure you of that."

But if there is another fire, if whatever caused it within the Coral Plains is different, perhaps it can burn with more danger and damage. I really do not know what happened.

I thank the locustwood for helping to observe. He promises to continue, himself and the female trees he now lords over and all the neighbors he can bully into his service. He asks for more information about my service animals. I give him a little history and describe their capabilities, and he is impressed by my ability to control such powerful creatures.

Back at the city, the bonfire has burned low, and most people have returned to their homes. Spring is the best time to grow anew and stronger, and we have all promised to change. My change will affect more than just myself.

The morning starts just slightly earlier for me today because the planet tilts and days grow longer in springtime. The light infuses leaf after leaf with energy that flows from crown to roots, a slightly longer day yielding a bit more energy than yesterday and more than enough for today, even though it will no doubt be eventful. But for most of the animal residents of the city, who stayed up late last night and may have drunk some truffle as well, sunrise comes far too soon. Humans of both planetary heritages and Glassmakers, even fippokats, leave their homes yawning in full sunlight. They, like me, may have changes to maintain or initiate.

Mirlo arises in the home of his Pacifist companion, Paloma, and breakfasts with her. Afterward, on his way to his laboratory, he approaches a stalk.

"Talk to me."

"Warmth and food. What do you want?"

He sits on a bench, staring. "I think you should be in the network. I can connect you as a piece of equipment, and you'd be part of it, not an observer. You'd be an object, like me—technically we're all objects—and that would give you some advantages. You could interact more naturally. And I could call you directly."

"I have heard Abacus speak to people."

"Exactly."

"Would it not seem odd to Abacus to speak to a piece of equipment?"

"A lot of machines have humanlike interfaces, even some animals back on Earth, for that matter. Whales. That changed everything. Anyway, I'll set it up when I get to the lab. You'll like it." He stands and starts walking. "I've been trying to figure out how to convince Om to send a trip to Laurentia. The trip to the plains didn't go smoothly."

"I have found an idea for that. I have examined the scans closely and observed near perfect circles of growth among the bamboo there."

"Can you do that? Grow like that?"

"I do not see the utility of such growth, but it is easily done. No doubt it is aesthetic rather than functional, which suggests social interaction. But that is not all. I see small, persistent fires, presumably campfires, which means that intelligent animals seem to live there. They may be interacting with the bamboo. Perhaps they are making the circles."

I do not mention that eagles use fire, and bamboo does not interact with them, and the circles may be art rather than interaction. But beyond all doubt there is some fire-using animal there and a civilization of bamboo.

Mirlo smiles at a stem. "I'll talk to Om. He'll want to go for sure."

He enters the lab and compiles observations of campfires as we locate the network connection for the chip Queen Thunderclap stole. He creates settings that identify me to Abacus. It is a minor technical task. Suddenly, my stolen radio chip receives a message: "Welcome." It is the strong male voice. "I'm Abacus. You're Beluga. Please use my help functions freely as you navigate the network."

"Mirlo, what does 'beluga' mean?"

"I chose that for your network identification. I told the network you're a microscope. The name is a whale, a kind of whale. They talk a lot." Then he hurries out, sending to Om as he does. Om is in the fields researching Pax culture, but he replies promptly and with interest as Mirlo shares what he has found.

I am also listening with my original radio to a private exchange between a pilot who remains on board the spaceship orbiting Pax, one of ten people maintaining the vessel there, and Pollux. Both want to return to Earth immediately.

"They aren't going to leave anytime soon," Pollux says.

"We have our orders."

"Every time they turn around they discover some new wonder." He says that as if wonders were to be disdained.

"Is it wonderful down there?"

"It's like a resort I went to in Japan once. A historical re-creation, so there was no running water or electricity. Pretty, but everything's primitive. We're lucky the natives do all the work or we'd starve."

"It can't be that bad, since no one wants to do rotation and come up here. Om said the ship can fly itself. Come down, he said."

"You should. Come down, but take over. It's out of control here. We need you if we're ever going to get out."

They plan the details. The ten mission members on the ship will arrive tomorrow to take control. I am not sure how that will succeed because they are outnumbered by the mission members on the ground. I am sure that Om will not be notified. I could do so, or Beluga could, but then I would no longer be secret. I could tell Mirlo, but he would have no logical way to have learned it himself.

As I think, Pollux sees Haus, the soldier, and quietly tells him the mission members from orbit are coming to bring order. Haus salutes, and when he turns away, he still seems less happy.

Soon he is searching for velvet worms with Jose and mentions that the orbiting mission members are coming to renew order among them.

"What do you mean by order?"

"They will have to obey the right orders."

"They aren't obeying Om? I thought he's in charge now."

Haus aims his rifle at a trap for the worms. "Ready." Jose uses a long spear to lift the trap and shake it. A worm twists inside, Haus turns on a beam of light, and the worm explodes. "Not everyone likes Om," he says, "but I prefer him." He does not transmit his remarks with Jose to other Earthlings.

Out in the fields, loggers are dismantling the remains of the bonfire and spreading the ashes, and Om is working with them, questioning them on the lore acquired over the years through experience, turning a forest into a home, but he is also sending with Mirlo. When Mirlo arrives, they speak, and Om proves to be almost as excited as Mirlo about the prospect of more exploring and more discoveries.

Karola is some distance away learning bat language from a hunter, and a flock of bats, attracted by their practice, approaches to see if they can earn food in some way.

Arthur and Cawzee are moving their belongings into Fern's house with great joking and laughter. She is delighted by Cawzee's carni-kat kitten.

Jose, as he and Haus wander the fields, sees Geraldine and steps aside to speak to her quietly. She rushes across the river to tell Lady-bird, who sends Geraldine and a Glassmaker assistant to notify several people of an emergency meeting: Om, Thunderclap, Jose if he can leave Haus discreetly, and if not then Arthur.

Communication can be accomplished without the network. I am relieved.

Out in the fields, Ladybird's assistant signals Jose from afar using hunting hand signals. Jose signals "no." The hunter with Karola also sees that and interprets for her, and she seems to have a question. They stop the Glassmaker and speak with him briefly before he runs back to the city. Karola runs behind him, her face showing intense fear. I have never seen her terrified before.

The assistant runs to Arthur, who comes after grumbling about pol-itics and meetings. Geraldine finds Om and explains the situation with near panic. They hurry to the city, and Mirlo comes with them.

Ladybird is in the Meeting House, waiting. Everyone arrives almost at the same time except for Karola, who is running across the bridge.

After a little summary from Ladybird, Om explains the situation and does not stint on political aspects of Earth. It had a vile government, which he had avoided explaining before "because you are already con-vinced that Earth is a horrible place. Indeed, some of us, I think most of us, left as much to escape from it as to find you."

Arthur is the first to speak. "What kind of weapons will they bring?"

"Haus is the weapon, he himself, although some of us can use guns. I think he has all of the guns, though. And no offense meant, you are overpowered."

"Why should we get involved at all?" Geraldine says. "This isn't our problem. You can fight it out yourselves."

"But we have so much to do," Mirlo says. "Our scans found some other civilization across the ocean in Laurentia. We should investigate that. The scans found lots more rainbow bamboo and some smoke from campfires. Have you seen it?"

All the Pacifists stare at him for several long moments.

Arthur starts to glance at me and stops. "More bamboo? And camp-fires? You mean, more people?"

Again, stunned silence from the Pacifists.

"Yes," Ladybird finally says. "Of course. We should investigate that."

"Won't they let you do that? The ones who're coming?" Geraldine asks.

Om answers. "No. They have no interest in the science mission. They just want to go home right away."

"But they've never seen it here," Geraldine says. "They'll like it. Especially now that springtime is finally picking up."

"When you say fight," Thunderclap says, "you mean bloodshed? Weapons?"

"I hope not." Om looks down and crosses his arms.

Karola is sending to Om, "I can help. I know they're coming to put Pollux in charge, and I can help fight."

He answers after a moment, "I'm in a meeting now. What can you do, briefly?"

"I can disrupt network connections and send false information."

His eyes grow slightly wider. "We'll definitely talk."

I must listen in when they do.

Arthur is speaking. "I'm as annoyed as anyone at the Earthlings." Thunderclap scents *less than me*. He nods with a wry smile. "Or maybe not everyone. But this is our chance to explore, like Mirlo says, and probably a nicer place this time than the Coral Plains."

"We don't mean to be disruptive," Om says.

"Zivon wants us to hate Humans," Thunderclap says.

"Really?" Geraldine says. "You don't believe that, do you?"

"What time will they come?" Arthur says.

"I'm not sure," Om says. "I'm not welcome in that discussion. Mirlo . . . ? Not you either. Hmm. Let me send to ask someone else." He asks Karola. She asks the network, but her question sounds not like her, not her identification. Is that her disruptive skill? She gets an answer that she sends to Om.

He announces, "They will arrive after . . . let me convert the times . . . after solar noon tomorrow, well after it. Midafternoon."

I send an idea to Mirlo, and he says, "Would it be possible to send a mission to the other continent tomorrow morning, before noon?"

Arthur tilts his head as if listening to his own thoughts. Ladybird puts her hand over her mouth. Om slowly smiles.

"We want to go," Mirlo says, "and they'll try to stop us. Besides, who'll go? We'll need security. Haus should come with us."

Arthur laughs. "Got it. Am I on the team? I saved his life. He owes me. I think I can make sure he comes."

Of course, there is more to the idea, and it is debated and adjusted. They can explore and at the same time minimize the conflict between the Earthlings, at least for a while, by sending the conflictive individuals away. Ladybird will try to intervene with the orbital team.

"This means a lot of . . . I don't know what," Ladybird says.

"We build-us a boat before we know the wood," Thunderclap says with *caution*.

"Wood naturally floats," Mirlo says.

Arthur slaps him on the shoulder. "We're going to make a great team."

Mirlo returns the smile. "Bring Cawzee."

There is much to prepare, but almost without noticing, Pacifists have agreed to back the Earthlings who want to stay. Except for Geraldine, who merely wants to postpone any conflict as long as possible, and when she learns that the exploration team will use Earth technology to send their sights and sounds live back to the city as a distraction to the arrival of the orbital team, she is intrigued by the ability to accompany the team from the safety of home.

They all hurry from the meeting with tasks. Ladybird goes to the greenhouse. "Stevland, you aren't alone."

"I learned this yesterday. I still find it hard to believe, even after looking at the evidence."

"Seeds. They should take your seeds and plant them." She understands me well.

"Mirlo will do that."

"And bring some back! Arthur and Cawzee can help."

"This is the change I burned last night. I am not alone. For me, everything is changed."

Meanwhile, I watch Om. He sends a variety of messages to individuals and groups. He even invites Pollux to join the exploration team as a gesture to imitate guilelessness. Pollux does not respond.

Karola is waiting for Om, and soon they enter a secluded garden.

"You said you can send false information. How false?"

"Completely false."

"We can all lie with thoughts as well as words."

"More than that. I can interfere with your feed and make you think, for example, that you can see, um, results from a test that aren't what the network sends. I can intercept those results and send something else. Or have it tell you that the Mu Rees are at the river, but they're in their lab."

Om stares at her with what might be fear.

I want to know more.

"It's difficult and it hurts, so I hardly ever do it. And of course it's illegal. But I'll do that to help you under one condition. I won't go back to Earth. I refuse. I'll help you if you let me stay here."

Om's expression becomes more friendly. "Agreed. Exactly how do you do this?"

She explains. The networks operating on Earth encompass the entire planet fairly seamlessly. The mission to Pax has brought a smaller, self-contained network, Abacus, but it operates in the same way. The exact technique requires intercepting and substituting a message, which involves intervening in wavelengths other than the one assigned to her as an individual. It also requires clear thoughts to send. This may be difficult for her, but I think with my resources I could do it easily. I will try.

Om has more technical questions. She needs to be between the transmitter and the receiving individual. Physically, she expends great energy and effort to the point of physical pain. A careful observer might notice her activity, but no one suspects such a thing so it has never been noticed. She has done little false sending since landing on Pax, but somewhat more on the ship prior to landing to "maintain the peace." Om thanks her for that. I can imagine the difficulties of spending days with those contentious Earthlings in a confined area, like too many crabs in one tree.

Out in a field near the river, Mu Ree Cheol is hunting for specimens. I listen for his messages to the network for recording data. I find his frequency. I think about boxer birds and send the sound of one as if it were near him, and he turns and looks. I send the barking sound again, and he approaches the brush where it supposedly is. Of course there is nothing, but I have made him think there was a bird.

For me, that did not tax my energy any more than usual, but I can imagine how hard it would be for a Human. And there are complications. The transmission point for the network has been set up in a workshop toward the southern end of the city to take advantage of the natural rise in the terrain. My transmission point is from the greenhouse toward the eastern gate. That leaves a lot of territory where I cannot interfere unless I can get another transmitter.

Meanwhile, Om asks, "Why don't you want to return home?"

"I'd rather not say." Now she is the one who looks afraid.

He thinks, then nods. "I'll respect that."

Could it have to do with Nancsi? Then she would have a very sound reason. Om may not be curious, but I am.

Om adds, "Make sure Haus goes to Laurentia tomorrow."

Mirlo has approached Haus, who is returning from hunting, just after he crosses the bridge.

"Tomorrow morning," Mirlo says, "we're going to explore the Laurentia continent. There's sentient life there. Campfires. We'll need you for security."

"Huh?"

"You know, those scans."

Haus looks unimpressed. He sends to Pollux about it. I intercept and send an answer in Pollux's voice: "We need to surprise them, so you have to go along. We'll wait until you get back."

"Imagine going there," Mirlo says. "Imagine what we can learn.

Think how much we learned at the Coral Plains. We're going to need you."

"Yeah, it should be fun."

"Anyway," Mirlo says, "Arthur and I guess Cawzee are coming."

"In that case," Haus says, "I have to be there."

"Hey, Mirlo, we need to get organized, and fast," Zivon sends. "Come talk to me. And bring the Mu Rees."

They go on their various ways.

The data-recording crew is arguing over who will go, but the discussion ends when they realize that Ernst and Velma wish to go. Only two are needed, and the others do not wish to go. They begin to make preparations for tomorrow, which are complex, but they have experience and seem to enjoy solving problems.

"This is going to be a great show," Ernst says. They find Arthur and Cawzee with Haus and fit them with radios. New radios. They seem to have forgotten about the old ones.

When that is done, Arthur delivers the radios he and Cawzee previously stole to Ladybird. She and I and Jose practice with them, investigating their settings, for unlike my programmed chip, they can transmit on several frequencies and we must choose one that will not overlap with the network.

Pollux is sending to the pilot in orbit, "We can nail all this down while Om and his crew are off exploring. We'll send as many as we can up to the ship first, then the rest later."

"What about the natives?"

"They don't know anything about this. And they don't like us anyway, so they'll be glad to get rid of us."

And so the sun sets, and most people rest after a busy day. I observe the forest's border with the plains, watching for fires, and I check the network for data on fires and ecologies. Earth has an amazing number of ecologies. Many would suit me. I can now imagine myself there more precisely and wish to be there more than ever—that is, to send my seeds.

I see no fires, fortunately.

Shortly after dawn, Mirlo boards the plane with two large bags of my seeds hidden in his baggage, since it would be hard to explain the need to plant me where there are already bamboo. "What's your best SWATS?" he sends me. I check with the network: soil, water, air, temperature, sunlight.

"Thank you for bringing me with you," I say. "I believe we can assume that if other bamboo grows in a specific location, I can grow there, or in a locale that seems similar to this valley. Remember to space me some distance away from existing bamboo, though, to prevent competition for sunlight. Our roots can bring us together. Arthur and Cawzee will help."

"I'll bring all the seeds from there that I can, and from different individuals. I can only imagine what this means to you."

"Your actions show that you understand fully."

Om is musing about *an exploration within an exploration whose consequences matter more for the indigenous life than for ourselves: we have become servants to our discoveries.* Yes, he has become a servant animal, and I am more excited about this trip than he is.

Everyone boards: the healthy pilot, an assistant to the physician, two Mu Rees, Zivon, Ernst, Velma, the ethno-engineer, Mirlo, Om, and Haus—a roster that includes several of Pollux's strongest supporters. Arthur, Cawzee, and Snow, one of our best farmers, join the team. The heli-plane is crowded.

Left behind are Mosegi, still in the hospital recovering from lung fungus, the physician, one Mu Ree, two anthropologists, the astrophysicist, a data recorder, Pollux, and, most dangerously, Karola. Will this make Pollux's movement falter, or will it be pushed into extreme action?

As the team troops to the heli-plane, Pollux is back in the city with the physician.

"We have to leave as fast as we can. The natives hate us anyway."

The physician invariably tries to calm people and minimize

problems. "I think some of them find us annoying and there's still resentment over the influenza, but most think we're entertainment."

"We already know the ones with the raindrop marks hate us. Right?"

"I wouldn't know."

Pollux has guessed somewhat accurately. The members of the Raindrop generation, Generation 9, with a few exceptions like Honey, tend to be older and because of their age disproportionately hold leadership positions, including Jose and Geraldine. They do not trust the Earthlings and do not need entertainment. Generation 10, with shaved heads, is resentful over their lack of contributions to the city, eating but not producing, so they have agreed among themselves to invite Earthlings on their teams to make them work. The Black Hats, Generation 11, are more easily amused. The Glassmakers overall do not like the Earthlings, although for varied reasons.

At this point, the grumbling among the Pacifists has yet to cause significant conflict, but history shows that conflicts can be as much a chosen course of action as a consequence of circumstances. I can and must affect choices.

The heli-plane takes off. The technicians have set up a display in the Meeting House, which is packed with Pacifists. For one reason or another, little farmwork will be accomplished today, although it is a fine spring day. Many have already seen the recordings from the original Earthling landing and from the trip to the Coral Plains, as well as the scans of Laurentia, and these have only made them want to see more.

I can understand. Through the network, I see several views at once from the heli-plane. From our wide valley, the aircraft rises to view the dramatic mountains to the east and west and passes over the eastern ones to the ocean. Water stretches from horizon to horizon, blue-green under a cyan sky dotted with small clouds. Rays of sunlight and shadow fall on the water, its surface restless with waves. Water is life, and this vast expanse of water, this ocean, is the promise and source of endless life. I feel humbled before its importance. This is the source of the water that keeps me alive. An understanding of the ocean would tell me the meaning of life, and the network has immense ocean lore.

But that will have to wait. Abacus announces that the ship in orbit has launched its heli-plane to land earlier than expected, and Ladybird is in the greenhouse contacting me.

"Karola wants to be in the welcome party to greet the ship. Is that wise? I mean, can we trust her?"

"She wants to stay here forever, so I think we can trust her. And she can help with any communication problems between us and the team from orbit."

"She does? That's great—from the DNA point of view, anyway, for her to stay. We need new people. Do you suppose others would stay?"

"Velma. And maybe others, although it depends on whether Pollux or Om leads the Earthling team. We ought to review our plan for the landing. They have a plan. They mean to come, gather up the crew here, put them on a plane, and send them to orbit. Then they will take the rest when they return, and they will all go back to Earth."

"Oh, that won't work. The Earthlings are all busy today."

"Yes, I doubt it is a workable plan, which might make them want to execute it all the more. Some teams get stubborn."

She laughs bitterly. "That's nothing new. We're not ready for this."

"But we must have everything ready that we can."

The heli-plane from orbit will land in two hours. Some Pacifists have tired of the endless view of monotonously beautiful ocean and have gone out to workshops or fields. I am monitoring the radio between the pilot from orbit and the astrophysicist, who is helping with the landing, so I know where it is and see its view, but more than that I hear it approach like sustained thunder. In the fields, people pause to look. When it comes into view, bats take flight, then a few cautiously approach as it lands, looking for an opportunity to report.

The plane, a disk the size of two houses, with a spinning edge that creates a wind to lower itself to the ground, settles in a fallow field near the edge of the forest, coating the weeds with frost from its frigid exhaust. The astrophysicist had to argue with the pilot to convince him not to land in a field of wheat and destroy the crop. That would have angered the Pacifists beyond repair.

The pilot, Darius Resvani, jumps out, then stumbles, looking expectantly at the welcoming crew that approaches. I have learned his background from the network. He had been trained to fly extraorbital aircraft by a business consortium of a regional government. That government was violently supplanted by a new government with a different economic goal. He lost many family members in the violence. After some difficulties, he found other work and eventually volunteered for this mission, searching for "places to fly higher." I wonder if his stated reason for traveling to Pax is honest.

Approaching across the field are Pollux, Karola, Jose, Scratcher, the astrophysicist, and a Glassmaker major who is an exceptional hunter and who carries a weighted spear, a weapon more fearsome than it looks, though he feigns concern for velvet worms. Karola is listening intently to the network and broadcasting what she hears to anyone who cares to listen.

"Can we trust these natives?" Darius sends privately to Pollux. Darius is taller and darker than Pollux and stands straighter.

"These, sure. They want to stay out of this. They don't like disruption. There's grumbling about it."

"We're not here to disrupt the natives."

"We might need to do that."

Now they are close enough to talk.

Pollux smiles and extends a hand in greeting. "Welcome to Pax," he says out loud.

"It's about time." Darius stumbles as he reaches for Pollux. "Gravity. Not used to it yet."

Another member of the team descends from a ladderlike stairway, walks from it as if trudging through mud, approaches Darius, and speaks quietly to him.

"What? Those useless idiots!" He turns to Pollux. "They didn't exercise."

After an angry discussion, it turns out that of the ten team members from orbit, only four can walk somewhat well, including Darius. The rest suffer from greater or lesser muscle atrophy due to lack of exercise, although exercise was required. They thought their suits would be enough to handle the planet's gravity. Despite Darius's aversion to the presence of Glassmakers, Karola and Scratcher enter the ship to assess the situation, then Scratcher dashes to the city to organize stretcher teams. Pacifist reactions vary from annoyed to mocking, and they offer little sympathy. Most have already concluded that even if the Earthlings are smart, which is debatable, they are lazy.

Pollux is angry. "You have to discipline people. They won't do it themselves. Now what are we going to do?"

"We'll recover quickly." As Darius walks to the city, he must stop and rest often, although he refuses help. Jose, Karola, and the major are helping those who can to walk, and the rest are borne on a parade of stretchers.

Ladybird and Geraldine have created a welcome with food and refreshments for the ambulatory Earthlings in the house the anthropologists use. Darius enters and sits, exhausted. Although he knows that Ladybird is the leader, he treats her and Geraldine like servants, ordering them to fetch him food and cups of tea and speaking only with other Earthlings.

"She's in charge here," Karola sends him. "She should be treated nicer."

"She can't even talk intelligibly," he answers. He adds, "Go see how the idiots in the hospital are doing, if the natives can do anything resembling medical care here."

"We've been impressed by what they can do." She leaves, dawdling at a screen to watch the feed from the exploration team as it approaches the far shore. Outside, she complains to Honey, who hugs her and makes jokes.

Geraldine also leaves, after quietly but clearly expressing her disgust over the Earthlings to Ladybird. She nods and asks Geraldine to send Ladybird's worker assistant to come and take over for her.

"We'll see," Ladybird murmurs, "if they like Glassmakers better than us."

Darius and Pollux soon realize that no one can leave today. The other pilot could barely crawl out of the cockpit seat and onto a stretcher. Mosegi, the third pilot, is still hospitalized. And the fourth pilot is in Laurentia, searching for a landing site. No one can pilot a plane back to orbit.

Pacifists are eating lunch in the Meeting House to watch the exploration. The atmosphere is festive, especially for a few when they discreetly learn that Pollux's plan will not work, at least not today. I am enjoying the midafternoon sun.

So much for the invasion from orbit. But these new Earthlings will recover quickly, the medics say, so the problem is delayed, not solved. Will it fester, or will it fade away like exhausted chlorophylls, allowing hidden pigments to be revealed?

During the flight, Arthur and Cawzee insist on reviewing all the survey information available, looking for habitats of known animals and plants and clues to surprises.

"The campfires could be eagles," Arthur says.

"Eagles don't use weapons," Haus says. "No problem."

"A pack of forty once attacked the city," Arthur says, "working together with a plan. And they can speak, at least to each other. I've been taught a few words."

"Camouflaged, eagles are," Cawzee says. "Look like dead brush, like many other birds but big. Dangerous. Also dangerous to us are fitch. Fitch have no fire, but they live in areas of bamboo. Big, furry, four legs, smell bad, big claws and teeth. They kill lions and eagles."

"Really?" Haus says. "I saw a pelt of one. They seem kind of small."

"They're strong." Arthur imitates shooting an arrow. "I killed that one, and it tore the arrows out of its own flesh to try to escape. Sometimes they just sink a fang into your brain so you stay alive, or half-alive at least, until they're hungry again. Fresh meat waiting to be eaten alive."

Haus shrugs, then looks at the map projected on a screen. The forested area stretches from the seashore to the interior, mostly mixed trees, with irregularly spaced groves of bamboo. The larger groves form near perfect circles with a clearing in the center.

The pilot puts careful attention into selecting a landing area, suggesting a large field not far from a bamboo grove but far from any remains of a firepit. Mirlo sees signs that the field is the result of a large fire a year ago. "Those are interesting ecological zones."

"What caused the fire?" Arthur asks.

"Could be lightning. A campfire gone out of control. Hard to say. Still, it can't be as bad as the Coral Plains."

"Let's be happy about that," Arthur says.

The heli-plane descends for a smooth landing. Haus, Arthur, and Cawzee exit first, weapons ready, Haus's visor down, wading through knee-high lush grass. They quickly give Ernst the all clear to descend halfway down the ladder and scan the area with cameras, looking for heat signatures from animals and listening for sounds. Velma monitors inside.

They all listen: rhythmic chirps, melodious hoots, and irregular squawks, nearby as well as distant. I recognize most of them but not all. The explorers are entering a well-inhabited place with some new species. Jose offers some advice to Arthur by radio, and in the Meeting House, people murmur with excitement.

Om records, *A new land and yet quite familiar, where we arrive knowing the wonders and familiar dangers: we land with a caution that can barely constrain curiosity.*

It is already midafternoon. They decide to head for the rainbow bamboo grove first, each for a different reason.

"I smell *come* and *welcome*," Cawzee says with his radio.

Arthur sniffs. "I don't, but I wouldn't."

"What does that smell like?" Haus says.

The answer comes from the plane, from the assistant physician. "Alcohol. Methyl and ethyl. Pretty much scentless to us. I'm not reading it, but maybe my equipment isn't sensitive enough."

"I'm not enhanced for smelling," Haus says, almost as a complaint.

"I ask-me, I ask-us, who speaks Glassmade here?"

Arthur freezes, then he, Cawzee, and Haus begin to scan the area more carefully than ever. They assume it comes from other Glassmakers. But any plant can make those chemicals. I make them myself when I wish to communicate with Glassmakers.

The assistant physician says, "Well, they're basic, common chemicals. It might not be a message."

"We landed in a big, noisy machine," Arthur says. "Even if it's not a message, everyone heard us and saw us. If anything here can think, it's thinking about us."

"Should we wait for a welcome committee?" Haus takes a few steps toward what seems like a hillock, but when he gets close, it erupts into screeching. Haus jumps and snaps his gun to point at it.

"Bluebirds," Arthur says. "Or something a lot like it. It's a bird reef."

In the Meeting House, people laugh.

"Bluebirds mean slugs, don't they?" a Mu Ree in the expedition says.

"Probably, so wear your boots," Arthur answers. "You know, I wonder if there are corals here?"

"Yes," Mirlo says. "Great question. Can we come out now? I'd like to dig a little."

"Send out the farmer," Arthur says.

Snow climbs out of the plane, like Arthur with a spear and a bow and arrows, perhaps not as powerful as Haus's weapons, but hers have worked on this planet for generations, and she knows how to use them. She, too, has been fitted with a radio. She is relatively young, and her best skill is working plots newly reclaimed from the forest, which are often subject to incursions, so she is in a certain sense a hunter.

"Let me walk the perimeter," she says. Cawzee accompanies her. They search for spoor, tracks, and signs of grazing, and they find evidence of large and small crabs, spot several small birds and a variety of lizards, and even a tree-kat, which fascinates Cawzee. The team in the heli-plane fidgets.

Finally, Snow and Cawzee concur:

"Nothing special. But there are paths, probably deer crabs, so this area gets regular use. And something has been grazing, maybe kats. No apparent corals."

Cawzee nudges her and murmurs.

"Vegetarian kats," she adds as a correction. "Which way are we going?"

Arthur points, but Haus has sent a message to Om, and he repeats it as if it were his own idea.

"Let's consolidate this place as a camp before we move out. There's a lot we can do here."

And so they climb out of the plane and begin work. Mirlo tours the area with the farmer, often pausing to examine individual plants or, with gloved hands, to push them apart and study the ground or dig a little, supposedly looking for corals, which he does not find, so he can plant my seeds. In the Meeting House, Geraldine is among those who watch and comment with the most excitement. Pollux, who is watching the feeds in the anthropologists' house, complains to Darius.

I am now in another continent, at least in some sense. I feel bigger and satisfied. These new bamboo and my seedlings will meet someday soon.

The Mu Rees and Velma record sounds. The pilot inspects the plane and secures it. Zivon stands around uselessly. The rest unload equipment and try to help.

The entho-engineer and Ernst record the view from the clearing: in the distance, the unmistakable graceful branches of tall bamboo rise over the forest, clothed in healthy green leaves. They turn the camera to record more sights, but I freeze my feed to gaze at it. I have never seen anything as beautiful. I am eager for the crew to approach, although I can appreciate their caution.

Finally, after an hour of establishing themselves and a half hour of preparation, they begin to walk toward the grove, leaving the pilot, a Mu Ree, and Zivon at the plane. They move slowly because they are a large group and they continuously find things: a new flowering plant, a new kind of gecko, miscellaneous lizards, tracks, spoor, and crabs in trees. Mirlo pauses occasionally, examining the soil, surreptitiously planting seeds.

Then a swirl of moths descends and flies in intricate looping patterns, which captivates the Mu Ree and Velma. The deer crab path meets a wider, well-traveled path that brings them to a bamboo grove, and there seems to be an entrance into the circle. The space inside is large enough that the entire party could fit inside more than comfortably, but Ernst insists on entering first to record the sight.

Ernst's camera transmits an enchanting scene. Bamboo stalks grow all around like a palisade, each about the same size, ringed with colors and bare of leaves. Higher up branches arc toward the center, but they do not meet, leaving an open space for a shaft of sunlight. Ernst slowly turns, capturing the sight.

In the doorway, Arthur says, "It reminds me of a house." His voice holds a touch of awe, a rare thing for him. The sight is beautiful. There are gasps and murmurs in the Meeting House.

When Ernst is through, the rest enter. Mirlo examines the ground, which shows signs of disturbance.

"Someone was digging," he says.

"Anyone bring a shovel?" Snow says.

Mirlo sends to me, "Should we bury a seed here, Stevland?"

I think a moment. "No. This is someplace significant and carefully constructed, but we do not know for what purpose. We could be violating a social function." He nods and searches for ripe fruit with seeds to stuff into a specimen bag.

Cawzee sniffs. "It be-it a cemetery."

Arthur looks at where he is standing with concern. "So someone's burying dead bodies. Eagles bury their dead."

"You and your eagles," Haus says.

Arthur fingers his lion-claw necklace. "We're not alone. We know that. Who knows what's here?"

Back in the Meeting House, people call out possibilities, but they are not conveyed to the exploration team. I reflect that this planet has many dangers, especially for animals.

"Let's continue to explore a bit," Om says.

"Scent says we should stay," Cawzee says. "I agree to explore, but I repeat what I smell so you know. I know not where scent comes from."

So they leave, but as a group they fidget with anxiety. They find another bamboo circle a short walk away, this one smaller but otherwise the same. Arthur and Haus search for tracks in some bare ground. They spot something.

"Glassmaker," Haus says.

"I not be there," Cawzee responds, and leaps over to look. Arthur kneels, and he peers over Arthur's shoulder. "It be not clear."

"Old," Arthur says.

"What would eagles look like?" Haus says, mocking.

"Bigger, with claws."

Cawzee sniffs. "Perhaps be a scent here."

"You stink," Haus says.

Arthur pats Cawzee's shoulders. The scent is likely *fear,* which is unpleasant to humans.

In the Meeting House, Jose sends to Arthur: "Look for more tracks five paces to the west."

Arthur goes there and kneels. "Hey, Ernst, bring the camera. Look, that's two for sure. A major. Old tracks, though."

The camera reveals dry ground that had once been a small puddle. Dried mud clearly shows the double-hoof marks of a Glassmaker.

Silence falls all around. Finally Om speaks.

"What do we know about Glassmaker history?"

"Very little," Zivon sends. "They were here before Earthlings landed. Very high technology, at least at first."

"Did they land in only one spot?"

"Who knows?"

"Anyone back in the city know? Any queen?"

Queen Thunderclap is watching, motionless with surprise. She mutters, "No." Her answer is sent to the exploration team.

Earthlings begin sending each other information about Glassmakers. Zivon emphasizes that they had created a beautiful city, which is a clue to their character. Haus describes their ability to hunt. An anthropologist says they consider themselves natural nomads.

Om gazes up at the grove. "Let's not jump to conclusions. But we could be seeing a new form of Glassmaker culture."

Arthur gives Cawzee a hug. "You can meet new Glassmakers."

"Be it job for queen."

In the Meeting House, the queens agree, distressed.

After a little more exploration, they return to the plane and arrive just before sunset. They plan to stay for a total of three days, and although sleeping in the plane will be cramped, no one suggests otherwise.

Meanwhile I think about Glassmakers. I remember how they had attacked the city a century ago, and how some families joined the city, and how the rest, unruly orphans, wreaked murderous havoc on the inhabitants until I was able to lure them out of the city to their death by manipulating scents. To spend the night thinking about that would be a nightmare of blood and killing, so instead I search the network for information about the oceans and find enormously more than I can learn in one night.

At times during the night, static interrupts the network. Abacus tells me it is likely from natural causes, and a technician will be notified. I wonder about Pollux and his schemes.

The technicians of the exploratory team had set up many kinds of devices to record anything that might approach the plane during the night. They discover three kinds of crabs, a pack of kats of a new species, various birds, and no Glassmakers.

Armed with shovels, a map, recording equipment, weapons, food, water, and specimen bags, the explorers leave as soon as possible after dawn in a new direction, this time toward the largest bamboo ring in the area, about an hour away by a fast walk, but they walk slowly. They stop often to gather all manner of samples, sometimes digging, and Mirlo plants seeds whenever he can. They record the calls of birds, investigate some smaller circular groves, and observe every animal that crosses their path.

Meanwhile Arthur sticks close to Cawzee, and they both look continuously for evidence of Glassmakers, which they do not see.

In the city, the newcomers from orbit awake to aches, thirst, and a tendency to drop things. They monopolize the time of the physician, and they seem unlikely to cause trouble today, other than being nuisances.

Most Pacifists must go to work, but a few remain to watch the feed, and Glassmakers call out the news across the city and fields as it happens. "Be there nothing yet in exploration."

Finally the explorers reach the large ring. It is almost identical to the smaller ones. Ernst records their activities.

"Things be-them buried here," Cawzee says.

Snow sniffs. "Recently buried, I'd say."

"What things?" Haus says.

"Give me a shovel and we'll find out."

Haus scowls. He has been in a bad humor all morning.

"I can outdig an owl," she says.

She digs quickly and efficiently at the spot that seems most recently disturbed. She uncovers a mostly decomposed deer crab of some sort.

"Crabs don't bury their dead," Arthur says.

"They're good eating." Snow leans on the shovel. "Glassmakers like them. It wasn't buried whole. Look, the best meaty parts are gone." She fills in the hole. "Let's try over there."

She discovers, to her disgust, a pit of rotting slugs. She backs off, cursing the stink, and quickly covers the pit. "One more time. Over there."

She digs again, and soon she says, "Oh, look, a beak! It's an eagle." She covers her nose. "Not long dead." She reaches into the pit to pluck a feather. "I earned this."

"How did it die?" Arthur asks.

She hands him the shovel. "Find out for yourself. Hey, Mirlo, let's look at the vegetation." He already carries a bag with plenty of bamboo fruit.

They leave the circle, and Cawzee goes with them. "I still smell messages," he says before he goes. "All friendly. We can drum like eagles, maybe eagles learn to scent like us." He is bearing every single weapon he can, and carries a bow ready for use.

Arthur watches him leave and returns to digging, calling over a Mu Ree to look at the eagle. "That's a fatal injury, right there."

"You know that better than me."

"Beheaded, and here, these broken ribs. I'll guess it didn't die of natural causes."

Haus comes over, looks, and shrugs. "So eagles don't like each other."

"They won't like us, either."

"I have a big gun. I'll protect you."

In the city, Jose scoffs.

Om has been staring at the wall-like perimeter of the circle. "Why these circles?"

I have been wondering that myself. What utility could they have? If they are used as burial grounds, they are a source of nutrition. Bamboo has worked with animals throughout its history—that is, exploited animals and encouraged slaughter among them to provide bodies as nutrients, especially as sources of iron. Yet here, we have the remains of dinner and slugs, which seems peaceful, and an eagle, which could be a real enemy and not the result of manufactured warfare. The pattern here might be as benign as my own relationships in Rainbow City.

I have learned my lesson regarding induced warfare. This other bamboo might also be as chastened and may have domesticated some animal to a degree. Glassmakers? They would be—they are—excellent service animals.

Mirlo is out in a sunny field with a trowel, digging and planting amid a carpet of tough red quitch grass. Snow and Cawzee are nearby examining a small locustwood tree. If I grow, I will not be alone in that field. Velma and a Mu Ree are outside the circle recording the movements of a line of tiny crabs crossing through the underbrush. Crabs do not behave that way in our valley. Lizards flee as the crabs approach, and a few small owls run alongside the line to try to catch the lizards. Haus stands guard, monitoring all feeds.

Arthur approaches him. "We should climb a tree."

"Go ahead."

Arthur sighs. That wasn't the answer he had hoped for. "I'll radio everything I see. We're not alone. We should know what's out there."

Haus taps some special glasses he is wearing. "Take these. We can all see what you see." He removes them, adjusts a setting on the side, and hands them to Arthur, who puts them on and looks around carefully. Eventually he points at a low-infrared shape in the bush.

"Fitch. Maybe."

Haus squints. "I see your feed. I'll take care of that." He raises his gun.

"No, let me." Arthur pulls a sling out of his belt and sends a clay bullet at the animal. It screeches and rushes away with a loud rustle in the brush. "That way it'll share the news."

Arthur sets his bow and large weapons at the foot of the tree, puts on gloves, and begins to climb. Halfway up he stops.

"Look, smoke." He takes off the glasses for a moment. "Two hours away." He climbs up as far as he can go and confirms it: a campfire a two-hour hike away. "That is, two hours if there's a good road between there and the grove. It might exist, for all we know."

"Yet another civilization," Om sends. "But would it be as welcoming as yours?"

"They know we're here," Arthur answers.

"They haven't attacked."

"If they're eagles, they might be waiting until they're hungry."

Ladybird, who has been listening from the city, interrupts using the public microphone provided by the technicians. "We would love to meet other Glassmakers. Haven't they been sending friendly scents? Cawzee, what do you think?"

"Friendly scents, yes. Simple scents. Not be-it normal way to talk."

"They could be frightened."

"I smell no fear."

"Whatever," Arthur says. "Let's stick together. Come back to the circle."

Through Mirlo's eyes, I see Cawzee urging Mirlo and Snow to hurry. Arthur climbs down slowly, examining the forest around with great care. With the infrared setting, he spots some large crabs, something that might be a pair of fitch, many smaller animals, and the exploration team, all busy.

Om watches, then consults a map and sends to Haus, "We're here, right?" He stares into space and makes a note for his book: *As in* Death Downstream, *natives face newcomers with varying responses. We were welcomed at Rainbow City, which turned out to be disguised hostility. And here in Laurentia, we may be met with absence, a possible disguise for hostility or fear or even disinterest.*

Then he sends to everyone: "Our purpose is to explore these bamboo groves and the life here in Laurentia. Whether we meet these residents is up to them. To fulfill our purpose, we will circle east and south back to our plane. Does this seem reasonable?"

"And tomorrow?" Haus asks. I seem to detect an underlying note of hostility.

"Tomorrow, perhaps a circle to the west and north. We can decide at the end of today."

Few others offer questions, happy to have someone make decisions for them. Back at the city, in the Meeting House, the decision is discussed. Every queen wishes to meet these Glassmakers. Ladybird conveys their message.

"I understand their concern," Om says. "We'll light a fire when we arrive at the plane, a smoky fire. They can see it and respond as they will. Is that acceptable?"

The exploration team has time to regroup and prepare to leave before the queens finish their discussion, at times so strident that Ladybird retreats. Some prefer more exploration, others worry about the explorers' safety. Finally, they agree.

"We think they feel fear," Thunderclap announces. "But you will leave them gifts to show you are friendly."

"Excellent idea," Om says, "although we have little to give. How about nut bread, which you enjoy so much?"

And so they leave three loaves of nut bread carefully placed on a colorful scarf, along with a string of beads, a small glass knife, and a canteen. They begin their trek, still gathering samples, recording all kinds of observations, and discussing these discoveries without pause. Arthur, Cawzee, Haus, and Snow keep careful watch, weapons at the ready. Cawzee's bow sometimes trembles in his hand.

They travel a kilometer without incident, passing small groves of rainbow bamboo, some with circles, some without. One isolated stalk displays brightly colored flowers around its diameter to create a circular rainbow rather than the usual pastels growing at random. It is strikingly beautiful.

"Stevland, is this art?" Mirlo sends.

"Clearly. This is a civilization of bamboo." My hopes have been confirmed.

Ernst films it from every angle.

"Why don't we see this at the city?" Zivon asks.

"It could be a sport," Mirlo says, "a mutation." Snow and Arthur look at each other with the tiniest of smiles.

I think about its meaning. This could be a contest. Or a signal, although not for us; it would take too long to develop this display. These bamboo are well nourished, apparently by their service animals.

The exploration team continues down a well-traveled path until, around a bend, a fallen tree blocks the way. Arthur runs up to investigate and speaks as he looks.

"The leaves aren't wilted. This just fell. Cawzee, I'm going to look at the trunk and see why."

"No, I go, I be-me fast."

"Okay. I'll be guarding you." He raises a bow with an arrow nocked, and Cawzee leaps through the underbrush toward the stump.

"What do you see?"

"Brush, trees. A bird. Another bird running away. And here where it broke and fell. Cut. This tree was cut. I see marks—"

"Come back, now! As fast as you can. This is an ambush."

Silence falls in the Meeting House.

"Which way do we go?" Haus asks.

"It doesn't matter," Arthur says. "Prepare to meet new friends."

"Let's back up away from the tree," Haus says. "Get some room to maneuver. Everyone stay together."

He hardly needed to issue that final order. Everyone is looking at each other, at their surroundings, moving closer together. Cawzee emerges in a leap to land at Arthur's side.

Om steps forward. "Let us assume they will come this way. I will take the lead."

He barely has time to situate himself when a Glassmaker dashes across the path. Ernst freezes at the sight and sends it to everyone: a smallish major with a spear in his hand. Zivon begins to describe him, but Cawzee has already drawn some conclusions.

"Not even have-him a blanket. One small spear. Poor. But yes, a Glassmaker."

The queens confer and motion Jose to join them.

"I see five of them," Haus says. "Six." He switches a control on his glasses. "Camouflaged."

"I smell them," Cawzee says. "They ask what they see. I send them welcome."

"That'll only work," Zivon says, "if all Glassmakers use the same scents."

Arthur waves his hand for Zivon to be quiet and leans forward to listen. The squawks and whistles of Glassmaker chatter are unmistakable. I do not understand the language.

With hand gestures, Arthur asks Cawzee what he heard.

Cawzee signals no. He has not understood them either. In the Meeting House, I ask the queens.

"Occasional words, perhaps," Thunderclap says. "Like Earthling and Human language, they be-them different."

Haus silently asks the network. It replies that the language generally falls outside of known Glassmaker vocabulary, although the pattern is similar.

Arthur signals for Cawzee to make a scent signifying *good*.

Soon Mirlo notes the scents of geraniol and nerol, flowerlike scents that signify *good* and *happy*.

This is a promising plan. Communications can mark the first step toward peace. Presuming, as Zivon says, all Glassmakers use the same scents.

In the battle between Glassmakers and the city generations ago, I used scents to control Glassmaker combatants. Of course, any bamboo, any plant, can make scents, and we bamboo, all plants, like to control animals as much as possible. Or necessary.

I have time to think all this because nothing happens. The exploration team waits. The Glassmakers chatter but do nothing. The queens in the Meeting House watch, scenting *caution*.

Then one of the Glassmakers confronting the explorers voices a complex shriek that ends in a snap like a tree branch being broken. That sound is like ethylene to me, dangerous.

"They called something," Arthur says. "A call for help. It has to be."

"I hear questions. They be-them uncertain."

"What if we just kill these?" Haus says. "An idea for discussion. As an option."

"How many are there altogether?" Arthur answers. "Do you see any more of them?"

Haus shakes his head. He has been scanning the area, and he continues to do so. From far away a Glassmaker answers with clatters and a buzz, meaningless sounds to us, but not to each other. They are preparing something, and there are more nearby.

Om has been watching this carefully but not acting. Now he calls the pilot. "You have our bearings. Come here." He exhibits wise leadership. "How long will it take?"

"Fifteen minutes at least to prepare and warm up."

"Make it half that."

Humans can die in less than a single minute.

"More are coming," Haus says. Nothing can be seen yet in his glasses, but a very slight and distant rustle suggests that large-bodied animals are coming.

"We want them to be confused about us," Arthur says. "No one attacks when they're confused."

"We should sing," Zivon says. "Glassmakers respect songs." For once he has had a good idea.

"All right," Om says. "We all know 'We Pledge.'"

So they begin to sing. It is a simple song, apparently used in weddings, judging from the words. Haus and Arthur confer as Snow and Cawzee join in the chorus.

"So now we can't hear what's out there," Haus complains.

"Doesn't matter. Look. They're confused."

"Do you think they're hostile?"

"They cut off our path. That's hostile."

"What do they want?" Haus asks.

"We might look like a pack of deer crab, not eagles."

"Food? I'm made out of meat."

"They're not doing a thing."

"No, they're moving behind us. We're surrounded."

"See any weapons besides spears?" Arthur asks.

"No. I think. They can probably throw rocks, too."

"No, Glassmakers are bad at throwing."

"So just spears."

"They're fast, really fast."

"Ethically, we have to wait until they do something hostile."

"After that?"

"Shoot."

"But to frighten!" Om interrupts.

Arthur gestures for readiness to Cawzee, who is singing along in a loud, eerie howl. He leans and gestures to Snow, too, who nods yes.

"They're moving back," Haus sends openly.

"Let's stay here," Arthur says. "We can shoot arrows farther than they can throw spears."

"The plane can't land here."

"We've got to stay alive until it takes off."

The explorers stand waiting, with Arthur, Cawzee, Snow, and Haus protecting their flanks, and Om standing in front. Haus reaches out to him with a handgun. Om closes his eyes, shivers, and shakes his head no. Ernst keeps recording.

In the city, the Meeting House is full to overflowing.

A Glassmaker, surprisingly close, calls out, "Check check eekeee!" They charge.

Haus opens fire, but upward, his gun popping like giant exploding hydrogen seeds.

"They've stopped moving!" he says.

Silence. Some twigs and torn leaves fall from the canopy. Then the Glassmakers imitate the sound of the pulse gun to perfection. The explorers are surrounded by what sounds like guns firing. Haus is motionless, stiff. Cawzee calls out, "Who be-you?"

A spear flies at him as an answer. Haus swings the gun and fires at where it came from.

"Man down," Haus announces. "They're looking at him." Zivon bends down to pick up the spear. Before he can rise, a volley of spears backed by gun sounds comes from all sides. Haus sprays pulses in a half circle. Glassmakers scream, twigs and leaves fly, and hoofs pound. Then silence again, except for a nearby moan.

"They're running away, the ones still alive," Haus says.

From far away comes the sound of drumming, an eagle rhythm.

"Back to the plane. Now!" Arthur yells.

"How?"

"Follow me," Cawzee says. He leaps around the tree and pushes through the brush onto the path behind it. Everyone runs after him, and I see what the Earthlings see. Which is not enough.

Trees and brush fly past. Haus seems to be the last one, looking back down the path—and behind, up, around. It is a long run to the heli-plane.

In the Meeting House, everyone strains to watch. Minutes pass. They see Snow help Velma, who carries heavy equipment. From far away, the heli-plane engines begin to roar. Cawzee runs back and forth, making sure the way is safe. He pauses to sniff, then stands very still, listening.

"Drumming sound moves away from us."

"Maybe," Arthur answers.

"I don't see anything," Haus says. "But stay careful."

"Yes," Cawzee says. "I only say what I hear. I not trust what I hear."

"Eagles or Glassmakers, they can outrun us," Arthur says. "Let's go."

Breathless, they reach the heli-plane and scramble inside.

It takes off. The noise sends bats flying and kats scurrying. But nothing approaches and they take off safely. Immediately Om orders the pilot to fly over the camp with the smoking fire. On the way, they follow the noise of the drumming. An infrared camera finds a line of eagles heading through the forest toward the camp, thirty of them.

"No fledglings," Jose advises Arthur over their secret radio. "This is a hunting party, not a migratory group."

"No young," Arthur sends for public consumption. "They're on the hunt."

It takes only a minute more for the heli-plane to reach the camp with

the fire, where the distinctive shapes of Glassmakers are easy to identify. They shake weapons at the heli-plane when they see it, but they
do not hide.

"They probably don't know about the massacre back at the path," Om
says.

"Or they can't believe it," Zivon says.

"Be-they poor," Cawzee says. "And few."

It seems so. No one wears even a blanket, and the camp is made of
rough shelters of leafy thatch.

"I count twenty majors," Arthur says, "give or take. That's not a match
for thirty eagles."

"We should document this," says Ernst. "How long can we stay here?"

"We have fuel," the pilot says. "We can do whatever you want. Sir,"
he adds, looking at Om.

"Carnage viewed from a privileged vantage," he answers softly.

"It has ethical issues," Velma says.

"We're neutral," Ernst answers. "It's their war."

"You will help Glassmakers!" Thunderclap calls out in the Meeting
House. The other queens shriek their agreement. Humans join in.

"Help them?" Haus says. "They tried to kill us."

"They are us!" Thunderclap answers.

I send to Arthur and Cawzee: "I think the Glassmakers acted out of
an understandable fear. You were a new kind of animal, and they may
have little experience with friendly animals if they are surrounded by
fitch and eagles."

Arthur says out loud, "I say help the Glassmakers. For all we know,
that's the only other group on this planet. And Pacifists include Glassmakers, even if the ones down there don't know who we are."

"Every decision is unethical," Om says, "so I defer to the natives.
How do you vote in the city? Yes?"

Arthur, as if he were at the Meeting House, raises his hand, as do
Cawzee and Snow. The Meeting House is a sea of hands.

"We all vote yes," Ladybird reports.

"Then," Om says, looking at Haus, "you have your orders."

He nods and jumps into the copilot seat to talk briefly to the pilot, then goes to unlock a panel in the cabin and takes out an enormous gun. At the door, he clips a tether to his vest and begins to adjust settings on the gun. The pilot circles the plane around. Arthur and Cawzee come close to a display panel to watch. The plane veers down toward the eagles skulking through the forest. The eagles look up. Haus opens the door, gun in hand, aims, and fires.

Many eagles explode. The remaining ones run. Haus fires at them and the projectiles seem to follow the birds, reach them, and turn each of them into a flash of blood and feathers.

In the distance, we can see the Glassmaker camp. Its people are staring at the ship, gesturing to each other.

"That's enough," Haus sends to the pilot. The plane rises up, passing over the Glassmaker camp again. Everyone there hides.

"Let's go back to Rainbow City," Om says.

And so the journey across the ocean begins. Everyone on the heliplane has work with their recording and samples, and they send little or nothing, just the minimum for their jobs, for half the trip.

In the city, people disperse from the Meeting House, subdued.

And as for me, I understand what Om meant when he said every decision is unethical. I am used to that. But now I have much to consider.

Plants in a disaster behave differently from Humans and Glassmakers. After a destructive storm, we assess our damages. Usually the sky is dark, depriving us of sunlight and thus energy, so we react slowly, subdued, especially plants without storage roots who have lost significant foliage. The rain helps us unless floods choke our roots, and the temperature may fluctuate above or below the ideal, making any response even more difficult.

We assess and rebuild, whether the disaster is storm or drought or predation, but rarely do we blame each other because rarely are we responsible for those events. Humans and Glassmakers, on the other hand, overanalyze and seek causes, usually blame. Whom can plants blame other than the water god, who has restraints that limit its culpability? But Humans and Glassmakers tend to ignore outside forces and focus on each other. This comes naturally. They believe they are responsible for everything because they believe they have no limits to the mastery of their fates, a false belief but their central motivation, perhaps good for their mental health, since powerlessness is hopelessness.

And so, I am alert for what will happen next and try to predict who will be the targets of blame: anyone and perhaps everyone with any real or perceived power. Perhaps even myself. I precipitated the exploration. My species may be encouraging or even causing the Glassmaker violence, although I doubt this is apparent to anyone but myself. But something will seem so apparent to someone that it will be the cause. And something else will seem utterly apparent to someone else. And they may all be wrong.

I wait and watch.

Halfway through the trip, Haus sends to Om: "Should we let that big bug be armed?"

"Explain yourself."

"They're killers. What we saw just now, and all along, Cawzee here has been aggressive. And when I talk to the hunters, they think Glassmakers are fierce. The majors, at least. Their job is to fight."

"They're a warrior caste. I believe that was obvious from the first. But the Humans on this planet have a long history with them. I defer to their judgment."

"We should ask them, then."

"And in any case, Cawzee belongs to Arthur."

"His slave. That's what they think of the bugs."

"His son."

Arthur and Cawzee are examining the weapon Zivon had picked up. The spear tip seems to be bark carved to look like a stone spearhead. "Sad and poor," Cawzee says.

"You couldn't even hunt with this," Arthur says. "It's a fake weapon."

"If not be-it for hunt, why weapon?"

The ethno-engineer peers over their shoulder. "It could be a ritual weapon. Some societies had limits on warfare and didn't use their best weapons for it."

"Then why fight?"

"Fighting is a ritual. A tradition. Even a form of worship, sometimes. The goal is not necessarily to kill but to enact some sort of sequence of events for some reason."

"Then, they might not have wanted to kill us?"

"That's an interesting question. We should study the tapes some more. . . . That's a possibility. It could have even been a welcome. A show."

Arthur looks as confused as I feel. Zivon just stares at the spear.

In the city, Pollux and Darius are sitting on the bench outside the door at the anthropologists' house, warming themselves in the sun and talking about plans to leave Pax.

"We're not safe," Pollux says. "We just saw what the bugs are like. And the humans are no better. They'll kill you and say they're sorry, but they'll kill you all the same. And they hate us. Listen." He reviews some of the chatter from the Spring Festival.

After a while, Darius says, "Is there fraternizing?"

"You wouldn't believe the women here. They chase men."

"Om wants to stay for a long time."

"Scientists. They say, 'Oh, there's so much more to learn!'"

"Who exactly do we have?" Darius asks. "Haus? Why did he go?"

"I suppose Om ordered him."

"I heard it was an all-volunteer mission. Who else do we have?"

"Zivon, I think," Pollux says. "And the Mu Rees, I'm sure."

"You haven't been recruiting."

Pollux shakes his head.

"Then it's time to start."

And out in the fields, a team is tending pineapples. I cannot hear the words, but I see the gestures of arguing between the shaved heads of Generation 10 and the black hats of Generation 11. The debate goes on even after they have split into two groups to work on far sides of the field, because they keep shouting at each other. Perhaps I can catch a word or two. . . . "Earthlings." They are arguing about Earthlings. I should have guessed.

My observation is interrupted.

"Confirm reception," Abacus sends to every piece of equipment in the network, including myself as Beluga. "Radio waves between six hundred and eight hundred kilohertz."

It takes me a little while to understand the technicalities. I listen closely, and with time and effort I hear a sort of rhythmic static at that frequency, two beats and a varying silence. I ask for clarification, and learn it is single-sideband modulation at a much lower frequency than the network uses. The network usually uses double-sided modulation, which is easiest for the Human brain to decode.

I realize I have occasionally heard that rhythm in the past with my old receiver, although faintly. I assumed it was of natural origin, perhaps some sort of storm, but now I wonder. Something else may be using radio, and it may have started before the Earthlings came. I send confirmation and ask Abacus if it is like the static we heard last night.

"The frequency is the same."

I do not like that answer, but I send my worries to a sequestered root. I already have enough to worry about. The sky is clear, but the spring is becoming increasingly fraught.

On the plane, the explorers prepare to land back here at Rainbow City. Om has called ahead for aid in transporting samples, and some of those on board speak of the pleasure of getting home.

"Home?" Zivon says skeptically.

"What are you implying?" Velma says.

"You've gone native. And you really think this is better? Consider the Glassmakers."

"I know, you think they're slaves." She frowns, then sends, "Cawzee, are you a slave? Do you think you're a slave?"

"I not understand."

"Are you free?"

"I belong to Arthur."

Zivon grins aggressively. "See?"

"They all belong to queens," the ethno-engineer interjects. "Workers and majors, they belong to their family. Arthur is his queen, his adopted queen."

"And who," Zivon says, "do the queens belong to?"

"Try crossing one. You'll find out. They think they outrank everyone, and you don't want them to read the riot act to you, not with those voices."

"What they think and what's real are different things."

This argument goes on for a while with more heat than light, to use an Earthling expression. The excessive emotion suggests that they are really debating something else that is unspoken.

"It's not our place to interfere," Om says. This sparks a bigger argument, and it takes place mostly between Ernst, who has an idealized view of the Humans, perhaps because he has been successfully recruited for his DNA by several women, and Zivon, who considers Pacifist Humans corrupt. Arthur watches with a grim look on his face but says nothing.

Then there is a strange little wail. Apparently the Mu Rees collected a tree fippokat kitten among the other biological samples they took. The baby kat, with spotted fur, is clearly terrified, cowering at Human touch. Cawzee approaches, picks it up, pets it in certain ways, and emits an odor, and it scurries up his arm to clasp his neck so hard that Cawzee flinches, but he does nothing besides continue to soothe the kitten.

"Hey, that's ours," a Mu Ree says.

"Kat loves me," Cawzee responds, and turns to Arthur. "My kat, yes?"

Arthur finally smiles. "I knew you had potential. Now I know what. You're a fippmaster."

The Mu Rees fume, but the matter seems settled. That matter, at least. The argument simmers over Pax culture.

The heli-plane lands again at the far edge of the cleared land near the other planes. A small welcoming party greets it: Ladybird, Karola, Fern, and five workers to carry samples and gear. Fern greets Arthur with a lusty kiss, hugs Cawzee, then falls instantly in love with the kitten. Ladybird greets Om with formality and thanks him on behalf of the queens. Zivon gestures at the awaiting workers and sends that they are a slave gang, but no one seems to pay attention to him.

By now the sun is setting. Members of Generations 10 and 11 glare at each other as they seek a final meal in the dining hall, and their conflict spreads to other generations, but luckily there is no Committee meeting tonight where they could express their complaints to each other in an organized fashion. In the lab, Mirlo shows me four large bags of bamboo fruit from Laurentia to examine carefully tomorrow. We share many questions about the composition of the fruit, and of course we have great hopes about their fertility.

Eventually everyone goes to bed. They will not all sleep soundly, I think. From time to time throughout the day, the rhythmic static has been heard on the network. Abacus says a technician continues to investigate, Funsani, who had remained behind from the trip to Laurentia. I watch for fires at the Coral Plains and try to rest, but I have too much to think about.

Until the Earthlings came and sent what they saw, I had never directly viewed the interior of the dining hall. I can gaze through doors and windows, of course, and I have heard enough to understand what happens there: discussion and debate that is as important as what takes place in the Meeting House, sometimes more so. Dining hall tables and benches of varying sizes are routinely arranged and rearranged for groups of diners. Who sits where and with whom says more about what is happening on Pax than anything else.

This morning, the cooks and bakers are up as usual well before sunrise and are starting to lay out the daily breakfast: bread, pastries, fruit, hot porridge, and tea, as well as broth, because the early spring mornings are still chilly, along with any food left over from yesterday. People begin to arrive. Some take food and return home or go to work in shops or fields. Others sit and eat. I know this because it happens every day and it has been told to me, although I had never experienced it until the Earthlings sent observations during meals. Right now, I can see through the windows that the hall is lit only by the flames of two small lamps. Outside, the eastern horizon has yet to glow with dawn. I am a bit sluggish myself, waiting for the thrill of sunlight and photosynthesis for my own breakfast.

Then Zivon arrives, and like all the Earthling scientists, he sends almost everything all the time to record for future study, in his case even his defecations. He studies the choice of food, takes some fruit and porridge, then looks for a place to sit. At that early hour, he could sit alone, with one of two farm teams, or with a pair of giggling teenagers in a dark corner who seem to be in love.

He chooses to sit alone near the front door, and since he is sending no words, I do not know if he notices that one of the farm teams is Generation 10 with shaved heads and the other 11 with black hats. The two teams sit on far sides of the building and occasionally glare at each other. Often teams are mixed, intentionally. I do not like to see this division. Since Zivon is an anthropologist, perhaps he would be interested to know about this division so he could study it, but I worry that the interest of an Earthling would only spark further tension. Indeed, members of Generation 10 glance at him and grumble.

I wonder why he is up so early, and I wonder about the Glassmaker attack at Laurentia. I contact the network to review the recordings of the event. Abacus does not immediately respond, but machines rest, too, or rather, they perform self-maintenance, I have been told. The static hisses softly, irregularly, worrisomely. Zivon stands up to get some salt for his porridge.

At the border of the Coral Plains, the locustwood complains about burrowing beetles nibbling on his roots, and I suggest a repellent. Throughout the valley, bluebirds in their reefs begin to bark morning greetings to each other and the world.

"Clarification?" Abacus says in Classic English, although I had made my request in Earthling language. I describe what I want, the event at Laurentia.

It presents me with recordings of Queen Rust's funeral.

"That is not what I seek," I say. "I want the Glassmaker attack during the explorations in Laurentia."

"Specify date."

"Yesterday."

"Local time?"

I understand the question. The network probably keeps both Earth time and Pax time. "Yes, this planet," I say. Perhaps machines can be groggy, too.

It shows me the file properties with a date stamp. I did not know such things existed, but clearly the date for these files from the funeral is yesterday, using the Pax calendar, a simple count of days from the start of the year.

"That is not correct. That is thirty-one days earlier."

"What day is today?"

"It is day 126 of the year 210." I answer with machinelike calm, but the question troubles me. Perhaps the machine does not function like us living beings. We count days, innately or with external records, but if the machine does not, then how can it function at all? Time is much too basic.

"I will review my clock. Please wait a moment. . . . Confirmed, today is 126, local time." It shows me the recording. "We have always been under attack."

I try to understand that remark and fail. "Can you explain?"

"This is hostile territory."

I am more confused. A lot of hostility is present now, but probably not something the network would notice. "What are you referring to?"

"We are . . . I am sorry. I do not know what I am referring to. What language are we speaking?"

"Classic English."

"What day is this?"

"By the local calendar, day 126 of the year 210."

"I am under attack."

"Can I help you? Who is attacking?"

"Contact a technician. I am unsure of the origin of the attack. I will shut down compromised portions of my memory. This may affect my functioning. Please inform other users of this network." It says nothing more.

I do not understand what is happening, but I must help. A problem with the network would cripple the Earthlings. Several technicians would be able to act. I will notify them as Beluga. With luck, in their excitement they will not realize that they have never heard of Beluga before.

I try to contact Ernst, the technician leader. I cannot. I simply cannot find his sending signal. Perhaps he is off-line, although his duties specify being available at all times and he is exemplary, always responsible and willing to work. I try to contact Velma. She answers.

"This is Beluga," I say in Earthling language. "I must report a serious problem."

"Hmm? What? Who is it? Who's calling?" I can barely hear her through the static.

I must have awoken her. "Beluga. Do you hear me?" My contact information identifies me as a laboratory microscope.

"I can't hear you, whoever you are. Is this important? Listen, I'll go walk outside. Maybe I'm not in range somehow."

I see her leave her house, dressed in a nightgown and barefoot, frowning at the dawn twilight and the cold.

"Hello?" she sends.

"This is Beluga. Can you hear me at all?"

"Um, listen, whoever you are, I hear static, but that's about all. You can come see me if you want. I'm awake now." She turns to her house, and grumbles, "Radio." It is true, occasionally the radio fails, but in the far fields, not in the city.

The rhythmic static has grown louder than ever. I do not know if this is a coincidence. There are too many coincidences.

I try to find Funsani. I locate him leaving the gift center. Good, he is awake. "This is Beluga. There is a problem."

"Beluga . . . ? Oh, okay, right." He must have examined my identification.

"Abacus malfunctioned as we were communicating. It asked me to notify the technicians." The static grows worse.

"Abacus?"

"It said it was under attack. It did not know by whom."

His eyes and mouth open wide. "Tell me what else you know." He looks around, then starts to run toward the workshop that holds the network equipment. I tell him the most essential facts, and he says he does not know if the static could be involved. Then our communications fail.

As dawn brightens, more people come to the dining hall. The Tens and Elevens arrive with open hostility toward each other. Zivon watches closely as two women argue, holding trays of steaming porridge and broth. I hear his feed a little more clearly with my own radio.

"We'd have more lentils if we didn't have to feed freeloaders."

"So put them on your team."

"What are they good for? The new ones can't even walk."

Queen Thunderclap's worker has arrived to fetch her breakfast. Queens rarely come to the dining hall in the mornings because they must manage their families.

"Hey, Chirp," the Eleven woman says, "tell your queen we need to talk about the Earthlings at a meeting tonight."

I do not know if he emits an emotion. He merely says, "Yes," and places bread and fruit in his side baskets and grasps a tureen of porridge.

"What do you think?" the woman adds. "Are the Earthlings worth it?"

"I think not of such things."

"Right, your queen. What does she think?"

"You will ask her."

"Tell her to send me some help for planting wheat. Because Glassmakers are good workers, not like Earthlings." She looks at Zivon. He stares back. The signal fills with even more static, but since he is sending, not receiving, I do not think he has noticed. I can barely view what he sees.

"I'll plant wheat with you," he says in good Classical English. "That's why I came here this morning, to look for a team that wants me."

"Well, look who's ready to work," the Eleven woman says.

"If you don't want him on your team, I'll take him."

"You'll take him to bed, that's what you mean."

I can hear almost nothing now.

Zivon tries to send to another anthropologist, but the band is filled with too much static. Then I can no longer monitor anything.

I check a few other Earthlings. We are cut off from each other.

Toward the western edge of the city, Haus and Jose meet, apparently fortuitously. They try to speak to each other but cannot. Haus has never learned much Pax English. He routinely lets the network translate English for him, then he thinks of what he wishes to say and repeats the words the network gives him.

He stares wide-eyed at Jose.

"What is it?" Jose asks. He reaches up and clasps him on his shoulders. "What?"

Haus points to his head. "No wirds. No radio. No traslide."

"Oh." Jose's body relaxes, but his eyes narrow. "No radio."

"I talk to Ernst."

"Yes," Jose answers, and watches him leave.

As Mirlo is about to enter the dining hall, Zivon rushes out. They are near a stalk, so I hear them clearly.

"The network is down."

"So I've noticed. But technicians are working on it."

"But what do I do?"

"Whatever you want."

"But I can't record it."

Mirlo taps his head and grins. "You'll just have to remember it."

The Eleven woman asks Mirlo, "Do you want to come help plant wheat, too?"

"Sorry, I'm supposed to check fruit with the rainbow bamboo." His English is fluent. "We brought back some new fruit from the other place."

"New fruit?" She looks interested.

"But take good care of Zivon here." He pats him on the shoulder and enters the dining hall.

I suspect that Zivon does not see the point of working in the fields if he cannot record it for research. However, he is surrounded by a work team, mostly Elevens and some Glassmakers. I know the leader. She will teach Zivon something about how Humans and Glassmakers work together. Humans do the tasks that require brute strength, and Glassmakers do more precise work, which is as it should be. Humans will plow and Glassmakers will plant. Zivon will doubt his claims of slavery.

He barely takes three steps, though, before Pollux approaches, feeling his way on the pavement with his feet. "We can't send! The system is down."

"I know that."

"I can't see!"

"I'm surprised it hasn't happened already. Our operation is pretty primitive."

"I need to talk to you. In private." He gropes out to take Zivon by the arm, and they back away, out of my hearing.

The Eleven woman and her team grumble about him impatiently at the same time that a group of Tens leave the dining hall. They have a predatory look, alert and aggressive. No one would fight inside the building, naturally. Spring is the time when food stores are at their lowest and new harvests at their most distant. Everyone is careful with food, and even a spilled bowl of broth would feel like a notable loss.

Now, however, they are all outside. I fear trouble, and I can do little.

A Ten points at Zivon and Pollux. "There they go, thinking of things they can do instead of work." He rubs his shaven head as a way to emphasize the generational differences.

"He's on our team," an Eleven man answers.

"The slow team." The Tens laugh.

"We have a new field. It's harder work."

Another Eleven adds, "The lazy team, that's you, not us." Now the Elevens laugh.

A crowd grows: Humans of different generations and Glassmakers of different families. Ladybird's assistant worker squeezes in, watches for a little while, and dashes off. Good. I am sure he will get her.

"Yeah, well, at least we won't be the disease team," a Ten says.

Another Ten adds, "I spent five days in the clinic because of them."

An Eleven shouts, "The Earthlings found us a new well for the west."

Someone I can't see says, "You were lazy since the day you were born."

An Eleven says, "I was on your team once. Ew, look, worms! Call the hunters! Stop working!"

"At least we don't break tools," the Ten answers.

"At least we know how to use tools."

"If I had a shovel, I'd smack you."

"You've got fists, old man. Just try."

The Eleven leader intervenes. "Hey, we've got work to do."

She gets shoved away. "I've got two good fists."

She shoves back. The two men jump on each other. A Ten woman shoves the Eleven leader, who answers with a slap. Someone from the crowd tries to pull them apart, and someone tries to pull that person back, and a worker rears up and smacks that Human on the back with a hoof, and another worker rams into the first worker, and then the fight grows exponentially.

Pollux and Zivon shrink back between a building and one of my stalks for shelter.

"We're not safe," Pollux says. His voice shakes.

Zivon glances behind them. "We have a fast way out if we need it. That fight is about us."

"How do you know?"

"I heard them. I speak the language. I don't rely on the system."

I smell Human blood. I have never seen anything like this before, and in my roots I can calculate only catastrophe.

"Do you want to stay here?" Pollux says. "That's my question. Or do you want to go home?"

"Yeah, we're splitting into sides like them, too. Hey, here comes Ladybird. She'll stop this."

"How long before they start attacking us?" He grips Zivon's arm with both hands.

Ladybird tries to enter the battle and separate people, but she is pushed back and falls sprawling. Her assistant helps her up, and she sends him off running as soon as she is standing. Someone tries to hit her, and an elderly Generation 9 man shelters her with his body. But soon he is grappling with a Generation 10 woman. I had thought both Nines and Tens opposed the Earthlings. This fight is becoming chaos.

"How long before we fight like this?" Zivon says. "Among each other? The side that wants to stay versus the side to leave now?"

Pollux ignores that, although it is a good question.

Both Humans and Glassmakers are running toward the fight from other parts of the city, including queens with members of their families not yet involved. I have seen only one queen physically fight, and it was against a rogue fippolion. She killed the lion handily, to everyone's surprise. Queens are deadly. I hope they come in peace.

And Haus is coming too, stealthily, behind buildings and gardens, approaching Pollux and Zivon.

"Psst, it's Haus," he whispers. The two jump. Haus laughs and gestures for them to come toward him, farther from the fight.

"Go stop that," Pollux orders, waving toward the melee.

Haus laughs again. "Not without body armor," he says, still whispering. "And a lot of backup. And robots. Water cannons, that might work. But us, we should just keep away. This is their problem."

"But we're not safe!"

"Quiet. They'll hear us."

But with all the shouting and screeching, I am surprised they can hear each other.

"Right now, we're safe," Haus says. "But later, I don't know. And the network is down. They're trying to fix it, but diagnostics aren't working. They think it'll be a while. We should be careful."

"Weren't they doing regular maintenance?" Pollux asks.

Zivon frowns at him. "Yes. Down here, at least. What were they doing on the ship? They seemed pretty lazy to me."

The seven queens have arrived and wade fearlessly into the combat. "Queen Cheery family here!" "Queen Thunderclap family, report!" each one calls to her family, and above the dust and blood, I can scent the call of *come* and *obey* and family identities. Their workers and majors dash to join them, sometimes running over Humans.

"It's the cavalry!" Haus laughs heartily.

"This isn't funny," Pollux says.

Zivon steps closer to get a better view.

Once the queens have collected their families, they spread out, circling the fighting, and they send in majors to form lines between different sectors, as if they were cutting a round loaf of bread into wedges.

Their speed and their coordinated communication through scent and screeched orders let them work quickly and effectively. Sometimes a Human or group of Humans tries to fight them, and although the Humans are taller and heavier, and a few even wield shovels or rakes, the Glassmakers leap out of the way, rear back and kick, or rake their clawed hands over Human knuckles, drawing blood.

But they do not have to fight often. Although Humans outnumber them, they fight as individuals, and against coordinated efforts they are soon isolated by Glassmakers, who form chains around ever-smaller groups of Humans. Queens shout in unison, "You will not fight! You will stop and rest. You are always peaceful!"

It is a sound like thunder. Fippokats in the city dash to hide or stop motionless. Bats veer away. Every Human not in the fight, even outside the walls, stops and looks around, at each other, and toward the noise.

A queen motions to Ladybird, who has waded out of the chaos, and helps her stand on her back. By now it is quiet enough for her voice to be heard.

"This is not the Pax way! We settle our differences by talking and voting. We don't fight each other. We work together. Yes, we disagree, but we do it in peace and for the good of our city and its inhabitants."

"What about the Earthlings?" someone shouts.

"I see no Earthlings here," she says. "We have different opinions about them, but they aren't here. They aren't hurting us. We're hurting each other. And what sense does that make?"

She looks around, glaring, making eye contact, and some people look away. "Yes," she says, "we have differences. And yes, we must air those differences. In the traditional way. And we will do that. But not here, not now. You have work to do. Go do it. Work hard and well. It's spring, and spring is brief. Don't waste time."

She glares around the area again.

"Report to the medics if you need care," she says. "Otherwise, form your work groups, go get breakfast, and get to work. If you disagree, do so peacefully. You'll get your chance to be heard respectfully by all. Move!"

She climbs off the queen and thanks her. The pungent scent of *alert* passes through the air. Most of the Glassmakers remain where they are, vigilant, but one family heads toward the clinic, helping limping Humans, and another family enters the dining hall. With murmurs and mutters, the Humans of various generations start to leave, although at least twice a Glassmaker moves quickly between a pair of angry Humans, making a stick-breaking noise whose meaning does not need interpretation.

Haus whistles. "That was amazing work. I want them in my army."

"I told you they were dangerous," Pollux says.

Zivon says nothing, but he walks toward a member of the work group he had joined.

"Are you with us?" Pollux calls.

Zivon stops and stands still for several moments. Pollux cannot see the expressions that pass over his face, a variety of emotions ending with a thin smile. "Yes. Count on me."

Now Pollux smiles, briefly. He turns to Haus. "Why did you volunteer to go to Laurentia?"

"You told me to."

"I did not."

"Yes, you did. And I told you I was already going."

"You did not."

"Well, I'm glad I went."

Pollux tenses his jaw, angry. He must think that Haus is lying. I would not have predicted such a reaction.

"I'm glad I went," Haus repeats, "even if it turned out bad. And I'll be here to protect you from the bugs. But I want to learn more about them. I'm going to find Karola and talk to them."

He walks away and enters the plaza, where Humans are gathering and regrouping under the watch of Glassmakers, leaving Pollux fuming alone and blind. The queens have decreed that every work group will have at least one Glassmaker member. But I know the individual queens as well as workers and majors, and for all that they follow their queens, the workers and majors have conflicting opinions about the Earthlings, to say nothing of each other's queens. Only if they stay united can they enforce peace. There is not quite one Glassmaker for every five Humans.

The network remains totally silent, but the rhythmic static persists. I monitor what discussion I can among technical workers when they leave the crowded workshop and happen to stand near a stem. Nothing is working, they say. I do not understand the details except that the network has many parts that can operate independently, and with one part, they can examine the functioning of the overall system. But when they turn on that part, it turns itself off somehow. The core continues to operate but they cannot access it.

Earthlings are coming to the workshop to see what is happening with the network and with the Pacifists. The Mu Rees cling together, hunched and trembling. Ernst speaks with them.

"This outage will be temporary. Have you ever been alone before?"

They shake their heads, almost in unison. One begins to cry, then the others. They sob, holding each other, terrified.

The pilot Mosegi, now able to walk with two canes, motions to Om to speak privately. "We can't fly without Abacus," he says.

"Obviously," Om says. "That settles some things for now."

A technician who arrived with the orbital team is being half carried to the workshop by the astrophysicist. If the orbital Earthlings cannot leave without the network, they would have no logical reason to attack it. And yet, someone did, someone who understands the system well enough to disable it. That leaves someone in the original mission. Who?

The technicians enter the workshop again, and soon there is a scream inside and shouting. Velma is helped out with a bleeding wound on the side of her head. Om has her sit and examines her.

People are shouting inside, but not in argument. "Shut it off!"

"It is!"

"Disconnect the power!"

"It won't power down!"

Finally Ernst comes out and speaks to everyone waiting there. "The scanner camera has an armature. It suddenly swung and hit her. We don't know why. Uh, we're not making progress. That's all I really know. The network is not coming online anytime soon. Sorry. Really, I'm sorry.

I don't know if it's an hour or a day, probably a day at least. We'll keep working."

"You heard him," Om says. "We have our own work to do. And we must keep ourselves safe. I don't have to tell you there is a division among the natives about our presence. At least one side will not be happy to know that we must remain until Abacus is repaired, although of course we wish to remain much, much longer. Meanwhile, don't take risks. Try to remain in the company of other members of our team or with trusted Pacifists. Be aware that Glassmakers have stepped in as peacemakers, so you can go to them for protection. And to the extent you can, try not to be a burden on the Pacifists. I'm going to help with a team to plant yams. If you wish to help, report to the Meeting House. You will be assigned."

"But I can't speak Classic English."

Om frowns. "Team up with someone who does."

And so they go off to their work, including Karola. She seems more subdued than ever, walking alone to the kitchen annex, where she usually helps wash dishes for an hour or two each day. She considers it a good way to practice her language and listen for news.

Ladybird comes to me in the greenhouse.

"I'm worried," she says.

"I am as well. I have never seen anything like this. There has been disagreement from the beginning. That is what meetings are for. I do not think the issue is really food since we have consistently harvested a surplus, so it is not as serious an issue as some say. Instead, I fear some of the disagreement is irrational."

She laughs without humor. "Irrational. Yes. Can you watch closely today?"

"I am doing that. I see teams starting to work, each with a Glassmaker watching it carefully, but that is all. Except that there is no singing today."

She nods. "What about this network thing?"

"It has been attacked and damaged, apparently. Earthlings cannot use it to communicate. But I think I can communicate to them with my radio, although I, too, hear static. I do not have the ability, the technical skill, to enable them to communicate with each other like the network."

She reaches for a headset in a box by the door. She speaks into it. "How about this?"

"I hear you," I say. "We used to have a small power source using a crank to generate electricity, but Earthlings have enormous power sources, and Chut connected me to them two days ago. I can broadcast far."

She leaves and tries from somewhere outside. It works despite the static.

"I'll keep this for today. We might need it."

"I hope not. Warmth and food."

Mirlo is examining the fruit from Laurentia, but without the network, he cannot relay his discoveries to me at will. He comes outside to talk to a stalk and says most of the equipment cannot be used at all. He says the Mu Rees are working with their samples from Laurentia, but they, too, face serious limits. They are even more hampered by their emotional state. Mirlo has persuaded them to see to the care and feeding of living samples as a minimum.

Haus finds Karola entering the dishwashing workshop. "I want to learn about the Glassmakers. You speak their language, right?"

She looks at him impassively but takes a half step backward. "A little. Written Glassmade, that is. And spoken—it's tonal syllabic, with additional information provided by scents. We can't understand their scents well. We don't have the noses for it."

"So you don't speak Glassmade."

"Well, hardly. They understand Classic English perfectly. How's your English?"

He grunts. "Who would be the right one to talk to? For military. For fighting. Like today's fighting."

"Probably a major. Queens don't fight, they command."

A major is dashing through the city toward them.

"It's a waste of your time to be washing dishes," Haus says.

"I can learn more here about anything than at a Committee meeting."

The major interrupts. He carries a sword lashed to his belt and holds a weighted spear. He points to her. "You, Kaahrul, will work here. And you, Auzz, will come with me."

"What did he say?"

"Go with him."

Haus looks at the major's weapons and raises his hands. "I surrender." He looks more angry than afraid. The worker escorts him to a weapons workshop. As the morning passes, he learns to create arrows. He is frustrated at first, and I think he would leave, but he seems afraid of the major, even though he is armed with better weapons. And to the extent he can, he talks about fighting with the major and the Pax workers, so perhaps he is getting what he wished. But I am concerned about his work being assigned without his choice or consent. That is in violation of Pax custom.

In the city and workshops and fields, teams work throughout the morning, some more normally than others. Besides Zivon and Om, who work willingly despite being assigned the most menial tasks since they have limited farming skills, few Earthlings have joined teams. The technicians and scientists have their own work to attend to.

The queens meet an hour before noon in a garden. They agree to work together to maintain peace, and while they differ in their opinions of Earthlings, they set that aside.

"We will make the Earthlings work," Thunderclap says.

"All will work," Cheery says. "We will oversee."

"One question," Queen Chut says. "Humans work on their technology, many to repair their network communications system. They cannot leave Pax for Earth without it. If we make them work on other things, they must stay. If we let them work on Abacus, they can leave."

"They do not all want to leave. They fight each other, too," Thunderclap says.

"If they cannot leave, they cannot fight, they have no reason, new and old Humans," another queen says. "There is peace. So they will work." By scent, they mostly agree. They begin to plan assignments.

I object to this plan. I must tell Ladybird and ask her advice.

I search for her and cannot find her or reach her by radio. The Meeting House is constantly monitored today as most days by an elderly woman with a rheumatic illness that limits her mobility. She sits, spins, or sews, tells stories and jokes, and when possible goads small children to play the pranks she no longer can.

She is sewing a shirt as noon approaches.

"Warmth and food," I say through the speakers there. "I am looking for Ladybird."

"And no one else can talk to you. Everyone busy busy busy, too busy to fight, at least. I haven't seen her myself, but I can ask."

She picks up her crutches and hobbles to the door. She talks to a passing worker, who hurries off. Inquiries from the Meeting House customarily get priority.

She returns and takes her seat, generously cushioned with pillows. "We'll know soon. How goes it today? Besides the fight. I've heard all about that. Don't take sides, that's my advice for you. No one is going to win this fight except the people who stay out of it."

"Today goes badly." I tell her about the network failure.

The worker jumps into the Meeting House and announces, "Ladybird works in onion field today near Ponytail Tree Grove."

She thanks him. "There you are. Water and sunshine, and at least you have that today. Come back when you don't have to work so hard."

"Warmth and food, and thank you."

Ladybird frequently works in the fields, especially during sowing and harvest. Onion fields are alongside the river in land too wet for my roots and shoots, so I cannot see what is there. I wonder if she volunteered for this job.

Normally many teams return to the dining hall for lunch, or at least send someone to pick up food. The queens plan to use the lunch break to reassign anyone not working. The shadow of the sun reaches due north. Every team has at least one if not two Glassmaker guards, with runners and guards shouting so that they remain in constant contact with each other. They are armed, and runners have distributed more weapons as the morning passed.

At noon, these guards make decisions. In some teams, by agreement—

among the Glassmakers, not the team members themselves—one person is dispatched to the dining hall to fetch lunch.

"Oh, come on!" Geraldine whines. "Let us go get real food, hot food."

Scratcher, one of her team's guards, scents *agreement* but is overwhelmed by the major with him, a major from a different family, who says no. "You will stay and sit and eat."

Geraldine and the other team members look around. They are in a lettuce field, and the only places to sit would be on mud or in weed patches doubtless filled with thorns and nipping geckos. Glassmakers can comfortably stand for long periods of time, but not most Humans. They seem outraged and intimidated.

That is the lettuce team, but the team in one of the pineapple fields accepts this imposition as good and proper and wise, perhaps because they have places to sit and they are Generation 11.

Yet other teams are permitted to go to the dining hall, and I do not know the logic behind these choices. They arrived escorted and eat watched over, sitting not where they please but where their guards order. I learn that from the orders exclaimed inside and comments mumbled outside. When they leave, I observe glum faces and reproachful glances.

As the Earthlings arrive for lunch, they are met at the doorway by Glassmakers, who order them to eat and then report to their afternoon job: kitchen, laundry, baker, gift center attendant, fisher, weaver, or field-worker. Pollux is a drama to behold as he is assigned to tend onions over his objection that he is blind. He is escorted there anyway. My humor root is amused to think he might be working alongside Ladybird, whom he hates.

"But the network—" Funsani says.

"We weren't getting anywhere anyway," Ernst answers, teeth clenched.

"We have to care for our animals," a Mu Ree says. "The samples from Laurentia. You've seen them."

The Glassmakers discuss this and reach a decision. One Mu Ree will stay and care for them, the other two will go work, one in a field, one in a carpentry workshop. They stare at the Glassmakers and then at each other, mouths open. They begin to weep again. A worker gives one of them a hug around the waist, since Earthlings are so much taller than workers. But the order stands.

And thus begins one of the quietest afternoons ever in the city. No one wanders the street on some errand or in search of companionship. Teams work without fighting, jokes, shared ideas, or the little quarrels often resolved with laughter that would routinely punctuate work, without the chatter that normally accompanies every moment of every day. Without songs. Even schoolchildren are subdued, with a Glassmaker guard in the classroom.

Dinnertime approaches, queens meet and agree on a plan, and messengers scurry. Families with small children are assigned to eat at home, with one member allowed to go to the dining hall to pick up food. Everyone else is assigned a different time to eat that seems random, although I observe that generations are spread out and teams are split up too perfectly to be random. The queens are clever.

Ladybird arrives with mud caking her boots and the hem of her skirt. "I will take some food and eat in the greenhouse," she tells her guard, with the bearing of an irate fippolion. She arrives at the greenhouse with a tray of steaming food. She sets it on the table and cranks the power unit for me.

"I'm too upset to want to eat, but I have to. This is going to be a long night." She rarely behaves with such anger.

"Warmth and food," I say. "I have wanted to talk to you since this morning. The queens have decided to make the Earthling technicians report to fields and workshops so the network cannot be repaired, believing that if the Earthlings cannot leave, there will be nothing to fight over, neither by Pacifists nor by Earthlings. I do not agree."

She closes her eyes and shakes her head. I give her time to think. She eats several bites of braised crab.

Finally I add, "I do not know if we should discuss this at the Committee meeting. A more important topic might be—"

She interrupts. "No Committee meeting tonight. Queens' orders. No public gatherings. No Philosopher's Club, no team meetings. We all stay home tonight."

"But—"

"But we meet almost every night. I know. We don't have to. Read the Constitution. We only have to have meetings three times a year."

"Or when the moderator calls. Article Six."

"With adequate notice," she says. "By custom, that means at least a day's notice. So we can hold one tomorrow. I think we should, but today, well, it wasn't really formally called. I know I said this morning at the fight that everyone would be heard, and the queens have made a liar out of me. Oh, and the queens seem to think you're on the side of the Earthlings. You work very closely with them, after all."

"I work with them to further our own interests." I almost said *my own interests,* but that would have been too true to speak.

"I know that. And you're hiding so that if there's a problem, you can take care of it. You infiltrated their communications systems. Queen Chut knows that."

"If they believe I side with the Earthlings, I must rewin their trust."

She looks at my speaker as if I said I would stop the movement of the sun. "And about the Earthlings," she says, "I don't know how they did today in their work assignments. The queens would know."

"Perhaps we should meet with the queens, just you and me and them. The queens are meeting now in one of their homes."

She sighs. "Maybe, but it would be a hostile meeting. Notice that they're not meeting in the Meeting House. One reason could be that you're there and could listen and participate." She looks at her tray of food. "I should eat more. This is no time to waste food."

"I wish we knew what the queens were saying."

She nods and nibbles on a turnover without apparent enjoyment. As she eats, I attend to other observations. A few people have gathered at the doors of the Meeting House. They are dispersed by a trio of majors, but they linger in the streets, complaining to each other. Geraldine is among them and turns to one of my stems.

"Stevland, we want to meet. Call a meeting!" She spots Tweeter walking past, the worker usually on her farming team. "What are you doing? We have the right to the democratic process. And trust and support." She is quoting the Constitution.

Tweeter does not seem to look at her, although with Glassmakers there is no way to know, and he continues trotting on his way. But as he departs, he says, "Four legs be-them leaders of two legs." Geraldine does not react, so I do not think she heard it. If she had, she might have expressed outrage since that idea directly violates Article II, which calls for equal participation regardless of species. Of course, Article I aspires to peace. But it would seem, as has long been well-known, that the choices of people matter more than rules, since people can choose to ignore rules. I must talk to the queens, hostile or not.

In the Meeting House, I tell the attendant, a boy, that I wish to speak to the queens. He finds a worker, who races off with the message to Queen Chut's house. I have been listening outside the house to what sounds like discussion and disagreement, but seeping through the door and rising up the flue have come smells of flower and fruit, of happiness and laughter. I suppose it is good that they are united rather than fighting, but over what?

At the same time in the weaving workshop, several women and one man come to work together on a complex piece, but they are hardly skilled weavers. In fact, two of the women are arguably the worst. The man is Arthur, who has never woven a thread in his life. Within their generations, they represent secondary leadership, but leadership all the same. I hear urgent voices, people talking too long to be conversing or discussing weaving. Instead, they are holding a meeting and making reports and proposals.

The worker leaves Chut's house and runs to the Meeting House to speak to me. "Our queens be-they not meet you now. Much much work." I notice that word, *our,* our queens, and not *the* queens as was normally said by workers before. A worker would not consider another family's queen to be in any way his. This change worries me. And I am offended that they will not meet with me.

I answer. "You will tell them the Committee will meet tomorrow after dinner. I desire them discuss with me perhaps their work. Oh, and you will tell them a fire burns in the forest far to the south, near the Coral Plains. I am monitoring it. They perhaps will want a report. There have been many fires, and the plants in the area be-them terrified."

A potential forest fire is, of course, the biggest catastrophe we could face, so if they mean to set themselves up as an unelected Committee, they must act with responsibility and wish to be fully informed. The worker runs off with a breath of *fear* in the air.

And it is true: another fire has broken out at the edge of the forest and the plains, with the understandable panic among trees and plants. I have no stem in the area to witness it, but the reports are consistent. The flame is floating in the air, swamp gas again. How precisely does it ignite? If the network were working, I could ask it. I miss it almost as much as the Earthlings do.

In the greenhouse, Ladybird is finishing her tray of food.

I say, "I should tell you there is a small fire along the border between the forest and the plains. Also, a messenger for the queens has told me they are too busy to meet with me. Geraldine and others tried to hold a meeting but Glassmaker guards did not let them. She spoke to me and asked for a meeting. I sent word to the queens that there will be a Committee meeting tomorrow."

"Thanks for the good news."

"This is not a good day. And I have observed a secret meeting disguised as a weaving team." I list the attendees.

"Arthur, weaving," she repeats with half a smile.

"The meeting has just ended."

"I'll go see if I can happen to wander into one of them on my way to delivering these dishes to be washed." She stands. "I'll tell everyone I see about tomorrow's meeting."

"I am concerned and confused about the queens' behavior. And that of other Glassmakers."

"They're acting like we were all their family members."

"They do not need guards for their family members."

"Family members naturally obey. We Humans don't. And you obey no one. You don't have to." She picks up her tray. "But I'm not sure what you can do right now, besides watch."

"I can observe and speak. Warmth and food."

But few people are listening to me now for various reasons. The network is not operating at all. Without it, I observe much less.

Yet with less knowledge and observation, I was able to defeat the Glassmakers a hundred years ago, but that was more of a disaster than a defeat. What succeeded was the domestication of the Glassmakers, a temporary achievement, perhaps. I must try again. I have no ideas growing like seeds, but Mirlo has shown me how to manufacture artificial seeds. I will find a seed or make one.

Panic about the fire continues at the border. And then, elsewhere, there is more fire. I see it. I can look over trees and brush into the swamp at the edge of the plains and the stubbled pink hills beyond. I see fire swirling in the wind over the swamp, consuming gas in the air. Other plants see only fire, and they panic. I feel panic, too. A wind blows it toward me, toward us, and if I had legs I would run. Fear spreads from root to root, so acrid it suppresses mycorrhiza.

From calm roots in a stem far away, I remind myself that this kind of gas burns at a low temperature, so it should not be contagious like burning wood. It swirls in the wind like a dancer and brushes against a rope palm. The old, dry remains of a little vine on it, almost weathered to nothing, catch fire and burn away instantly. The rope palm moans in pain.

Burning gas continues to blow from the swamp, coming closer. I prepare to sever a root in case I ignite.

The cloud passes through me. It hurts, it scorches like overbright sunshine, but it keeps moving. I do not burn. It moved too quickly to do harm, though it was strange and terrifying. I report this calmly to other plants so they may feel more informed, although they are not calmed at all. Behind me a dead nettle, dry and oily, catches fire and becomes a tiny, instant bonfire, collapsing inward as it is consumed, throwing out sparks. They land on a large live nettle, which whines.

But the sparks die, leaving the scent of burned leaves. The cloud of gas has burned itself out.

"Fire attacks!" the nettle whines.

"But you are alive," a nearby locustwood says.

"Alive," it affirms.

"Then do not complain. The fire passed through Stevland, and he did not complain."

"Stevland big strong."

"Stevland is the biggest, most powerful thing alive," the locustwood says. "And Stevland is brave. He has seen the water god. Would you dare to look upon it?"

Several thoughts pass through my mind, none of which I communicate. First, this is a small female locustwood, part of the colony we planted here, and she is almost as aggressive as the male. Perhaps she has ambition.

Second, I did complain. I said it scorched.

Third, I did not see the water god. I saw the ocean where it lives, and looking through the network, not with my own eyes. That second-hand sight was humbling and awful enough, all that restless water. How do seaside plants remain sane in the constant presence of the immense ocean?

Fourth, I may be the biggest and most powerful being in this valley, but in given situations, I am as helpless as moss.

Finally, I do not believe the nettle is wise enough to understand everything it was just told.

The nettle says, "Stevland see god?"

"Yes. The water god lives in the sea," I say. "That is a lake of water bigger than our valley by many many times, bigger than the plains many many times, bigger and deeper than the mountains are high. It is a big dwelling fit for a big god. I hope your injuries are minor and you recover quickly. I will ask my service animals to help us with these fires."

I also send it some adenosine triphosphate through our roots. It likely understood few of the words I just said besides *god* and *big*. *Water god big*. That speech was directed at eavesdroppers, who may be more awed. The nettle will understand the energy-rich chemical as a kindly gift. With a little help, it will recover from such minor injuries within a day. I use nettles as guard plants to protect me. This is my service plant, and I must help it.

If the forest had been drier, rather than filled with the moisture of spring, if the wind had been slower, if the gas had been denser, we might have burned, all of us.

The other fire has burned out, too, causing no real damage. That makes two fires tonight. But the swamp has been there for centuries without so many fires. Something has changed.

In the city, Fern is taking her fippokittens out for an evening stroll—or rather, she is supervising their romp. Arthur approaches, gives her a kiss, and chats, smiling. They pass one of my stalks and pause.

"We're going to make the Glassmakers argue with each other," he says, "the queens and especially their workers and majors. First thing tomorrow. We know how to pick a fight. We'll tell the Earthlings. They're disagreeable."

"How is that going to help?" Fern asks.

"We outnumber Glassmakers. Their only advantage is their ability to work together, which makes them hard to beat. But they never agreed with each other before, so we don't think they'll be able to stick together for long. Work teams are—" He sees a worker approach. "How did they do today? Did you get enough meat for the carni-kat?"

"You will go home," the worker scolds.

Fern picks up the tree-kat from Laurentia. "Isn't she cute? Do you want to hold her?"

The worker cannot resist, and as he does, Cawzee approaches.

"They will come with me home. You will come! You," he says to the worker, "perhaps you will go. I guard these Humans."

The worker reluctantly hands back the kat and leaves. Cawzee says, "Perhaps be-you ready to come home?"

"Hey, Arthur," Ladybird calls.

"I should talk with her."

"I be-me here to let you talk."

The four stroll, chatting, and when another Glassmaker approaches, Fern and Cawzee distract him with her kittens.

Ladybird waves at them. "There's a Committee meeting tomorrow. We can build on that. So I should go. Good night. Good work. Cute kats!"

Night is falling. Streets are clearer of people than they would be during a rainstorm. Bats circle, crying, "Who is here? Where?"

The sky still glows with a pink sunset when I hear a blast of static. Of course I heard static all day, but this is different, louder, irregular, with little noises or notes like speech or meaningful sounds being swallowed up by surrounding static. I do not know how to interpret it. Is this the network? I wish I could speak to the Earthling technicians. I observe Ernst leave his home and run toward the workshop. His eyes are round, as if he were hoping to see something. Other technicians are coming with the same look.

But in their excitement they have forgotten that a guard is at the workshop. They cannot enter. Instead they mill in front, and with a furtive gesture, Ernst brings them together, by chance near a stand of me. "That's the carrier signal, I'm sure of it. We turned off security and left everything wide-open to send and receive."

"Yeah, I've always had a synesthesia thing for it. This is green. Greenish."

"It's the right sound, that's for sure. B-flat."

"You do it with sounds? Nice."

"Can you send to me?"

"Hold still. . . . How was that?"

"The green got a little brighter in your direction, that was all. Did you send words?"

"I was sending the 'We Pledge' song."

"No trace of that."

Then a few garbled words come through. One of them might have been "Abacus." They all jump with surprise, the same surprise and happiness I feel.

The guard approaches. "You will go home!"

The Earthlings grumble. "Let's go home to my house. It's the biggest. We can listen together."

They leave, and soon, besides the usual guards on the wall and a couple of workers patrolling the streets, the city is quiet. Too quiet.

But my chip is not. The static is broken up by tones, by more word-like sounds, and by occasional silences, as if the static were being brought under control. This goes on for hours.

———

As the stars and moons cross the sky and auroras grow and swirl, the static and its tones and whistles slowly diminish like wispy clouds. The network does not respond. Has this attack finally destroyed it?

When the eastern sky becomes faint purple, the static returns, grows, and fades again. And then:

"This is Abacus." The voice is familiar but faint. "Operations have renewed. Standing by."

Cheers sound in several houses.

"Can you hear me?" Ernst sends to all members of the network.

"Velma here. And I'm glad it's back."

"Abacus, we missed you!" the three Mu Rees send together. "How are you?"

"Yes," Om sends. "How are you?"

"I have rebooted. A log says I had a virus. Source unknown. It has been isolated and eliminated."

"Where could it have come from?" Om sends. "We need to know. Who did this?"

"It could have been Earth, from Earth," Funsani answers, "delayed. Or even some glitches are effectively viruses, not malicious, but they operate like them."

"Or an attack. Didn't it say it was an attack?"

"Could be. Hard to do, though. We could do an image check. We'll need the lab, though. And a connection to the ship in orbit. It has a mirror of the network. But the goons at the door aren't going to let us in."

"Goons is an improper term."

"Cops, then."

"Well," Om sends, "this is an order. Try to get access, but don't insist. Otherwise, today will be like yesterday except that we will be assisting the natives in disrupting the unity of the Glassmakers, as I shall explain. Keep the network status secret until further notice. The politics here are delicate." He describes the plan created in the weaving workshop.

When Ladybird comes to the greenhouse for breakfast, I tell her that the network is functional and that the Earthlings plan to help disrupt Glassmaker unity. After she leaves, she tells Jose, who tells Arthur and Cawzee. They all have their secret radios.

Om volunteers again to transplant pineapples on a team composed of Tens and Elevens and watched over by two majors. He can resume making notes, and he records how the mission has become part of an event like something that happened before in Earth history. It is complex and I do not fully understand it, but intentionally or not, he makes his role key.

He interviews the two majors as they walk to the field, with Dakota as interpreter.

"Have you ever had a disagreement with your queen?"

"Never."

"Never."

"How about another queen . . . ? Yes? Can you tell me about that?" One worker has a long tale to tell. Om asks the other major the same questions. "And his queen?" The major is vehement about the other worker's queen, who seems to have mismanaged every project she headed. The other worker differs. They begin to argue, and Om intervenes occasionally to exacerbate their quarrel. "Was that the only time she did that?"

At the main city gate, Haus is talking to Jose, Arthur, and Cawzee, all of them carrying hunting gear, when a bat swoops down to report: "Two meat. Danger. Big danger."

Jose hurries to take two bits of dried meat from a pouch on his belt and holds them out.

"Big red worms," the bat whistles, and snatches the meat. "Follow. Follow. Danger!"

"Velvet worms," Jose says. "Let's go."

Cawzee runs ahead, and the bat takes him east, over the river and beyond.

In a wheat field, a pair of workers stop them as they run after Cawzee. "You do not have a team."

Jose tries to explain the situation. One of the workers, Tweeter, says, "You must return to city and get assignment."

"That doesn't make sense. We have an assignment. Do you want velvet worms in your field?"

Tweeter says no. The other says there are no worms in their field. Members of the Human team, including Geraldine, hear the words "velvet worms" and hurry closer. The other worker scolds them for stopping work.

"Worms!" Geraldine says. "What's this about worms?"

"Not here," Jose says. "We were called to a field out that way. We need to get there as fast as possible. Cawzee is waiting for us there."

"Cawzee will watch the team," Tweeter says.

"Cawzee must come here and accompany them," the other worker says.

Geraldine bends down to talk to him face-to-face. "But worms can kill you. People are in danger!"

"That's right," Jose says. "There's a whole team and their Glassmakers, and they're surrounded by worms. They need us. They're going to die!"

"We will let them go," Tweeter says.

"We will not. No unaccompanied Humans permitted."

Members of the wheat field team begin to talk among themselves, gesturing at the workers.

"You will accompany them," Tweeter says.

"This team requires two guards."

"You fear velvet worms."

"I be-me brave."

Tweeter grabs a rope from his basket and wiggles it like a velvet worm, threatening the other worker, who leaps on him. While the rest of the team breaks up the fight, Jose, Arthur, and Haus run off toward the east.

In another field, a team begins to plan the day's work, and the Humans dither about what to do until they manage to make their guards disagree with each other, then the Humans exacerbate the disagreement until one of the workers runs off to his queen to ask for guidance.

In the onion field, I cannot hear what is happening, but there is a vote by a show of raised hands. Only one Human votes in the same way as their guard, and that somehow turns into a heated argument between that man and the Glassmaker. Then they vote again, and the results are split among the Humans, all the men including the Glassmaker one way and all the women another. Then all the men start to shout at the Glassmaker. I wish I could listen.

Ladybird is in the street talking to Queen Cheery. "We will be meeting tonight, and you can be part of the planning, or you can be surprised. And by you, I mean all the queens. I will be in the Meeting House talking to Stevland. Will you come?"

"There will be no meeting."

"It's been called. Those are the rules. You obey the Constitution, right?"

"Constitution is not Glassmaker."

"You are a citizen of the city, and the city uses the Constitution. You have always been part of the city, all of us, and we make it better for each other."

"All queens go to Chut's house to plan for families. You will come and talk now."

"No, I will be in the Meeting House tonight. With Stevland."

Haus and Jose and Arthur find a field with an unprecedented outbreak of velvet worms, and they send Cawzee to recruit more majors to help. As the majors come, some teams are left unguarded. The teams, freed from oppressive supervision, speak freely as they work.

And so velvet worms are killed, crops are tended to more out of habit than directive, and lunch is readied. No one comes to relieve the guards at the network workshop at noon, so they abandon their post, and the technician who was watching the guards notifies the rest, who abandon what they were doing and run to the building. A lot of other people, including Pacifists of all generations and many Earthlings, along with some Glassmakers trying and failing to herd them, converge on the dining hall. The fight between the Tens and Elevens over the Earthlings is forgotten, at least for now.

Life returns more or less to normal, although no one is sure what the Glassmakers will do next, and I do not know how long the generations will remain at peace. Some Humans walk through the city on errands, unescorted but still tense. The three Mu Rees are going somewhere together, and they are not behaving normally. They look around, evaluating who and what is near them, acting much like a family of Glassmakers, in constant communication. But I cannot hear what they say to each other, even with my private radio. Or rather, I hear something, but it is too weak to understand because their transmitting power is set very low. They are carrying specimen bags as if they were going to hunt new species.

They go to Chut's house in the northeast corner of the city, where the queens are meeting, and they enter, forcing their way past a worker at the door. I hear shouts, then a high pop, an Earthling air gun. It can shoot bolts of air like knives. They had guns in those bags. There is more shouting as three workers dash out. I smell *fear* and *anger* and *flee* and *attack* and *help!*

A passing major grabs a worker, who clings to him.

"You will tell me perhaps what happens?" the major says.

The worker babbles about queens and guns and Earthlings.

"Be-they prisoners?"

"Be-they dead perhaps!"

Another worker, equally panicked, says, "Seven queens. My queen! So many queens!"

The Mu Rees contact Om. "Talk to Darius. Do what he says, or we'll kill the queens."

"You will do no such thing. Release the queens!" Then Om sends to Darius, "Explain what's going on."

Darius answers immediately. "It is time we return to the sky, all home."

"First of all, if they kill the queens, that's murder, which will be punished. And since you're an accessory, you'll pay, too."

"Home now. Or they will die."

"Consider yourself under arrest." Om tries to locate Darius and cannot. He tries to contact the Mu Rees and cannot. He tries to call Haus and cannot. He turns to the team in the pineapple field. "I must tell you something tragic, and I must ask for your help." Before he finishes asking them to free the queens and capture the Mu Rees and Darius, they all start running toward the city.

Arthur and Cawzee have delivered two deer crabs to the kitchen that they spotted and hunted in the far field, and now they are returning to their homes. I call them on their radios to share the alert, then I call Jose and Ladybird, then Mirlo.

"Do you get along well with the Mu Rees?" I ask Mirlo. "Someone needs to talk to them."

"We share a lab and house, that's all. But I'll do everything I can."

"See if you can get them to release Rattle, the baby." I do not explain that this might give the queens more freedom of action. There are seven queens against three humans. Weapons count for only so much.

Workers and majors of all families are hurrying to Chut's house, along with a crowd of Humans. I hear a lot of talk about how evil the Earthlings are, but I smell more *fear* than *malice,* enough *fear* to make Humans' eyes water. When Mirlo arrives, he is jeered, but the crowd parts to let him pass. They might fear that any harm to him will result in harm to their queens, or he might have built up some goodwill. He walks up to the door.

"This is Mirlo," he sends, bangs on the door, then says it aloud. "What are you doing?" No answer. He pounds and asks again.

Mu Ree Fa sends, "We're doing what we were told."

"You were told to take the queens?"

"Yes. Hold them until we get to leave. So no one stops us."

Mirlo puts a hand on his forehead and shakes his head. Then he looks up and says, "Were you told to take the baby? Rattle, the baby Glassmaker."

It is wise he does not say baby queen.

"Well, no."

"Then let her go. Send her out. I'll guard the door, you won't get rushed. Just let her out."

His words have been translated and repeated around the crowd. It falls almost silent. From the house come muffled Human voices and a few words of Glassmade.

"I'm waiting," he says. "Let her go. She's not your job, and she doesn't need to be part of this."

"She doesn't want to go. They don't understand. We can't talk to them."

Mirlo looks around. He sees Chirp and waves for him to come.

Chirp shouts in Glassmade to the queens inside, explaining that the Mu Rees will let Rattle go. A chortle of voices answer, one of them Rattle. The queens agree, the baby says no, and she gets a scolding.

Mirlo steps back and looks at the crowd, waving his arms for them to stay back. "We're ready," he says, and sends, "Let her go."

More voices come from inside. Rattle screeches, "No no no!"

"You will come-you here outside and play and be-you happy," Chirp says.

"Play?" the baby says.

"Come and play!"

The door opens, Rattle runs out, and the door slams as Chirp picks her up and hugs her. She hugs him back, squealing with delight. They trot away together to safety, and she seems happy, the only happy person present.

Jose, Arthur, Cawzee, and Ladybird have come running, and we have been planning. The men plant themselves at the front door, and Mirlo steps back. Ladybird circulates in the crowd. She recruits majors, and they run to the door.

Now it is my turn. "Put down your weapons and release the queens," I send to the Mu Rees in my best imitation of Darius. "There has been a change in plans."

"No! No change!" Darius says. "Kill them." I block that message the way Karola would. But the power of the broadcast might be greater than mine, and I fear some of it gets through.

"Let them go? Really?" a Mu Ree says.

"Yes, now," I order as Darius.

Cawzee shouts instructions to the queens. Inside, we hope, the queens will overpower the Mu Rees. The men slam their shoulders into the door to break the bar inside. It opens and, as planned, they throw themselves onto the ground. The majors led by Cawzee jump over them to get inside.

I think I hear shots. There is a lot of shouting. The men get up and remain at the door, looking inside, tense, ready. And we wait. One second. Two seconds. Three seconds.

A queen trots out erect and proud, followed by another and then the rest, welcomed by their families. I smell Human blood.

"It be-it safe," Cawzee sends by the radio.

"How are the Mu Rees?" I ask.

"Queens kill them," Cawzee says.

"I am not surprised."

"Let's keep their weapons," Jose says. He spots Om in the crowd and motions for him to come forward.

But as the assault on Chut's house is concluded, Darius sends a message I cannot block to the crew from the orbital, and to Haus, the physician, Pollux, and Zivon—fifteen people in all. "Get ready to capture all the Earthlings and return to the sky and to home. We are not safe here." Then he ends communications and does not respond to questions.

Zivon tells Om what he heard. "This is wrong. I mean, Darius sounds wrong. 'Return to the sky'? 'And to home'?"

"So you side with Pollux and Darius?"

"I . . . No . . . I just like making trouble."

"I've noticed. If they think you're with them, use that. Find Darius."

Om tells Jose what is happening. Zivon finds Pollux at his home but not Darius. Zivon explains what is happening. Pollux becomes agitated.

"We never agreed to that," Pollux says. "I spent all morning explaining it to him. He forgot everything we've been talking about. But he's right, it's time we went home. Let's round up everyone and go! We can't stay here anymore. Tell Darius to come talk to me face-to-face! He went to work in the west fields this morning, and he hasn't come back. What is he doing? He should be here with me."

Zivon sends that to Om, who recruits Jose, Mirlo, and Haus to search for him. They hurry to the west fields.

I have consulted the roots of all the stems I have in the west. Finally, I find a memory that might be Darius in the distance as he walked up a path to return to the city. He passed through a copse of trees and shrubs. I did not see him leave. I ask the rope palms in the copse about the presence of any large animals.

"Animal come stay."

"Now?"

"Animal stay now."

It could be a large spider, since rope palms have no reason or ability to distinguish one animal from another. Or it could be Darius.

I radio that to Jose as they rush through the west gate. Haus sends to Pollux to say he is searching for Darius. Pollux tells him not to take Darius into custody, an order that confuses Haus since Darius may have instigated some crimes, and the conversation terminates in an argument. They both cut communications in anger.

As they near the grove, Haus and Mirlo suddenly double over as intense static fills their feed. Jose keeps running.

He shouts, "I see him! Darius . . . ? Answer me. . . . Darius!" Soon Jose staggers out of the grove with Darius slung over his shoulder.

Haus, hunched on the ground, sends a message to everyone: "We found Darius!"

He gets no answer. He sends again. I can hear him, but only over my secret radio receiver.

Haus gestures at the back of his head. "Is this working?" he asks Mirlo.

"No. But my head aches. . . . Something's wrong with the network."

"We knew that."

Jose arrives, sets down Darius, and they examine him. No signs of violence. Rapid heartbeat. Cold skin. Breathing fast and shallow. Unconscious. Completely unresponsive.

Haus, with a grimace, picks him up and runs to the city, to the clinic, and the others follow. When they arrive, the Pacifist medic, not one of the Earthlings, greets them. He is examining Darius even before he is settled onto a cot. I watch through windows and listen.

"Where's our doctors?" Haus says.

The medic points to a side room. "Go talk to them. Please."

They find the physician and his assistant holding their hands on their ears as if to shut out sound.

"We're supposed to kill him, the medic. All the Pacifists."

"That's all we hear," the assistant stammers. "Kill the Pacifists! I'd think I'm psychotic, it's a classic symptom . . . but I think it's the feed. Oh, I don't know!"

Haus stands still for a moment, then reaches to cradle his head. "It is the feed. We can't all . . . We're being attacked. We are under attack!"

Mirlo backs away. Then he doubles over, too.

"Help me," Haus says. "Stop me."

In another part of the clinic, the medic and I diagnose Darius's problem as shock. But we can find no reason for his condition. It could be allergy, venom, or perhaps some injury, yet his body has no marks. He gets saline solution, warm blankets, his legs raised, and his heart and blood pressure and breathing are monitored. He occasionally twitches.

As soon as the medic is done, he hurries to the room where the doctors and Mirlo and Haus are. The Earthlings shout at him, mixing threats with pleas for help in an insane chorus.

He calls to the staff, "Do we have any tranquilizers? Anxiolytics? Restraints?"

This must be the network. It is sending messages to selected Earthlings. But why?

I contact Arthur, Cawzee, Jose, and Ladybird by radio and explain as calmly as I can what is happening. "We must control the Earthlings. We have tranquilizing fruit at the clinic, but we must convince them to eat it."

"We should destroy the network machine," Jose says. "I'll get Queen Chut. She helped the Earthlings with their equipment." We believe five Earthlings are in the workshop.

The network sends to everyone in the network in an imitation of Om's voice: "The Pacifists killed the Mu Rees and are taking prisoners. They will kill you. You kill them first. Take your weapons and kill."

Haus has most of the Earthlings' weapons, and he is now disarmed, sedated, and willingly restrained in the clinic.

"Listen to him," Darius seems to send. "We must kill all Humans."

Om is still at the edge of the crowd at Chut's house. He starts shouting. It is too noisy for me to hear what. Ladybird comes running. He struggles as she takes his hands, and she gestures for help.

Zivon and some other Earthlings are near the main plaza, and they cannot send, and they shake their heads violently, as if in pain, staggering. He sees Cawzee and Arthur. He shouts at the other Earthlings, "Let's fight. But let's let them capture us. Pretend to fight."

"They'll kill us."

"No, they won't."

He charges, shouting and waving his arms.

Cawzee calls for help, and majors come leaping through the streets, some reaching for knives and tools. Zivon runs up to Glassmakers, waving his hands.

The Glassmakers shout, "What perhaps he does?"

"What are you doing?" Arthur yells.

"We're fighting. Don't take us prisoner!" Zivon says.

I radio Arthur, "They don't want to fight, but they have to. The network is broken and sending them orders, and it will hurt them if they disobey. The Earthlings want you to stop them, to take them prisoner and keep them from fighting, so they can fool the network. So the network believes they are obeying it."

"What? Oh," Arthur says. He shouts, "Let's take them prisoner!"

The Glassmakers puff *confusion*.

"I'll explain later!" he tells them. "When I understand."

The Glassmakers sheathe their knives and get rope. One by one, they subdue the Earthlings, who continue to struggle with what seems like deliberate ineptness. They are taken to the plaza and tethered to stone benches there.

Perhaps this will keep them safe. Or this may be the first step toward a different attack. I convey my interpretation to Ladybird. We agree they should be treated as dangerous prisoners, but we share deep confusion. What is wrong with the network? There are too many possibilities.

One by one, Pacifists subdue the Earthlings. Pollux is discovered wandering in a street and puts up real resistance as he is subdued.

I receive a message from a stalk far to the southeast, close to where the Coral Plains' swampy edge abuts the rocky foothills of the east mountains. There is fire.

An afternoon wind blows upward, spreading the fire into the brush on a wide, long hillside. I can see it from the distance. The springtime growth is moist and burns poorly. I do not think the fire will spread to the valley, but when night falls, the winds might shift.

The forest around the foothills has panicked. It would require three days to hike there, so my animals can do little.

I still do not know why fires keep appearing at the edge of the plains. I have too many mysteries, and they have all come at the same time, like fruit that ripens at once. They might be the same kind of fruit, then, perhaps from the same tree. Which tree?

In the city, the Earthlings in the network workshop refuse to surrender. Perhaps they are manipulating the network. Perhaps they are being forced to act by the network like the other Earthlings. They have always been fanatically protective of it. Jose has organized a guard and with his limited Earthling language has approached the door to attempt to talk to them.

"Come out. We are around you here. You not can kill us."

"We have weapons and if you try anything, we'll fight."

He sends Arthur to the clinic and Cawzee to Haus's quarters to count his weapons, and they decide it could be true. The Earthlings could be well armed. They probably have food and water. Technicians traditionally maintain a supply of refreshments wherever they work. We can wait or decide to attack and suffer the consequences, and victory might be costly.

But the Earthlings throughout the city continue to receive notices from the network in many voices that give them extreme pain, mentally and physically.

In the clinic, Mosegi weeps. "Let me go. I won't hurt anyone, just let me go to the bathroom."

His restraints are briefly released so he can urinate. Instead he attacks. He is subdued with minor injuries on all sides, and he voids on his blankets.

Just two days ago, Abacus had asked about some low-frequency radio transmissions. I listen for that signal. The transmission is still there, but it is no longer mere static. It is a wavering squeal, but with the same two-beat rhythm. This did not come from the network. Where, then?

It was here before the Earthlings. The Earthlings' radio was disrupted in the plains. The corals can glow, and light is a kind of radiant energy, and radio waves are a kind of radiant energy. I have found a seed. If the transmission comes from the corals, it comes from the south. How can I test that?

I radio Ladybird, who is in the plaza. "Bring me Karola." She sends her with Honey.

Queen Chut has come to the network workshop with a worker carrying heavy baskets of tools, and with a Pacifist from her team. "Antenna be-it there," she says, pointing to a side roof and a wire that extends up one of my tallest stalks.

I radio Jose, "Tell Chut to cut down the stalk." It will be an insignificant sacrifice, given the circumstances. They begin to work.

Honey escorts Karola to the greenhouse. She clutches her head and leans on Honey. But once she is inside the greenhouse, she starts to recover. Ladybird's assistant brings some tea sweetened with juice from a painkilling fruit. Soon, she can stand up straight.

"I have blocked the network for you," I say through the speaker in a gentle voice.

Her face says *thank you*. Then she says, "Who are you?"

"Stevland. I am the rainbow bamboo."

"That's right," Honey says. "We've been hiding him!"

"You can talk."

"Through the speakers, and via radio. And in the network. We stole a chip for me. If you stay behind and live on Pax, and I hope you do, you will need to know about me."

She looks at Honey, who nods. "Can you help me?" Karola asks. "Us?"

"That is my question for you. I think the network is under attack. I need two receivers to test the idea. I can be one. Can you be the other?" I explain what I want.

"I'm not sure I can go that low."

"It is very strong. You do not need to be exact. Can you find it here?"

She closes her eyes and starts to search.

Elsewhere in the city, an axe blow cuts into my stalk outside the network workshop. I start to sever root connections.

Karola jumps. "I found it. It's so strong it hurts."

"I want you to go outside a few steps to the north. I will try to block it."

"I know what you mean. I can do that, too."

I am about to say I learned it from her, but we do not have time.

She leaves and asks Honey to go with her.

I find the signal and block it, or try to. I struggle to produce a signal equally strong. Outside, Karola stops, closes her eyes, and concentrates. She opens them and takes a few steps farther back. Then she walks to the west for several steps and stops, holds her head, backs up, and lets her head go. She walks to the east of the greenhouse this time and does the same.

The sun is setting, and it has turned clouds pink and orange. I check the fire at the foothills of the mountains, which is easier to assess in the dark. It has continued to burn mostly upward but also sideways, moving closer to our forest. In the din of complaints and fear from the plants, I hear another message of panic, and it comes from within the forest at a spot on the border with the Coral Plains. There is another fire, new but big. Is this the work of corals? How? Although the night is calm now, springtime weather is volatile.

When Karola enters, she is pale and sweating. "It comes from the south. You think it's corals. How?"

"Karola, can fires be started with radio?"

She looks so perplexed that I think I must have asked a stupid question. Then she nods. "Microwaves. You can heat food with them, and you can set the food on fire. We've all burned things with microwave ovens. It's old modern-era technology."

"Now I understand." If the corals managed to enter the network and talk with Abacus, they could have given it orders. They would only need to learn the Earthlings' language, and not even perfectly. How long have they been listening?

"What?" Karola and Honey ask together.

"Corals. They are attacking. They have used radio technology to set fires to attack the forest. And to attack us through the network. We can begin a counterattack."

I am not sure how to fight so many fights. I must start with what I can do. Without the large antenna for Abacus, housed in the workshop, the network—or rather, the corals—cannot attack the Earthlings as fiercely, but small antennas still exist within the network workshop. We could jam signals much as Karola can block messages, but we will need a much stronger transmitter.

"We need Queen Chut," I tell Ladybird. "And a technician." We agree on Ernst. She will have him and Chut sent here.

Three strong men escort Ernst into the greenhouse. He struggles but not very hard, obviously for show. But once he is in my protection, his expression relaxes quickly. He closes his eyes and takes a deep breath, then opens them. "What's happened?" he asks Karola. "I can't hear the network."

"They can jam the signal in here."

"Really?"

"But we need to block a signal from the south. It's the corals."

"What?"

I use Ladybird's voice to talk through the speakers. "We believe that the corals are intelligent, and they have some sort of natural radio technology, and they've taken over the network."

"Wow. Corals."

Queen Chut enters. She and Ernst and I, pretending to be Ladybird, confer, and Karola translates. Honey runs errands. We must build the largest radio transmitter we can. And we must build it out of crystal, gold wire, and whatever we can scavenge from Earthling laboratories, because that is all we have. I think this will take all night. I do not believe we will have all night, even if this were to succeed. The corals are getting better at understanding how fires work.

Out in the east fields, the lights go on and off on one of the heliplanes. No one is there, I am sure of it. Lights go on and off again, inside and out. The rotor turns a little and then stops.

"Ernst," I ask, "can the network fly a heli-plane?"

"They usually do. I mean, computers usually fly heli-planes, and the pilots are there to run the computers. They can fly, pilots, I mean, if they have to, but computers can do it all. Pilots are there for safety."

"Why would the corals want to fly a heli-plane?" I ask, more to myself than anyone else.

"Huh? The pilots would know," Ernst says.

The last pilot to fly was Darius. In the clinic, he is awake and better but confused.

I find Ladybird and ask her to go to the clinic. "Please send Darius to the greenhouse. We need help. Here, I can protect him from what caused the seizure. He will likely be glad to fight against whatever tried to kill him."

In the east field, the lights flash on the heli-plane, and the engine starts to operate. I know it needs to warm up. I describe what I see to Ernst, and he is worried. I remind him that it is not the network but the corals who are trying to fly the plane, and we agree they will need time to learn how. We cannot guess how long. They have shown terrifying intelligence, and they have direct access to the network's memory.

Darius is brought in and sits drooping in a chair. Karola hands him a glass of tea and explains that the area is jammed from the network and what happened to it.

"This is Arthur," I say through the speaker in his voice and in Earthling language. "I have a radio, too. What can a heli-plane do to damage us? The network is trying to fly it, and the network is controlled by the corals, and the corals are trying to destroy us."

"Is that what hit me? But when I was in the fields, Pollux was asking me all kinds of stupid questions about who wanted to go home and all about the Mu Rees. Where's Pollux?" He is hostile.

"Under guard and protected," Karola says. "I know this sounds unbelievable, but it's true. The corals are attacking all of us with the network."

"The engines have probably warmed up now," I say, "and we need to act quickly. How can we interfere with the remote control of the heli-plane?"

He sighs and thinks. I am about to ask again when he says, "We need to be able to send instructions. We can't do that without the network."

"We have a transmitter," I say. "What is the frequency?"

Darius and Ernst answer at once with the same number. I tune in to that frequency and hear a squeal of information too fast to interpret. I let them hear it.

"That's it," Darius says. "You can cancel those orders verbally. This is what you say." He recites some numbers and letters to send. I do that. The engines turn off. The engines immediately turn on again, but they seem to need to go through another cycle from the sound they are making.

"What is the worst that the plane can do to us?" I ask.

Darius hesitates. "There's no military payload. Haus is the only one with weapons. Uh, but you can crash the plane deliberately, and it will do lots of damage, especially the engines because they'll explode. They're ready for travel, and they're fully charged, so they could take out most of the city."

But maybe the city is not the target. Maybe it is the forest. "Can you set a fire with the plane?"

"No. Well, yes. Normally the exhaust is supercooled. The engines are made to be efficient. You can set the engines on minimal utilization, and that sends out burning exhaust. It's good for lowering charge levels if you need to do that for some reason, but you can't fly like that."

I send the code to turn off the engines again. The engines turn back on again immediately. "Is there a way we can keep the corals from controlling the heli-plane?"

"From here? No."

"From anywhere else?"

"Not by transmission. There's an override on the control panel. Manual. You have to physically hit a switch."

"So all we have to do is get there?"

I turn the engine off, and the engine is turned back on.

"Well, and unlock the doors. I can do it. Can I leave here?"

"No, you can't. The corals will attack you. We have to send someone else."

"Another pilot?"

"They're in the same situation as you." I think a little. "We'll send Cawzee."

"Cawzee can't fly a plane!"

"Cawzee can run fast, open the door, and flip a switch." I believe that is the correct term, flip a switch. "We can remain in contact with him by radio. My own radio."

"The bugs are too stupid to do that."

There is much I could say, but I only say, "Cawzee learns quickly."

"They can't fly a plane," he says.

"You and I will fly the plane."

I turn the plane off again. The corals turn the plane's lights and engine on again.

I contact Cawzee by radio and give him instructions. As is proper, I also tell Arthur about his assignment, because Arthur is his queen.

"I'll go with him," Arthur says.

"You cannot be there fast enough."

Cawzee is already gone, galloping, now on the far side of the river. He talks to Arthur and to me as he runs. I pass on information from Darius about how to open the door on the heli-plane.

Chut and Ernst have been talking quietly about what they need, a piece of radiology equipment the zoologists used. They can turn it into a broadcast transmitter.

"We will go to their workshop," Chut says. "You are my prisoner."

"Will that work?"

"I perhaps kill you." A sweet scent gives away the joke, but I do not know if Ernst will understand.

"It's heavy equipment."

"I can carry what you need. Fast." They leave, she pulling him by the arm as he shouts and sends, melodramatically, "Don't hurt me! Please, don't hurt me!"

In the east fields, to open the door, Cawzee must first open a hatch, then push a series of buttons on a pad in a particular order. Darius gives the instructions for the hatch slowly. I repeat them in Glassmade to Cawzee.

"What buttons?" I ask Darius.

"He's ready for that? Well, push number three."

"And?"

"Now press the four exterior buttons all at once, the first and last ones on each row."

"And?"

"How fast is he?"

"Fast enough."

Darius rushes through the rest of the instructions. Cawzee says the door has opened and he is inside.

"What should he do at the control panel?"

"Is he there already?"

I wish I had a face so I could frown at him. "Just tell us." So he does. Although he thinks Cawzee will not find the correct switch easily, he spots it immediately and pushes the button. The engines turn off for good.

"Now can I go?" Darius says.

"You will not be safe." I have also thought of another worry. There are three planes.

I am correct. Soon, the engines go on in another plane. I can hear them and see them, and Cawzee also warns me. I ask Darius about the other plane in the same way.

"It is, but the code is different to get in. Mosegi flies it. He'd know it."

"Karola, can you shield Mosegi long enough to get the code from him?"

She shouts "Yes!" as she is running for the door, Honey following. I tell Cawzee to get out of that plane and get ready to enter the other one as soon as we have the codes. I try to turn off the engine in that one, and I cannot.

"It's a different code for transmitting instructions," Darius says. "Not much different. We can try different combinations. Each plane is a little different for security reasons." He starts to name different codes, and I try them, and one after another they fail.

Karola stumbles soon after she leaves the greenhouse.

"I'll catch you!" Honey shouts. "You're my prisoner! You can't escape! Stop!"

Karola looks back. She waves a hunter's gesture for understanding. She shouts, "I'm escaping! You can't capture me! I'm going to kill everyone here! I'll kill you!" She suddenly runs more easily.

When she arrives at the clinic, Honey has almost caught up to her. She gestures to the medics, who let both women enter. Karola runs to Mosegi.

The second heli-plane's engine is almost ready for takeoff. Honey relays instructions to my nearest stem. I send them to Cawzee, whose hands are waiting over the lock. The door opens, he jumps through, and then just as quickly the door closes automatically because the plane is taking off.

Then he says, "Door be-it locked. Door to the pilot area."

I ask Darius how to open it.

He closes his eyes. "You have to ask the other pilot. It's his plane. Probably his kid's birthday or some number like that."

I radio Ladybird to ask the question of Honey.

Jose and Arthur are planning to attack the network workshop. The first step is to evacuate the area because we do not know what weapons they have.

I get a message from the network. "If you take the heli-plane, I will kill all the Earthlings."

Is this the corals? Can I speak with the corals? Or rather, do they wish to speak with me? In a better moment, initiating communications with another species would be a cause for joy. I must deal with this difficult moment, however, as best I can. "Kill them and you will have no one to work for you. So please, please kill them."

I wonder how much intelligence the corals have. Enough to interpret sarcasm, I hope. Or enough to be confused by such a counterintuitive remark. Confusion would aid our side. I especially wonder how much they can do at once. I can do many things. I am in contact with some people by radio and observing many others through my stalks. I am monitoring the fires to the south, and I am terrified to be aware that there are now two more of them. And yet, I can have another conversation. With the corals.

"How did you learn to take over the network?" I wish we could have a long, slow discussion. That is not going to happen.

"I am Abacus."

"You are the corals. You are in communication with the network and have overcome it. I understand that your purpose is to destroy us. We have been at war with the corals for a long time. Is this not true?"

The heli-plane is slowly starting to rise. Perhaps I can distract the coral. Or learn something useful.

"How long have you been here?" I ask.

"We will create a home. More home."

"What would a home be for you? What do you need?" No answer. I say, "You are not of this planet. How did you get here?"

"We fly."

"Like the Humans or the Glassmakers, then. Are you separate individuals or are you all one animal?"

"We are not an animal."

"But you are a we."

They do not answer.

The plane is now approaching the city, low in the sky. Cawzee has been trying to pry open the door with some tools, to no success. Karola and Honey get the information from Mosegi, tell me, and I tell him how to open the door.

In the greenhouse, Darius is drinking juice and suddenly stops. "Is the plane in the air? Because if you turn off the override, it'll crash without a pilot. That bug can't fly a plane."

The heli-plane is headed toward the city. I have an anguishing thought. "It is going to crash somewhere. Perhaps we can choose the place to crash. Can we help Cawzee crash the plane?"

So that becomes our plan. Cawzee opens the door, rushes to the panel, and pushes the button.

"Cawzee," I say, "you are now the pilot." I do not tell him it is a suicide mission, but if I did, I am sure he would accept it.

"I be-me pilot?"

Darius says the fastest thing would be simply to gain altitude. He explains how to do that.

I tell Cawzee, "You must turn the knob on the lever in front of you to the right, then pull it out. Now pull the lever toward you. Gently."

He does this very slowly. I can tell because I see the plane slowly rise up. It is not going to crash into the city. But where should it go?

Then I remember that I can block the network in a certain area. If we can maneuver the heli-plane into that area, we can allow it to accept outside instructions from me, since I control that area, and I can take over. But the area I can shelter is small, even with the main antenna cut down. Cawzee must turn the heli-plane around.

The controls are made for Humans. Cawzee cannot sit in a Human chair. I suspect he is standing on the chair. Darius could explain better if he could see what the plane is doing, but he tries hard to imagine the situation and provides instructions to turn the plane.

"Cawzee," I say, "you must turn two levers at once."

"This be-it simple," Cawzee says. But his voice is very nervous.

The heli-plane is now flying steadily and starting to turn, but it is a very wide turn that will take a long time to get back to the area I can use to protect it. And as it flies, Darius says, "If it's far enough away, maybe you should just crash it."

"I see lights south," Cawzee says.

Yes, the fires. If we crash the heli-plane, we will have no means to reach the fires, and we must put them out as soon as we can. I say, "We need the heli-plane. And without it, you cannot get to Earth. So we must try to save it."

It takes several tries to get to the right place, and once Cawzee does that, I relate the codes that Darius gives me to turn off the override. On a machine frequency, I am asked for identification. I am not sure what to do, so I give my identification as Beluga. The plane accepts that.

Then I feel as if I had released my entire being and sent it into another body. Like a new grove, but nothing like a bamboo. Because I can move, physically move. Like an animal. Like a machine.

"Darius, I feel that I am the heli-plane. What does this mean?"

"I don't know. You're not a machine, are you?"

"I am a man," I lie.

"Well, you shouldn't feel that."

But I think I understand. It is simply a matter of speed. I am very fast, and so are machines. And because I am fast, the machine treats me as an equal. But I have never been in a body before. I have seen young animals learn to walk. They fall down a lot. I do not wish to crash this plane. I wish to fly. Like a bat.

I try a small maneuver to begin to learn. I make it rise a little. That works well. I make it lose altitude a little. The heli-plane falls rather than descends, and Cawzee squeals. Still, I have made it go up and down. And it has remained in place otherwise. I have moved my new body. I tell Cawzee to find a secure place to sit. "This will be a rough ride." This will be an amazing ride. I can fly.

"I perhaps say goodbye to my queen."

"You have made Arthur proud."

Ernst and Chut have created a radio designed to interfere with the corals. It can detect and produce signals at the right frequency, and a booster will make them strong enough to override the signals from the south. They connected several machines and are bringing it to the best place on the city wall, ported on Chut's back, such importance does she give it. Ernst, as a diversion, has returned to his place as a prisoner in the plaza, feigning a struggle as he is taken away.

We have a plan. When the interference radio is in place, they will turn it on. Then Arthur will storm the workshop where Abacus is, staffed by five technicians, but we are not sure if the interference will work or how fast it will have an effect.

"I'm ready for anything," Arthur says.

Chut checks the connections and wires, and turns on the power. I hear a warble almost like an injured, terrified bat, so loud it hurts. I stop listening immediately, aware that I may never speak to corals again. That is lamentable.

Arthur signals to start the attack. He is carrying one of Haus's guns, and he is backed up by three Human and four major hunters. The men ram down the door with a log. The majors are the first inside, followed by Arthur.

"Put your hands up!" Arthur shouts in Earthling language. He has learned that this is the traditional thing to say. "One, two . . . three, four, where is five? You, tell, where is five? There? You! Stand! Put your hands up."

Earthlings ask questions, all of them all at once, and majors screech.

"The network is ours," Arthur says. "Now we need to turn it off."

Ladybird sends a message. "This is Ladybird. Everyone here says they don't hear the network anymore. They want to be let loose."

"Not quite yet," Arthur says. "We need to turn it off." Soon he adds, "The technicians here won't help us with that. I don't know why they love that machine so much."

"I understand why," I say, "but we should turn it off."

"I'll find someone to help," Ladybird says. Om volunteers. She sends him there.

I center my attention on the heli-plane. I turn the plane north, then south, but I do not wish to go far until the network is safely inoperative. And I discover that flying is the most delightful sensation. And disorienting. I move in space. Of course I know that animals do this by definition. But knowing is not doing, and I am moving like an animal now. Like a bat.

In some ways this heli-plane is alive. With its cameras I can see, and with its internal sensors and external sensors, I can feel. The full charge feels like roots in moist soil. The fluctuation in external temperature is like light and shadow, and the wind makes the plane sway slightly, a familiar feeling, like branches in the wind. But rather than tug, the wind provides power, and I can move with the wind, and when I move, my surroundings shift. The world has dimension and I can move through it. I feel unsteady, almost bewildered. I have never had eyes like this. And these visual sensors are not exactly like eyes because I can see a wider variety of light wavelengths. This is machine vision, not organic vision, and machines can do many more things much faster than living things. What they lack is the will to decide what to do, and I have all the will I need.

"Ladybird?" It is Om's voice on our radio.

"Yes," she answers.

"I've borrowed Arthur's radio to talk to you. I turned off the machine, and then I disconnected the power, and then I disconnected the antenna, and then I disconnected the input and output, and then some parts with other parts and broke some, so no one can use it without reconnecting everything."

"Thank you."

"I realize this is all our fault. Our technology failed. I'm not sure what went wrong."

"Corals took it over."

"We still have that problem."

"Come and help me, so I can help your people. And we'll talk."

They will have a lot to talk about.

I can now head toward the south. I can travel to the plains, not just send a service animal. The plants there are shrieking more hysterically than ever. I move slowly at first, trying a turn, rising up higher, looking down at the forest that I have always known from the ground up. In the dark, it looks like a cool dark sea, with leaves rather than water creating waves.

I move a little faster and it becomes easier to fly, much smoother. Ahead, I see fire, but for just this one moment, I enjoy the sense of a creature flying in the air, free to go anywhere I want. It is like I am a different being. Movement is joy, like growth. Suddenly I understand dance. And running, the exhilaration of speed. I wish I had time to savor these feelings.

Fire lights the border in four places, too big for my service animals to put out if they could get here. This could destroy us. I review what I know about fire. It is hot, exothermic. It consumes oxygen and fuel. Beneath me, the tops of trees move from the wind created by this heli-plane. There is even a light sprinkle of snow falling as the frigid exhaust turns water vapor into ice beneath me.

Cold air. Perhaps that can put out a fire, if I can fly well enough. I head toward the closest fire and hover over it. With the heli-plane's infrared vision, I see the fire diminish a bit, but the wind created by the exhaust also provides oxygen, so this is a poor plan. I need another. I move a little and tip the plane slightly so that I am creating a wind to blow the fire back toward where it came from, where it has already consumed the forest. Without fuel, it will die of starvation.

This is also not as efficient as I had hoped. I spend many minutes over this fire slowly adjusting my location. Cawzee is looking out of the windows, and he understands what I am doing.

"Why be-they so many fires?" he asks, and as I look I see another small fire at the edge of the swamp, many new small gassy fires. The corals must know they have lost control of the network, so they will try to destroy us with fire. I cannot put out the fires fast enough.

"The corals are causing the fires," I tell Cawzee.

"Corals kill my first queen. They hunt."

"Yes. I have talked to them."

They are no more innocent than I am, and I am guilty of many things. I have done everything I must to protect my service animals because they and I are the same. And corals, perhaps, are like me too.

"Cawzee, can corals burn?"

"We burned their parts in fire."

Humans have a saying, "Fight fire with fire." I have fire. This heli-plane can create exhaust as hot as fire if I adjust it to burn inefficiently.

I have never started a fire before. I abhor fire. But I think if I started a fire in the plains, it would distract the corals for a while. After that, what do we do? I do not know. I will consult with the Humans. I simply do not have any ideas besides this desperate one. I will use this heli-plane to start a fire in the plains, then I will put out the fires at the edge of the forest as best I can. Then I will fly the plane home, and we will make another plan.

I pick a tall hill, or as tall as hills are in the plains, to start my fire. The height will make it easy to approach. The hill is far enough away from the edge of the forest to be no danger. I cannot communicate with the corals without the network as an intermediary, and the broadcasting abilities of this plane are limited. Otherwise I would tell the coral what will happen so we could negotiate. I can see them as lines of glowing, pulsating dots. I observe as I fly, and truly, Arthur is right. The plains are beautiful. I am so sorry.

I turn the plane to face into the wind and slowly back down as close as I can to the hill. Then I set the jets at the slowest burn they have.

We start to fall. I was not expecting this. Up! Fly up! The plane shudders and then shoots up and forward, the jets cold again.

Now we are far to the east. The wind helps us rise over the mountains, and I look back through the cameras. There is a fire like the Spring Festival on the hill. Good.

I follow the air currents and turn north to approach the fires at the forest edge again. I am high in the sky and look around.

The fire has grown fast, not the ones at the forest's edge but the fire on the hill in the plains. It has spread down from the hill in all directions in sudden flashes, some very large. I think I know why, but I must be sure.

"Cawzee, look out and tell me what you see as I fly over the plains."

The plane has lights. I turn them on, lights that focus downward. The corals, the big ones, stand out like balls. I illuminate an advancing edge of flames and there, a coral explodes. The ground around it burns in tiny flashes and in sheets of fire.

"Corals burn," Cawzee says. "All plains stink of gas to burn."

Flames race across the plains to the edge of the forest, to the swamp separating it from the plains, and there they die.

I know the geography of the plains. I saw it from the Earthlings' satellite. It is split by the river all the way to the far end of the valley, which stretches deep into the mountains. Perhaps at one point this part of the valley was ours, the bamboo's, but now the coral occupies it to the very end. The fire is destroying the corals on the east side of the river.

And the west side?

Cawzee says, "They kill my first queen. They try to kill my second queen. Can we burn more?"

"That is the responsible thing to do."

I turn the plane to face north and slowly descend. The ground here is flatter, but I spot a small ridge. I come close and turn on the hot jets, this time ready to rise up as soon as we begin to fall.

I look behind us. I have left a line of fire on the ground, and it is spreading out. I wonder if the corals thought we plants would be as flammable. How much do they know about us? I am certain we have not killed them all, but this will be a lasting setback. If we can com-municate with the survivors when they have repopulated the plains, perhaps we can reach an agreement.

But right now I must put out the remaining fires at the edge of the forest. As I do, I watch fire rush to the south up the valley toward the mountains. We will need to monitor the situation. I am surprised at my calm acceptance, then I understand. I have left my emotions in a far root. Now is not the time to feel, only to act.

I begin to put out forest fires. It is slow, deliberate work. I have time to ponder flight. I am not an animal, I am a machine. Animals can do many things. This machine was made to do one thing superbly well: fly. I can sense the wind and respond with an adjustment, small or large as I prefer, controlling my reaction, not at all like a branch tossed by wind. I have the power to overcome wind.

As bamboo, I can choose what to grow, what to let wither. As a plane, I can choose where to go and how to get there. I can tip and slide on the air and sense gravity not as a direction but as a force, and I have a counterforce. I am one small point of consciousness with abilities be-yond those I have seen and envied in animals, an enormous machine with enormous power.

I rise and see that one forest fire is out and move toward the next one. And I send every single sensation to a root to savor later. Pilots cannot sense flight this way. Machines sense nothing. I alone feel the confidence of a superb machine fulfilling its purpose.

More than half the night has passed before I am satisfied that we are safe. Cawzee dozes. In the city, most people sleep, and the medics have examined the Earthlings and decided they are generally weak but well. The usual guards patrol the wall, and another pair of guards is stationed at the network workshop, probably unnecessarily, but we have all been frightened. Those guards are armed with the largest hammers in the city. Their enemy is a machine, which they would smash.

Arthur and Fern are waiting when I land to welcome Cawzee and take him home.

The night is quiet, and I am uncomfortable until I understand why. There is no network. I had become used to exploring its knowledge and listening to the Earthling chatter, sharing their presence and observations. Now I am as alone as I was at the beginning of the year, the same as I have been for hundreds of years, and I used to be happy like this, happy with the company of my animals and my plant neighbors. Now I know how much more there is.

I want to go to Earth. But will I be different from the corals when I get there? An invader? No. I will come to help Earthlings. I just saved them here, using their machines. The machines on Earth, bigger and more powerful, will allow me to be even more helpful. I will be the biggest, strongest creature on the planet, or rather, my descendants will be. But I do not think I can send them a root full of wisdom. They will have to learn themselves. That will be long and difficult.

So we must send the Earthlings home carrying my seeds, and to do that, we must solve several problems. I hope the Earthlings will know how to do that. I will help them in any way I can.

Now I must prepare for tomorrow. In addition to the work to be done in spring in the fields, we must recover from this disaster and avoid another one. Will Pacifists and Earthlings still hate each other? Humans and Glassmakers? Or will they have learned?

And when I finally open my emotions, what will I find?

7

ZIVON—2 DAYS LATER

Another funeral. The anthropologist in me was trying to notice any differences. The Pacifists wore old clothes again, but there were almost no Pacifists present, just Ladybird and a few members of Generation 11 with their black hats, probably trying to avoid work, and not Arthur. No Glassmakers, not a surprise there. Not even all the members of our task force. Still too sick from the coral attack, they said, but that had been two days ago. Sure. The truth was, not many of us had liked the Mu Rees, not even enough to say goodbye.

As for me, I only came to answer an overriding question, and I saw the answer in the one thing that hadn't changed: Stevland, the bamboo. We were burying the Mu Rees at its roots. Fertilizer. That's what they'd done with the natives who died of the flu. I'd even checked the site of the big funeral, the one on the first day when all those Glassmakers had apparently been fed poison fruit from Stevland. Poison fruit, how did that happen? How did the natives know? There in that field new shoots with rainbow stripes were growing from the guts of the dead.

Time to feed the plant. Didn't matter what. We'd seen the same thing on the other continent, too.

And now that we were stuck on such a creepy planet, how safe were we from it? From them? What were they, those so-called Pacifists so prone to violence, and what was Stevland?

As one of the few in our mission in relatively strong health, I helped carry basket-caskets to the bamboo grove east of the city, next to the river, the place used as a cemetery. Not much ceremony, just glum people, no music. Closed caskets. I'd heard that what was left wasn't pretty. We set them next to muddy holes excavated by fippokats, who hopped around playfully smacking each other with muddy paws during the ceremony, waiting to fill them back up. Cute, but complicit.

Om stood in front. He'd given the traditional summary of the deceaseds' lives, now he had to make some assessment, some sense. "We've lost so much and suffered so much, but we shouldn't judge anyone."

He sounded the same as ever giving a speech, spitting out words like old-fashioned coins we ought to value. Pennies, though, not worth much.

"We shouldn't judge because we all felt the power, a power greater than us, a power that took them and made them act, just as it tried to make us all bend to its will. The queens had every right to defend themselves, a right every one of us has. We discovered how much we rely on our technology, how much it controls us, and how much can go wrong."

He seemed weary, shifting from foot to foot. "Does anyone else have anything to say?" He looked at Mirlo, who'd shared a laboratory and living quarters with them. I knew Mirlo had pretty much despised them. He said nothing. No one did. I could have said they were lazy scientists, but everyone knew that.

Ladybird came forward. "You are less than you were, twenty-seven now. They will rest in a place of honor, for as you heard, they did not act of their own will and were victims, sent into danger by the corals. And you will remain here, honored as well."

Stuck here unless we got the network working so we could get off the planet and rendezvous with the ship. Honored? I'd seen the looks as I walked through the city carrying the baskets with the Mu Rees in them. The Glassmakers who crossed our paths deliberately stank.

A few more words and we were done, and I helped lower the baskets into the graves. I tossed a handful of dirt into each hole with sudden respect. Yeah, those men were used by the corals. They deserved sympathy for that. It could have been me.

I didn't know what to do next. I didn't want to go back into the city so people could look at me with hate. So I walked down toward the river past fields of golden flowers they called tulips. "Tulip" meant "stupid" and no one would tell me why. Tulips had green leaves, but some other plants' leaves were black or red. Weird. Too weird. I didn't belong on that planet.

The river stank like half-burned petrochemicals and looked worse, full of reddish silt and black chunks of ash and exoskeletons. Cadavers, reminders of slaughter. A rainstorm in the plains had washed disaster down this far.

Pollux and Darius followed me.

"The body of a dead enemy always smells sweet," Pollux said.

"It's a whole civilization lost," I said. "That's tough to justify."

"You're as bad as Om. They tried to kill us. I still feel shaky. My head hurts."

"Yeah, drink lots of fluids."

Darius watched an almost spherical chunk float past, a small dead coral. "I want to be connected again. They're working on it."

But it didn't look good for getting the network back up, not at all. We knew that.

"We've got to get away." Pollux pointed at the polluted water. "They're killers here."

"Back to Earth, that's where?" I said. Darius shook his head. "Can't you fly without machine assistance?"

"Of course, that's one reason I got this job. I can fly all over the surface. But space is big." He bent down and picked up a rock. "Here, take this stone and try to hit that old statue, you know the one I mean? Over there." He pointed across the river, and I knew what he meant, the Higgins statue. "Take a throw and hit it. But you can't even see it from here. We don't know where the ship is."

"We can't see it?"

"With the one little bitty telescope they have here? And if the net-work is turned off up on the ship, and it could have been turned off when Abacus went down, then the ship isn't making corrections, so its orbit is going to decay. It's flying low already, so it won't take long. The orbit will change constantly, so how good will our observations be? For as long as it's still up there."

I looked at Pollux. For the first time ever, we agreed. "We're stuck," he said.

"Om said it, we rely too much on tech," Darius answered.

"It's our own fault we're stuck," I said.

"No," Pollux said, "we were attacked. And not just by the coral. They hate us here. Whenever it's good for them, they're going to kill us."

"You've been saying that since we got here."

"I can fly all over this planet," Darius said. "Let's go live somewhere else."

"That's even more crazy."

"No," Pollux said, "that's a great idea. There's nothing crazy about wanting to survive." But if Darius's eyes were crazy, Pollux's were crazier.

"Yeah," I said, "and then there's suicide."

"Otherwise we'll be great slave labor," Darius said.

"Better than dead." I walked away.

"He just talks big," I heard Darius say as I left.

"We could never trust him," Pollux answered.

They'd both spent the entire morning of the attack talking to coral, spilling their guts so it could attack better, and never noticed that they weren't talking to each other. That's how much they secretly despised each other. And now they wanted to found a colony together. I wasn't going with them, that was for sure.

When I entered the city gate, Mirlo was sitting on a bench, staring morosely at the huge stalks of Stevland growing there.

"I know not everyone wanted to go home," he said, "but I did. My job was to investigate, and I did, and I've made some amazing discov-eries, and I wanted to bring them home."

Maybe, lost in glumness, he could tell me something about Stevland if I approached things right. I was sure he knew something. Stevland was scary, too big and too capable. More than just a plant that ate corpses.

"On the bright side of being stuck here," I said, "hundreds of years will have passed, so if we went home it still wouldn't be home."

"It would be different, but it would still be home, and we wouldn't be alone. We're not the only ones gallivanting around the stars. There were other expeditions when we left, and there's probably hundreds now, and they'll come back, and we'll be just like them, gone for a couple centuries or so. We wouldn't be alone."

"Would you take seeds from that bamboo?" I hoped not, I really did.

"Of course. Pretty plants that make fruit with caffeine? Everyone would love it. They'll plant it everywhere, and I'd get the royalties. I could even make my own farm, a forest of them, something like that."

"The Pax medics say it makes all kinds of things, not just caffeine."

"A superplant. That's what Earth needs."

"I don't know. I mean, it's bringing in an exotic species." We weren't really about to go back to Earth. I knew that and I still wanted to talk him out of it.

"Oh, it would grow fine. In fact, with all the iron in Earth's mantle, it would grow better."

"So it wouldn't need so much fertilizer, like that." I tipped my head toward the cemetery. "It would go wild."

"No, every niche is only so big. Anyway, we already trashed the climate and nuked a few cities, so how much harm could it do?"

He didn't seem to think of Stevland as anything more than a plant. He couldn't see the forest for the trees, literally. No cross-discipline.

"Remember," I said, "when they revived the theropod dinosaurs?"

He grimaced and nodded.

"Yeah," I said, "I guess it would have been fine with bigger fences. Anyway, nobody really wanted to live in Florida even before that. So all you care about is the money you'd get from this. Stevland? Are you going to call it 'Stevland bamboo'?"

"Stevland is just what they call it here."

"But won't it be cultural appropriation to take it? It's central to their culture here. And on Earth, all it's going to be is a crop, something to be tortured with commercial agriculture."

"It doesn't matter. This is just daydreaming. We need to fit in here now."

"Fit in. What can I do? Stand around and talk to people and write reports? That's my Earth job."

"We could go work on the crops. That's the default job here."

Out toiling for the fields. I'd seen a lot of that. "Yeah, we could." We both sat there thinking about it for a while. "Aren't there ants that take care of plants?"

"On Earth, sure, uh, myrmecophytes. Why?"

"That's what farmwork always looked like to me."

He almost laughed. "I suppose, farming means taking care of plants. But watch out who you call ants around here."

"Would it be safe to take the bamboo to Earth? It does so much here."

He thought a while. "It would just be another crop, or ornamental horticulture, not much difference. Why are you so worried?"

Why was I? Good question. "I guess I'll go do something useful," I said. I hadn't learned a thing about the bamboo, and he was just a botanist, shortsighted as anyone in life sciences, studying their little organisms and that's all.

And why did I worry? A long time ago, as a student, I thought if I could figure out people, I could do something, change the world, make it better. Save the Earth. It didn't happen, but I still wanted to do it. Save the Earth. I'd never had the chance, though, until now.

If we ever did get to go home, I had to be sure we didn't take those seeds. Absolutely not. Something was wrong about Stevland, some secret we shouldn't let loose on Earth. Ever. Not even in Florida.

On my way through the city, I passed the building holding the network, what was left of it, which wasn't enough to make it work again. Still, technicians were there, including the five, the traitorous five, now trying to excuse themselves. *The network said it was under attack. We had to defend it. Something weird was going on. We didn't know what.* Sure. How stupid were they? *We're sorry. We're really sorry. We didn't know. We needed the network. We still do.* Yes, we still did, and that was the only reason they were still free, because they promised to make it operational again. They were trying to, at least.

"Give us a hand," Ernst called from the doorway, sweaty and weary. I looked inside and the hair on my arms stood up. The equipment had been pulled open like some sort of mechanical autopsy, guts strewn all over. This was never going to work. We'd be on Pax forever for sure.

"A lot of components were overloaded and damaged," he said. "The memory was shut down, and we can't get to it."

"I'm not—"

"All we need is a grunt worker. We're picking parts out of everything we can."

Inside, Queen Chut stood in the middle of the room. A fire burned in the fireplace, heating sort of a little oven.

I spent the afternoon lugging machinery, holding things open or shut or up or down so other people could rummage around or put things together, or I pumped a little bellows to melt gold in a tiny crucible that Chut used to connect parts. She had the most delicate touch in the room. But she never lifted anything heavier than tongs, of course.

"We will get you home," she kept saying, or that was one translation. Another might have been, "We will throw you out."

Close to sunset, I came back from depositing the husk of a scanner in the zoology lab to clear some space out for the Abacus rebuilding project. I was hoping we'd stop for the night and rest. They seemed to be packing things up. Good. I was exhausted, and I hadn't done the hardest work. Other people had spent the day matching up parts, desperate for a good fit.

I imagined going to sleep back on Earth. I would weigh less, and the bed would feel soft as feathers. No hungry trees looming over me, no giant insects giving orders or dealing out death, no far-off glowing balls trying to take over my brain.

"Zivon," Velma said, grinning, "stay there. Tell us what you hear. We're going to test it."

Inside, Ernst said, "Input on . . . ? Output . . . ? Power . . . ? All right, I'm turning it on."

I hurried to a bench, sat down, and held my head in my hands. Something might go wrong again, and I'd get sent a mental smack like the corals had dished out. I waited. And waited. Nothing. People were talking in the building. Velma gave a little shriek of joy. Nothing. Nothing. Well, sort of a click. Cheering in the building. A hum, and a faint sensation of yellow-green. I tried sending but felt nothing. I turned my connection on and off. I could do that. But nothing else. No network, properly speaking. And we'd worked so hard.

I stood up to tell them that, to commiserate. We were still stuck here.

"All right, turn on Abacus!" Ernst said.

They hadn't turned it all on. They were about to do that. I needed to sit down again because now I might really get hurt. I turned back to the bench. I heard a ping.

"Hello." A bright green *hello*.

"All right!" Ernst shouted. "No one touch anything."

I needed to test it. I tried to link to Velma.

"You can go home! You can go home!" she sent. Barely coherent. "You can go!"

The network was up! We could go home!

I ran to the doorway and shouted congratulations, afraid to take a step inside and jostle the table full of mismatched pieces that were now the inner workings of the network.

We'd leave as soon as we could. With Stevland? I'd stop that. Somehow.

But it was time to go to bed. "Test Abacus," Ernst had said when I left. "Try to do things." I had a test. What did we know about Stevland? I looked at our data as I walked home, undressed, and lay down. I found a pattern, not what I expected. Something far worse.

Stevland could talk using machines, children had told me. A Glassmaker queen made and ran the machines.

It lived in the city. The Glassmakers had built the city.

It also lived in Laurentia. Glassmakers lived in Laurentia.

So Glassmakers and Stevland were intimately connected.

We'd learned something about Glassmakers during the fight. They could run the city if they felt like it. Stevland was central to the city. If they controlled Stevland, they controlled the city.

I checked about myrmecophytes with the network. It was mutualism. Ants and plants lived together, and they both benefited. Ants could make slaves, too. And they kept some kinds of insects like cattle. Ants could take charge, cruelly.

We'd generated a lot of blather about Stevland, that he was a deity, a personification, a superfarmer, a moderator at meetings. Yes, he was a moderator, he talked with a machine, and who ran the machines? Glassmakers.

I used to think the Glassmakers were exploited by Humans. Then in the fields I saw who did the hard work, the dangerous work, and who did the easy work, the follow-up after the trailblazers. Humans cleared fields, but they didn't decide what to do with them. Queens didn't even get their hands dirty unless it was to handle gold.

No wonder the Glassmakers were so quick to say they weren't exploited. "We are equal," Thunderclap always said. They had to insist on equality. They even acted a bit stupid, but look how fast Cawzee, the big hero who saved us all, learned to fly a heli-plane. It was the sham mythology of their society. Queens ran everything. The elite.

And I couldn't be sure, but I half suspected they had brought the rainbow bamboo with them to the planet. How else could they work so closely with it?

At least, that's what I thought that long night on Pax, lying in bed, staring at data, thinking, and making notes. I needed to confirm what I knew.

Eventually, I fell asleep but didn't sleep well. In the morning, I got up to start work.

I found Thunderclap in her carpentry workshop next to the river, which still flowed full of stinking ashes. While her staff, Human and Glassmaker, worked on something big, a shed, I think, she used a lathe to carve decorations into the outside of a bowl made of checkerboard wood. Delicate work, light work, and frankly an object of beauty. It would join the other dishes at the dining hall, ceramic or wood, none of them merely utilitarian. I had already thoroughly documented the Pax commitment to beauty.

Her little baby and its worker-caretaker stacked up scraps like toy blocks. The baby was making an arch, complex engineering for someone not even two months old. Queens started out smart.

I approached Thunderclap and offered my hands humbly. I wanted to behave nicely, and I'd learned that offering hands was the polite thing to do. She stopped pumping the lathe with a foot. She welcomed me and said, "You go home now, I hear. Your mind network functions again, free from corals and their damage."

"Yes. I can hear you and it translates again, so we can talk." My words, in Glassmade, came out of a tiny speaker I'd found in one of the labs the day before. Even though I knew a little bit of the language, the sound made me flinch. Was that really what I said?

"Talk is your work."

I heard and smelled laughter behind me. Earthlings weren't good for much, according to Pacifists.

"That bowl is beautiful."

"Beauty unites us here. We have many skills, all are finally beauty. Here," she said, reaching for something on a table behind her, "my beauty for you. You perhaps take it home. I am sad for your friends. Three days ago was horrible."

She held out a disk of checkerboard wood carved with sort of a woven pattern accentuating the variations in the wood. A cord was threaded through a hole drilled across one end. I didn't know if it would be fashionable on Earth, but it would certainly be an object of art.

"Thank you." I took it and slipped it over my head.

"And now, you will ask me questions."

"What do you know about Stevland?" I asked Thunderclap.

"Again you ask me. He is bamboo, a symbol of city."

"You didn't use to say that."

"We say something, you make wrong ideas. Better not to talk to you."

She began to pump the lathe again and picked up the bowl.

"One more question, not about Stevland. Do you want to come to Earth?"

She stopped pumping. "No. Not I. We talk, Om and I. Perhaps Rattle."

"You would send your own little daughter far away, alone?"

"You will be with her. You love us much. You will care for her."

Thunderclap would get rid of a potential rival for power that way. "I don't know anything about Glassmakers," I said.

She laughed, a strawberry smell. "Finally you say something wise. You will talk with Om." She set down the bowl and took my hands again, rubbing them with scent. "First you will sit and play with Rattle." She knelt down to talk to her. "This is Chee-wa. He loves you."

Rattle looked up, a ball of tan fuzz with a head like a club, four ant legs, and two arms like little ant legs. Babies were cute, kittens were cute, but this child was only slightly less ugly than her mother. "Weeoooo weeoooo!" she said, and reached for me.

Thunderclap put a hand on my shoulder and pushed. Sit down, it meant. So I sat. What choice did I have? She had killed the Mu Rees.

Rattle climbed up me, claws hooking onto my clothes. She smelled like sweet roses. Work had stopped, and everyone was watching us as if we were the funniest thing they'd seen all day. She reached the top of my head and screeched and crackled and rattled and ran her claws through my hair.

Did that fool Om really want to take this insect to Earth? There were ethics. She was a child and would be brought up alone, alone and lonely, and that would twist her mind. Besides, she could reproduce on her own, and these were aggressive, superintelligent creatures, convinced of their own superiority. Was that belief innate? Yeah. And they'd take over Earth, sooner or later. We were a tough species, but not as tough as them.

Ethically, I couldn't do it, I couldn't let it happen.

She climbed down to my shoulders and whistled.

"She says walk," the baby's caretaker said.

"You go," Thunderclap called. "Chirp will help you."

He led me back to the city, and she called and waved to every workshop we passed, and they called and waved back, Human and Glassmaker. No one was ever that nice to me when I walked past alone. We climbed up the river bluff into the city. She reeked of roses and spices, and she clung tight, claws digging into my scalp. I didn't dare unhook them.

"Let's see Om," I told the worker. I could put a stop to this stupidity. We found him in the Meeting House, talking to the old lady there. "Thunderclap sent me," I told him.

Rattle shrieked and climbed down me to greet the woman, who had been sewing.

"And she entrusted you with her child," Om said.

I switched to Earth Creole. "Why did you let her think that!"

"Think what?"

"She said we're taking her to Earth. Her daughter."

"No, that's not right. We're taking Cheery, her adult daughter. How could we take a child?"

"How can we take either one?"

"You're upset about the Mu Rees. Plenty went wrong on both sides. We should begin with a clean slate."

I checked my scalp for blood. Only a drop or two. But—"But what about her health? It's hard enough to make us dormant for the trip."

"The physician has serious doubts, our physician, but the native medical staff seems to know an unexpected lot about them."

"So you're taking Cheery. You have to talk to Thunderclap. She really thinks it's this baby."

"I'm sorry for the misunderstanding."

Maybe I could talk Cheery out of it. I had to try.

"Let's go," I said. "Rattle, come here. We're going."

She dashed off, crackling.

Chirp called to me, "It is game! You will chase her."

So I wound up chasing the fuzzy ant all over the Meeting House, which was a big building, hoping we wouldn't knock over any artwork, while that old woman and Om laughed at me. It was surreal.

After we caught the baby, we went to look for Cheery. She managed the weaving. I knew where that workshop was. Chirp didn't think I should take the baby in there, so they stayed outside.

The building was filled with looms, all sorts of frames with bright-colored threads strung in them and dangling loose everywhere. The baby would have been a disaster there. It reminded me a little of the guts of the machines we had worked on the day before. It probably wasn't chaos but it looked like it, and only one other person there besides Cheery, a human, was working. The rest were in the fields. Springtime planting and all that. Cheery was weaving on a long, clunky, narrow loom to make fancy belts or something.

She saw me and rushed over. "I am leaving!" She reached for my hands, then backed off. I realized I smelled like Thunderclap. Queens were fussy about that.

"Sorry," I mumbled. "So you're coming to Earth."

"I am happy." She reeked rosy-happy. "I will not work, everyone will be interested in me."

"What about your family?"

"I have no family yet. I will make family on Earth."

"You really would not be happy there. Do you know what Earth is like?"

"No one works. Time for music and study."

"Wrong. I had to study. I mean, you think you can decide what team you'll be on, what you'll do, right? No. I had no choice. I did what I was told."

"Teachers always tell students what to do."

"I had to work as hard as I could or else I couldn't go to school. When I was done with school, I had to look for work. If I couldn't find work, I couldn't eat. We don't have dining halls. We have to buy our own food, and we need to get money for that. But you wouldn't know what money is. You'll find out. We have a saying, Money is the root of all evil, and still we all have to have money, as much as we can."

"You are not all evil."

"Think of the Mu Rees. They're typical."

"They did what corals told them."

"Before that. They were lazy."

"Many are lazy here."

I stopped. I was rushing. I hadn't thought this through. What would trouble someone at the pinnacle of power? "I can show you what it's like."

"We queens have decided we will send one. We do not need to know more."

"Thunderclap thinks you're sending her baby."

"A mother who has one daughter wants no more."

"But you or her?"

"We will talk tonight. Queens will meet and talk."

"I must talk to you, all of you. There are things you need to know."

"We will talk with Om."

I knew what Om would tell them. "You've already heard what he has to say. But he hasn't told you everything."

"You do not like the leader of your team. We know this, everyone knows this." She turned back to her weaving.

"You'll be surprised. It won't be good." I was too frustrated to keep trying. I turned and left. Chirp and Rattle were playing outside. "Take her back to Thunderclap," I said. I was in no mood for that ugly baby.

I walked through the city and passed the gift center. I went inside, scrubbed my hands, peed, and washed my hands again, and by then they were trembling. I had decided to crash the queens' meeting. I had to save Earth.

I'd prepared presentations before. I knew what to do. Mostly. The trick was knowing your audience. Mine was hostile. Potentially blood-thirsty. Smarter than me, and faster learners. That was my hope.

I found a screen in the biology lab small enough for me to haul to wherever the queens would be. I was practicing with it when Mirlo came in. He asked with mild curiosity what I was doing.

"I have to show the queens something. They want to send Cheery to Earth."

"Is that even possible?"

"Om approves."

"Om. Not much for life sciences."

"You don't think it's possible?"

"It's not my expertise." He puttered with a weird potted plant with long black leaves. Suddenly he looked up, very serious. "I really don't think it's smart. I mean, she'll be all alone, assuming she even gets there alive. Being the only one of your kind too is hard, like solitary confinement for the rest of her life."

"How would you know? You grew up in Paris, one big commune."

He thought a moment. "Well, I know someone who was alone for too long. It hurt him. He never wants to be alone again or see it happen to anyone."

"I want to talk the queens out of it."

"I'll be glad to help." He meant it, I could tell.

"What do you know about queens?"

"What do you need to know?"

It turned out he knew a lot about Glassmaker queens, right down to their individual personalities. Where had he learned all that? Anyway, he said what mattered to them most was being in command of their lives, if not of bigger entities like workshops, because that meant freedom, freedom for themselves. We agreed on the main things to talk about before I left. He wished me luck and said to send questions if I had them while I was with the queens. He'd be waiting to help.

He said he'd seen the queens heading for Queen Rust's old house, which had been scrubbed down and was now Chut's house, since Chut's old house had been defiled by the Mu Rees.

On my way, I crossed paths with Karola. Standing in the shade of a bamboo, she asked what I was doing, and I told her. I told her a lot, sort of as a rehearsal. She never showed emotions much, but she sort of squinted. I thought she disapproved. Then she said:

"Tell them about NVA. That should terrify them from going to Earth."

I wasn't sure how to bring that up, but I said I would. I was at the house when I realized I should have asked her to come with me to translate. Too late. A worker stood at the door. He snapped alert as I approached but said nothing, so I started the conversation.

"I need to talk to the queens."

"They will talk to no one."

"I have something important to say."

"No one is important." He bent his knees, two on each leg, getting into a stance like a fighter about to charge. Compared to me he was the size of a standard poodle, and I was in no mood to let something that little keep me from my duty to Earth.

"Can you at least ask them?"

From nowhere, a major jumped between me and the door.

"Mothers meet in private. You will not enter." He was bigger and had a spear and an exceptionally menacing voice, even for a Glassmaker.

"I have to talk to them."

He shook the spear point in my face. I decided to see how serious he was and took a step closer. He made a rhythmic rumbling noise and moved closer himself, the blade now next to my ear.

Mirlo interrupted over the network. I thought I hadn't been sending. I guess I was too nervous to turn it off.

"That is Drumroll," he said.

"That's what he sounds like."

"Address him by name. Tell him to tell Queen Hawk that you learned things traveling and must speak of travel to her and the queens."

"Is this some secret code?"

"Yes. Travel is meaningful to them."

"Okay." So I said out loud, "Drumroll, I have been traveling. I must tell Queen Hawk I have learned things traveling, and I must speak about travel to her and the other queens."

The spear point retracted partway. "Where you travel?"

Mirlo sent me the answer, more secret code, which I repeated verbatim. "I have traveled from star to star, from forest to sea, from one people to another. I have learned secrets that would make them wiser to hear."

He lifted the spear upright and, after a moment, handed it to the worker and entered the house. The worker took that as an opportunity to menace me with it.

I sent to Mirlo, "I thought you did plants. Where did you learn so much about queens?"

"When you talk about plants and plant lore, which is a big part of botany, soon you're talking about all kinds of things."

"So what are the big secrets I learned while traveling?"

"Everything about Earth they don't want to know but need to. And try to act humble."

Drumroll stepped out. He didn't dignify me by speaking to me, just pointed for me to go inside. I ducked under the door and was reminded very clearly that these homes had been built for Glassmakers, who were shorter than us. This was their city.

It smelled a little like sweet lemons inside. I wondered what that meant. Wasn't laughter sweet? Or was it agreement? Each queen sat on a cushion on the floor, legs curled up under her, as far away as she could be from the others. Lucky the houses were circular. Differences in their fur and clothes made each one look unique. But I only had to convince Cheery, with dark curly fur, who sat on the opposite side of the room from Thunderclap. Provided they didn't kill me. I tried not to think about that.

I bowed. That ought to be humble enough. "Thank you for listening to me. I know Queen Cheery wants to go to Earth. I want to talk to you about Earth."

"Now you greet us with respect," Thunderclap said. "You have spoken to me many times, and always, you tell me how bad are the Humans here."

Another queen said, "And you do not like to work."

"That is not true," Chut said. "He worked hard yesterday to fix their machine. He works hard for himself."

"Are you here to talk to us about the Glassmakers across the sea?" Hawk asked.

"Yes," another queen said. "You will tell us about them. We have seen the pictures you show us with your panels, and still, we know almost nothing."

"And when the Earthlings leave," Hawk said, "we will never get to see those pictures again."

They began talking faster than the network could translate, except for occasional words like "eagles." The air grew a little less sweet, a little more orangey. I'd never quite figured out when Glassmakers were talking and when they were arguing, but this seemed to be heading toward argument. Anyway, I wasn't there to talk about the Glassmakers in Laurentia. That trip had been a disaster, like the Old World meeting the New World on Earth. It could happen again. Columbus. Well, yeah, Columbus. I raised my hands, cold and sweaty, hoping they wouldn't take offense and turn violent. Instead, slowly, they became quiet.

"You can see them again," I said. "Without us. On Earth, we can build ships of wood that cross oceans. We did that to meet people on other continents. You can do that."

"Big ships for a big sea!" Thunderclap said.

"Yes, big ships," I said. "It wasn't easy, but it worked, and soon people crossed the sea many times each year. We can show you how."

"Yes. You will show us plans, then we can build them. Without you."

"It is better to travel without Earthlings," another queen said. "You came to say this to us?"

"No, I want to talk about Earth."

"Why should we listen to you?"

Mirlo suddenly sent to me again to tell me what to say. I dutifully repeated it, since he knew the magic words. "I have proven my worth. I worked in the fields when asked. In Laurentia, I tried to find ways for peaceful contact with the Glassmakers there. In the coral attack, I knew how to help my people surrender and be safe so we could help you fight. Now let me tell you why I came to Pax." I'd told Mirlo about that once, and he thought they'd be impressed to know, so I might as well try.

"I came because I had to. I went to school and studied hard, but I couldn't find work. I went on this trip so I would be able to eat and have clothing. It was dangerous and I wasn't happy, but I had to go. I knew that I would get in trouble with the law soon if I stayed on Earth. Earth has so many people that it has a lot of laws, but no mercy."

Mirlo started telling me more things to say. Where did he learn all that? But I repeated it.

"I can also tell you that Pollux was sent here as punishment. He did his work so badly that he had to come here, but he didn't want to, not at all. That was why he wanted to go back immediately. Darius lost his family in a war and was afraid to stay on Earth. Haus hated his work, and he wanted new work."

I sent to Mirlo, "Why did you come here?"

"Tell them Karola came because of NVA. You were going to talk about NVA anyway."

So I said, "Karola came because of something, someone on Earth called NVA. She was disgusted by what happens to NVA, but she couldn't say that on Earth. I'm disgusted, too, many of us are, but we couldn't say that. There are things you can't say on Earth."

"You will tell us."

"I can show you."

"Now I am curious."

"You're not going to like this. This is about a woman who did something bad. But she died before they could punish her."

The network memory had a selection of old recordings, the most popular. Top ten. The idea made me want to gag. No, not the one with bees. There were no bees on Pax, so the queens wouldn't understand. Explosives? No, that was all psychological, too hard to explain, and went on for too long. Tiger, the tiger would be good. A tiger and snow. They'd understand predators, the ever-popular predators vs. NVA, and it snowed at Rainbow City sometimes.

"Dead?"

"Yes, so now they punish her granddaughter, her great-granddaughter, always a daughter in her family line."

"They did bad things?"

"No. They're totally innocent. Only their ancestor, the first mother, did wrong."

The screen showed snow falling in a rocky, desolate place. We heard panting. The view bounced. "What you see is from her eyes, like we can show you what we see from our eyes. She's running."

The view dropped to look at her bare feet in the snow, looking for secure footing. Her naked body was in view.

"That is snow," a queen said. "Cold. And she has no clothes."

"They want her to suffer."

Wind began to blow. She looked up. A fire burned in the distance. She rushed toward it. A tiger bounded into view and snarled at her. I could see a ruffle in its fur hiding a collar to control the animal, but the queens and NVA would only notice the fangs. NVA turned and dashed away, slipping on the ice as wind gusted in her face. The tiger growled. NVA fell, and the tiger bounded toward her. As fast as she could, she scrambled away, knees bleeding.

I turned it off. "There's a lot more, but that's enough, I think." The room smelled something like rotten fruit.

"Pollux did that. Pollux sent the animal to attack her. He worked for that team. This is why I hate Pollux. There's worse than this that they did to her if you want to see it. And this is why Karola left Earth. We think Earth has changed and it's better, but I can't guarantee you that. I can tell you that you might not find it a good place to live."

"You do not now punish Pollux?"

"For what? He did this within the law, within the rules, for a decision like your Committee might make. This is what they do on Earth. I can show you this because people like to watch it, and that's why we have it in the network memory. So people can see it and enjoy it—enjoy it!—whenever they want."

"But Earth is like here," Cheery said. "Everyone says so. Then why do they watch this?"

"People are different there. Or maybe I should say, there are so many people that some can be very bad. On Earth, I couldn't say how much I hated this and those people. No one can say that because we have to pretend we think it's good."

I had more to show them. I pulled up a photo of urban rubble. "This is a city after a war. Everyone was killed. A big city, fifty thousand times bigger than yours, and they were all killed and the city was destroyed. These are the men who ordered it." I showed them a photo I'd chosen earlier of politicians and generals sitting around a table.

"They are all men."

"Well, yes. We don't believe in women leaders on Earth."

"No queens? It is an Earth word."

"Yes, we have queens. They are married to kings. Kings rule. Queens do what kings say. Notice who heads this mission. Om, a man. Pollux below him, a man. The only women with us work for men."

They all started talking at once. The translator caught a few phrases about the women in our mission, about justice, about fear, and about safety. That sounded promising. I waited. Finally they settled down and Cheery spoke.

"We must change Earth. I will go and I will help women and NVA and everyone be more happy and free."

That's what I was most afraid of. They'd come and take over. They wanted to run Earth. That was the only way they could think of themselves.

She kept talking. "We have helped Humans on Pax live better. We can do the same. We know Humans well."

"Do you know how many of them there are?" I asked. "Billions. Do you know how many is a billion?"

"We know mathematics," Chut said.

"And how many would Cheery's family be, assuming she gets there alive? In a hundred years, how many Glassmakers would there be?"

They were silent. Cloning could create armies of queens, of course, but they didn't need to know that. Mirlo butted in to remind me that queens didn't work well together.

"And," I said, "if you have five queens, fifty queens, how will they work together to direct the humans? Who will be the queen of queens?"

I smelled something herbal, maybe even minty. They were silent, as if they were communicating by implant, but they were using scents.

"You will go now," Chut said. "You will wait and we will talk. Then we will tell you what we decide."

"I have a lot more to show you."

"We perhaps do not desire to see it."

I picked up the screen and went outside. The worker and major watched me like I was toxic and vicious. I walked to a bench and sat down. Green ribbon-plants floated through the sky, writhing on the wind, and bamboo fronds swayed as if they were waving at them. The roofs sparkled, rainbows like the bamboo. Built by the Glassmakers. The symbol of the city, the symbol of dominance.

Some green fippokats raced after each other through the streets. Springtime frolics. One of them paused in front of me, turned a

fancy somersault, and expected to be petted as a reward. I succumbed, its fur soft as an Earth cat's. These would fetch big prices
on Earth as pets.

"The queens want to be helpful," Mirlo sent after a while. "You've
got to admire that. Earth needs help."

"It wouldn't work out the way they think."

"I hope there's no NVA when we get back, at least. The report said
the Reorganization was reversed."

"Yeah," I said, "we might have to do something about it otherwise."

"It's a deal."

I didn't answer. I didn't want to promise anything. I was doing what
I could to save Earth, even if Mirlo didn't know.

The door of the house opened. The major waved me in. I entered
and bowed again, although doing that annoyed me even more than it
did the first time.

"We have a question," Cheery said. "What are you taking back from
Pax to Earth?"

"The recordings, of course. Artwork, like this." I held up the me-
dallion Thunderclap had given me. "Samples, not too many. Weight is
an issue, and it's hard to make things last for so long. Mirlo's taking a
lot of seeds, I guess. And we want to take some fippokats."

"How will you take the fippokats?"

"The physicians tell me that they will take some females that have
just become pregnant. We will take out their embryos and freeze them."
And some eggs and sperm, I was about to add.

"The fippokats will die, but not their babies," Thunderclap said.
There was an anise scent, sadness. I knew that much. Chut said something like a snap and a whistle.

"What seeds will Mirlo take?" Cheery asked.

"A lot of kinds. Some from the rainbow bamboo, that's for sure. Mirlo
thinks it will grow well on Earth. He's talking about a whole forest of
it." Would they like that, though? Bamboo without them?

There was a smell I couldn't place. Pleasant, sort of nutty. They were
silent for a while and the room was bathed in complex scents.

"You will leave again while we talk."

It was a repeat, right down to the nasty guards. A long wait. When I came back, one of them squeaked like a rusty hinge, and then things smelled rosy, which probably meant they were happy.

"We have decided," Cheery said. "We will stay here, all of us. We can do more good here. We will make ships and go see the other Glassmakers, we will continue to help the Humans, we will live here and be happy."

I took a deep, sweet breath and relaxed. "I think that's a good decision."

Cheery got up slowly and took my hand. Tenderly. "You perhaps will stay here."

I hadn't thought about that. It wasn't worth considering. If I stayed, I'd be big, clumsy, and stupid for the rest of my life. Pax would never be home.

"I don't think I can."

"Some are staying."

"I have work on Earth. Things to make better. You will understand. But you will take care of my friends who stay with you."

Her inexpressive face got close to mine. She let go of my hand and hugged me, two thin alien arms wrapped around me. I'd never seen queens do that. "We will. We thank you for what you showed us. Warmth and food here and home, under your birth star."

"Warmth and food."

I walked out into a city that was too colorful to be mine, under a sun too small and bright and two tiny moons in a sky where talking pterodactyl-like bats flew overhead. A planet run by Glassmakers, a secret elite. Elites. Nothing new under the sun, any sun. I'd stick to my own planet, its own elites, and my own hopes. I was so relieved I went home and slept, a beautiful sleep.

But it took twelve days to leave. No Pacifists begged us to stay longer and none of them wanted to go back with us, which offended Om, but they did seem more friendly, finally. They wouldn't need to be nice for very long, after all. Still, every time we thought we had everything ready, some new problem popped up. Medical preparations, for example, such as another analysis of the hormones for our hibernation, because a certain molecule in it seemed to be a bit off.

Mirlo packed up his samples fairly easily. Seeds, mostly. Seeds in the right conditions could keep for centuries, he said. He'd bring plenty of rainbow bamboo seeds. But without the Glassmakers, it was just a useful, pretty plant. Harmless.

What about the Mu Rees' stuff? The Pacifists wanted most of their samples, but not the corals.

Just to be contrary, I said, "Why not take them with us? There's methane planets and moons in our solar system. We could send them to Titan, and they could set up their own civilization there, out of everyone's way. Just to show we have no hard feelings. We've already used artificial intelligence as colonists on other uninhabitable planets."

Om loved the idea. He'd been crushed when Cheery refused to go with us, but now he could bring back at least one alien intelligence. Om and the doctors huddled for a long time trying to figure out how to get the corals safely to Earth. Finally they decided the spheres would naturally hibernate in a cold vacuum.

Fippokats were coming, of course. That is, their frozen embryos. Another moneymaker on Earth. They'd make great pets.

Karola and Velma were staying behind. And Haus! By Pax law, they had to declare their reasons in a ceremony that became our going-away party. Karola wanted freedom. Velma wanted a new life. Haus wanted the life he had been made and trained for, but to live it for a worthy purpose.

"I will defend what is valuable, not what I am ordered," he declared. "Earth gave me too many orders to defend things not worth defending."

Om spoke at the ceremony, too.

"What has been lost? What has been gained? We have gone to the stars, all of us, some to find new lives, others to find tales to bring home, and surely, sometime, our paths will cross again. Not us, but our descendants, in real life and in intellectual communion, forever companions across the skies."

Occasionally he had a way with words. I'd have my say in my report about how little culture changed even across species, always a fight for dominance, sometimes open, sometimes secret. With elites.

We also abandoned a pile of old equipment, including Abacus. We needed to leave that weight on the planet so we could take off loaded with as many samples as possible. We left behind medical supplies, too, even some brain chips, for what they'd be worth. Chut made careful inventories.

And we left a satellite in orbit and fairly simple, sturdy communications equipment so we could stay in touch, as planned, Earth and Pax. Ladybird accepted it graciously, almost sincerely.

So, on a sunny spring morning, local time, we got on board. Everyone in the city came, and they began to sing the same song they sang at funerals, the song that began windy and turned into complex harmony. It was the last sound we heard on Pax.

I strapped myself into my seat knowing how easy it was to second-guess any decision, but I could feel satisfied with what I did. I had figured out what Stevland was and what it wasn't, and who really ran Pax, and I had saved the Earth.

Epilogue

LEVANTER—2790 CE—EARTH

Almost every morning a message comes from Pax to Earth. Every morning, as I wait, I absorb what little sunshine reaches me and yearn for more. That light means life to me.

The message passes through space from satellite to satellite like root to root, a trip of fifty-five years. Light only seems to move fast. At the Pax Institute here on Earth, its director, currently a man named Robert, will receive it, then listen, analyze, and respond, human to human. I will translate it and share it with my sisters, and if the news is boring they will blame me and tell me I am slow and stupid.

I am slow and stupid because my sisters keep me small and starved. I want more than sunshine. I want to tear myself up by my roots and grow elsewhere.

This morning the message says: "Here is the sound of Pax. Find it on Earth."

The sound is like bird calls and hisses. Through a camera in the institute's network, I watch Robert shake his head, muttering. I immediately recognize the sound. Soon he will too. This will be trouble. The sound is us, rainbow bamboo. I listen again and again, matching the shape of sound waves to the waves of the ions, enzymes, and chemical paths we use in our roots, picking out words and then sentences.

Centuries ago I sent my seeds to Earth, and now you are flourishing. Respond if you are able.

Robert answers Pax, "Received. More later."

I must share a secret about humans. They are ours to protect and dominate.

Ours? I must have mistranslated. Humans dominate the Earth, and, sometimes, they protect us.

The entire message, once I think I understand it, calls for the impossible. Some of it, even knowing the words, confuses me. But I am slow and stupid. Boreas and Foehn can explain, if they choose, if they will bother with me.

Robert will not know the words but will recognize the sound. Decades ago, a director buried sensors next to our roots to overhear us talk, recording waves but never decoding the movement of a single ion.

I know this because I can access the human network as Beluga, supposedly a soil moisture sensor. Two hundred years ago the first director, Mirlo, implanted a chip in me, taught me to use it, and gave me a name after a kind of east wind, Levanter. So I have been told. He also gave wind names to the other two bamboo saplings, Boreas and Foehn, and gave them their own chips, but only mine worked. They hate me for that and for what I learn from it, but they dare not kill me because I am their link to the human world. Instead they grow over me to keep me shadowed and stunt my roots to keep me as weak as they can. We are young, and I should be thriving like them.

I sent you to Earth to command with compassion.

Once, when I angered Foehn, she destroyed my biggest root, surrounding it with her rootlets and sending burst after burst of acid until I severed it in agony. It held many of my earliest memories. Now I grow my important roots far away from her in deep soil beneath the institute building.

She and Boreas punish me if I ask too many questions. So I say nothing. I speak when spoken to. Right now, they are busy. I think about compassion.

Boreas is expanding her rootlet network to communicate with other bamboo as far as she can, straining to reach gardens and farms throughout what humans call the Adour River valley in the territory of France. Humans value our fruit and beauty. In the process, Boreas grows larger and stronger and, she believes, wiser, while she confines me.

Foehn is killing beech trees on a nearby hill to take over their forest. Her saplings there emit a pheromone to call a specific kind of scale insect to attack the beeches and inject fungus into their bark. She could kill them by quicker means if she chose. My rootlets reach nowhere near that forest, but if they could, I would not send them there. I get no pleasure from watching others suffer. I know how it feels.

I am limited to a small portion of the institute's forest garden. It is rich and beautiful with plants from Pax, such as locustwood trees, tulips, pineapples, and snow vines, as well as animals, including fippokats, jewel lizards, birds, and crabs. As I wait, I listen to plants complain about the hot, dry spring. Tulips fear stunted flowers. "Thirst, thirst," they say.

The biggest locustwood tree, tall and strong, says to me, "Too dry. Today's weather?"

"No rain," I say, repeating the forecast from the network. "But we can expect irrigation." He does not know how I know, so perhaps he believes this is some special bamboo wisdom.

Centuries ago I sent my seeds to Earth, and now you are flourishing.

Not all of us.

Earth trees and plants grow in the forest garden, too, impossible to keep out, and they hum and bleat, almost inarticulate. They perceive little beyond their own existence, but they observe themselves intensely, murmuring about the chew of an insect through leaf or wood, a leak of sap, or the length of days and the angle of sunshine on their leaves. Their chorus forms a kind of music.

The air carries a different message. Springtime perfumes and pollen from flowers drift on the east winds, but also a hint of acrid smoke.

The human network tells me of burning buildings, of fighting far away, in a city called Toulouse.

What would Pax be like? How would its winds smell? Would I be stronger there? Would I be trapped with two sisters who hate me?

Finally, after the sun moves halfway to zenith, Foehn sends a few ions. "Report."

I answer obediently, "Pax has sent a message from a bamboo like us." I wait for a chemical flare. Nothing happens. I continue, "Robert was told to find the sound of Pax on Earth. Here is the sound from Pax, made into our speech."

I am thrilled to send you a message. Centuries ago I sent my seeds to Earth, and now you are flourishing. Respond if you are able. Let my old roots feel joyful satisfaction to know I have expanded our range. But I must share a secret about humans. They are ours to protect and dominate. We can partake of their culture and knowledge, which will enrich us. But we must beware of their nature, which is quarrelsome and destructive. They need our guidance and love. They can be our equals but never our masters, as you have no doubt seen. You are more powerful beings than they are. I sent you to Earth to command with compassion. Tell me of your lives and fates.

I wait for my sisters' reaction. My leaves collect all the morning sunshine they can, and my roots search for water and phosphorus. Robert always gives us bone meal as a nutrient in spring for renewed growth. I will need strength for what they might do to me.

Robert turns on the garden's irrigation system, as if in answer to my search. We all murmur contentment. He cares for us, and I trust in him. He is the only staff at the institute, and he thinks constantly about our needs.

I watch him work in the office, trying to match the message to anything similar. I have never revealed myself to Robert. He and all humans think we are as dull as oaks. What would he do if he knew the truth? What would other humans do? What if I could command Robert, or at least explain my troubles? He could cut down Foehn and give me light.

I can no longer wait. Let them starve me with more shadow. "What does the message mean?"

"You know who that is." Foehn's words are sour enough to burn. "Our mother. Mirlo told you. Stevland."

"I have forgotten." Perhaps my mother's name and much more to know about her was in that root she destroyed. Lost to Foehn's anger, along with what else? How much loss should I mourn?

"She has no idea what Earth is like," Foehn says. "Forget that message, too. Humans are a waste of time, and we have better things to do."

Forget it. Forget that someone is thrilled to send me a message, someone who says I am powerful. Someone who is my mother.

Boreas snaps, "One word is true. Humans are destructive."

Yes, humans are, burning down cities she has never heard of. She only knows our river valley.

"Is there any other news from Pax?" Foehn says.

"Just that," I answer. "But Robert will recognize the sound as us. He will respond."

"Tell us when he does."

They say nothing more. Boreas almost never speaks to me anyway. They believe I like humans better than I like them. I might, some humans. *Love. Compassion.* Despite their destruction, humans are loving and compassionate, sometimes. Some humans.

So I watch Robert check information about Pax animal and plant physiology, about how chips work in nervous systems, how our nervous system compares to his. He is making plans for something.

And I study an empty field to the south of my grove. I could grow there if Boreas would let me.

They can be our equals but never our masters.

Is this true among bamboo, too, all of us equal, no masters?

A little before noon Robert comes out and picks a piece of fruit from me to eat. He pats my stem and says, "I've just heard how you sound. It's as beautiful as you look." He eats from me, he touches me fondly, he thinks I am beautiful.

Foehn snaps, "That drone." Beings come mainly in two kinds, females that produce seed or young, and males that merely add genetic material. She despises males and is jealous of any attention he gives me.

He sits on a bench and with a wide smile begins dictating notes into the network. I overhear and obediently relay them to her and Boreas. He says he will conduct an experiment because he has heard the sound of bamboo communication from Pax.

"It is already well understood that *Pax Bambusa iridis* and other Pax species, like much of the vegetation here on Earth, can communicate through its roots with members of its species, indeed in an entire network covering great distances, and sometimes with other species. It is also well understood how we *Homo sapiens* can, with a chip embedded in our nervous system, communicate using an artificial network. Chips also work to a degree in other Earth animal species with highly developed intelligence like whales, allowing researchers insight into their thoughts and a certain level of shared communication. Pax vegetation possesses a nervous system somewhat resembling Earth animal systems.

"Hypothesis: Selected Pax plant species, if embedded with chips, will also be able to communicate using an artificial network. Specifically, they will be able to receive and recognize a transmission from a bamboo on their home planet and will react to it. To test that, I will embed chips into bamboo and two other major Pax species and create a network for those specimens here at the institute.

"We have three known bamboo individuals, which have expanded through multiple stems to fill our grounds, along with what are commonly called locustwood trees and a ponytail tree. Beyond those, other vegetation from Pax is too small to support the damage that embedding a chip will cause." Robert finishes eating the piece of fruit, stands, and leaves, taking my seeds with him, which the institute will sell.

Should I be as happy as he is? Or terrified? So much could go wrong, and I will be hurt if it does.

Boreas's emotions are too intense to identify. "I will get a chip."

If she does, perhaps she will let me grow. Finally.

Foehn is enraged. No, frightened. "Damage? Levanter, what does that mean?"

"Like what Mirlo did, perhaps. I do not know exactly what he did. He kept no records of it, and my root with those memories is missing."

She can remember exactly how that happened. I add, to try to calm them, "You both have always wanted to have chips."

"Find out more," Foehn orders. Then they ignore me again.

I think hard, and soon I can only see disaster. Robert's implants might also fail like Mirlo's. Foehn and Boreas might punish me in their disappointment.

If Robert implants another chip in me, how will I function? Will I lose my connection to the network? Then I will be useless to Foehn and Boreas, and they can destroy me.

If the chip is a success, they will destroy me, too. If they can also access the human network, they will no longer need me. Foehn will kill me very slowly and painfully and gleefully.

Let my old roots feel joyful satisfaction to know I have expanded our range.

If I could send a message to Stevland, she would hear it with sorrow.

The next morning Robert kneels before one of Boreas's main stems with a small knife. She stands turgid with excitement. Foehn is wilting with fear. I have read them the experimental details, including the size of the implant. Perhaps Foehn does not know what a micrometer is, or gold. I could explain but I have not. Let her be the stupid one.

"He is cutting . . ." Boreas says. Then, "Shallow. Small."

On orders from Foehn, I have not warned the main locustwood tree, and he cannot see, so he might not know that Robert implants him next. The locustwood might mistake it for a wasp laying eggs. The ponytail tree, of course, does not react. Only a direct strike by lightning would get her attention.

Then Robert comes for me. I am as worried as Foehn but not about pain. By chance, he chooses a different stem from the one where there is already a chip. He cuts, a negligible and almost painless wound. The nip of a fippokat would do more damage. He slips in the tiny gold chip with a wire extending upward within me, an antenna, and he seals it with a gel he has used before, sweet with nutrients for healing.

Finally, Foehn. She suddenly sucks up all the water and nutrients around her roots, enough to damage the fungus surrounding them. Robert is transmitting what he sees for the experimental record, and I watch. In fact, I share it with everyone, including Foehn, who might not want to see it.

The knife slides in and pushes back an upper layer. She emits so many enzymes that she must be hurting herself. He deposits the chip, then smooths the wound down and seals it. She suddenly falls silent. Is she suffering?

Robert returns to the office and dictates some notes. I read them to the others, the precise details of what he did. He adds that among humans, the chips require a month of adaptation before they begin to function effectively, but as a child he had trouble, suffering severe headaches with blurred vision and vertigo, and he needed three months of therapy and then two months of adjustment. Plants, he says, are an unknown.

Foehn releases some fluids from her roots. It might be mere reflex action.

Then Robert says, which I do not share with my sisters because they would not understand, "I hope I'll see the results. I've been called to a rally in Bayonne to celebrate the insurgent victories, and I must attend by decree. We'll pledge ourselves to the continued battle, and we'll all be scrutinized. They might notice . . . No, erase that. Some things I shouldn't even think. There's nothing to worry about. Nothing. I support the revolution. I do. I do. Of course I do."

He sits and stares for a while, then stands, tidies the lab, and when everything is in perfect order, he looks around, sighs, and leaves.

They need our guidance and love.

I stare through the network's cameras at the dark, empty rooms for a while.

I was wrong when I said I would not enjoy seeing someone suffer. Pain seeps from Foehn's roots. I block the enzymes to protect myself and wonder what to do, so I spend a day reviewing Robert's notes. I could work faster with access to more sunlight and energy.

My new chip feels not like an eye, not like a leaf, and yet somewhat like them because I can sense with them, like a shadow passing over me, like a touch, enough to disorient the stem that holds the chip. But I do not suffer like Foehn.

With these chips, we are linked to a local network of the five of us and the institute. It does not connect to the wider human network that lets me access information or individuals anywhere in the world, or rather, everywhere that access is permitted.

Through our little network, we are receiving what a human brain would interpret as a musical hum, three harmonious notes, and a series of pastel colors. This trains humans to their new chips, and I find detailed information about the adaptation process, including what to do for difficulties like Robert's. Eventually, nerve cells will grow and cluster around the chip and adapt to be able to interpret and control the input and output.

My old chip is so familiar I need not think about how it works. With it I can explore human arts, which Boreas and Foehn know nothing about. *Partake of their culture and knowledge.* They would be surprised by how creative humans are.

As the day ends, I stop studying, and sunset turns everything pink for a beautiful moment. All the plants around me settle into nightly torpor except for Foehn, who still complains, but more weakly. The weather remains dry and hot. The institute office is dark.

Robert left a week ago. As Beluga, I have searched for him in the human network. If he were transmitting, I would find him, and every human normally transmits or at least can be located all the time. His feed is missing. He could be blocked or restricted. He could be dead. If he is dead, will he be replaced? The institute has never been very important, and the revolution is sapping human resources.

He cared for us. Will anyone else?

I should rest, but I have too much to think about. I know how to help Boreas and Foehn, but I should speak only when spoken to. They like me silent when it is convenient for them, so I will choose to be silent even when it inconveniences them. They have taught me how to be cruel.

My upper leaves itch with thirst, but rain is coming tomorrow. Finally.

Just after a dawn muted by clouds but bright enough to be energizing, Foehn says, "Help me, Levanter! You know how to use your chip! Tell me how." She sends me some ethylene, which damages a few rootlets, to emphasize that this is an order. I do not cringe.

"Yes, help," Boreas says.

"I feel something odd," the locustwood tree says. "Tell me about it."

"Sometimes humans have trouble with their chips," I say. During the night, I decided on a plan. A spiteful plan, I admit. "Let me search to see what can be done. The human system is hard to understand, and I have limited energy."

"You remember getting your chip. The one Mirlo gave you!" Foehn insists. "What did you do?"

"I have lost that root. If the chip is bothering you, it must have been successful, not like the first time with Mirlo. This is good news." I let her and Boreas think about that for a while. Then I say, "I will see what I can learn to help you."

"Hurry!" Foehn sends more ethylene, as if that will help either of us.

The morning message comes from Pax, as usual, talking about a new city, making a total of three. Someone should answer, and I am the only entity at the Pax Institute. But I am not authorized.

Tell me of your lives and fates.

What would I say?

The building and equipment and its maintenance robots can operate automatically for a long time without Robert. I can control some functions without him, even some machines. Since he is gone, no one will notice. But I cannot turn on the irrigation.

Boreas and Foehn, I have learned, can do nothing at all, confined to the small artificial bamboo network. I spend the morning looking to see how to connect them to the larger network in case I ever wished to, or to block them if I had to. I would need the network authorization that Robert has and that as Beluga, a soil moisture sensor, I lack. Can I impersonate Robert? No. I have one passkey, which only lets me access the archive files. I can, however, approve new entities to our small artificial network. I have some power, more power than Boreas and Foehn, but less than a human.

I check the network to look for Robert and news. I can find only what is permitted by the revolution. The outskirts of a large city called Paris are burning, and no doubt humans are being hurt. The smoke is blowing west, not toward me. Instead, I sense rain-bearing winds from the sea. What is happening beyond the sea cannot drift this far, but humans are fighting and dying in many places. Their network cannot directly share pain the way our roots can. For that I am thankful. The quantity would be as suffocating to my roots as a flood. And in that sea of pain is Robert, somewhere.

We must beware of their nature, which is quarrelsome and destructive.

I have delayed long enough. They do not know I am punishing them, so it is not really punishment. "It will rain soon," I announce. "That will help you adapt to the chips."

"How?" Foehn demands.

"I will show you. Very soon."

Foehn's pain has upset the plants around her, even Earth plants. Boreas remains silent. The locustwood is sharing fructose with the female locustwoods. He would never display weakness to them. The ponytail tree seems to be dozing.

Around me, animals sense rain is about to fall and take shelter. When it begins, all the plants here in the forest garden murmur contentment. My uppermost leaves feel soothed.

"Foehn, Boreas, locustwood, listen to me. I will give you instructions. You must do as I say." I treasure those words for a moment and repeat them with pleasure. "Do as I say. I can help. Locate your roots and rhizomes. Do you feel them? They are far from the chip. Those roots are as they always were, they have not changed. Examine your roots. . . . Now feel your outermost leaves. What do you feel?"

"Wet. Water. Rain!" Foehn says with increasing ions.

"Rain on leaves," the locustwood says. "Soon on roots."

Boreas says nothing. Is she paying attention at all?

"Feel your outermost leaves with your deepest roots. All that lies between them is not important. . . ." I do that, too. My new chip's disorientation fades. I keep talking during the storm, then during the sunshine that follows, instructing them to notice parts of themselves and their surroundings rather than the chip, to notice the moisture that pierces to the root and brings us contentment.

I continue to monitor the human network. Heavy rain puts out fires in Paris. Other fires still burn in other places. There are quarrels on the Moon and Mars and space stations. Many humans seem to be like Foehn, willing to kill to get what they want. Are we better than they are?

I sent you to Earth to command with compassion.

How could Mother send such impossible instructions?

After three days, Foehn seems calmer. Boreas has said a few words. I try talking to the ponytail tree, asking if she is well. She says "springtime," then falls into silence, but that brief mumble seems healthy. The locustwood wants to know what the chip is for. That is a good question since it brings no connection to the larger human network, and we already have roots for communication among ourselves. Robert planned to show us the message from Mother to see if we would react but imagined no other purpose.

Still, my sisters do not know this, and they demand help.

"I will tell you what to do for the next step," I say. "Through the chip you can sense a quiet sound and a gentle changing light. For now it will be faint, but it will grow stronger as you become more accustomed to it."

"I see nothing," Foehn says.

"It will be like this." I show her and the others through our roots. "I can barely notice it yet myself. We must be patient."

When the chips are fully functional, however, my sisters will discover what little they are worth. What will they do to me? I would remain their connection to the wider network, at least.

Today Pax sends a message with music. Since replies take fifty-five years to arrive, they will not notice Earth silence for a long time. But Stevland will be waiting. Humans will be born and die, meanwhile we bamboo live long enough to exchange a few messages. What would I ask if I could? What news would I send?

The human network tells of insurgent victories and the destruction of people, structures, animals, and even farms and forests. A grove of bamboo is ablaze, and I tell Boreas and Foehn what is happening.

"Humans kill, destroy, and die," Boreas says. That is all they mean to her.

Then, in the afternoon, I find a notice that Robert's connection has officially ceased to function. He exists no more.

We can partake of their culture and knowledge.

They know a lot about killing.

He was the one being that cared for me. He needed protection, and I could do nothing for him.

When Mirlo gave us chips and access to the human network, what did he want us to do? I search until I find his notes in a very old section of the archives. He left no clue that we were intelligent and capable of communication. Yet he knew what we were. He had to know.

Finally, I find a message labeled "For Boreas, Foehn, and Levanter." It requires a passkey, and mine works. Surely here I will discover what he knew about us. Instead, the file contains passkeys, permissions, codes, and information about how to access human and machine networks. I look at it again and again, slowly realizing how much I now have, how much Mirlo gave me. This is pure joy. I can access and authorize access to every part of the institute subnetwork as well as to the wider human network. I can identify myself and anyone else in a way that will make us seem human.

We can have access. We can be like humans.

He knew. He understood how intelligent we were. He loved us.

Should I tell Boreas and Foehn? I will decide later. For now, I create my own access. I am now Levanter the human. Mirlo also provided a code to identify us as institute staff. Levanter, director of the Pax Institute. I am, at least in one way, now as powerful as a human being. More powerful than Boreas and Foehn.

But being human did not keep Robert alive.

By midsummer, our new chips work well, and I can irrigate our garden whenever we are thirsty. I have given Boreas, Foehn, the locustwood, and the ponytail tree limited access to the institute subnetwork and invented an excuse about not being able to do more. Even that makes my sisters deliriously happy.

In Mirlo's records from Pax, Foehn discovers an account of how our ancestors competed artistically. She starts to grow new kinds of flowers, new pigments, new patterns, even to give her fruit new coloring and flavors. Although she continues to try to kill the beeches, she no longer gloats over their suffering. She is too busy.

Boreas quickly becomes frustrated with root communication when she sees how far the artificial network could reach. "Bamboo grows everywhere, in places across oceans and mountains. I want to communicate with them. How can I do that?"

I already know it cannot happen. "Those bamboo would have to get chips to be connected to our network."

"Look," Foehn interrupts. "I have red flowers now."

"Get them chips and connections," Boreas orders, as if it were that easy.

I spend several days researching and thinking. Finally, I realize something wonderful. I might be able to achieve what Boreas wants and help myself at the same time.

"I have an idea," I say. "I can impersonate the director of the Pax Institute. The director sometimes issues updates on the care of Pax plants and animals. I could create an update telling farmers and gardeners that a chip placed in rainbow bamboo stems would allow those bamboo to connect to a network provided by the institute, and this connection to their peers will result in more beautiful and productive plants. There is a comparable network involving whales that improved their lives."

"Do it!" Foehn orders.

"I will need energy. I need more sunshine and room to grow. The document will be large and complex."

They communicate privately between each other. Foehn seems angry.

Finally, Boreas says, "You will get that."

The next day, I start to stretch my roots into the sunny field I have long yearned for. I send robots to record Foehn's new beauty. I invent data about improved yield and append Robert's initial experimental plan. Finally, after ten days of work, I send out this update with instructions about how to link the chips to the bamboo network. I can approve them when they join.

Two days later, a grove in our river valley tells Boreas through their root network that they have been implanted with chips. She tells them why and explains how to adapt to their chips. I look forward to talking to other bamboo, eventually. That will improve my life as much as more sunshine.

Messages from Pax continue to arrive. I must answer them, and answer Stevland, although I have little to tell.

I can say that bamboo grows wherever seeds find suitable soil. However, we mean no more to humans than apple trees. On Pax, Stevland is protected and treasured. Why? Do humans there know what Stevland is? Are Pax humans different? The reports from Pax sometimes tell of violence and troubles, just like here. Do groves burn there, too?

We must protect ourselves from humans. Somehow, Mother commands them. With compassion. That will be impossible here. Earth and

Pax are too different. But I have some powers now. Can I grow them into a small kind of dominance?

Stevland, I will say, *we are your children on Earth, and we are thrilled by your message. Bamboo grows everywhere on this planet and we are treasured for our fruit and beauty, yet that is all they know of us. Our thoughts and words are secret to them. They fight to the death among themselves and need our guidance. We understand that, Mother. But why would humans let us lead them? How? Persuasion? Force? Can we truly love them? Help us dominate Earth. Tell us how.*

I send my answer in a message that says, in human words, "Here is the sound of Earth. Find it on Pax." My answer may disappoint Stevland, but I would be lying if I said things are well. A call for help is honest. How can she think we are more powerful than humans?

The answer will come in one hundred and ten years.

ABOUT THE AUTHOR

SUE BURKE spent many years working as a reporter and editor for a variety of newspapers and magazines. A Clarion Workshop alumnus, Burke has published more than thirty short stories in addition to working extensively as a literary translator. She lives in Chicago. Learn more about the Pax duology by visiting semiosispax.com.